PRAISE FOR MARY KAY ANDREWS
and *Savannah Blues*

"I really loved *Savannah Blues*. Mary Kay Andrews has perfect pitch when it comes to endearing, smart-mouth heroines, and she has caught the languid looniness of the Low Country perfectly."
—ANNE RIVERS SIDDONS

"Disarming—entertaining." —*Washington Post*

"Delightfully breezy—richly atmospheric." —*Publishers Weekly*

"*Savannah Blues* is a shining novel of wit, love, and hilarious—yet poignant—vengeance. Mary Kay Andrews writes with great spirit and vitality."
—LUANNE RICE, bestselling author of *Dream Country* and *Safe Harbor*

"A flat-out enjoyable novel. . . . Andrews displays a great eye for detail."
—*Raleigh News & Observer*

"A great heroine, [a] steamy Savannah setting, a hunky chef, antiques galore, and an intriguing mystery. It doesn't get any better than this."
—SUSAN ELIZABETH PHILLIPS

"Deft plotting, sly humor, and appealing characters. . . . Pure fun."
—*Kirkus Reviews*

"A woman with revenge on her mind, corporate conspiracies antiques to die for (literally!), and a m̶ore could you want? *Savannah Blu*
—ANN B. ROSS, *Ne*
author of *Mi*

Billy Howard

About the Author

MARY KAY ANDREWS is a former antiques picker and a recovering journalist who reported on the trial made famous in *Midnight in the Garden of Good and Evil*. She lives in Atlanta. Visit her at www.marykayandrews.com.

Savannah
Blues

Mary Kay Andrews

Perennial
An Imprint of HarperCollins*Publishers*

A hardcover edition of this book was published in 2002 by HarperCollins Publishers.

SAVANNAH BLUES. Copyright © 2002 by Whodunnit, Inc. All rights reserved. Printed in the United States of America. No part of this book may be used or reproduced in any manner whatsoever without written permission except in the case of brief quotations embodied in critical articles and reviews. For information address HarperCollins Publishers Inc., 10 East 53rd Street, New York, NY 10022.

HarperCollins books may be purchased for educational, business, or sales promotional use. For information please write: Special Markets Department, HarperCollins Publishers Inc., 10 East 53rd Street, New York, NY 10022.

First Perennial edition published 2003.

Designed by Nancy Singer Olaguera

The Library of Congress has catalogued the hardcover edition as follows:
Andrews, Mary Kay.
    Savannah blues / Mary Kay Andrews.—1st ed.
      p. cm.
    ISBN 0-06-019958-X
    1. Savannah (Ga.)—Fiction. I. Title.
PS3570.R587 S28   2001
813'6—dc21   2001016749

ISBN 0-06-051913-4 (pbk.)

07   ❖/RRD   30 29

This one is for my big sis, Susie, with love.

ACKNOWLEDGMENTS

 *I* ran away from home in the summer of 2000 to write and research this book. So, to those I left behind in Atlanta—Tom, Katie, and Andy—I send a thousand thanks and kisses and hugs. And to those who helped me find a temporary home in Savannah—more of the same. Jacky Blatner Yglesias and Polly Powers Stramm offered food, friendship, estate sales, and invaluable connections. Jan and Jay Bradley were the world's most gracious landlords. Anne Landers and the Ardsley Park supper club gave me more than they'll ever know—including the recipe for crawfish cakes with remoulade. And the Wednesday night "needlers" at Twiggs of Savannah kept me in stitches—literally. Thanks are also due to Chatham district attorney Spencer Lawton and the deputies of the Chatham correctional institute, who locked me up for authenticity's sake. Any errors, misrepresentations, or outright mistakes are my own fault and not theirs.

The rapping at the front door of the carriage house was unmistakable. Her. I could see Caroline DeSantos's slender profile through the frosted glass inset of the front door. She had started by ringing the bell, once, twice, three times, then she began rattling the doorknob with one hand and banging at the brass knocker with the other.

"Eloise? Open up. I mean it. That beast of yours did it again. I'm calling the dogcatcher right now. You hear me? I've got my cell phone. I'm punching in the number. I know you hear me, Eloise."

She did indeed have something that looked like a phone in her hand.

Jethro heard Caroline too. He raised his dark muzzle, which has endearing little spots like reverse freckles, his ears pricked up, and, recognizing the voice of the enemy, he slunk under the pine table in the living room.

I knelt down and scratched his chin in sympathy. "Did you, Jethro? Did you really pee on the camellias again?"

Jethro hung his head. He's just a stray, but he almost never lies to me, which is more than I can say for any other male I've ever been involved with.

I patted his head as a reward for his honesty. "Good dog. Help yourself. Pee on everything over there. Poop on the doorstep and I'll buy you the biggest ham bone in Savannah."

The banging and door rattling continued. "Eloise. I know you're home. I saw your truck parked on the street. I've called Tal. He's calling his lawyer."

"Tattletale," I muttered, putting aside the box of junk I'd been sorting.

I padded toward the front door of the carriage house. The worn pine floorboards felt cool against the soles of my bare feet. Caroline was banging so hard on the door I was afraid she'd break the etched glass panel.

"Bitch," I muttered.

Jethro barked his approval. I turned around and saw his tail wagging in agreement.

"Slut." More wagging. We were both gathering our resolve for the coming barrage. Jethro crawled out from under the table and sat on his haunches, directly behind me. His warm breath on my ankles felt oddly reassuring.

I threw the front door open. "Sic her, Jethro," I said loudly. "Bite the bad lady."

Caroline took half a step backward. "I heard that," she screeched. "If that mutt puts a paw in my garden again, I'm going to . . ."

"What?" I demanded. "You're going to what? Poison him? Shoot him? Run him over in that sports car of yours? You'd enjoy that, wouldn't you, Caroline? Running over a poor defenseless dog."

I put my hands on my hips and did a good imitation of staring her down. It wasn't physically possible, of course. Caroline DeSantos stands a good four inches taller than I do, and that's without the four-inch spike heels she considers her fashion trademark.

She flushed. "I'm warning you. That's all. For the last time. There's a leash law in this town, as you well know. If you really loved that mutt of yours, you wouldn't let him run around loose all the time."

She really was quite lovely, Caroline. Even in Savannah's ungodly summer heat, she was as crisp and fragrant as a just-plucked gardenia. Her glossy dark hair was pulled off her neck in a chignon, and her olive skin was flawless. She wore lime green linen capri slacks and a matching linen scoop-neck blouse that showed only a tasteful hint of décolletage. I could have gone on living a long time without seeing her that way, that day.

"Oh," I said. "Jethro is running around. Is that what's bothering you about my poor little puppy? But you're an expert at running around, aren't you, Caroline? I believe you and my husband were running around on me for at least six months before I finally wised up and kicked him out."

I'd kicked Tal out, but he hadn't gone far. The judge in our divorce case was an old family friend of Tal's daddy, Big Tal. He'd given our 1858 townhouse to Tal in the property settlement, and only after my lawyer raised the god-awfullest ruckus you ever heard, had he tossed me a bone—basically—awarding me the slim two-story carriage house right behind the big house.

Tal installed Caroline in the big house the minute the paperwork was completed, and we've had a running back-fence spite match ever since.

My lawyer, who also happens to be my uncle James, talked himself blue in the face trying to persuade me to sell out and move, but he knows better than to try to make a Foley change her mind. On Charlton Street I'd make my stand—to live and die in Dixie. Move? Me? No sirreebob.

Caroline flicked a strand of hair out of her face. She looked me up and down and gave me a supercilious smile.

It was Thursday. I'd been up at dawn cruising the still-darkened lanes of Savannah, trying to beat the trashmen to the spoils of the town's leading lights. I looked like hell. My junking uniform, black leggings and a blue denim work shirt, was caked in grime from the Dumpsters I'd been digging through. My short red hair was festooned with cobwebs, my nails were broken, and peeling paint flakes clung to the back of my knuckles.

The day's pickings had been unusually slim. The two huge boxes of old books I'd pounced on behind an Italianate brownstone on Barnard Street had yielded up mostly mildewed, totally worthless Methodist hymnbooks from the 1930s. A carton of pretty Occupied Japan dishes rescued from a pile of junk at a house on Washington Avenue hadn't turned up a single piece not chipped, cracked, or broken. The only remotely promising find was an old cookie tin of buttons I'd bought for two dollars at a yard sale I'd nearly passed up on my way back to the carriage house.

It was that box of buttons I'd been sorting when Caroline had mounted her assault on my front door.

Now there was a soft pooting noise behind me. Caroline literally looked down her long, Latin nose at me and curled her full-blown upper lip. "My God," she cried. "What is that wretched smell?"

I sniffed and looked over my shoulder at Jethro, who was slinking in the other direction.

"It's not Jethro," I said, leaping to my dog's defense. I pointed over at the wrought-iron railing in the entryway, where I'd draped the tattered hooked rug I'd been trying to air out before bringing it inside.

"It's probably the rug," I said. "I got it out of an old crack house on Huntingdon. I think maybe it's got fleas."

Caroline jumped back as though the rug were a live skunk.

"I can't believe the filthy garbage you drag back here," she began. "It's appalling. And it's no wonder I have to have the house sprayed twice a month. I told Tal, 'Weezie is infesting our house.'"

Behind me, in the vest-pocket living room, my telephone was starting to ring.

"Gotta go now," I said. "Got a business to run." I slammed the door in her face and turned the dead-bolt lock.

Jethro licked my toe in gratitude. "Ro-Ro," I said gently, not wanting to hurt his feelings, "that was bad. No more bologna sandwiches for you, little buddy."

I caught the phone on the fourth ring.

"Weezie, wait 'til you hear."

It was BeBe Loudermilk, my best friend, whose mother, exhausted after having had eight previous children in ten years, had settled upon the name BeBe, and the French pronunciation of "Bay-Bay," for her ninth and last child.

To BeBe, being last meant she was always in a hurry, always trying to catch up. She was a human hurricane who never wasted time starting a conversation with any conventional pleasantries such as "Hey" or "How've you been?"

"Go ahead and guess," she urged.

"You're getting married again?" BeBe had only ditched husband number three a few months earlier, but like I said, BeBe's a fast worker. And she never liked being without a man.

"This is serious, Weezie," BeBe said. "Guess who's dead?"

"Richard?" I said hopefully. Richard was BeBe's second husband, the one who'd had the unfortunate proclivity for phone sex. BeBe was still fighting with the phone company over all the bills Richard had run up calling 1-900-YOU-SKRU.

"Be serious now," BeBe demanded. "Emery Cooper called me this morning. You know Emery, don't you, darlin'? He's a Cooper-Hale Cooper, you know, from the funeral home? He's been pesterin' me to go to dinner for weeks now, but I told him I never date a man until he's been divorced for at least a year. Anyway, Emery's cute, but he's got children. You know how I am. And I don't like the idea of necking with somebody who works with the dead. Is that awful of me?" She didn't waste any time waiting for an answer.

"Anyway, Weezie, Emery let it drop that Anna Ruby Mullinax died last night. In her sleep. Ninety-seven years old, did you know that? And still living in the same house she was born in. Of course, Cooper-Hale is handling the funeral arrangements."

Jethro was licking my toes again. He wanted out. But I hated to have him pee on any more camellias until Caroline cooled off. I cradled the phone to my ear.

"That's nice, BeBe," I said. "Listen, could you call back? I've got to take Jethro for a walk right quick."

"Weezie," BeBe exclaimed. "Don't you get it?"

"What? Emery Cooper wants to get into your pants? Does he smell like formaldehyde, do you think?"

"No," BeBe said. "He smells lovely. Like money. But child, I'm worried about you. Didn't you hear what I said? It's Anna Ruby Mullinax. That house she lived and died in? It's Beaulieu, honey. Now what do you think about that?"

I felt a little tingle on my neck. Beaulieu. I looked down at my forearms. Goose bumps.

"You said she was ninety-seven," I said, my voice shaking. "Were there any survivors?"

"Not a living soul," BeBe said triumphantly. "And Emery says the house is jam-packed with old stuff. Now. Who's the very best best friend in the whole wide world?"

"You are," I assured her. "I'll call you later."

 Of course, once I'd calmed down from my encounter with Caroline, I was able to put Anna Ruby Mullinax in context with Beaulieu, the crumbling Mullinax rice plantation on the Skidaway River, seven miles outside of town.

She was the last of the Mullinaxes, one of those "fine old families" whose members claimed to have come over in 1733 with General James Oglethorpe's first shipload of Georgia settlers, who, incidentally, were definitely not the deadbeats Yankee history books would have you believe. Don't ever mention the words "debtors' colony" in Savannah—not if you know what's good for you.

At one time, according to my mother, who keeps up with this sort of thing, the Mullinaxes were the richest family on the coast, and Beaulieu was the grandest plantation house in the South, the very last working rice plantation in Georgia, up until 1970, when Hurricane Brenda rampaged south out of Charleston, and the tidal surge blew just enough salt water into the rice canals to ruin the crop and the Mullinax fortune.

Funny. The year the Mullinaxes lost their money was the same year I was born.

I've looked it up. Nineteen seventy was also the year the Beatles broke up, Nixon was president, US forces invaded Cambodia, and *The Partridge Family* was a smash hit on television. Hard to believe that was also the year Jimi Hendrix and Janis Joplin both died. And they were only twenty-seven. Not to mention it was the year of Kent State and four dead in O-hi-o.

For the rest of America, 1970 was a year of revolution. For the Foleys of Savannah, it was the year my forty-year-old mother produced a living miracle—me.

Up until my mother realized a really rotten case of heartburn was actually a pregnancy that was six months along, nobody had ever really expected any big surprises from Marian Foley. Having a baby at forty was the last thing my mother expected out of middle age. I know, because whenever I've crossed her over the years, she's told me so.

"Forty," she always says, crossing her arms over her bosom in the classic martyred-matron pose. "To think I waited all those years for you. A miracle. That's what it was. Father Keane said you were a gift from Our Lady. Because of all the novenas I made."

Once, at a family party, when my father got into the Jim Beam with the bad uncles, he heard my mother tell that story once too often.

"Bullshit," he bellowed. "It wasn't the damned novenas. It was a busted Trojan!"

Mama didn't speak to him for six months.

And so, more than thirty years after that precipative prophylactic incident, on the hottest day of July, I set out for Beaulieu to pay my respects to the late Anna Ruby Mullinax. And, of course, to see the treasures of Beaulieu.

Ever since I can remember, the place has fascinated me. We used to pass it on our Sunday-afternoon drives, and Daddy would slow the car down so we could get a good look down that long, live-oak-lined driveway. You couldn't see the house from the road, just the trees dripping Spanish moss and the rusted wrought-iron gateway with Beaulieu written in arching cursive letters.

Once, when I was a teenager, a boyfriend took me for a boat ride on the Skidaway River and pointed out the ruins of the plantation's old slave quarters, barely visible through the green-and-gold swath of marsh grass that separated Beaulieu from the river. There had been a long dock once, stretching out over the marsh to a landing on the river, but all that was left by the late eighties were rotted pilings populated by giant brown pelicans who sat in the sun and blinked and yawned in the relentless heat.

It was high tide, so we ran the boat up on the gray mud riverbank and snuck onto the property. The boyfriend's name was Danny Stipanek. We only lasted three months as an item, mostly because Danny, who was nineteen and getting ready to enlist in the Marines, was perpetually horny, whereas I was afraid of getting pregnant, or worse, in Savannah, getting a bad reputation. That day, though, something came over me. Not the terminally tumescent Danny Stipanek, but the cool, velvet beauty of Beaulieu.

I didn't get pregnant, just sunburned and chigger-bit in the worst possible places. Danny Stipanek drifted out of my life and into the Marine Corps just as it was time to start my senior year of high school in the fall. I always think of him now when I see those television recruiting commercials for the Marines. The few. The proud. The horny.

My father always calls the obituaries "the Irish sports page." The day after BeBe's phone call, I saw the funeral notice for Anna Ruby Mullinax. Just as BeBe had promised, there were no survivors. And as she'd promised, there'd be a memorial service at Beaulieu. A chance for an advance showing.

That Friday, I slipped my best dress into a plastic dry-cleaner's bag and hung it carefully over the passenger seat of the truck. I thought of the dress as my homage to Zelda Fitzgerald—buttercup yellow ankle-length silk voile, with a matching silk underslip. I'd found it in a plastic garbage bag full of old clothes a year earlier when workers were tearing down an old Victorian house on East Thirty-eighth Street.

Dressed in my favorite baggy khaki shorts, faded T-shirt, and sneakers, I made my usual Friday-morning rounds. I'd circled four estate sales in the classifieds of the *Savannah Morning News* but only one turned up anything worth buying. After the sales, I hit the Goodwill store on Victory Drive, the St. Vincent DePaul Thrift Shop, and finally, the This N' That.

Mr. Meshach Greenaway runs the TNT. It's a homely little concrete block box that used to be a lawn mower repair shop, until Mr. Greenaway discovered he could make more money hauling away white people's junk than he could fixing black people's busted Snappers.

The TNT is over in what my mama calls "the quarters" —one of her typical euphemisms for Roosevelt Park, a modest, mostly black neighborhood a few miles from my parents' own all-white suburban ranch-style neighborhood.

Mr. Greenaway saw me coming. He opened the door and cracked a smile, his blue-black face dripping with perspiration. He pointed toward a towering pile of boxes that blocked the entire front of the shop.

"Been waitin' for you, Weezie," he said, taking a sip from his ever-present plastic foam cup of ice water. "Take a look over there, girl. That there's all the attic and garage of Mr. Arnold Lowenstein of East Forty-sixth Street." He lowered his voice, in case of spies.

"Mr. Lowenstein, he the one owns Low-Low Liquors. Used to anyway. He dead now. Got that big old redbrick house with the hedge around it, over on the corner of Atlantic Avenue."

The address he'd mentioned was prime territory, a wealthy settled neighborhood, big houses, and old money.

Mr. Greenaway nudged me. "Take a look."

Oh, the junk!

The Low-Low Liquor Lowensteins were prominent in all the right circles in Savannah, and they'd had four kids. They were big wheels at Temple Mickve Israel. Cissy Lowenstein had been a grade ahead of me at St. Vincent's Academy, Walter a year behind me over at Benedictine. In case you're wondering, the way it works in Savannah, rich WASP kids go to Country Day School and working-class Catholics and rich Jews go to the parochial schools.

Anyway, the kids would have taken all the "good" stuff, I knew. So there was no sterling silver, cut glass, or bone china, nothing with an English pedigree or a French accent. It was just a good old bonanza of baby-boomer Americana.

The Lowensteins had been savers, bless their hearts. Practically nothing had been thrown away since Mr. Arnold had gotten back from World War II. Of course, none of it was stuff my local dealers would touch.

There was a whole carton of Fire-King jadeite dishes, with sectioned luncheon plates, matching coffee mugs, cereal bowls and chop plates, enough to stock a small 1950s diner.

Another box yielded mint-condition magazines from the thirties and forties; *Field and Stream, Boys' Life, Argosy, Collier's* and *Vanity Fair*. The covers were original color illustrations by the biggest names of the era. The *Field and Streams* alone would bring fifteen dollars a pop from my antiquarian book guy in Charleston.

I pawed through the boxes like a woman possessed, rejecting thirty years worth of *National Geographic*s and all Mr. Lowenstein's banking records from the 1950s, but separating out a stack of hemstitched Irish linen bedsheets and pillowcases, yellowing lace curtains, and a pile of women's satin and silk slips, nighties, and peignoirs. When I opened a metal foot-locker containing Mr. Lowenstein's World War II army uniforms, I knew I'd found something good. Stashed under the uniform was a fabulous cache of forties and fifties pinup girl calendars, playing cards, and magazines. As soon as I spotted the first Vargas girl calendar, I began to appreciate the fact that Arnold Lowenstein had been a true connoisseur of nudie art. I loved him more when I found the first issue of *Playboy*, dated 1951, and the subsequent issue that featured the famous Marilyn Monroe pictorial.

After an hour, I was filthy, smudged with dust and mildew, my clothes littered with dead silverfish. I reeked of mothballs, but I was happy.

I sat back on my heels and looked up at Mr. Greenaway, who'd been pretending to read the newspaper.

"How much?" I asked, gesturing toward the pile I'd accumulated.

He sucked his teeth, closed his eyes, took a pencil stub, and scribbled numbers on the margin of the newspaper page.

"Look like a hundred seventy-five to me," he said. "And that's 'cause you a regular."

I felt a stab of Catholic guilt coming on. The stuff was worth at least four hundred dollars, even buying wholesale, which I was doing. I was fairly sure I could make at least three times that, if my usual dealers were in a buying mode and if I hadn't made any stupid mistakes. But I had exactly two hundred dollars in cash on me, and I was trying to budget my buying to free up enough cash for the upcoming Beaulieu sale.

"It's worth more than that, Mr. Greenaway," I said. "Those green dishes are jadeite. Really trendy. The plates alone go for thirty-five dollars apiece in Atlanta."

Mr. Greenaway pushed his sweat-stained baseball cap to the back of his head. "That right?" he said, picking up one of the diner dishes, looking at it with new respect.

I took the roll of twenty-dollar bills out of the black leather fanny pack I wear strapped around my waist, peeled off seven bills, and handed them to him. "I'm kind of strapped this week," I said. "How about I take everything but the dishes for one hundred forty dollars. If you don't sell them, maybe I can come back next week, after I turn this stuff around."

Mr. Greenaway took the money and tucked it into the bib pocket of his overalls. "Go on ahead and take the dishes, Weezie," he said. "You good for it. Think I don't know that?"

By the time we got everything loaded in my truck, it was already eleven-thirty. I'd have to rush to my parents' to get showered, dressed, and over to Beaulieu.

I whizzed in the kitchen door, past Mama, who was at the sink peeling tomatoes for my father's lunch. Daddy always has the same lunch during the summer; a tomato sandwich on white bread with Blue Plate mayonnaise, Lay's potato chips, and a Diet Pepsi.

My father was taking his midmorning nap, I knew. Since he retired from the post office, he has a regular routine; breakfast, newspaper, coupon clipping, nap, lunch. Then, yardwork, nap, television game shows, dinner.

"OK if I take a shower?" I asked, not waiting for an answer.

"Weezie?" Mama said, looking up. "What are you up to?"

"In a hurry," I said, grabbing a handful of potato chips as I passed.

My hair was still damp from the shower when I came back into the kitchen, wearing my yellow Zelda dress.

Mama put the plate of sandwiches on the kitchen table and eyed me with suspicion.

"You goin' to a dress-up party in July?"

"No, ma'am," I said. "I'm going out to Beaulieu. To Miss Anna Ruby Mullinax's memorial service."

As soon as I'd said it, I knew it was a mistake.

"Jean Eloise Foley, don't you dare," Mama said, setting her iced tea glass down on the table with a thud. Her thin, blue-veined nostrils flared from the outrage of it all. "That's the most sacrilegious thing I have ever heard. I won't have it, you hear?"

When she's drinking Four Roses watered down to look like iced tea, something she usually does 1 to 4 P.M. year-round, Mama thinks everything is either outrageous or sacrilegious.

"The paper said family and friends would be received for the memorial service at Beaulieu starting at one P.M. today," I pointed out. "She doesn't have any family left. Who's to say I'm not a friend?"

"You're not," Mama said. "We don't know any of those people. People like the Mullinaxes don't know people like the Foleys." She leaned in closer to me, sniffed my dress, and made a face. "People like the Mullinaxes don't know people who pick through other people's garbage for their clothes."

I ran my hand down the front of the dress, which I'd spent hours hand-washing, mending, and pressing. Suddenly, I didn't feel like a Zelda. I felt like a zero. Mama has a talent for that.

"This dress has the original Hattie Carnegie label," I said quietly. "If I decided to sell it, I could get at least two hundred dollars from one of my vintage dealers in New York. Maybe more if I auctioned it on eBay."

"You can't go out to that woman's house," Mama insisted.

"She's dead," I said. "She won't mind a bit."

Mama sipped her bourbon/tea. "It's disgraceful," she said. "What if one of the Evanses is there? Tal's mother and daddy run around in that crowd. What if one of them sees you there?"

I forced a smile and dipped a phony little curtsy. "I'll say 'Hello, Genevieve. Hello, Big Tal. So nice to see you again. I'm just here to see how the other half lives, now that your son left me and ripped me off for most everything I own. Please give my regards to Little Tal, and tell him I hope he and his darling Caroline rot in hell."

Mama got up abruptly, went to the refrigerator, pulled out an aluminum tray of ice cubes, and clinked more cubes into the tall glass already standing on the kitchen counter.

"I still can't believe you've ended up like this," she said accusingly. "Tal was perfect for you. You had the perfect life." Her nearly nonexistent upper lip quivered, the fine downy hairs rippling like a miniature crop of wheat. "Now look at you. You live in a garage. No job, no husband, no prospects. What kind of life is that?"

Daddy walked into the kitchen as Mama was launching into her "no prospects" spiel. He had the television listings folded into a neat square, his afternoon viewing plans all mapped out. He stared down at Mama's drink on the countertop, frowned, then looked over at me.

"If you'd just get a job and then quit, I could tell people what kind of work it is that you're out of," Daddy said, chuckling as he always did when he pulled this line on me.

He reached around to his back pocket, took out his black leather billfold and extracted two ten-dollar bills. "Here," he said, giving me a wink. "To tide you over."

I pushed the money away. "I'm fine, Daddy. Really."

He looked at my dress, grabbed my hand, folded my fingers over the bills. "Buy yourself something nice. A new dress."

Like twenty bucks could buy a new dress. Daddy still thought Cokes cost a dime. I tucked the bills in the breast pocket of his short-sleeved dress shirt. "Keep your money," I said. Be sweet, Weezie, I thought. Even if it kills you. "Tell you what, Daddy. Play my numbers in the lottery. It's up to eleven million this week. If you win, you can give me half."

He was getting annoyed now. He did that when I showed signs of having outgrown my training bra and my pink princess telephone—both of which were still ensconced in my old bedroom at the back of the house.

"Just keep it 'til you get a job and move out of that garage," he said, shoving the money back into my hand.

"I'm self-employed, not unemployed. And it's a carriage house, not a garage," I said, my voice tight. "My carriage house is a historically signifi-cant structure on the most beautiful street in the historic district."

"For Christ's sake! It's a garage behind the house your husband lives in with his girlfriend," Daddy said.

"Ex-husband," Mama said, always helpful. "I guess we should be grateful she's got a roof over her head, Joe. If it weren't for your brother James, she'd be out on the streets. Or back here, living with us."

Be sweet, Weezie, I thought, biting my lip. But I knew I'd live in a Dumpster in hell's back alley before I moved back into that princess pink shrine at my parents' house.

From their point of view, I was a mess, I knew. I was over thirty, newly divorced, with no money or direction or marketable skills. Dropping out of the local community college to marry Talmadge Evans III had seemed like a good idea when I'd done it ten years ago. The ink on his Georgia Tech architecture degree was barely dry, and we were tired of having sex in the back seat of his mother's big white Lincoln Continental.

Genevieve Evans has always driven Lincolns, and his father, Big Tal, has always driven Cadillacs. Tal's family are what Mama likes to call "well-fixed."

In Savannah, that's a euphemism for old, Episcopalian money. "Filthy rich" on the other hand, is new, Yankee money. "Stinking rich" is Jew money. If a woman is "popular," it means she puts out. If a man is "artis-tic," he's gay. If a rich kid is "troubled," he's a sociopath. It's easy if you've lived here long enough. And the Foleys have always lived in Savannah. Well, always since Aloysious Francis Foley came here from county Kerry, Ireland, in the 1850s to help lay track for the Southern Railroad.

Daddy turned on the television on the kitchen counter, sat down at the chrome-and-Formica dinette table, and unfolded his television viewing chart. He frowned. *Jeopardy* would not be on for another half hour. He would have to settle for *Wheel of Fortune*.

"Selling junk!" Daddy muttered. "What the hell kind of work is that?"

"I'm a picker," I told my father for the bazillionth time. "I buy antiques at the source and fix them up and sell them to antique dealers. It's a real job and I make real money."

"Garbage picker," Mama said, lapping up her bourbon/tea.

"Look at the time," I said, edging toward the door. "Bye-ee."

"What's your hurry?" Daddy asked. "Have lunch. You look like you could use a free meal."

I snatched another handful of potato chips and dashed for the door. "Thanks!" I called over my shoulder.

ames Aloysious Foley leaned back in his chair and studied the wooden fan blades doing slow circular laps around the high pressed-tin ceiling over his head. He sighed, then looked back at the woman sitting in the wing chair opposite his desk, who was waiting for him to say something profound.

"You see, Father James," she began, dabbing nervously at her forehead with a crumpled tissue, "I don't want a divorce. Divorce is a sin. I just want you to fix it so that Inky brings his paycheck home like he's supposed to."

"Mrs. Cahoon, *please*," James said. "I'm not *Father* James anymore, remember? I'm out of the priesthood. I'm a lawyer. Now, from what you've told my secretary, you haven't had much of a marriage for a long time. It's time you ended it. Start a new life for yourself and let Inky get on with his."

Denise Cahoon jumped from the chair, her face flushed beet red. In her early fifties, she was a good-looking woman by James's standards; nice trim figure, sleek dark hair pushed back behind her ears, soulful gray eyes. Why she wanted to cling to some beer-soaked lout like Inky Cahoon was a mystery.

"That's not true!" she said in a piercing voice. "Our vows are sacred. I don't want a new life. I want my old one back. You make Inky do the right thing. Call his boss down at the newspaper and tell him Inky's spending his paycheck on whores and liquor. Tell him they're to send that check right to the house instead of letting Inky spend it all."

James looked back up at the ceiling fan. Sometimes he swore he could see patterns in the dust motes as the blades cut through them. Running horses, majestic oak trees. Today, as Denise Cahoon implored him to salvage the unsalvageable, he swore the dust swirls looked exactly like the holy card of the Immaculate Heart of Mary, the one that was pierced by a flaming sword and bound in chains. He shook his head and looked back at Denise Cahoon.

"Mrs. Cahoon," he said, his voice taking on the gentle note of the confessor he'd been for twenty-four years (one year shy of his silver jubilee, he'd up and quit, turned in his cassock, surplice, scapular, and holy-water font), "Inky moved out five years ago. You told my secretary he's been living with a girl from the composing room. They have a four-year-old child and another on the way. That doesn't sound like a good sign for your marriage."

"It's probably not his kid," Denise said belligerently. "That girl sleeps with anything in pants. I've seen her, the slut. Inky just wants to think it's his. He always wanted kids."

James reached into a tray on his desk, got out the divorce forms, handed them across the desk to Denise Cahoon.

"It's probably for the best," he said. "No children involved. Look over those papers, call me, and we'll get them all filled out. We can file for the divorce; everything could be taken care of in six weeks."

She stared at James as though he were an alien, beamed down there to that dusty little office on Factors Walk by whatever unholy forces had already been at work destroying her life for the past five years.

"That's it? That's all you can tell me? No counseling, no family therapy? Just boom, sign here, it's over? Twenty-two years and now I'm no longer Mrs. Bradley R. Cahoon Junior?"

Her voice rose a little with every syllable she spoke, and her face got pinker, and she loomed higher and higher over James's desk. It occurred to James that Inky had possibly been wise to get out while the getting was good.

"You can call yourself whatever name you like," James pointed out. "But I'm afraid divorce is probably your only option now. If you drag things out, it'll just cost you more money in legal fees. After five years and two children, it's doubtful to me that Inky is going to have a change of heart."

Mrs. Bradley R. Cahoon Jr. reached across the desk and snatched the papers out of his hand. "Never mind. I came here because your mother and my mother were friends. My mother was at your ordination, you know. Right there at the cathedral. I thought a priest would see the right thing to do. Ha! Bernadette Foley would roll over in her grave if she could see you right now, James Foley. Divorce! Shame on you." She wagged her finger at his face. "Shame."

James pushed his chair backward, away from that thin, fleshy finger. "Good-bye, Mrs. Cahoon," he said.

He swiveled the chair around and looked out the dirt-streaked window at the muddy brown Savannah River.

A sleek black tanker glided by, its bulk seeming to dwarf the people and cars on River Street. Japanese registry. The name Shinmoru Sunbeam was painted on the ship's bow.

He heard the door to his office slam. Good.

He'd had lots of clients like Denise Cahoon since he'd moved back to Savannah from his last church in Naples, Florida. People just wanted to hear what they wanted to hear. And he wasn't in the penance business anymore.

The door opened again, and he smelled perfume—gardenias this month—and cigarettes.

"Christ!" Janet drawled. "That woman doesn't get it, does she?"

James swiveled the chair around so that it faced the door again. The river mesmerized him. It always had. He couldn't get any work done if he could see the river from where he sat. And there was work to be done. Thank God.

Janet had a stack of files in her arms. She piled them on top of the wing chair, then put a pink message slip in front of him on the desk. She ran her fingers through her short, wiry, gray hair, and the cigarette she'd tucked behind her ear fell to the floor. She tried to kick it out of the way, so he wouldn't see it.

"I thought you were going to quit smoking," James said, trying to look stern.

"Don't start," she warned.

Janet Shinholster was his secretary, oldest friend, and business manager.

They'd dated all those years ago, back when he was a cadet at Benedictine and she was at St. Vincent's. After he'd entered the priesthood, he'd seen her only occasionally until he returned to Savannah from Florida.

They'd had a tentative date or two right after he came back two years ago. There was even some fumbling around on the sofa in Janet's apartment, until James reluctantly confided his suspicions that he probably wasn't terribly interested in sex.

"You're gay," Janet had said, not acting the least bit surprised. "I understand, James. Totally."

Her reaction annoyed him, actually. He'd never thought of himself as swishy, not in any way. At all.

"What makes you think that?" he'd demanded.

"You've been shut up in a seminary or a rectory your whole life," Janet said. "Since you were eighteen. And then you quit the priesthood. Just like that. I figured, you know, finally. He's ready to cut loose. Explore the alternatives."

"Do I act queer to you?" he'd wanted to know. "Interested in boys? Is that what you thought? That I was one of *those* priests? A pedophile?"

"Never mind," Janet had said, turning on the lights and straightening her blouse. "Let's forget it ever happened."

What annoyed him even more was that Janet was right. He'd started seeing someone, a year later. Not some faggy little boy-toy. Jonathan was a successful lawyer, chief assistant district attorney. It was all very discreet, except that Janet knew, the first time Jonathan came by the office to take him to lunch. Damned Janet knew everything.

"Weezie called," Janet said. "She wanted to know if you were busy this afternoon."

James smiled. His niece was the real reason he'd come back to Savannah. They'd always been close. "You're the father I never had," she liked to tease. "The mother too."

"What's Weezie up to?" he asked.

Janet shrugged. "She said she was going out to Beaulieu for a memorial service for Anna Ruby Mullinax. Wants you to meet her there, if you don't have anything better to do."

"Do I?" James asked, looking meaningfully at the stack of files on the wing chair.

"I think you should go," Janet said. "Anna Ruby Mullinax knew a lot of people in this town. Influential people. People who need legal work."

Janet took his blue blazer off the brass coat hook on the back of the door and held it out to him. "You'll have to wear a necktie, you know."

He shuddered. It was ninety-six degrees outside, the humidity at 100 percent, as usual.

"And don't forget to take some business cards with you," she added. "This is called networking, James."

CHAPTER *4*

 *I* turned up the air conditioner on the pickup truck and glanced anxiously at the temperature gauge. The needle hovered below "simmer."

"Just let me get to Beaulieu and then you can go on the fritz again," I said, giving the dashboard a pat for encouragement.

Before I was divorced, I never talked to inanimate objects. Not out loud. Now I talk to my truck, the toaster, and my bank statement, anything that promises not to talk back or to act snotty. I've had a lifetime of snotty.

Jethro's tail thumped on the vinyl seat. One thing about Jethro, he loves the sound of my voice. "Good boy," I told him. Thump. Thump. "Sweet, precious boy," I said. Thump, thump, thump. He was really getting hot and bothered now.

One of Jethro's best qualities is that he is the least critical dog I have ever known. He loves everybody, hasn't got a mean bone in his body. I found him one morning right after Tal left, when I was taking my usual predawn curb cruise.

There was a huge mountain of junk in front of a stick-style Victorian somebody was renovating on Habersham. I was poking around, pulling out bits of wooden porch rails, chunks of wrought-iron fencing, even a gorgeous stained-glass window transom, when I heard a faint squeal. I backed away from the pile fast. The squealing continued, too loud even for Savannah's brashest wharf rats.

I edged closer, kicked aside a length of rusted-out gutter, and saw a little black-and-white wriggling hairball. He had a pink nose with black spots and he was no bigger than a one-pound sack of flour. At first he looked like he was covered with flour. It turned out it was just plaster dust from the junk pile. It was also instant love. I left the stained glass, tucked the puppy and the porch rails under each arm, and ran like a thief back to my carriage house.

As for the puppy, the vet said he was part beagle, part German shepherd, and mostly mutt. It cost me two hundred dollars for all the shots and the deworming medicine. He's the only dog I've ever owned. Daddy would never hear of a dog, him being a mailman and everything. I named him Jethro, for Jethro Tull, the rock group, and Jethro Bodine, the *Beverly Hillbillies* hunk.

Tal called his lawyer and then my lawyer the first time he glanced out the back window and saw Jethro lift a leg on a camellia bush in his half of the walled garden.

"That crazy bitch is keeping animals," Tal yelled. (James played the message-machine tape for me.)

"Weezie's not a tenant," James reminded him when he returned Tal's call. I was sitting right there listening in, of course.

"Look at the property settlement papers," James told Tal. "The judge awarded Weezie the carriage house. She can keep elephants and giraffes if she wants to. So if I were you, I'd keep quiet about the dog. No telling what she'll come home with otherwise."

We were almost at the gates to Beaulieu. I could feel my dress wilting like week-old lettuce. The temperature inside the truck was at least ninety. I pulled the truck off right where the crushed-oyster-shell driveway began, directly under the open Beaulieu gate, leaned over, and rolled the window down. Jethro is just tall enough to see out the passenger-side window. He stuck his head out, sniffed, and gave one short, appreciative bark. I believe that dog can smell an antique.

I gave myself a quick glance in the truck's rearview mirror. My short, dark red hair was plastered to my head and my face was almost as red as my hair from the heat. My brown eyeliner had started to run in the corners, like Pagliacci.

I was dabbing at my melted makeup when a white Mercedes pulled up beside me and tooted the horn.

James. The electric window on the passenger side glided down. "You better ride the rest of the way with me," he called.

"Jethro too?" I asked.

He looked over at Jethro, who had jumped into my lap and was trying to stick his head out my window to say hello to his old buddy James.

"Will he stay in the car and not chew up the upholstery?" The Mercedes had been a retirement gift from James's parish in Florida. I call it the pimpmobile, but James says he gave up his vow of poverty and intends to start making up for all those years of driving Chevys.

"He'll be good," I promised.

James's car was divinely cool. It smelled like new leather and Beech-Nut chewing gum. I held my damp head in front of the air-conditioning vent and pulled my fingers through my hair to try to get it dry.

"I didn't know you knew Anna Ruby Mullinax," James said, one eyebrow raised, the way he does.

"I didn't," I said. "But this may be the only chance I ever get to go inside Beaulieu. Mama says that's sacrilege."

"Your mother's an expert on sacrilege," James said.

"But you knew Miss Anna Ruby," I said. "Janet told me."

"Did she tell you how we met?"

"Don't think so," I said.

"It was a long time ago," James recalled. "The year I helped start that little church in Metter, Christ Our Hope. Must have been 1978, something like that. Miss Mullinax called me, said she'd heard through some of 'her people' that we were building a new church."

"I thought the Mullinaxes were Episcopalian," I said, interrupting.

"They were. By 'her people' she meant the black folks who'd been family servants. Slaves, originally. But people like the Mullinaxes didn't like to call it slavery after civil rights got fashionable. A whole crowd of those black folks were living up there in Metter. Most of them Catholic, most of them in my new parish."

"What did she want?" I asked.

James smiled. He has the Foley family jaw, long and squared off, and when he smiles, which is frequently, it makes creases all the way up to his eye sockets.

"She wanted to give us something for the new church. In memory of a woman named Clydie. Clydie Jeffers. She'd been Miss Anna Ruby's housekeeper until she died at the age of eighty-eight. So I came out here, to Beaulieu, and we talked, and Miss Anna Ruby ended up donating the pews for Christ Our Hope. Had them made out of cypress trees they cut out here on the property. And a little brass plaque said they were placed there 'In loving memory of Clydie Jeffers.' No mention of the donor. Miss Anna Ruby strictly required anonymity."

A slight breeze stirred the moss from the trees overhanging the shell drive. The live oaks were spaced sentinel style, ten yards apart on both sides, their bases covered with a creeping carpet of ivy, their canopy nearly blotting out the blazing blue sky overhead.

I squinted, and up ahead, at the end of the tree tunnel, I could see the shape of the house, rising over the treetops. I sat up and waited for the house to come fully into view. I'd waited a long time to see Beaulieu.

"She was nice?" I murmured, keeping my eyes on the house.

"Different," James said. "She was dressed in pants, I remember that. I'd never seen such an old lady wearing pants. And barefoot! Your grandmother Foley never went barefoot outside her own bedroom, let alone walked around in front of a stranger, and a priest, at that. Miss Anna Ruby was her own person, and careful with her money."

By then I wasn't listening. We were there.

Three-story-tall Doric columns, twelve in all, stretched across the front of the house, supporting a carved balustrade, and above that were three gables, and beside that, there was a one-story wing on each side. The house was raised up, on a foundation made of tabby, the crushed-oyster-shell masonry you find on old houses along the coast in South Carolina and Georgia.

There was a double stairway winding from the entry porch to the portico. Not white, like the Hollywood version of a Southern plantation house, Beaulieu was painted a pale golden pink, with black-green shutters on the wide six-over-six windows. It was imposing and breathtaking—and it was crumbling.

Paint hung in shreds from the columns, whose bases were chipped and rotted, like a bag lady's teeth. A fine sheen of green mold had worked its way from the foundations up the front of the house, and the wooden slats of the window shutters had rotted and fallen away. One of the gable roofs had collapsed, the portico sagged, and the only windows not gray and cobweb-streaked had missing panes of glass.

"Oh," I said, feeling the wind go out of my sails. I blinked. "How sad."

"Yes," James said quietly. "Very sad."

Jethro pressed his nose against the window, and I gently pushed it aside.

"It wasn't this decrepit when I came out here in the seventies," James said.

He followed the driveway around the side of the house, to an unpaved area used as the car park. There were ten or twelve other cars parked around. One of them was a buttercup yellow Triumph Spitfire that was carefully parked in the shade of a sweet gum tree.

My stomach lurched, as it does every time I see the Spitfire.

"What's she doing here?" I said, grabbing James's arm. "She doesn't even like old stuff."

He'd left the air-conditioning on, but he was fumbling with his necktie. "She who?"

I pointed at the Triumph. I knew the car well. After all, it was parked under the carport beside the carriage house in the space that used to be mine. James had won me the carriage house and half the walled garden behind the big house on Troup Square, but the judge, inexplicably, had given Tal my parking slot.

Every night I heard the vroom of the Triumph as it jetted up the alley and slid neatly into the slot—my slot—while I now had to take my chances parking the truck out in front on Charlton Street—if I could find a space at all.

"Caroline," I said. "She's here."

James shot me a look of concern. "Do you want to leave?"

"I'll be fine," I assured him. "As long as she doesn't start anything."

James got a little pale. I patted his hand reassuringly, then turned around and scratched Jethro's muzzle.

"Be a good boy and don't eat Uncle James's nice pimpmobile." I rolled down the windows and gathered my resolve. "Let's go," I said.

The front door had been covered with an ugly 1950s aluminum screen door. Attached to it was a wilted wreath of ferns and daisies. Beneath it was a small handwritten card. "Please come in," it said.

We stepped across the rotted threshold and into another era. Not the antebellum South, unfortunately. More like the late years of the Eisenhower administration.

The wide hallway was dark and cool. A fake colonial chandelier with only one lightbulb still burning hung from a dropped ceiling. The beautiful old plaster walls were painted pale pink; the elaborate egg-and-dart plaster cornice boards and moldings were a dull gray. Venetian blinds covered the tall floor-to-ceiling windows. I looked down at the floor. Thank God. They were coated with grime, but the original heart-pine floorboards had been left intact.

James took my elbow and guided me gently inside. Twin parlors opened off either side of the hallway. The room to the right was piled high with furniture, three long folding card tables were pushed together, every inch of tabletop covered with crystal, china, silver, and pieces of bric-a-brac. Naturally, I started toward the room. But James pulled me back. "Other side," he whispered.

The parlor to the left had been cleared of furniture. A cheap box fan hummed in one of the open windows, pushing more hot, damp air into the already saunalike room.

The gathering was small, no more than twenty people. Most of Anna Ruby Mullinax's friends looked to be candidates for their own memorial service. They were white haired, stoop shouldered, frail. The men mopped at their glistening faces with handkerchiefs, the ladies fanned themselves with the memorial booklets that had been stacked on a table by the front door.

A tall, thin woman wearing white minister's robes stood at a wooden lectern in front of the fireplace. Her shoulder-length white hair stood in a frizzy halo around her head.

But I wasn't really looking at the minister. I was looking around for Caroline.

She saw me first and gave a little wave. I nodded politely and felt my insides curl up and my scalp start to tingle.

Caroline was dressed in a pale gray linen suit with a short, tight skirt that hit four inches above her fabulously knobby knees. As always, she radiated cool elegance while the rest of us were drowning in a puddle of our own perspiration.

An older man stood beside Caroline, his hand resting lightly on her shoulder. He had dark wavy hair styled in a bad comb-over, bushy graying eyebrows, and a tennis tan. I'd met his type at Tal's parents' parties. Christ

Church. Oglethorpe Club. He was wearing a college class ring. Probably Duke or University of Virginia. Definitely Kappa Alpha.

"Who's that with her?" I hissed into James's ear.

He glanced over, nodded solemnly at Caroline's friend, who was watching the two of us watch the two of them.

"That's Gerry Blankenship. The Mullinax family lawyer. Shh."

Anna Ruby Mullinax died at the age of ninety-seven, but her going-away speech took less than ten minutes. "A quickie," my father would have called it.

Within another five minutes, a blond-headed young man gussied up in a white dress shirt, black slacks, and black bow tie was passing around a tray with thimble-sized glasses of sherry. A black teenaged boy in the same outfit offered a silver tray heaped with cheese straws, the traditional Savannah cocktail/funeral offering.

The guests stood and chatted quietly, as though they were outside a church instead of inside the last vestiges of a nearly vanished way of life.

I edged over toward the parlor doorway, heading for the room where all the goodies were stashed. James grabbed my arm just before I reached the hallway. "Eloise!" he said, a little too heartily.

Caroline DeSantos and Gerry Blankenship stood beside James. I couldn't tell who had cornered whom.

James nodded toward the lawyer and then toward me. "Gerry Blankenship, meet my niece, Eloise Foley. Gerry is Miss Mullinax's attorney, Weezie. He was just telling me about the plans for Beaulieu. And of course, you already know Caroline DeSantos."

The faintest tinge of pink flushed across Caroline's lovely olive face. She brushed a strand of glossy black hair away from her forehead.

"This is awkward, isn't it?" she asked, looking from me to Gerry to Uncle James. "Ex-wife and wife to be. Living practically on top of each other. Did you know that, Gerry? Weezie lives in the carriage house behind our house. But that's Savannah. We'll just all have to be very grown-up about this kind of thing, won't we, Weezie?"

Blankenship coughed. I heard James inhale sharply, waiting to see if I'd keep my promise about nonviolence. I felt my fists tightening. Caroline was taller, but I had at least twenty pounds to my advantage. I could beat the stuffing out of her right now, I thought. Slap her into another time zone. Pinch off her head with my bare hands.

"We're all adults," I said, shrugging. Of course I wouldn't attack Caroline in public. Private revenge is so much sweeter.

 ames Foley held his breath as he watched the two women sizing each other up like a pair of alley cats circling the same scrap of mullet.

James had met Caroline months ago, long before Tal's announced shift of affections, at a dinner party Weezie had hosted at the townhouse. He gathered then that Tal and Caroline were inseparable. Weezie had fluttered about from guest to guest that night, offering drinks, hors d'oeuvres, and of course, a running commentary on the house, which was her pride and joy. She'd been totally blind to Tal's attentions to Caroline DeSantos.

Weezie was a born hostess. Where she got her talents from, James would never know. Certainly the Foleys were not party givers. Not even very good cooks. Take Bernadette Foley, his own mother. Her idea of dinner was a pot roast cooked to cinderlike dryness, a nice plate of boiled turnips, and carrots on the side.

His sister-in-law, Marian, Weezie's mother, wasn't much more comfortable in the kitchen. And for the last ten years or so, Marian had been too tipsy most of the time to pull off much more than a grilled cheese sandwich or maybe one of those jars of marinara sauce dumped on top of a plate of overcooked spaghetti.

It had been a mistake, James now realized, to help Weezie win ownership of the carriage house in the divorce settlement with Tal. But she'd been absolutely adamant on the issue. Tal, the lanky, thin-lipped WASP, had also dug in on the issue of the house, refusing to give up his half.

He'd even brazenly moved Caroline into the big house, betting it was the one thing that would force Weezie out. He underestimated the Foley stubborn streak.

Right now, with the two women glaring at each other, James felt as though he should be wearing a black-and-white striped referee's shirt instead of his good suit jacket and the tie Janet kept in his office for important clients.

He grabbled two thimbles full of sherry, handed one each to Weezie and Caroline, and then took one for himself. Gerry Blankenship declined with a shake of his head. From the red glow of his nose and the tang of his breath, he'd already had a taste of something this day, and it wouldn't be anything so mild as ten-dollar-a-gallon sweet sherry.

"You mentioned plans for Beaulieu," James said to Blankenship, hoping to distract the women. "I understood Miss Mullinax didn't have any surviving relatives. What happens to the property now?"

"Nothing's been announced yet," Gerry demurred, suddenly finding something interesting to stare at on the floor. "The will has to go to probate, plans have to be approved. It's all quite tentative."

Caroline smiled broadly. She had beautiful, even, white teeth and the biggest, darkest eyes James Foley had ever seen. A stunner, even though she was a home wrecker, he thought guiltily.

"Gerry loves secrets," Caroline confided. "But the cat will be out of the bag tomorrow, anyway. Go ahead and tell, Gerry. Or let me, please?"

Gerry Blankenship grabbed a glass of sherry that someone had left sitting on the edge of a sideboard. He downed it in one gulp, then looked around for another. "This might not be the time or place," he said.

"Pooh," Caroline said, waving her hand dismissively. "This will be a godsend for this town. Three hundred, four hundred jobs? A capital investment of over three hundred million dollars? Who could argue with that?"

She favored James with a dazzling smile. "You used to be a priest, Mr. Foley. So you know all about confidentiality, right?"

"I'm a lawyer," James said. "My clients trust me to be discreet."

"Now, Caroline," Blankenship started.

"What are you talking about?" Weezie demanded. She'd stopped casting longing glances toward the east parlor and was trying not to stare too hard at the large threadbare oriental rug rolled up against the wall opposite her. James could see her toting up its worth in that adding-machine brain of hers.

Now Weezie was glaring right at Caroline, eyes narrowed, ready to pounce. "What are you talking about?" she demanded, leaning in closer. "What is going to happen to Beaulieu?"

"Gerry?"

Blankenship rocked back and forth on his heels. "Go ahead," he said finally. "It's what Anna Ruby wanted. And that's what this is all about. What she wanted," he said, his voice taking on a belligerent tone. "Not what the hysterical society people want." He lowered his voice. "Anna Ruby was concerned about people. Not some moldering old pile of bricks and boards. Our local economy. Jobs. We talked about it often. How we could keep Savannah so that young people could stay here, make a decent living, become part of the community."

"It's going to be tremendous," Caroline bubbled. "All state-of-the-art technology. Coastal Paper Products wants to make this the finest facility of its kind in the world. And the environmental controls . . ." She rolled her eyes toward the ceiling. "We're designing it to meet standards the EPA hasn't even set yet. Nobody will even know it's here. Back off the road, no smokestacks, no emissions, nothing."

James swallowed his sherry, wincing at the sweetness. "Are you talking about a paper plant? Here? At Beaulieu?"

Weezie's jaw dropped. "You can't . . . Beaulieu?"

Blankenship harumphed. He squared his shoulders. "As I say, it was Miss Mullinax's wish. She was a practical woman. And Beaulieu had outlived its usefulness long ago. Have you any idea of what the upkeep on this place would be? And there was no money to do any of it, you know. Miss Mullinax was quite proud of her family's heritage. Coastal Paper Products wants to call it the Beaulieu-Mullinax Plant. A living memorial."

"Beaulieu. The house?" Weezie squeaked. "What happens to the house?"

Caroline cut her eyes over at Blankenship. He shrugged.

"Nothing has been decided," she said. "Coastal would *love* to restore the house. They're very preservation-minded. Do you know Phipps and Diane Mayhew?" she asked James.

"Uh, no," James said.

"Phipps is the president of Coastal Paper Products," Caroline went on. "Tal just finished designing a guest pavilion for their house out on Turner's Rock. And I'm designing the new plant. You remember the Mayhews, don't you, Weezie? Diane came out here with us today, to pay her respects to Miss Anna Ruby. Phipps had to be in a meeting in New York."

James knew Weezie knew the Mayhews. She'd complained bitterly about the efforts she'd taken to impress the couple back when they'd first moved to Savannah and Tal had gotten wind of all that Yankee money they intended to spend on their "country estate."

Weezie had told of peeling and deveining ten pounds of shrimp, sorting and picking over five pounds of back-fin crabmeat, even painting the downstairs powder room, all to impress the Mayhews during the "intimate little dinner party" she'd thrown for them.

"Phipps Mayhew gobbled everything I set in front of him. It could have been a bowl of soggy Rice Krispies and he wouldn't have cared," Weezie had reported. "And that wife! Diane Mayhew claimed to have a seafood allergy. She nibbled at a lettuce leaf and asked for some kind of imported mineral water I never heard of."

"Oh," Caroline said, smiling and waving at someone across the room. "Here's Diane now."

A short dumpy woman in an expensive black knit suit tottered over toward them and gave Weezie a tentative sort of smile.

"Well, hello, Mrs. Evans," the woman said. "I don't know if you remember me. I'm Diane Mayhew. My husband, Phipps, and I had a lovely dinner at your home when we first moved to town."

"Hello, Diane," Weezie said. "Of course I remember you. But my name isn't Evans. It's Weezie Foley. Tal and I are divorced, you know."

Diane Mayhew blinked. "I'm so sorry," she stammered. "I had no idea. Phipps never mentioned . . ."

"Actually," Caroline meowed, "Tal and I are engaged. I'm surprised Phipps didn't say something."

"Oh," Diane Mayhew said, laughing nervously. "You know men. If it isn't about business, they don't concern themselves with the petty details of other people's lives."

Diane Mayhew had mouse-colored hair, thin eyebrows, and watery blue eyes. Her hands clanked with thick gold chains and bangle bracelets. To James, she looked the essence of out-of-place chic in the heavy black suit. Her face shone with perspiration, and her hairstyle had fallen like a flat soufflé.

Now James saw Weezie's eyes narrow.

"Caroline has just been telling us that your husband's company has bought Beaulieu," Weezie said. "But surely it isn't possible you plan to tear down this wonderful old house."

Diane Mayhew gazed around and actually shuddered.

"Wonderful? I don't think I'll ever understand you people down here. Why, up home, this place wouldn't even merit a second look. My goodness, when you consider the history of places like Westchester County in New York, or Bucks County, Pennsylvania, this place is totally unimpressive. And the lack of maintenance, in my opinion, is shocking. Phipps tells me Caroline and her firm have designed a breathtaking new building that will be a real showplace for you people."

Weezie actually gnashed her teeth. "Diane," she said in a slow, deliberate drawl, "it may interest *you people* to know that Beaulieu is the oldest house of its kind on the Georgia coast." She turned to Blankenship. "Isn't Beaulieu some kind of historic landmark or something?"

Gerry Blankenship shuddered when she said "landmark."

"Not at all," he said quickly. "The architecture is totally unremarkable, and of course, the place is falling apart. But Caroline here is the architect; she can tell you much more about it than I. Those people from the hysteric society have been out here, snooping around, asking a lot of questions, but while she was alive Miss Mullinax would never allow them on the property. She was a free spirit, didn't believe in letting somebody else tell her what to do with her own property."

Caroline started to say something but stopped abruptly, giving a sidelong glance at a striking-looking woman who was standing in the hallway, staring raptly up at one of the crumbling plaster ceiling medallions. She nudged Blankenship. "Do you see who I see?"

They all turned to find out whom Caroline was looking at.

"Excuse us," Caroline murmured. She took Blankenship's hand, and the two of them glided away toward the far corner of the room. Diane Mayhew followed in their wake.

"What was that all about?" James asked.

"Merijoy Rucker," Weezie said, smiling like the cat that'd found the cream. "No wonder those three shut up so fast."

"Who is she?" James asked, staring at the brunette who'd spooked Caroline and Blankenship. Something about the girl's face, the pert upturned nose, the short, sleek dark hair, seemed familiar. She looked about Weezie's age, but dressed more conservatively, in a sleeveless black silk shift with pearls around her neck and at her ears. Very slender, with endless long legs encased in sheer dark hose. She looked like money.

"I've seen her before," James said.

"Well, she's Catholic, so I wouldn't be surprised," Weezie said. "Plus, she's the head of the Savannah Preservation League. She was a couple years ahead of me at St. Vincent's. She married the youngest Rucker; Randy, I think his name is."

"Rucker Freight," James said, remembering. "Mrs. Rucker was Catholic, but Mr. Rucker was just rich."

"Very good, James." Weezie patted his shoulder approvingly. Because he'd been a priest, James had been excused from playing the "who do you know" game. Now, though, he was a lawyer, and lawyers needed to know all the players. He'd come to depend on Janet and Weezie to help sort it all out.

"Why should Merijoy Rucker make Gerry Blankenship tuck tail and run for cover?" James wondered.

"The SPL is the group that makes sure nobody in the historic district plants so much as a petunia without checking its historical context. If they find out Beaulieu's to be sold and torn down to build a paper plant, they'll raise holy hell. Especially Merijoy. She's got all that Rucker money, and nothing else to do with her time and energy. The woman is a holy terror."

"You exaggerate," James said, watching Merijoy Rucker extract a penknife from her pocketbook and start scraping gently at the paint on the windowsill she was standing in front of. Acting casual, she slipped a small plastic bag out of her handbag and scraped the paint chips into it, zipped it shut, then tucked it back in her pocketbook.

"Blankenship never said anything about tearing down Beaulieu," James said. "Caroline said the company hoped they could save it."

"That's just a lot of public-relations baloney," Weezie said. "You heard what Diane Mayhew said. This house is toast. Most architects want to create their own structures, not glue together somebody else's. If Tal's firm is involved, they've probably already got some big grandiose scheme drawn up. And a tacky old plantation house with aluminum screened doors and plaster that crumbles when you so much as look at it are not a part of their plan. You can bet on that."

James was dubious. He'd seen this kind of thing before. "If Miss Mullinax left provisions in her will, the SPL can't stop the paper company from using the property as they see fit. Can they?"

"Merijoy Rucker could stop a herd of charging bull elephants," Weezie said. "And she wouldn't even chip a fingernail doing it. Remember that wrought-iron balcony that was on the front of the townhouse when we bought it? I wanted to tear it off, because it wasn't even very pretty. And it was a safety hazard. If it had fallen, it would have killed somebody. But Merijoy got wind of it and came over and made me apply for a permit just to take it down. From my own house."

"Good Christ," James said. He took a second look at Mrs. Rucker. She was so lovely, so harmless-looking.

"You had to get permission to do work on your own house?" James still could not believe it. He'd been a part of the most hidebound, tradition-worshipping bureaucracy in the history of the world, the Catholic Church, and still he had never heard of such a thing.

"The house is in the historic district. It's listed on the National Register of Historic Places. We got a tax break on the renovation work for restoring it to their specifications," Weezie explained. "So now the SPL is running the show. And Merijoy Rucker personally runs the SPL. She's a Nazi in Ferragamo pumps."

Weezie took a delicate sip of her sherry. "You know, I haven't talked to Merijoy in months. I'll bet she doesn't know Tal and I are divorced."

James laughed. "In this town? Everybody knows you're divorced. I had Denise Cahoon in my office today, crying and carrying on about how Inky won't come back to her. Denise Cahoon barely knows what day it is, but even she asked me how my niece was doing after the big split-up."

"Denise Cahoon," Weezie said. "Now there's a pathetic story. Is she finally gonna make an honest man out of Inky and let him marry the mother of his children before they go off to college?"

James sighed. "She just wants Inky back. Well, Inky and his paycheck and retirement benefits."

Weezie set her empty sherry glass on the sideboard and brushed her fingers through her hair.

"I'll be back in a little bit, Uncle James. I think I'll just go over there and have a word with my old classmate Merijoy. See what she knows about this business of tearing down Beaulieu."

James nodded. "Janet says I'm to walk around and give out business cards for my law practice. Don't you think that's crass at a memorial service?"

"Be discreet," Weezie said. "Look at that couple over there." James looked where she was pointing, at a couple, both in their nineties, so frail they looked as though a good gust might blow them away. One of the waiters had made the mistake of leaving a silver tray of appetizers untended on the sideboard. The woman was scooping up cheese straws and stashing them in a cracked black leather pocketbook.

"That's Spencer and Lorena Loudermilk. I heard Spencer had gall bladder surgery over at Candler Hospital six weeks ago, and he's had a fever and a bellyache ever since. He went to a doctor up in Atlanta who says the surgeon must have left a clamp inside Spencer. All their grand-children have been after Spencer to sue Candler, but Spencer says he doesn't trust lawyers any more than he trusts doctors."

She nudged James. "Why don't you go over there and chat?"

"Ambulance chasing!" James said quickly. "It would be totally unethical."

"Tell Mr. Loudermilk your niece is best friends with their grand-daughter, BeBe," Weezie suggested. "Just inquire about his health. And don't forget to let him know you're an attorney."

James fingered the stack of business cards Janet had tucked in his pocket. He hated this part of his new life. He just wanted to help people. But, as Janet liked to remind him, his landlord couldn't cash a check for good intentions, and that gleaming white Mercedes parked out in the yard wouldn't run on noble deeds.

The office on Factors Walk was his biggest expense, a luxury, really, to have the river to watch whenever he liked. He lived simply, in the two-bedroom wood-frame cottage on Washington Avenue Bernadette had left him in her will.

James straightened the knot on his tie. It wouldn't hurt just to intro-duce himself to the Loudermilks. They seemed like a lovely couple. He only hoped Weezie wouldn't get into a brawl while he was rustling up some new billings.

CHAPTER 6

Eloise Foley!" Merijoy Rucker's eyes went all crinkly with delight at the sight of me. I guess she'd forgotten the incident with the balcony. "How in the world are you?" she asked, giving me a big hug. She stepped back and looked me over. "And where on earth did you get this darling dress?"

Merijoy Rucker liked my Zelda dress. I was a success. "You really like the dress?" I said shyly. "It's Hattie Carnegie. From the late twenties, I think."

"It's adorable," Merijoy assured me. "Vintage clothing is one of my favorite things. Nobody but you could pull off a look like that, Eloise. After all the weight I've put on having babies, if I put on something like that, I'd look like Omar the Tentmaker."

"Oh no," I protested. "You're so thin, Merijoy. Thinner than high school, even."

Merijoy glanced around the room. People were saying their good-byes, moving toward the door. She was watching Caroline and Gerry Blankenship, who were across the room, their heads bent in earnest discussion, with particular interest.

"So sad about Miss Mullinax, isn't it? Did you know her well?"

It was the question I'd been dreading. I looked around for Uncle James, hoping he'd come over, strike up a conversation, and save the day. No good. James was schmoozing BeBe's grandparents.

"I didn't know her well," I said, trying to sound cool. "She was more a friend of my Uncle James. I just tagged along as company." I lowered my voice. "To tell you the truth, Merijoy, the real reason I came was out of concern for Beaulieu. Such a historic landmark. Losing it would be a blow."

"Lose Beaulieu? What do you mean? Do you know something I don't?"

Caroline had zeroed in on me now. Her eyes were shooting off hateful little sparks from across the room. She said something to Gerry Blankenship. Now both of them were staring at me. Caroline could probably read lips. She did everything else. Easy, girl, I told myself. Be sweet.

"You know Savannah. I've just been hearing rumors, that's all." I did a little sidestep to put my back to Caroline, so she couldn't read my brain waves.

I leaned in toward Merijoy.

"Paper mill." I breathed the words, hardly moving my lips at all.

"No," Merijoy said. She clutched at her scrawny chest and rolled her big dark eyes as though she might have a cardiac infarction. "There is no way in this wide world that could happen. Do you hear me?"

I'd really pushed a button.

"I talked to Miss Mullinax," Merijoy explained. "For months and months now. We had dinner at Elizabeth's on Thirty-seventh back in February. She showed me some of the original land grant documents for Beaulieu. She as much as promised Beaulieu would be left to the preservation league. We talked about a living museum. I've already started inquiring about grant money for the restoration. The place needs a massive infusion of cash. There are several foundations that've expressed interest. The plantation outbuildings would be restored, a small-scale rice-growing operation. She would never . . ."

"Maybe there's been a misunderstanding," I said hastily. "Please forget I said anything, Merijoy. If you say Beaulieu is safe, I'm sure that's right."

Merijoy pursed her lips thoughtfully. "Gerry Blankenship is Miss Anna Ruby's attorney. I thought it would be sort of, well, grasping, to call on him any earlier. Out of respect for Miss Anna Ruby. But I've been phoning his office, leaving messages, to find out about the will. And today, I've tried to get a moment with him ever since he got here. He won't look me in the eye. Do you know that woman he's been talking to? I've seen her around town, I believe."

"I know her," I said, my stomach twisting into knots. "Her name is Caroline DeSantos. She's an architect in Tal's firm. She's his new fiancée."

Merijoy winced. "Then it *is* true. I'd heard things weren't going well between you two. I'm sorry, Eloise."

"I like to be called Weezie," I said, lifting my chin. "The divorce was final last month."

"What about your house?" Merijoy asked, her inner alarm going off.

Merijoy knew every inch of every house in the historic district. She was always peeping in at people's windows and sneaking around in lanes.

"Your house," Merijoy said mournfully. "All your hard work. That place was a ruin before you bought it. I used to ride by there all the time and I'd say to Randy Rucker, 'That place is a disgrace. Somebody needs to buy it and rescue it before there's nothing left but a pile of brick dust.' You're not going to sell the house, are you? Because Adelaide and Malcolm Osborne have been looking for something around Troup Square for months. . . ."

"The carriage house isn't for sale," I said, from between gritted teeth.

Really. Some people are such vultures. Ever since word of our divorce had gotten out, people had been stopping me on the street. "So sorry about the breakup—does that house have a full bath on the ground floor, or is it just a powder room?"

"Tal got the big house in the divorce settlement," I explained. "But I got the carriage house. That's where I'm living. It's actually ideal for me. Two bedrooms, two baths, a study, and I got half the garden too."

"And that adorable little kitchen. I hope you didn't do anything to cover up those exposed brick walls." Merijoy cocked one eyebrow. "So you're living on the same property as Tal and his fiancée. How unusual. I've got to give you credit, Weezie; you're much more open-minded than I would be if my husband left me for another woman. Why, if Randy Rucker so much as looked at somebody else, I swear, Weezie, I'd have to take the law into my own hands."

Caroline and Gerry Blankenship were walking toward the front door. Caroline stopped once, looked over her shoulder at me, trying to figure out what I was doing.

Merijoy saw where I was looking. "I swear, Weezie, don't you want to just kill her?"

CHAPTER 7

ight after Tal announced he was in love with somebody else and wanted a divorce, I was so depressed, all my friends were afraid I was suicidal.

I ran around and did all the things women do when their lives are shattered into little pieces.

I talked for hours on the telephone to all my girlfriends. We speculated on who the other woman might be. BeBe offered to pay to have Tal followed by a private detective. When I wouldn't let her, she offered to do it herself, for free. BeBe loves intrigue.

I couldn't afford a therapist. Instead, I started reading a lot of self-help articles. The best ones are in the magazines they have at my hairdressers'.

"Picking Up the Pieces after Your Divorce" was the article I was reading in *Women's World* magazine during the time Tal had moved out of the house and was supposedly living with his college roommate. I didn't find out until much later where he was really staying.

The beauty-shop article said women going through a divorce should undertake something they called a "life skills inventory" so that they could snap out of any self-destructive postdivorce patterns.

Life skills. Like what? Accounting? Taxidermy? Automotive repairs?

For a few years, while Tal was clawing his way to the top of the firm his grandfather owned anyway, I'd worked in the usual assortment of jobs I'd gotten through relatives, friends, and friends of friends. In Savannah, that's how everybody I know had always gotten jobs. You didn't need a resume, certainly you didn't need any "life skills inventory." You just needed to know somebody.

I was a file clerk at my neighbor's uncle's insurance office, a data entry operator at the bank where Mr. Tal had always done business, medical records clerk at the dentist's office where I'd gotten my teeth straightened when I was twelve. The only job I'd ever gotten on my own was as a clerk at the public library. I'd passed the spelling test with flying colors.

I'm a great speller. Blessed Sacrament School fourth-, fifth-, and sixth-grade spelling bee champ.

But championship spelling probably wasn't one of the life skills *Women's World* was talking about in their article about picking up the pieces.

BeBe still can't believe I never suspected anything was up between Tal and Caroline. But why would I have? He didn't work any later hours, our love life didn't change (sex on Saturday mornings and Thursday nights), he never tried to hide his fondness for her—in fact, he was insistent that she and I should become new best buddies. The friendship thing didn't take, of course. We gave dinner parties together, went sailing, and played golf, the whole deal. Now that I look back at it, I realize I did the cooking for the dinner parties and Caroline bought the wine. Tal and Caroline crewed the boat; I packed the picnic lunch.

My resentment simmered, then festered, until late one Sunday, after a whole weekend of forced buddying up with Caroline, I let Tal know how I really felt.

"I'm sick of her," I told him. "We have nothing in common. She hates all my friends. She's always saying what a flake BeBe is. Whenever we have these stupid get-togethers, I do all the work and she sits back and looks fabulous all the time. The woman has no sweat glands. She's great at everything and she deliberately tries to make me feel inadequate."

Tal just laughed. "You're jealous!" he said. "It's natural."

"What's that supposed to mean?"

"You know exactly what I mean," Tal said. "If Caroline makes you feel inadequate, it's probably because you're so, well, unfocused. Face it,

Weezie, you go off in a million different directions. You piddle with this and that, but you're never serious about anything. Not anything I care about, anyway. You're . . ."—he took a deep breath—"You're a dabbler, Weezie."

If he'd picked up the fillet knife off the counter and plunged it between my ribs, Tal couldn't have wounded me any deeper.

Unfocused. Twist the knife; see if you can hit an artery.

A piddler. How about a major organ?

A dabbler. Rip out my heart and stomp it on the heart-pine kitchen floors I'd stripped and hand-waxed all by myself.

Coming from him, I thought, it must have been true. After all, everybody was always saying how Talmadge Evans III was so accomplished at everything. Architecture. Classical guitar. Golf. Fly-fishing. Sailing. And now adultery.

I'd stayed in the house until the last possible moment. The judge had given me a month to remove my stuff.

At 6 P.M. on a Friday, exactly thirty days from the day the property settlement was final, I finished moving out of the big house. The moving van with Caroline's furniture had made two passes by the front door already. To be perfectly honest, I cried more over leaving the house than I'd ever cried over the loss of Talmadge Evans III.

That day, I rolled up my threadbare oriental carpets, packed up every stick of blue-and-white porcelain I'd scrounged for the past ten years, boxed up all my antique reference books, including every Kovels' price guide issued for the past fifteen years, and then, sobbing, I hand-carried the pieces of furniture Tal had never liked over to the carriage house, my new home.

I didn't trust movers with my treasure, so I loaded up the little blue milk-paint goat cart I'd converted to a coffee table, and wheeled it back and forth until I was done.

The judge gave Tal the four-poster mahogany Charleston bed we'd bought for our fifth anniversary, all the silver flatware his mother and her friends had given us as wedding gifts, the eighteenth-century drop-leaf cherry table in the foyer, and all the living-room furniture.

After I'd made the last load I went back to the big house one last time. It was dusk. I unscrewed every lightbulb in every fixture in the house. I crawled up under the kitchen sink, and with a pipe wrench, I removed the grease trap from the sink. I put a crimp in the copper pipe leading from the hot-water heater. After some consideration, I opened up the refrigerator—the three-thousand-dollar Sub-Zero I'd gotten for half price from an appliance distributor I know, and I removed the little wire do-jiggey that tells the ice maker it's time to make more ice cubes.

An hour without ice in Savannah is like a lifetime in hell.

There was more I could have done, but I couldn't bear to inflict any really lasting wounds on my house. It didn't matter what the judge said; it was my house. I had found it, breathed life into it, made it my own. The paint on the walls were colors I'd hand-mixed, the old gas-light chandeliers were ones I'd taken apart, piece by piece, polishing the brass, washing the crystals, and rethreading the arms with new wiring. Since I'd rescued the house I'd taught myself to reglaze windows, strip woodwork, lay tile, repair plaster, do simple wiring, paint, and garden. Dabbling, Tal would call it.

Of course, there were things I'd learned I couldn't do. I'd burned my hand badly with a blowtorch the one time I'd attempted plumbing. I couldn't hang wallpaper straight, nor did I have any particular affinity for carpentry.

That afternoon I wandered aimlessly about the darkening rooms, my footsteps echoing in the half-empty high-ceilinged rooms. "It's time to go," I said sternly, after I caught myself looking around for a broom to sweep one last cobweb from one last bit of cove molding in the living room. "They're his spiders now."

The last box of my clothes was upstairs in our bedroom. His bedroom, now. I picked up the cardboard box and lifted the flap to see what was in this one. It was full of cheesy lacy lingerie; teddies, bustiers, French-cut and thong bikini panties; all gifts from Tal, who never seemed to notice that none of it was my taste.

I glanced in the bathroom, caught a glimpse of myself in the gold-leafed mirror over the vanity.

There were dark circles under my eyes from not sleeping. I'd lost weight, and my clothes hung from my hunched-looking shoulders. Two tiny earrings shone from my right earlobe. My fear of needles borders on the pathological, but BeBe had talked me into the second set of ear piercings. I'd gone for the idea because I've always loved earrings and have boxes and boxes of unusual vintage ones I've picked up over the years at estate sales and junk stores.

Tal, of course, had been horrified to see his wife with two sets of earrings. "You look like a Ubangi tribesman!" he'd said.

Tal had never seen me the way I really was. Maybe now I could see myself. I took the box of lingerie into the bathroom, set it down on the floor. One by one, I removed the panties; zebra-striped, red nylon, peach fishnet. I dropped a pair in the commode. It felt good. I dropped in five pairs in all, flushed once, and then again. The pipes made a gurgling sound, and water started to rise in the bowl.

Back in my new house, I fixed myself a vodka and tonic and gave Jethro a big raw steak. Then I pulled a chair up to the window and watched while Tal and Caroline pulled up and parked her Triumph in my old parking space. When the phone started ringing and wouldn't stop, I took it off the hook and fixed myself another drink.

erijoy Rucker knew something was up. Not for nothing was she the biggest snoop in Savannah. "A paper plant? And I bet I know who's behind it. It's that Mayhew person, isn't it?" she said. "Coastal Paper Products? Diane Mayhew was at the Symphony Ball planning coffee this week, and she wouldn't even look me in the eye. I knew right away something was wrong. She's been toadying up to me for months."

I looked around helplessly. The minister was shaking hands with people and making her way toward the door. Others were drifting that way too. If Merijoy Rucker kept me trapped here, giving me the third degree about Beaulieu, I'd never get back to the other parlor to check out the merchandise. Uncle James was no help. He was still deep in conversation with the Loudermilks.

"Do you think anyone would mind if we looked around the house a little?" I asked Merijoy. "I've never been inside Beaulieu before. I'd like to get a last look, especially if they're going to tear it down."

It was as if I'd issued a battle cry. Her nostrils quivered in indignation. "Nobody's tearing anything down," she assured me. "Let's go peek in that other parlor. I think that wallpaper in there may be an old Scalamandré pattern. Prewar."

We both knew she was talking about the only war that counted in Savannah. The War of Northern Aggression. The Late Unpleasantness.

As we turned right off the hallway, Merijoy stopped short—so short, I plowed right into the back of her.

"Lewis!" she exclaimed, backing up quickly.

The man she'd collided with seemed surprised to be recognized. He scowled in annoyance. His right hand moved quickly to the pocket of his blue blazer. But not so quickly I didn't see him slip a small black camera into the pocket.

"Well, hello, Merijoy," he said, his frown dissolving. He nodded curtly in my direction. "Hello."

Lewis Hargreaves knows my name. All the antique dealers in Savannah know me, even the ones who pretend they don't buy from pickers like me. Not that I'd ever sold much to Hargreaves.

Hargreaves owns L. Hargreaves. It's an "antique gallery"—nothing so plebeian as a shop. His specialty is big-ticket, one-of-a-kind early Southern antiques. Hargreaves himself is regarded as something of a boy wonder. We went to parochial school together, but whereas I was still a measly picker, Lewis had opened his own "gallery" his first year out of Georgetown University. It wasn't long before his shop was being written up in all the big shelter magazines like *HG* and *Architectural Digest*.

Merijoy Rucker leaned forward and gave Lewis a light kiss on the cheek. A soft pink suffused his pale face, and he blushed to the roots of his white-blond hair.

"Lewis, you naughty thing," she said teasingly. "What are you doing skulking around all by yourself in here?"

Hargreaves blinked rapidly. "Just paying my respects to Miss Mullinax."

"Bull hockey, Lewis," Merijoy said. It was the strongest language I'd ever heard her use. "You weren't in the room during the memorial service."

"I was invited by Gerry Blankenship," Hargreaves said. "It's confidential, that's all I can say right now."

Hargreaves walked rapidly down the hallway, toward the staircase.

"He's casing the place," I said, watching his immaculately tailored back disappear. "There's sure to be an estate sale, you know. I'll bet he's already putting in a bid for the good stuff."

Merijoy sighed. "I was hoping the furnishings would be left intact. It's really vital to retain the original pieces for an important house museum like this."

"Sure," I agreed. We turned in to the parlor. It was stuffed with piles of furniture, rugs, boxes, and crates.

"Oh!" Merijoy cried, running the palm of her hand against the wall. The paper was a robin's-egg blue, with murals of coastal birds: wild herons, marsh hens, egrets, and kingfishers. The paper hung from the wall in ribbons; large parts of it were obscured by spreading brown water stains.

"My God," Merijoy moaned. "This is a Menaboni mural. Hand-painted. And it's ruined." She pulled out her own pocket camera and snapped it.

"Maybe there's a way to mend it," I offered.

Over in the corner of the room, a stack of boxes obscured a large piece of furniture. It was a cabinet of some kind, loaded with bits and pieces of old blue-and-white china.

I pulled the boxes away from the cabinet, sliding them against a moth-eaten braided rug on the floor. My hands were filthy from the dust and mildew on the boxes. Nothing in this room had been used in a very long time.

Even in the dim light of the parlor, the corner cupboard stood out like a diamond in a handful of pebbles. I held my breath while I ran my palm over the satiny wood. It was burled elm, eight feet tall at least, with three scalloped shelves behind a pair of wavy glass doors. Below were carefully wrought doors and a scalloped apron. Bells went off in my head. This cupboard was the work of a master cabinetmaker, early nineteenth century. The craftsmanship would hold up to that of any of the famous Philadelphia or Boston artisans of the time, but the design looked Southern vernacular.

"That's nice," Merijoy said, flicking at the cabinet door. "I'll bet it's original to the house. Look at the way it fits in that corner. You're into antiques, Weezie. What kind of china is that?"

"Canton ware," I said, my eyes still on the cupboard. "From the 1700s. Very valuable."

Merijoy sighed. "The neglect. The ruin. I could weep. I really could. Look at that mantel."

I tore myself away from the cupboard and walked over to the mantel enclosing the fireplace. It was highly carved, with bas-relief nymphs and caryatids and all types of doodads.

"Nice," I murmured. I wasn't really into Victoriana. I kept glancing over at the corner cupboard. It was calling me, seducing me.

"It's horrid!" Merijoy exclaimed. "So tacky! And it's all wrong for this house." She poked a pencil into the wood, which seemed to crumble like stale cake. "And it's riddled with termites." She snapped another photo.

She stamped her foot on the floor. "I hate it when the owners fool around with an old house like this. There should have been a cypress mantel here. Or marble, maybe. Not this." She flicked her hand over the carving. "Grotesquerie."

"Maybe the original is up in the attic someplace," I said. "Or in one of the outbuildings. I saw a barn and what looks like a smokehouse outside. And that building right next to the house. A summer kitchen. All those sheds are probably packed with old stuff." I looked around the room, at the dusty piles of books and papers, the boxes of linens and kitchen utensils, glassware and photo albums. "I don't think the Mullinaxes ever threw anything away."

"Maybe," Merijoy said, unconvinced. "Of course, the rest of the house could be a pile of sawdust too—just like this mantel."

"Let's go, Weezie," she said, catching my sleeve in her hand. "It's too depressing to look around anymore. Just from what I've already seen, it could take hundreds of thousands to restore Beaulieu. Millions, maybe."

I took one last, longing look around the room. At the cupboard. It was what had drawn Lewis Hargreaves and his pocket camera into this room.

Fortunately, the main parlor was nearly empty, because we were both a mess. My hands were dirt-streaked, my dress a network of wrinkles. Merijoy looked like someone had swiped her favorite toy. Her elegant black linen was smudged, her hair mussed. She'd bitten off all her lipstick.

"That woman, Caroline DeSantos," Merijoy said. "Is she really living in your house with Tal? Right under your nose?"

Uncle James saved me from any more questions about our unusual living arrangement. He strolled up with Mr. and Mrs. Loudermilk trailing in his wake. He looked pleased with himself. Spencer Loudermilk looked happy too, for a petrified person.

"Weezie," James said, "I believe you already know Mr. Loudermilk."

I held out my hand to shake his withered little claw. "Your granddaughter BeBe is a good friend of mine, Mr. Loudermilk. She's told me a lot about you and Mrs. Loudermilk. And Mr. and Mrs. Loudermilk, this is Merijoy Rucker. Merijoy is quite active in preservation."

Lorena Loudermilk squinted up at me from behind a cloudy pair of eyeglasses that had been patched in two places with duct tape. She was bent nearly double with the most pronounced dowager's hump I'd ever seen, but her pale skin was smooth and pink, her teeth still even and white.

"I know you," Mrs. Loudermilk said, nodding at Merijoy. "You married that Rucker boy." She hardly paused. "My husband, Spencer, has got a clamp lodged in his lower intestine. This lawyer boy here is gonna sue the pee-diddly out of Candler Hospital."

Spencer Loudermilk looked like a liver spot with legs. He beamed and patted his abdomen. "That's right. You should see what I do to those metal detectors at the airport."

Merijoy's one-track mind refused to be derailed for long. "Weezie and I were just catching up on old times." She turned to James and gave him a dazzling smile. "Mr. Foley, you're an attorney. Have you heard any scuttle-butt about what's to happen with Beaulieu?"

James has a very good poker face. My father says it's because he was educated by the Jesuits. Daddy blames everything bad that's ever happened with the Catholic Church or modern civilization on radical left-wing Jesuits.

"Haven't heard a thing," James said blandly. "Excuse us, please, would you all? Weezie and I have an urgent appointment back in town."

He bowed and I said pretty good-byes, and as we walked out onto the front porch of Beaulieu, somebody grabbed my wrist. Caroline. Fine beads of perspiration dotted her upper lip. "What was Merijoy Rucker talking to you about?" she demanded.

"Preservation," I said. "She's very interested in preserving old houses."

I tried to pull away from her, but Caroline's nails dug deeper into the flesh of my wrist. The dark eyes were mere slits. "If she thinks she can turn Beaulieu into a museum house, she's sadly mistaken. We've got a deal with the paper company. Airtight. And if she tries to raise some stink about it, we'll raze this old rattrap to the ground. In a single morning." She released my hand. "Tell her that, why don't you? Tell her how single-minded I am."

I looked down at my wrist; there were red claw marks in the flesh.

"You don't know Merijoy Rucker, do you, Caroline? Well, I'm sure you'll get acquainted very soon. The two of you actually have a lot in common. It'll be interesting."

CHAPTER 9

Weezie was shaking and milky-pale by the time she got to James's car. Jethro stuck his head out the window and barked enthusiastically at the sight of her, but Weezie gave him only a halfhearted nod.

It worried James, seeing Weezie's moods shift like this. Moments earlier, she'd gleefully pounced at the opportunity to give Caroline a small measure of misery. Now she looked positively ill. Goddamn Talmadge Evans III.

"There was certainly a lot of old stuff in that house," he said, trying to sound enthusiastic. "Good loot—right?" To him the place looked like a hideous moldering pile of garbage, but then, as Weezie often reminded him, he didn't know shit from shinola when it came to that kind of thing.

"It's fabulous," Weezie said, picking at a bit of lace on the hem of the odd, drooping dress she was wearing. "Just in those three rooms I saw, there was enough for ten estate sales."

James started the car and busied himself with sliding a disk into the CD player. He turned around and asked, politely, for Jethro to *please* take his tongue out of James's ear.

The CD was the latest Clancy Brothers release. James sighed. It was a gift from one of his Florida parishioners.

Mrs. Finley had bought him a box of CDs for his new car; the Clancy Brothers, the Irish Rovers, like that. James had been enthusiastic about the gift at first; but now he thought he'd go mad if he ever again heard a bagpipe or a Celtic harp. It was terribly clangy, Irish music. He wished he had some Trisha Yearwood or Garth Brooks. Simple stuff about pickup trucks and lying and cheating and drinking.

Instead, he had the Yancy Brothers yammering away about some dreamy-eyed girl with a ribbon in her hair.

"I hate it here," Weezie said suddenly.

They were bumping along down the oyster-shell driveway, past some tabby ruins covered with the foamy green of resurrection ferns.

"Since when?" James said, shocked.

"I do," Weezie insisted. "Savannah sucks. It's always hot. The gnats drive me insane. The marsh stinks like dead fish. The people are so self-satisfied, it makes me want to puke. People in this town like to think they're so sophisticated. That Paris of the South stuff. What a load of crap! Nobody around here knows a damn thing about anything that really matters, like art or literature or music."

She ripped at the hem of the dress, and a strip of lace and a long patch of fabric came away in her hand. She threw the clump of fabric on the floor. "These assholes keep screwing it up. They tear down anything that's good or beautiful."

"They pave paradise and put in a parking lot," James said.

"What?" Weezie looked at him oddly.

"Joni Mitchell," James said, pleased at being able to surprise her. He'd always loved radical folksingers, especially the ones with ratty blue jeans and greasy hair who seethed with the injustice of life. Maybe it was the Jesuit in him.

He glanced over at Weezie. "Gerry Blankenship was half in the bag today. He reeked of gin. Drunk talk. Anyway, they won't have to tear down Beaulieu, you know. It'll fall down all by itself, any day now."

"Maybe." Weezie kept seeing Caroline as she stood in front of the windows in the parlor at Beaulieu, looking out to the marsh and the river beyond. Like she owned the place. One more home to wreck.

"I could make a lot of money off that estate sale," Weezie told James. "Get the good stuff and get out while the getting's good."

"Get out? What's that supposed to mean?" James asked, pulling the Mercedes alongside Weezie's rusted turquoise truck.

"Fuck 'em all," Weezie said. "Ticktock, James. What's that Bible verse, about a time to every purpose? Maybe all the stuff that's happening to me means it's time to get out. Go to a real town. Atlanta. Maybe San Francisco. I've never been out west. Hell, New York. Why not? I could open my own shop. Be a real dealer. No more dabbling. I just need to make one good killing at that sale, and then it'll be my time."

"Ecclesiastes," James said. "Originally, of course. Although the Byrds did a nice version too."

CHAPTER 10

*T*he day after Anna Ruby Mullinax's memorial service, I went through all my reference books on Southern furniture, looking for a piece similar to the cupboard I'd seen at Beaulieu. But most of the pieces I found were fancier, more high-style.

I sketched the cupboard from memory, then took my drawing pad down to River Street, to the unstylish end, to the last unrestored old cotton warehouse in Savannah.

Lester Dobie fished his glasses out of the breast pocket of his grease-stained cotton sport shirt and held my drawing only inches from his nose. He squinted his eyes, moved the drawing back a little, sighed, and picked his cigar back off the counter where he'd left it burning.

"Burled elm? You're positive?"

I wavered. Elm pieces were a rarity. The only ones I'd seen for myself were at the Telfair Museum in Savannah, and at the Museum of Early Southern Decorative Arts in Winston-Salem. A huntboard and a blanket box.

"Pretty sure," I said. "The color looked like elm. And the grain. The piece was coated in grime, but that's what it looked like to me."

"Double glass-front doors above, three shelves, fancy kind of cornice?"

"I'm not an artist," I apologized. "But I think the sketch is close. The glass was definitely old. Bull's-eye, probably. It had the waves."

He rubbed the two-day growth of beard on his chin. Sighed. "And Lewis Hargreaves was looking it over pretty good?"

"There was other stuff in the room. Really nice Canton ware. But I'm betting it was the cupboard he was interested in. He had a camera with him."

"Lewis knows his stuff. It must be the Moses Weed. Gotta be."

I looked down at the drawing, back up at Lester, waiting for his approval. Lester Dobie taught me everything I know about antiques. His junk shop, Dobie's—just that, not Dobie's Antiques or Dobie's Ye Olde Shoppe—had been in that cotton warehouse as long as I could remember. It was where I'd bought my first antique, a pink silk and Venice lace Victorian baby pillow. I'd paid two dollars for it, out of my baby-sitting money, when I was fourteen. After that, I was hooked. A week didn't go by that I wasn't in his shop, roaming among the old wagon wheels and local-dug bottles that were his specialty.

We'd hit it off because I wasn't afraid to ask questions. For years, I'd made the rounds of yard sales and junk stores, picking up promising bits and pieces and then taking them to Lester, either to find out about them or to sell them to make back my investment.

"You've got a good eye," Lester told me one day, after I'd tried to sell him a plastic bag full of coin-silver spoons I'd dug out of a kitchen drawer at an estate sale on Wilmington Island. "You can get better prices other places, though. Take that silver over to old lady Dreyer. She likes that snooty-hooty stuff. They're worth fifty apiece."

Before I knew it, my Saturday-morning hobby had grown into a business.

"You know who Moses Weed was, right?" Lester chewed his cigar out the right side of his mouth. His hands were busy polishing a small brass barometer.

"Not really," I admitted.

"He was a slave," Lester said. "Born at Ashton Place, right outside Charleston. Ashton Place was a huge spread. Moses Weed learned carpentry from an itinerant Philadelphia cabinetmaker named Thomas Elphas. Folks who owned Ashton hired Elphas to come down and make all the furniture for their library, dining room, and parlor. And they put little Moses to work in the shop as an assistant to Elphas. Later on, Weed was sold off the plantation. Brought a lot of money because he was so skilled at carpentry."

"Sold to the Mullinaxes?" I asked. "Beaulieu?"

"He would have been in his early twenties in 1860," Lester said. "He only made a few pieces at Beaulieu before the war started. Nobody really knows exactly when he left there, or where he went. Maybe a dozen pieces are attributed to him. Utilitarian stuff, mostly—some benches, kitchen tables, a huntboard, a pair of armchairs. There's a cradle, carved cherry, attributed to Moses Weed. I've seen pictures of it. It's in a museum in Philadelphia where they have a small collection of Elphas's stuff. "

"And a cupboard? Like the one I saw at Beaulieu?"

Lester nodded and jabbed my drawing with his stubby forefinger. "Miss Anna Ruby loaned it out to the High Museum in Atlanta for their 'Neat Pieces' exhibit of Southern-made nineteenth-century furniture back in the 1970s. Me and Ginger went up and saw it. Beautiful thing. That wood fairly glowed. They called it the Moses Weed cupboard."

"It's gotta be the same one," I told him. "How much? How much is a piece like that worth today?"

He sucked on his cigar and thought about it. "You'd have to have the provenance to sell it to a serious collector. According to Miss Anna Ruby, it was made from elm trees off the property out at Beaulieu. Ain't no elm trees anywhere around here anymore. That piece was made right there in the plantation carpentry shop. Hand-forged hinges. Moses Weed couldn't read or write, but they did teach him how to make his mark. Should be on the piece somewhere. But now, if you can't prove it came directly out of Beaulieu, you can't prove it's the Moses Weed."

"How much?" I repeated.

"Ballpark? Maybe two hundred thousand dollars. More if you sold to one of them museums rolling in dough. But remember—that's only if you can prove it's a Moses Weed."

I closed the sketchbook and put it back in my purse. "It's a long shot. Maybe there won't be a sale. Maybe they'll sell it off before the sale. To Hargreaves maybe. I probably couldn't afford it anyway."

Lester looked down at the barometer. The tarnish was gone and it shone with a soft gold luster. "That's a lot of maybes."

ithin a month it was in all the papers, the Atlanta ones too, about how Coastal Paper Products had announced plans to build this truly humongous paper mill in Savannah. But by the time the press got hold of the story, the plant's estimated cost had ballooned to $750 million.

"Nine Hundred New Jobs!" the *Morning News* trumpeted.

"State-of-the-Art Environmental Controls!" the local chamber of commerce bragged.

They were showing the ground-breaking ceremony on WSAV-TV news on Friday morning. I caught it out of the corner of my eye, waiting for the weather report. Tomorrow was the sale. Let it rain, I prayed. Keep away the tire kickers.

When the camera showed Caroline helping Phipps Mayhew lift the first shovel of dirt, I flipped quickly to the next channel.

"I saw that," BeBe said. She was sitting on a bar stool at my kitchen counter, separating eggs for the pound cake I was making.

"Saw what?" But it was no good. BeBe never misses a trick. That's why she owns half a dozen successful businesses, drives a Jaguar convertible, and has a full-time live-in maid.

BeBe cracked the last of the ten eggs, plopping them into the big stainless-steel mixing bowl on my KitchenAid mixer.

She picked up the remote control and turned it back to WSAV. It was a slow news day. They were still going on and on about what a good thing it was—to tear down a historic landmark and put up yet another stench-spewing wart on Savannah's landscape.

"Lookie, lookie," she said. "It's Miss Wonderful." BeBe studied the television screen critically. "You see that dress Caroline is wearing? That's a Briaggi."

"So?" I was watching the beaters whirl through the cake batter, keeping my eyes off the television and Caroline. After our last run-in, when she called the dogcatcher and reported Jethro for being outside without a leash, I'd backed off our mutual war.

"That dress cost three thousand dollars," BeBe said authoritatively. "They don't even sell it in Georgia. I saw it in the new issue of *Vogue*. There's a boutique in Palm Beach. Martha's. Only place you can buy it besides New York."

I added a teaspoon each of vanilla and lemon extract to the cake batter.

"You know what I could do with three thousand dollars?" I didn't bother to keep the bitterness out of my voice, since it was just BeBe.

"I could open my own shop. I mean it, BeBe. All the stuff I've got stored in my parents' garage? And at Uncle James's? Three thousand dollars. Rent a little place, fix it up. . . . Maybe live above the store. Have you ever been to Baltimore?"

My voice trailed off. It was not the first time we'd had this discussion lately. BeBe thought I was nuts to want to leave Savannah.

She frowned. "Listen, sweetie, you know I don't like to ask personal questions, but I can't understand why you're so broke. I mean, you did get some money in the divorce settlement—right?"

"Some," I admitted. "But James made me use a lot of the cash for an annuity—for my retirement, since I didn't get any of Tal's pension benefits. And the rest of the money's tied up in inventory. It's worth a good bit—but I have to sell the stuff before I can make the money. And without a shop, I'm still selling at wholesale prices."

"Open a shop right here," BeBe said. "There's a darling little place over on East Congress. That old lounge—remember? By the Lucas Theater?"

I wrinkled my nose. "The Lamplighter? The place that smelled like a toilet? Where every wino in town used to pass out right there on the sidewalk? No thank you very much."

"The old City Market is hot, hot, hot," BeBe singsonged. She stuck a finger in the batter, smacked her lips appreciatively. "Yummy. Speaking of . . . they came in the restaurant together last night, you know."

"Who?" I was fiddling with the oven thermostat.

"Give me a break. You know damn well who I mean. Tal and Caroline. You should see the ring she's wearing. Five carats, minimum."

I looked down at my own engagement ring. When I was nineteen, it had looked like the Hope diamond. Now it looked like the half carat Tal's mother had given him to give me.

"Is it a square-cut baguette? Two hunking sapphires on either side? White gold band?"

BeBe's big blue eyes widened. She'd tied a bandana through her frosted blond curls and her only makeup was lip gloss. She looked like a grown-up Rebecca of Sunnybrook Farm.

"Shit," she said.

"Great-grandmother Evans's ring," I explained. "Tal's mother kept it in a safe-deposit box. She always said it was too 'showy' for an itty-bitty thing like me."

"It's gaudy," BeBe said, a little too eagerly. "Caroline doesn't have the presence to carry it off. Everybody knows brunettes should wear yellow gold."

"Thanks, Babe," I said, recognizing the tactful lie for what it was.

"She hangs all over him," BeBe said. "It's nauseating. I wanted to ask her to leave last night because she was ruining my customers' appetites. I swear, Weez, she had her hand down his pants at the table. Everybody saw it."

The KitchenAid's heavy-duty motor hummed, and BeBe was quiet.

I oiled and floured the cake pans, then opened the oven door and slid out the twelve-inch cheesecake I'd already baked. Mocha swirl.

"You don't have to do all this, you know," BeBe said. "Just let me give you the money. I'll be, like, an investor. In your new shop."

"We've already been through all that," I said, setting the cheesecake on a wire cooling rack. "I've got no assets, other than the carriage house. Even if I move, I won't sell it. It's mine. And you know I've got no track record. I'm a horrible credit risk. I won't take your money, BeBe."

I put a finger to the cheesecake's glossy top and pressed down. The cake looked perfect; not too soggy, not too dry.

"Just let me do this. Bake desserts for Guale. I'm good at it. What do you think? Twenty-five for the cheesecake, maybe thirty for the pound cake?"

Guale was BeBe's latest business venture. A tiny bistro in what had always been a shoe-shine stand on Abercorn, at St. Julian. A year ago, drug dealers had conducted an open-air stop-and-cop in front of the stand. Now people lined up on the street, waiting to get in to try the trendy "coastal cuisine."

It had been BeBe's idea to have me bake desserts.

"All the eggs and cream cheese in these things? They're so rich, we'll have to slice them really, really thin. We can get twenty slices out of each one, charge five dollars a slice. That's a hundred dollars per cake. Your take is fifty dollars."

"For pound cake? How do you get away with that kind of thing? You can get a whole strawberry pie at Shoney's for eight bucks."

"But it's Shoney's," BeBe said, wrinkling her nose in distaste. "A lot of rednecks eating cheeseburgers and fried clams. This is Guale. People *want* to pay through the nose. They want something they think they can't get anyplace else."

"You're a criminal, BeBe Loudermilk," I said, shaking my head.

"A capitalist," BeBe corrected me.

"And speaking of which, wait until you set eyes on the new chef I've hired." BeBe licked her lips dramatically. "Talk about yummy. Dark hair falling over one eye. Big, soulful blue eyes. He's kind of skinny, but he's got the cutest ass you've ever seen. I'm thinking of opening up the wall between the main dining room and the kitchen, just so everybody can watch him at work."

BeBe hired and fired chefs every other week. They were always geniuses their first month. And by the second month they were deranged psychotics. The most recent one had chased BeBe down the lane with a copper saucier full of flaming bananas Foster after she'd dared to criticize the freshness of his baked sea bass.

"He's single," she said, taunting me. "And straight."

"How do you know he's straight?" I asked, eyeing the egg whites critically.

"Trust me," she said. "I can tell."

"How?" I said, challenging her.

"Daniel's into bass fishing," she said. "He's got a Bassmaster sticker on his truck. A Dodge Ram."

"Gay men drive trucks," I pointed out.

"Toyotas," she said dismissively. "Toy trucks. Besides, he was in the Marines. That's where he learned to cook so divinely."

I put the pan in the oven and closed the door.

"Just what I need in my life," I said. "A redneck who can julienne green beans. Forget it, BeBe. I'm done with men."

"Wait until you see him," BeBe said, fanning herself with one hand. "Lawsy me, I'm getting hot and bothered just thinking about him."

"That's the oven, not your hormones," I said.

"Speak for yourself," BeBe shot back.

It was time to change the subject. "A hundred bucks for the cheese-cakes," I said, sitting down on the other stool. "And I've got another eight hundred bucks saved up. It's not enough. Were you serious—before? About the money? It would just be an advance, for the desserts. I could bake a lot more if I did it in the kitchen at the restaurant with that commercial oven of yours."

"You'll take the money?" BeBe looked confused. "I thought it was against your principles."

"There's a piece," I said slowly. "At Beaulieu. The estate sale starts Saturday morning. If I could get it at a decent price, I know I could sell it, twenty thousand dollars rock bottom. "

I'd been thinking about that burled-elm cupboard. The one Lewis Hargreaves had been salivating over. The Moses Weed cupboard.

BeBe got up and poured herself a cup of coffee. "So you'll let me bankroll you? How much?"

I winced. Usually when I'm picking I stay away from the really fine stuff, mostly because it requires a bigger outlay of cash and thus a bigger gamble. I generally deal in what people in the business call "smalls," things like paper ephemera, glass, china, silver, linens, paintings, and accessories. When I have picked up a big piece, like a pine armoire or a dining-room set, it's always been because it was too good a steal to resist, and I knew I could turn it around quickly.

This time would be different. "Five thousand," I said, the words pain-ing me. "Cash. Sometimes you get a better deal if it's a cash transaction.

But it's just this one time. And remember, it's an advance. I'll probably be baking these damn cheesecakes when I'm a hundred and two."

She picked up her purse and skipped to the door. "Let's go to the bank," she called over her shoulder. "But remember, I get first shot at the good stuff."

"Like you have any room in your house for anything else," I said. Jethro looked up from his place by the kitchen door. "Not this time, buddy," I said, patting his head. "But Friday night, it's you and me. You and me all the way."

CHAPTER *12*

he doors at Beaulieu were supposed to open at 8 A.M. Saturday.

At 6 P.M. Friday, I loaded my equipment in the truck. The cooler, with sandwiches, diet Cokes, and a thermos of coffee, went first. Next came my sleeping bag, pillow, bug spray, a flashlight, my two biggest canvas L.L. Bean tote bags and my Kovels' price guides. Jethro hopped in the front seat as soon as he saw the cooler. He loves to play camp-out the night before the sale.

One good thing about being divorced was that Tal wasn't around to ridicule me for taking the hunt so seriously.

When we were married and I'd get up at dawn to stand in line for a sale that didn't start until 9 A.M., Tal told me I was crazy. And he hated the idea of my going from dealer to dealer "peddling my wares" as he called it.

Now, it was nobody's business but my own. I was throwing a lawn chair into the back of the truck when BeBe zoomed up. She got out of her red Miata with a sleeping bag in one hand and a bottle of wine in the other.

"What's up?" I asked warily.

"I'm going with you," she announced. "I can help you at the sale. We'll make it a party. You know I've never been inside Beaulieu either."

She locked the Miata, tossed her stuff in the bed of the truck, and opened the passenger-side door. But Jethro wouldn't budge.

"Sorry, pal," I told him, giving him a gentle shove. "The banker gets to ride up front."

"Turn here," BeBe said when we got to the corner of Charlton and Habersham.

"Why?"

"I need to run by the restaurant for a minute."

"Guale? What for?"

"The new chef's upset about the shrimp that was delivered this morning. He says they're too small. Now he's threatening to take the shrimp-and-grits cake off the menu tonight."

"So let him," I said. "What's the big deal?"

"It's our signature dish," BeBe said. "People drive down from Atlanta and Hilton Head for our grits and shrimp. It would be a disaster."

I shook my head, exasperated. "Can't you just call him? I wanted to get out to Beaulieu to claim a prime camping spot close to the house."

"We'll get there," BeBe said airily. She leaned over and gave me a critical look. "Don't you ever wear lipstick?"

"To camp out in ninety-eight-degree heat and a hundred percent humidity? No. Why should I?"

Instead of answering, she dug in her purse and brought out a lipstick, which she aimed toward my face.

I rounded the street onto Lafayette Square and pulled up to the curb in front of the cathedral.

BeBe frowned. "Now what?"

People were hurrying into the magnificent French Gothic Cathedral of St. John the Baptist for 6 P.M. Mass. I saw a couple of my mother's friends and waved. When Sister Perpetua, my eighth-grade homeroom teacher, scuttled past, I sank down in the truck's seat so she couldn't spot me and give me the nun evil eye.

"What's going on here?" I asked. "Why are you insisting we stop at the restaurant? And why is it so important that I wear lipstick? What are you up to, Babe?"

"Nothing," she protested. "Really, Weezie." She reached over and fluffed the top of my hair with her fingertips. "Much better." She handed me the lipstick. "Keep it. I can't wear that shade. Makes me look like Joan Crawford."

I peeked in the mirror on the back of my sun visor. Maybe she was right. A little color couldn't hurt. I slicked on the lipstick and tried to flatten the hair she'd pouffed up, but BeBe slapped my hand away. "Leave it alone," she protested. "Big hair is back this year. Don't you read?"

I shook my head and started the truck. We drove over to Guale without incident, and I was amazed to find a parking spot on the other side of Johnson Square from the restaurant. Normally, on Friday nights, you can't get within three blocks of Guale.

"My luck is changing," I said. "Either that or word got out about the shrimp-and-grits fiasco and nobody's coming tonight."

BeBe glared at me. "We don't open for dinner until seven. Come on."

"I'll wait here," I said. "Can't leave Jethro alone."

"He can come too," BeBe said. She snapped her fingers. "Here, Ro-Ro."

Jethro bounded out of the back of the truck and followed BeBe across the square.

For lack of anything better to do, I locked the truck and went after them. The square was quiet that time of day. Pigeons fluttered around the statue of Revolutionary War hero Nathaniel Greene, and a handful of Japanese tourists stood a few paces away, snapping photographs. A tour bus lumbered around the square, belching black smoke from its muffler.

"Damned tour buses," BeBe muttered. "The pollution is peeling the paint on the restaurant. It's outrageous."

I sniffed the air appreciatively. "Doesn't smell like pollution to me. Smells like money."

She grimaced. It was an old Savannah joke. Here we were, living in one of the most beautiful and historic cities in the country, and for as long as anybody could remember, we'd been fouling the air and water around us—first with the pulp and paper plants, and now with all the tourists who'd been drawn to Savannah by an outrageous tattletale true-crime book. Everybody complained that the buses were blocking traffic, creating noise and health hazards, but nobody minded the millions of dollars those tourists were dumping into the local economy.

Guale was on the corner of St. Julian Street. We skirted the front door and went around to the kitchen entrance in the lane. From a hundred yards away we could hear angry voices.

"Uh-oh," BeBe said. "Wait here. Daniel's on the warpath again."

A big black Dodge Ram truck was parked illegally in the lane. I propped myself on the bumper, crossed my arms over my chest, and closed my eyes. My stomach growled. Something wonderful was cooking in that kitchen. It smelled like garlic and rosemary and roasting meat. Maybe BeBe would bring me a doggie bag.

As I was standing there, sniffing and drooling, the kitchen door flew open. A man in black-and-white checked pants and a white chef's smock strode furiously into the alley carrying a huge stainless-steel vat in one hand. He flung the vat's contents against the brick wall of the restaurant, sloshing a river of steaming soup into the pavement.

I jumped out of the way and narrowly missed being scalded.

"That's what I think of your fish stock!" he called angrily over his shoulder toward the kitchen. "Who told you to use dried parsley in a stock? Who told you to use black pepper? Who? Did I tell you to use crap like that? Did I?"

"Hey!" I shouted at him. "Watch what you're doing."

He whirled around to face me. His white smock was spattered with grease and broth stains. His hair needed cutting. Brown waves of it fell into his eyes and he flicked it back impatiently with one hand.

"What? What do you want? We're not hiring and we don't open until seven." The way he said open, I knew he was a Southerner. And not just a Southerner. He was a Savannahian. You can tell. The accent's peculiar, almost like a Richmond accent, but quite different from, say, Atlanta or New Orleans.

"You nearly burned me with that soup," I snapped. "You ought to be more careful what you're doing before you start slinging boiling food around."

His face flushed. It was deeply tanned and the bright blue eyes were set beneath heavy eyebrows. He was tall, maybe six three. Embroidered over the left side of the chef's smock were the words "Guale" and "Chef Daniel."

BeBe poked her head out the kitchen door. "Daniel?" Her voice was meek. "Everything all right?"

I was astonished. I'd never heard BeBe talk that way before. Not to a man, not to anybody.

"Daniel?" she continued, inching slowly toward him. "Pete's sorry. He really is. He didn't see the carton of fresh herbs in the cooler, and he didn't realize you use white peppercorns in your fish stock. He was anxious to get it started before you came in this afternoon. He thought he was being helpful."

Daniel blinked. Long thin fingers pushed a strand of hair off his forehead. "He should try reading the recipe card. It's taped right by the prep sink."

BeBe stepped outside and patted Daniel's arm soothingly. "He knows that now. He's inside, chopping fresh parsley like mad. He'll get the new stock going right away. Okay?"

"It needs at least four hours of simmering."

"There's plenty of frozen stock in the freezer," BeBe said. "A whole gallon. That'll be more than enough for tonight, won't it?"

She smiled brightly and batted her eyelashes for extra effect.

"I suppose."

"Great." She turned to me. "Did you two meet?"

He had the grace to look embarrassed. "No. I'm afraid I was too busy trying to scald her with bad fish stock."

He extended his hand, thought better of it, wiped it on his smock, then held it out again. I shook.

"Sorry," he said. "I'm Daniel. Daniel Stipanek. I don't usually make such a bad impression."

My automatic smile froze. I felt my ears burn, and improbably, my hand felt icy in his. Stipanek? Danny Stipanek?

No. It couldn't be. The Danny Stipanek I'd rolled around with in the shadows of Beaulieu's live oaks was only a little taller than me. His ears stuck out from his head. He was a graceless goofball. The man clutching my hand in his right at this moment bore no resemblance to that Danny Stipanek. This Daniel person towered over me, the grin creasing fine lines around a square jaw, the blue eyes bright in his brown face. BeBe's description of him had been more than accurate. He was indeed gorgeous.

I tried to say something, but it came out as a choke. I took a deep breath and tried to recover from my shock, pulling my hand away. "Actually, this isn't really a first impression. We've met, you know. I'm Eloise Foley."

He took a step backward. "No way." The lazy eyes swept me up and down, but the slow grin came back.

"Weezie? Really? Well, I'll be damned."

I certainly hoped so.

BeBe looked from me to Daniel. "You two know each other? How?"

I watched him nervously. What did he remember? And how much was he willing to reveal to his new boss?

"We went to different high schools together," Daniel said.

"That's right," I said, relieved. "Years ago. I'm surprised Daniel remembered my name even."

That damned grin again. "How could I forget?" he drawled.

I had to get out of here. My heart was racing a mile a minute. The smell of garlic and fish stock was making me nauseous. Danny Stipanek! Of all the men to run into in all the alleys in Savannah. I groaned inwardly. Of course, he had to look great. And I? I had to look like I usually did. The baggy, wrinkled jeans. Faded T-shirt. I hadn't even bothered to put on a bra. Good God. I didn't dare look down. At least, I thought, I'd put on the Joan Crawford lipstick. So I wasn't a total hag.

"Uh, BeBe," I said, glancing meaningfully at my watch. "We really need to get going now if we're going to get a good spot close to the house."

"Just another minute," BeBe promised. "I was going to pack us a little dinner. Some cold roast chicken, a couple of biscuits."

"House? What house?" Daniel asked.

"It's a plantation house. Out on the river. We're going to an estate sale there in the morning. Weezie is an antique dealer, you know."

"No, I didn't know," Daniel said, raising one of those dark eyebrows. "We've sort of lost touch over the years."

I remembered his touch. It made me shudder.

"Oh yes," BeBe said airily, laying it on thick now. "Weezie is opening a shop in the fall. In the old Lamplighter Lounge space. She's buying stock for the shop now. This sale is really supposed to have fabulous stuff."

"Really?" he said. "Where's the sale? Maybe I'll drop by there myself. I'm looking for a few things for my place."

"It's at Beaulieu," BeBe said. "I can draw you a map if you like."

I wanted to die. Right there. Or I could step inside the kitchen and stick my head into one of the big commercial gas ovens.

Daniel was grinning again. His blue eyes danced.

"Beaulieu? I've been there."

"And you remember the way?" BeBe asked helpfully.

"Oh yeah," Daniel said lazily. "I remember everything about Beaulieu."

ell me the game plan again," BeBe said, slapping at a gnat.

I passed her my bottle of Avon Skin-So-Soft and she slathered the sickly sweet–smelling oil all over her body. We'd parked on the front lawn at Beaulieu and set up our folding chaise longues in the bed of the truck. It wasn't the Ritz, but it was free and I'd parked as close to the house as I could get. My brilliant idea about camping out had apparently been shared by at least two dozen other salegoers. There were real campers, trucks, vans, even a couple of pop-up tents, scattered all over the front lawn of the old house, despite signs everywhere that said No Trespassing.

I recognized most of the vans and trucks. They belonged to antique dealers and pickers from as far south as Jacksonville and as far north as Charlotte. The classified ad about the sale had run in the Savannah and Atlanta papers. "Magnificent Antebellum Plantation Estate Sale," it had read. The ad took up four column inches and promised everything from advertising tins to zinc-topped tables. Positively mouthwatering.

There were even a few "amateurs" camping out that night. I pointed out a powder blue Eldorado parked in the shade of a huge old live oak.

"That's the Einsteins," I said.

"Really?" BeBe was impressed. "Like in the genius?"

"They pronounce it Ein-steen," I said. "They run a jewelry store in Statesboro. They're both in their seventies and they're rabid collectors of cutglass. The newspaper ad didn't say anything about glass, but if they're here, they must have gotten the inside dope. They're mean as cat dirt too. Bennie, the oldest one, has a walker. He'll run right over you with it if you get in the way while he's after a piece of Fostoria. And I've had Sammy, he's the little one with the yellow mustache, snatch stuff right out of my hand before. So we'll probably stay away from glass. Although I did see the most fabulous Fenton punch set—the punch bowl, the stand, twelve cups. Flawless. OK, if you can get to the punch bowl, do it. Last time I was here, it was on a sideboard in the dining room. Don't just stand there and stare at it, scoop it all up and put it in one of the tote bags. There are some disposable diapers in there. Wrap 'em up in that. We can't afford breakage. Count, to make sure somebody hasn't snagged a couple of the cups. Ten cups is good, twelve cups makes it worth a couple hundred dollars more."

Then I showed her the shiny silver half-ton van with the words L. HARGREAVES on the side.

"That's Lewis Hargreaves. If you see him acting interested in something, be subtle, but try to grab it before he does. He's the competition. And he knows what to look for."

BeBe took out a cigarette and lit it. "Lewis. I know him. My God, Weezie. How do you know what's what? How can you remember everything? You're starting to intimidate me, and I don't intimidate easily."

"It's like that television game," I told her. "*Supermarket Sweeps?* You remember that one? Everybody stands at the starting line, they yell go, and the contestants run up and down the aisles grabbing stuff, hoping they'll make it back to the checkout in the shortest time with the biggest cash register tape. All these people here are after the same stuff as us, probably. We just have to beat them to it. It's kill or be killed."

I pointed my paper cup of wine at a red truck parked not far from ours. "Except somebody like Nappy. He's another specialist. Buys old records, paperback books, radios, clocks, and guns. Guy stuff. He picks for dealers up in Ohio and Indiana. Kind of weird-looking, because he doesn't have a hair on his head. But he's nice. He'll sometimes pick up something at a sale that he knows I buy. I do the same for him."

"OK," BeBe said. She poured another glass of wine. It was her third. I was still sipping my first. "We stay away from radios or clocks."

"Well," I wavered. "I buy them if they're cute. Like, if you see an old Bakelite radio, jump on it. For that matter, grab anything Bakelite. You know what it looks like, right? Sort of like old plastic, but with a glow to it? Usually it's red, yellow, green, or amber. Or one of those cute little old alarm clocks with the metal clangers, or a traveling clock in a leather case. Nothing big. Only cute and little."

"Cute and little," she mumbled.

"Smalls, we call them," I said. "Here's what you're looking for, BeBe: Anything blue-and-white porcelain. Miss Anna Ruby had a lot of that. Make sure it's not chipped, unless it's just marked rock-bottom, say a platter for ten dollars or under. English is best, American is OK, I don't buy Japanese. Silver—but only sterling. Look on the bottom for the hallmark. Linens. There should be tons of linens. Look for damask tablecloth and napkin sets, printed luncheon cloths from the forties, linen sheets and pillowcases, bedspreads, anything in the Victorian white category. Paintings are great. The walls are covered with them. Get the old prints, the—"

"Stop!" she hollered, plugging her fingers in her ears. "Enough already. God, I thought this was supposed to be fun. You're making it all so serious."

"It is serious," I said, pulling her hands away from her ears. "A sale like this comes along once a decade, if that. The Mullinaxes were true connoisseurs. They bought the finest of everything. And they never got rid of a single thing."

"All right." She sighed. "Smalls. Sterling silver. Oil paintings. I get the picture."

"You can get furniture too," I added. "I've got a roll of masking tape in your bag. I've written 'Sold—Foley' all over strips of it. When you see a piece you like, slap the tape right on the front. If the piece isn't too big for you to move, try to take it to the cash-out person. Tell her you're putting it in my pile. Try to find good old painted wood pieces, or oak or pine. Ignore the junky mahogany stuff from the forties. Concentrate on country kind of stuff. You know, like I have in my house."

"*Had* in your house," she said sleepily. "But I thought there was some cupboard you were after."

"The Moses Weed. I'll deal with the cupboard," I said firmly.

"Now. About the attic and the basement," I continued, "and the closets.

Very important. You know how I am about vintage clothes. Make sure you check closets. In every room. Grab all the clothes you can—everything except seventies polyester. I know it's in, but I don't do disco. Old hats, shoes, and handbags are good too. Look for alligator. I can sell that all day long. And don't forget to check dresser drawers. Vintage lingerie is wonderful."

"Dead people's panties? That's yucky." She yawned again. "Too tired. Tell me in the morning."

I looked over and saw that she'd nodded off, the cup of wine still balanced on her chest. "That's right," I whispered. "Sleep. We've got to get up at five to be in line."

"Weezie?" Her eyes fluttered open again. "You and Daniel. I sensed something there. Heat. Definite heat. Did you ever, sort of, date?"

It was hot, but I felt a chill creep up my spine. "Once, maybe. In high school. It was nothing, Babe. Go to sleep."

She yawned. "Can't believe you didn't hang on to a hottie like that." Then she was asleep.

I tried not to think of Daniel Stipanek. Tried not to remember that long ago summer day and the feel of Spanish moss on my back. I drank the last of the wine and drifted off to sleep myself.

A mosquito was droning around my face. I slapped at it, yawned, tried to roll over, and realized I had a pressing need to pee. Damn. Never should have had that second glass of wine. I looked at my watch. It was 2 A.M.

My lawn chair made a creaking noise as I sat up. Jethro heard me and sat up too. He let out a low-pitched whine.

"You too?" I whispered. He whined again.

Now what? I'd planned to make a run to McDonald's in the morning, for coffee, a newspaper, and a pit stop. But I needed to go right now. In another couple hours, people would start lining up to get into the sale.

I hopped down from the truck bed, and Jethro followed. I stretched and yawned and led him away to a nearby tree where the lucky dog got to empty his bladder.

More people had arrived since I'd dozed off to sleep. There were maybe seventy or eighty vehicles parked in and around the lawn. I looked up at Beaulieu's darkened windows. A bathroom, I thought. If I could just borrow a bathroom.

OK. I started out thinking about a bathroom. But soon I was thinking about that silent old house. And how in just a few hours, the place would be teeming with crazed antique dealers and collectors. What I needed was a little head start. A little sneak preview. I reached back into the truck, got my flashlight, and, on second thought, tucked the plastic sack that had held BeBe's wine in the waist of my jeans.

The house was absolutely dark. A single naked lightbulb shone on the backside of the house, over what looked like the kitchen door. I tried the doorknob. Locked, of course. Pressed my face up against the glass in the door and shined the flashlight. I could see a night-light plugged into a wall socket near the kitchen counter. All the contents of the cabinets had been emptied onto the counters. I could see gorgeous old yellowware mixing bowls, stacks of Fiesta ware dishes, mugs and platters, blue spatterware dishpans and roasting pans and coffeepots. Everything I saw I would have bought. On top of the blue enamel 1920s Charm-Glow stove somebody had set up a big commercial coffeepot, along with a stack of foam cups and packages of creamer and sugar. Supplies for the people running the estate sale. Was somebody in the house, I wondered? Nobody I'd talked to seemed to know who would be running the sale. None of the local people who ran sales had been asked. In fact, most of them were like me, parked outside, dying to get in.

I walked around to the parlor side of the house and up the steps to the covered porch. The floor-to-ceiling windows were all closed and fastened securely, the drapes pulled tight. Obviously, whoever was running the sale didn't intend to give any previews. I followed the porch around to the front of the house, stumbling now and then over a rocking chair or a stray garden tool. A quick flicker of my flashlight showed the porch had been packed with the kind of thing I usually find in garages at estate sales; yard tools, gardening equipment, old folding wooden chairs, galvanized tubs, wooden buckets of nails, dozens and dozens of flowerpots. One stack of flowerpots caught my eye. I bent down. They were pastel glazed, with playful patterns of tulips and bluebirds and sunflowers. I turned the top one over. Bingo. It was really the real McCoy. Pottery, that is. I sorted through the stack quickly. There were six McCoy flowerpots, two Roseville, all of them marked ten cents. Antique shops in Buckhead sold plain McCoy for thirty to fifty dollars apiece; Roseville like these would go for at least sixty dollars. Score one for Weezie.

But where to hide them? I looked around, saw a huge, overgrown boxwood at the edge of the porch. I took the stack of pots, lay down on my belly, and slid them underneath the shrub.

Now I really did have to pee. I did a kind of quickstep around to the porch on the other side of the house. The windows to the dining room were closed tight, drapes drawn. Double damn. This side of the house was in total darkness. A malevolent old magnolia towered over the porch; its topmost branches leaning up against and nearly covering the wall. I played the flashlight against the side of the house. A second-story window was nearly level with one of the branches. And it had been left open maybe six inches.

As a kid, magnolias had been my favorite climbing trees. The branches were thick and low and the foliage so dense you could never see a kid at the top of the tree throwing water balloons at kids riding by on their bikes.

I leaned down and got right in Jethro's face. "Stay," I said sternly. He yawned and lay down. I shoved my flashlight in the waistband at the back of my jeans, hitched a leg over the lowest branch, pulled myself up, and kept on going.

At ten feet in the air, the view of the branch nearest the window looked a lot thinner and scarier than it had from the ground. But the threat of wetting my pants—in public—and having to stay in said pants during the sale of the century kept me moving.

I shinnied out to the end of the limb, swung my left leg over, and leaned precariously in toward the wall of the house. Steadying myself on the branch with one hand, I reached out and pushed upward on the window. Stuck. I gritted my teeth, put both hands on the rotted window sash, and gave it a shove.

Slowly, it inched upward. When it was halfway open, I leaned my torso into the window and slithered through, tumbling in a heap onto the floor.

I was in! I snapped on my flashlight. I was in a small bedroom dominated by a massive carved four-poster bed heaped with stacks of old clothing and linens. Water-stained rose-trellised wallpaper covered the walls. But for the first time in at least twenty years I paid absolutely no attention to the stacks of junk piled nearly ceiling-high in the bedroom. Never mind the antiques. I needed to find a bathroom.

There were two doors in the room. One was narrow, painted white. I opened it, and a stack of hatboxes fell on my head. A closet. It was jammed with clothes. Faded cotton housedresses, drifts of netting and chiffon, silk and brocades. Reluctantly, I went to the other door. It led out into the hallway.

I didn't dare turn on a light. I played the flashlight around the wide hall. Four more doors. Lock-kneed and cross-eyed with agony, I opened two doors, found two more bedrooms. On the third try I found the loo.

High-ceilinged with yellowed tiles, a clawfoot bathtub and yes!—an ancient, but apparently working, commode.

Afterward, I stood in the hallway, listening. Had anyone heard the groan of the cast-iron pipes, the gurgle of water? The old house was still except for the creaking of floorboards under my feet and faint, skittering noises in the walls. Roaches. This was Savannah, after all. Everybody has roaches, except my parents. Pest control is one of my father's hobbies.

Well, I was in, wasn't I? No alarms had sounded. No harm in checking around. I headed down the stairs, clinging fast to the handrail, which teetered at every touch.

At the bottom of the stairs I paused again, trying to get my bearings. The people organizing the sale had been busy. Long tables lined the walls of the hallway, heaped with a hundred years' worth of bric-a-brac.

My hand came to rest on a mismatched pair of chunky Georgian silver candlesticks. One stick's base was squared-off, the other round. They were tarnished and dented, and the tape that bound them together said ten dollars. It was too dark to see the hallmark, but they were still a steal. I took the plastic bag out of my hip pocket and stashed the candlesticks there. My hip brushed against the table and I grabbed to catch the bibelot I'd knocked over. Holding my flashlight on it, I saw it was a Staffordshire porcelain shepherdess grouping. Without thinking, I scooped it up and checked for a price sticker. It was marked twenty-five dollars. Not dirt cheap, but I knew I could turn it at half a dozen shops right here in town. I took a dish towel from a stack of linens and wrapped it around the shepherdess, adding it to my stash.

The bag was getting heavy. It was time to go. Out of the corner of my eye, I saw a glint of metal amongst the linens. I bent down closer. A beautifully worked wooden box lay open on top of the linens. The box was fitted with faded purple velvet. Nested inside were two small, exquisitely inlaid pearl-handled revolvers.

I frowned. Firearms are not my specialty. There were too many knowledgeable gun dealers in south Georgia, and I knew too little about them to take a risk. But even my untrained eye could see that these were something special. I picked up the box for a closer look. A heavily chased silver plate adorned the lid. I squinted, but couldn't read the worn engraving. It didn't matter. From what little I could tell, these were probably Civil War presentation pistols. There was no price sticker. They went into the bag with the candlesticks and the china shepherdess.

Squaring my shoulders, I headed for the front parlor. I held my breath as the flashlight flickered over the far corner, the one where the cupboard had been.

It was there. I exhaled. The cupboard had been cleared of the china and its doors were flung wide. I tiptoed over, felt the satin-smooth patina of the wood. An index card was taped to the inside back. In block printing were the words "Elm corner cupboard, original to Beaulieu plantation. Signed, dated 1858, authenticated." The next line on the card made me gasp. $15,000.

I snapped off the flashlight, stuffed it in my back pocket. The adrenaline rush was suddenly gone. The price of the Moses Weed cupboard was fair, but it might as well have been $150,000. I'd come to Beaulieu ready to gamble, but somebody had raised the table stakes way over my limit.

It was time to go. I felt limp with fatigue and disappointment. I'd lost my heart and my nerve. No more death-defying tree climbs for me. I'd just go out the back door and slink back to my truck.

But what to do with my booty? Now that the Weed cupboard was out of my grasp, I might as well make a go of the other treasures. I needed a place to hide the bag, someplace off-limits, where prying hands and eyes wouldn't scoop them up before I came in at the legal starting time. Someplace as far away as possible from the card table near the front door where the checkout stand would surely be located.

Upstairs. There was a narrow closet in the bathroom. A linen closet, no doubt. I could hide the bag under the inevitable sheets and pillowcases. My knees wobbled as I climbed the stairs.

I went into the bathroom, shut the door, pressed the push-button light switch. I was too tired now for caution. Holding the bag with my left hand, I jerked at the closet door with my right. Stuck. Heat and moisture had made the wooden door swell and warp. I set the bag down on the tile floor, grasped the doorknob with both hands, and tugged. It gave a little but still wouldn't open. I stood back a little, bent my knees, and pulled again.

The door flew open and I heard something. Not the skittering of renegade roaches. Something heavy, sliding onto the tile floor. I looked down. Caroline DeSantos looked up at me, her head crimped unnaturally to the side, legs stuck straight forward. She was still wearing the three-thousand-dollar Briaggi dress. Only now the cream silk bore a huge crimson blossom in the middle of her chest. Caroline DeSantos wouldn't have been caught dead in red. Only now she was.

ethro barked.

"My God, no," I said aloud. But I knew that bark. It was high-pitched, anxious. "Weezie, come back to me," it seemed to say. Or maybe it was just his "Weezie, I'm bored and I've got a squirrel treed" bark. We were still working on communication skills.

I stood, rooted to the spot, looking down at Caroline. I felt dizzy, but I kept looking. Jethro kept barking. A horn beeped somewhere outside. That did it. I ran into the bedroom and stuck my head out the window.

"Hush," I called. "Hush, puppy." The magnolia leaves made a thick, nearly impenetrable canopy over the lawn below. The hot humid air was perfectly still. Jethro whimpered, and I heard his tail thump against the grass.

Then a beam of light sliced through the syrupy softness of the night. I put my hand up to shield my eyes, but the beam was relentless. Jethro whimpered again. I felt like joining in.

"Ma'am?" The voice below was loud, but not deep. "Ma'am? I'm from Paragon Security. An alarm went off. Are you the owner of this home?"

"She's dead." I meant Anna Ruby Mullinax, but I was thinking of that corpse on the bathroom floor too.

He cleared his throat. "Ma'am? Could you come down, please? And, uh, I think you should know, I'm an armed response officer. You're, uh, under arrest."

Under the circumstances, I decided to hide my bag of loot under the bed.

The magnolia tree suddenly looked threatening, the ground seemed miles away. "How about I come downstairs and meet you at the front door?" I tried.

"Come down the way you came in, please," he said. He shone the flashlight up into the treetop again. I took my time climbing, putting one foot gingerly beneath the other, not looking down. From below, I could hear the buzz and drone of a radio. He was talking into it. Calling in reinforcements, probably.

When I was about four feet off the ground, I saw a car with flashing blue lights speeding down Beaulieu's front drive.

"That's fine," the security guard said. "Jump on down, please, ma'am."

My foot slipped, and I fell in a heap, rolling away from the base of the tree, scraping a long patch of skin from my right thigh and my right hand when I tried to cushion my fall. Jethro trotted over and licked my face.

"Stay right there," the guard said. I got the impression of youth, of a tan uniform, and of a big gun barrel, pointed politely, but resolutely, in my direction.

Jethro started in to howling when he heard the police siren. One by one, lights flickered on around the darkened grounds of Beaulieu. The first police car was followed by a Paragon Security Armed Response vehicle, which was really just a battered tan Chevy Blazer with a gun rack in the rear window.

"I was just looking for a bathroom," I told the skinny young guard. It sounded lame, even to me. "I saw a window open, and I went in the house, and I used the facility, but then I needed something to dry my hands on, and I opened the closet." I paused and took a gulp of soupy air. A gnat flew into my mouth. It was that kind of night. "Officer? You might want to call the real police."

A beefy older guy grabbed me by the arm. "Ma'am? We're as real as it gets. And we're gonna swear out a real honest-to-God warrant against you for breaking and entering."

I winced and tried to twist out of his grasp, but he held on tighter. There was no good way to bring up the subject of a dead body for somebody in my predicament. Still, I'd been raised Catholic. Confession seemed only natural.

I swatted at the gnat cloud around my face. "Officer? There's a dead woman in the bathroom closet upstairs."

"Oh." A vein throbbed in the skinny guy's neck. The beefy guy produced a set of rinky-dink handcuffs that looked like he'd gotten them with cereal box tops.

You could hear the police sirens coming from a long way away. People around the grounds began to stir. A crowd gathered there around us, at the base of the magnolia tree. People whispered and pointed at me. My head was pounding. I needed coffee and ibuprofen because I was not thinking clearly. I should have been thinking about a lawyer, about who put that big ugly bloodstain on Caroline's chest. Instead, I was wondering whether or not they'd postpone the estate sale until after I got out of this messy little jam.

CHAPTER *15*

 he redbrick police barracks was at the corner of Habersham and Oglethorpe. James made it there in under ten minutes.

He was worried about his niece. On the phone, she'd said something about finding a body, out at Beaulieu, and about being arrested and charged for breaking and entering. Oh yes, and possibly homicide. She was hysterical and, he fervently hoped, overreacting. Although it wasn't like Weezie to overreact.

He pushed the heavy plate-glass doors open. A sleepy-eyed black woman looked up from her perch behind the front counter. At one time, this had been a high varnished-mahogany desk, and the face behind the desk would have been one of the meaty-faced Finnegans, or maybe BoBo Kuniansky. But the Finnegans had gotten out of police work, and the last he'd heard, BoBo Kuniansky was selling real estate at Hilton Head Island. This woman was someone he'd never seen before. And she was separated from the world by an inch-thick shield of bullet-proof glass. James sighed. This was not the Savannah of his youth.

The black woman told him he needed to see Detective Bradley.

Upstairs. The elevator took a long time. A heavyset man in a brown short-sleeved shirt seemed to be the only person in the detective's office.

"Are you Detective Bradley?" James asked.

"I'm Jay Bradley. You Father Foley?"

"Just James, if you don't mind."

"I had you for freshman English. At Benedictine," Bradley said. "Class of eighty. I guess you don't remember."

"It was a long time ago," James said apologetically. "And I only taught the two years. Were you good at English?"

"Nah, I sucked," Bradley said. "You wanta see Eloise?"

"I do," James said quickly.

Bradley gestured toward the door opposite where he was standing. "She's in there. Kinda shook up."

"Weezie would never kill anyone," James said, his voice sharp, authoritarian, like the former English teacher.

"Yeah," Bradley said. "Whatever. In a little while, we're gonna book her, and I'm gonna go home and get some sleep. I'm wiped out."

"Book her?" James could not keep the alarm from his voice. "Weezie's not a murderer. You can't keep her overnight."

Bradley shrugged. "We keep her until a judge says otherwise," he said. "You're a lawyer, right? You know all this stuff."

Actually, he didn't. But he knew somebody who knew criminal law backward and forward. Did he dare call Jonathan at this hour? Their friendship was still so new, so tentative. He winced. But this was Weezie. And blood was thicker than water.

His niece was huddled in a chair in the corner of what looked like a conference room. It was Savannah, midsummer, which meant every public building in town had the mean average temperature of a meat locker. This room was freezing, and she had her arms wrapped around her chest, her knees drawn up in a fetal position. Her face was red and blotchy from crying, and her arms were covered in red welts.

"Uncle James!" It was a whisper, really. She stood up, and he folded her into his arms, the way he'd done when she was six and had scraped her knee riding her bike.

"Weezer," he said, rubbing her arms. They were like ice. "It's all right, Weezer. I'm here. I'm here."

He got her calmed down finally. Went to the break room, got her a cup of coffee and a package of Little Debbie snack cakes. The Little Debbies were actually for him. Terrible habit.

James draped his windbreaker around Weezie's shoulders. She was pale and shivering. "Tell me what happened," he said, once she'd warmed up a little.

"Caroline's dead," Weezie said. "They think I killed her."

"I know," he said.

She covered her mouth with her hand. "Oh my God!"

"What?" James leaned over, alarmed. "What?"

"BeBe," Weezie said. "I just left her there. At Beaulieu. And Jethro. And the truck. They made me get in the police cruiser. BeBe was sound asleep. My God. She'll think I was kidnapped."

"No, she won't," James said, relieved that this particular crisis could be averted. "She called me right after you did. She saw the cops putting you in the cruiser, and one of your dealer buddies told her what had happened. Or, at least, what they thought had happened."

"That I'd broken into Beaulieu, stolen a bunch of stuff, and shot Caroline," Weezie said. "That's what everybody thinks."

"BeBe knows you didn't do anything like that," James said, patting Weezie's hand. "She drove the truck home. Jethro's with her. She just wanted to make sure I knew what had happened."

The door opened all the way. Bradley poked his head in. Coughed officiously. "Time to go."

"Go?" Weezie looked confused.

"Jail," Bradley said. "That's how it works when you get charged with murder."

CHAPTER *16*

 *I* spent the night in jail. That much I could remember. Everything else, my subconscious wiped clean. Thank God.

The next morning, James and BeBe bailed me out. James brought the Mercedes around to the jail's side door, and BeBe came bustling in carrying a huge garment bag and her own makeup case, which is as big as what most people use for a week's vacation.

"What's all that?" I asked wearily. "I just want to go home, Babe. I'll shower and change when I get home."

"Not in this lifetime," she said fiercely. "There's a whole mess of reporters waiting outside for you. All the television stations, the Savannah paper, Atlanta, Jacksonville, there's even a gal out there interviewing people who swears she's from *People* magazine. If you think I'm letting you walk out of here looking like something the cat dragged in, you better think again. Now come on, let's duck into the ladies' room and get busy cleaning you up. I don't know how I'm gonna be able to cover up those dark circles under your eyes. And those bug bites! I swannee, Weezie."

"No," I whispered. "Why? Why are they here?"

BeBe blinked. "Honey, I hate to tell you this, but this is a big story.

Not just for Savannah. For anywhere. Caroline's daddy is some big shot architect in Chicago. And Tal, well, you and I know he's just a little chickenshit pencil-pushing geek, but he *is* from a prominent old Savannah family, and he *was* engaged to her. And you *are* Tal's ex-wife. And let's face it, the two of you have a history. You had *issues*."

My stomach lurched. My best friend thought I'd killed Caroline.

"But I didn't do it. I was with you. You told the police that, right?"

She nodded vigorously. "I told 'em. I told 'em over and over again. We were together all evening. Right up until, what? Midnight? The trouble is, Weezie, we drank all that wine, and I fell asleep. You know how I am once I get a snootful. I could sleep through a hurricane. In fact, I did sleep through Hurricane Floyd."

"But you don't think I killed her, do you?"

"Did you? I mean, I wouldn't blame you if you had."

I groaned. "BeBe!"

"OK, OK," she said hastily. "No. Of course you didn't kill her. Absolutely not. Eloise Foley is not a person who kills another person."

"Thank you," I said lamely.

"Although if you'd asked me to help, I would have bought the bullets."

"Don't even joke about that," I said. "Did I tell you they made me wear handcuffs? And while I was riding in the back of that police car, another car pulled up beside us? Guess who looked right at me?"

"Who?"

"Patti Dowd."

"Who's she?"

"Patti Dowd, president of my class at St. Vincent's. And Marcia Watts was sitting right beside her. And Janisse Haddad was driving! You can't miss that yellow Viper her husband bought her for her thirtieth birthday."

BeBe groaned. "If Marcia Watts saw you, she's probably the one who alerted the media."

"It's no joke. The deputies frisked me. I had to wear jail shoes. And my cell had a stainless-steel bench that was part toilet."

"Eeeww," BeBe said, wiping her hands on her slacks. "I wish you'd told me that before I hugged you. No offense."

While BeBe kept the ladies' room door barricaded I stripped off every stitch of clothing I'd worn the night before, and threw them in the trash barrel. I took a birdbath right there in the ladies' room in the Chatham County Jail, scrubbing at my skin until I was the color of a tomato. Then I put on the panties and bra BeBe brought me from home. She unzipped the garment bag and pulled out a navy blue linen sailor dress, complete with bib collar and red bow and hip pleats. I swear, the thing had puff sleeves.

"Ick!" I said, holding it at arm's length. "Where are the jeans and T-shirt you were supposed to bring me?"

"At home," she said firmly. She unzipped the zipper and tried to pull the dress over my head, but I pushed her away.

"Where in God's name did you find that rag? Punch n' Judy?" It was a Savannah boutique that sold high-priced kiddie clothes. My mother had force-fed me frilly Punch n' Judy dresses until I was twelve years old and sprouted breasts no amount of smocking or flounces could hide. Mama wept when the saleswoman told her they didn't carry a B-cup training bra in the Teen Time department.

BeBe tried to look hurt. She couldn't sell it.

"This happens to be from the Young Careers shop. It's a very nice dress."

I crossed my arms over my bra. "Fine. You wear it. I wouldn't be caught dead in that thing. Where are my jeans?"

She sighed. "Your uncle James suggested this. We have to think about your image, Weezie. You can't just blow out of the jailhouse in your raggedy-ass jeans and tie-dyed T-shirts with all those reporters and photographers out there. You've got to look sweet. Demure even. Innocent."

"I don't have to look innocent. I *am* innocent."

"Well, they don't know that." She reached back in the bag and brought out a pair of navy blue pumps. With blue grosgrain bows at the toes. Swear to God. Bows.

"Here. Put these on too."

I gave her a murderous look. "What, no white anklets?"

Once she had me dressed, BeBe applied about a quart of concealer, a quick dusting of powder, and the faintest coat of pale pink lipstick.

I frowned when I saw what she'd done. "Give me some blusher, will you? And some mascara. I look like I need a blood transfusion."

"That's the look we're going for," BeBe said. "Pale. Emaciated. Heartsick."

When she'd finished dressing me up like Dolly Dimples, BeBe stood back and studied her handiwork. "I like it. Simple. Virginal, even. Let's go."

A sheriff's deputy walked us out to the back door, but when he pushed it open, a surge of people pressed toward me.

A dozen long-lensed cameras were pointed right at my face. I spotted half a dozen TV cameras. People were calling my name. "Weezie! Eloise Foley! Did you kill the other woman? Why'd you do it, Weezie?"

James pushed his way through the crowd and grabbed one arm, and BeBe grabbed the other. She was in her element, shoving cameras out of the way. "No comment!" she bawled. "Miss Foley has no comment!"

James yanked the back door of the Mercedes open, and before I knew it, BeBe had shoved me inside. She jumped into the front seat beside James, and a moment later, we roared away from the curb.

BeBe was laughing like a banshee. "That was great!" she crowed.

James turned around and gave me a sympathetic look. "Are you all right?"

I shook my head. "OK. Tired. Humiliated. You think they'll really put it on TV?"

"Afraid so, sweetheart," he said. "Reporters have been calling all morning. They came to my house first thing, banging on the door. And they've got your carriage house staked out. Tal's house too, of course. So we can't go back to Charlton Street right now."

I bit my lip. For the first time all day, I felt hot tears welling up in my eyes. "Where are you taking me then?"

"My house," BeBe said quickly. "Not a soul will know where you are."

"All right," I said, defeated. My body ached and my eyes burned from lack of sleep. I put my head back against the cool leather of the headrest. And then I remembered something. The dress.

"BeBe?"

She turned around. "What is it, sugar?"

"Where'd you get this dress? The Young Careers shop closed years ago."

She smiled. "Your mama brought it over. She's been saving it for you."

When I stepped inside BeBe's front door, Jethro jumped up and nearly knocked me over. He barked and wagged his tail—and piddled all over the floor.

"That dog is going outside," BeBe said, grabbing for Jethro's collar.

"Please, Babe," I said, trying to look pale and virginal and innocent all at the same time I was mopping up the piddle with a paper towel. "He won't do it again. He was just excited to see me. Please don't put him out. I just want to lie down and have a little nap. He'll lie down with me, won't you, Ro-Ro?"

Jethro stood on his hind legs and rested his paws on my shoulders and licked my face soundly. It felt grand.

"How are you gonna get some sleep with that big ole hound slobbering all over the place?" BeBe fussed. "And what about fleas? If he gives fleas to my cats I'm gonna skin that hound and nail his hide to the back door."

"He doesn't have fleas, do you, Ro-Ro?"

Jethro wagged his tail vigorously.

"That means no," I explained.

James kissed the top of my head and I gave him a hug. "I'm gonna go see if I can earn my keep now," he said. "I've been doing some research. I'm pretty sure none of that stuff they found at the house—like the antique pistols or the plastic bag with the receipt for your wine—can be used as evidence against you, because those rent-a-cops let so many people in the house they can't be sure who touched what. But I'm gonna go out to Beaulieu and walk around, see if I can find out any more about what happened out there Friday night."

"The sale," I said. My heart sank. The biggest estate sale of the century, and I'd been in jail all day. "It'll be over by now. God. My one chance."

"Think again," BeBe said briskly. "The cops were all over that house like stink on a polecat. They canceled the sale, sugar. And you should have heard the ruckus the dealers raised. Lewis Hargreaves looked like he might have a myocardial infarction right there on the spot, his face was so red. I thought a couple of those folks were gonna storm the place. And they would have too, except for the fact that the cops chased everybody off the property and put yellow crime-scene tape all the way around the house."

I smiled and then yawned. It was the best news I'd heard all day. Of course, it *was* still the worst day of my life.

I slept the sleep of the angels. Or the damned. But it was sleep, and I was so tired I felt I might never wake up again. Somewhere off in the distance, I heard a phone ringing, and the tapping of BeBe's heels on the hardwood floors. I heard water running, and voices, and the faint drone of a television coming from a distant place. But I slept and slept.

When I woke up, Jethro was gone. I looked out the window of BeBe's guest room. It was dusk. Fireflies glittered in the fronds of a palm tree outside the window. I'd slept for nearly six hours.

I went in the bathroom and washed my face. Looked in the mirror and saw that I was still wearing the sailor dress. I left it in a heap on the bathroom floor and walked out to the bedroom, where I found a paper sack with my beloved jeans and T-shirt, even my favorite pair of flip-flops.

BeBe was in the kitchen, talking on the phone. "Oh," she said, looking over at me and covering the receiver with the palm of her hand. "You're awake. Just in time. Daniel sent supper over for you. I was afraid it would get cold."

"Daniel?" The hairs on the back of my neck prickled.

"He saw it on the news. He's called here twice, asking about you."

BeBe took her hand off the phone. "Look, Emery. I can't talk now. I've got company. Call me later."

I sat down on one of the bar stools at the kitchen counter. BeBe went to the counter and started lifting white cardboard take-out containers from a paper sack.

Warm smells wafted through the kitchen. Garlic, onion, some herb I couldn't identify. Jethro appeared from nowhere and put his paws on the counter beside BeBe, who pushed him aside.

"Isn't this the sweetest thing?" BeBe asked. "He's fixed you chicken country captain, and rice pilaf, and just look at this gorgeous Caesar salad."

She raised the lid on a box of crisp green lettuce leaves.

My stomach did a neat little flip.

"I'm not hungry."

"Bullshit," BeBe said. "I know for a fact you haven't eaten in at least twenty-four hours."

"James gave me part of a Little Debbie," I said weakly.

BeBe opened a cabinet and took down two white china plates. She set them on the counter and added napkins and silverware. Then she got a bottle of white wine out of her stainless-steel restaurant refrigerator and poured us each a glass.

When the plates were loaded with food, she took her place beside me and pointed at my plate with her fork. "Now eat," she said sternly. "Or I'll call up one of those reporters at Channel Three and tell 'em where you're hiding out."

"Blackmailer," I said. But I nibbled a bite of the chicken. Divine.

BeBe smiled angelically. "See," she said. "The man can cook. And he's interested in you, Weezie. Very interested."

"But I'm not interested in him," I said, taking another bite of chicken. "All I wanna do is finish my dinner, take my dog, and go home. And forget this day ever happened."

CHAPTER *17*

I closed and locked the door behind me and took a deep breath. I was home. Jethro nudged my knees with his head. I sat down on the floor and took his muzzle in my hands. "You thought I left you, didn't you, buddy?" He licked my chin. "You thought the bad guys locked me up for good, didn't you?"

Another lick. I put my head against the arm of my sofa and closed my eyes. But only for a minute.

I walked from room to room in the carriage house, switching on all the lights, letting my fingertips drift across tabletops. Everything was just the way I'd left it, what? Only a day ago?

In the kitchen, the red message light on my answering machine blinked furiously. I backed away from it as though it were a coiled snake. I knew that blink. Mama. I would call her back, later. Just not now. I didn't have the strength right now to cope with Mama's hysteria.

I wandered upstairs to the second floor. It had once been an unfinished attic space, but when I'd taken over the carriage house, I'd left the sloping ceilings open, painted the dark old exposed beams white, and turned it into a bedroom loft, complete with the master bath of my dreams—courtesy of a claw-foot cast-iron tub I'd bribed a garbage man fifty bucks to haul home from behind the burned-out shell of a Victorian row house on Thirty-eighth Street.

I'd placed a big antique brass bed in the middle of the loft space, where I could look out a pair of lace-draped windows to the tiny wrought-iron balcony facing the back of the big house.

I'd been in such a rush to leave the day before that I hadn't even made the bed—unusual for me. Making the bed was a ritual I loved. Over the years I'd collected baskets full of old sheets and pillowcases—Irish linen sheets with hand-crocheted edging, pillow slips with lavish monograms (never my own initials), pin tucks and embroidery and convent-made lace. I topped the bed with an old white matelasse spread with scalloped edges. At the head of the bed I had a mound of starched pillows. At the foot I kept the quilt my grandmother Foley had made as a wedding present for Mama.

I knew a lot about quilts, but this was a pattern I'd never seen anywhere else, probably a variation on an Irish chain. The colors were soft pastels, Depression era, probably made from old feed sacks.

The quilt had slipped to the floor. I picked it up and sat on the edge of the bed. Jethro jumped up beside me. I draped the quilt around my shoulders and buried my nose in the folds of cloudlike cotton. Even after all these years the quilt still smelled of my meemaw—of lavender and Ivory soap flakes. Mama didn't like anything as old-fashioned as a quilt, so she'd left it in her cedar hope chest for all those years, until I'd begged her to let me have it.

I lay back on the bed and closed my eyes again. Maybe I would sleep and this jumpy, unsettled feeling would disappear. Maybe I could shut out the image of Caroline's waxen face, and all the other horrors of the past twenty-four hours.

But sleep wouldn't come, not even after I took a long hot bubble bath and slipped into my coolest cotton nightgown. I was still restless, boiling over with some weird, pent-up energy. Finally I tossed the quilt aside and went back downstairs.

In the kitchen, I kept my back to the answering machine and rooted around in the refrigerator for something to settle my nerves. There wasn't much in the way of food, because I'd been too busy getting ready for the sale to go to the store. I had eggs, some half-and-half, some cheddar cheese, and a questionable foil package that turned out to be sliced ham Mama had sent home with me after Sunday supper the week before.

An omelette! I whisked the eggs and cream together and set the ham to sizzle in a scandalous amount of butter in a black iron skillet.

While the ham browned, I grated the cheese and beat it into the eggs and cream, along with some salt and ground black pepper. The smell of the frying ham almost made me swoon. Of course, Jethro demanded his share of the scraps.

When the omelette was done I poured myself an iced-tea glass full of chardonnay and went to sit at the tiny bistro table in the kitchen. But the air conditioning was suddenly too chilly. I shivered, then decided to sit outside in the courtyard to eat my midnight supper.

The worn bricks of the patio still held the heat of the day, and they felt good under my bare feet.

I put my plate and glass down on the wrought-iron table beneath the shade of the pink crape myrtle tree. Humidity closed over me like a blanket, but I welcomed the warmth.

I took a bite of the omelette and sipped the wine, willing myself to relax. I loved this time of night in the courtyard. Most of the time, the historic district these days buzzes with activity, with the roar of tour buses and traffic and the jackhammers of the never-ending restoration process. But now the streets were quiet. The tourists had been tucked into their pricey bed-and-breakfasts, and it was as though I had the town to myself.

I nibbled at the omelette and let my eyes wander around the courtyard. There was a white climbing rose clambering up the brick around the door of my carriage house, and the rose had been loaded with blooms six weeks earlier. Now it needed deadheading, and probably a good watering, since we'd had a bone-dry spring. I stood up and walked across the courtyard to the tiny goldfish pond by the tea olive shrub. I sat on the rock edge of the pond and dropped in a bit of omelette. The pond was so tiny there was room for only two koi—Rocky and Bullwinkle. Now they appeared under the surface of the water, nibbling at the egg.

I took another sip of the wine, and a slight breeze ruffled the back of my hair. I looked up and for the first time saw the light in the third-floor window of the townhouse, Tal's home office.

A face was silhouetted in the window. Tal. I could see him so clearly it nearly took my breath away. He was gazing out the window, but seemingly at nothing. As I watched, he buried his face in his hands. I looked away, hurt that his hurt was so naked, so visible. And then, unable not to, I looked again. He seemed frozen in that window, a strand of his thick, wheat-colored hair falling into his eyes, his fingers splayed across his face.

He was mourning Caroline. The stab of pain surprised me. Hadn't I battened down the hatches, wasn't I over all this moony shit? Our marriage had been over for more than a year. Time enough to heal, I'd told myself.

But it was so damned hard, not loving him. We had dated for two years, been married for a little over ten. Nearly half my life. I had loved Tal for so long, it was hard to remember what I had been like before we were us. Our split had been bitter, and at some point, I had forced myself to shut down any memory of what our life had been like before things fell apart.

Now the memories came rushing back unbidden, as I sat there, in the garden, in my nightgown, looking up at the only man I had ever really loved. As he sat in the home we had built together, mourning the woman who had come between us. Whom he thought I had killed.

He looked so damn vulnerable. So fragile. It was a word I never would have associated with Talmadge Evans.

I thought about the first time we'd met, in a club on River Street. I was eighteen, starting classes at Armstrong State College, living at home with my parents.

It was clear from the beginning that we didn't run in the same circles. Tal was preppy, Waspy. Country Day all the way. His parents lived in a big house in Ardsley Park, his daddy did something at one of the banks downtown. None of it mattered.

At closing time that night, he talked me into walking out to his car with him. He pulled me inside the little MG, sat me on his lap, and we necked like crazy. Oh God, I was so hot for him, I still blush at the memory.

He called me the next day, and we went to a movie and, afterward, drove out to the beach, and for the first and last time in my life, I had sex with a man on a first date.

It was fine.

When Christmas break was over, he went back to Tech, and I followed.

Tal graduated at the end of winter quarter. It was March. We moved back to Savannah, and in June we got married, moving into a tiny ground-floor apartment of a townhouse on Jones Street, which belonged to a friend of the Evanses.

And yes, I remembered it as bliss. I worked at jobs I didn't care about, and Tal and I planned our future. He sketched the beach house he'd build us on a barrier island off the coast. I filled our tiny rooms with my bargain finds, painted and sanded and wallpapered. After five years Mama started making noises about grandchildren, but Tal was still building a career, and besides, we were having too much fun to be tied down to kids.

When I found the townhouse on Charlton Street, I knew it was meant to be. Tal wanted something smaller, in Ardsley Park, near his parents, but once I saw the real estate agent tacking the sign in the window of the townhouse, I knew it would be mine. I stopped the agent, inquired about the price, and the identity of the owner, but the agent was reluctant to part with the information.

It didn't matter. By that time, BeBe and I were friends, and she knew everybody in town. Three quick phone calls later, BeBe called with the news. The house belonged to a woman named Jean MacCready.

I could have wept with joy. Miss Jean was in her eighties, a spinster who lived on my parents' block and who had been Mama's godmother. The Eloise part of my name was an old Foley tradition, but I had been named Jean for Miss Jean MacCready. And I never knew she owned downtown property. When I asked Mama about the Charlton Street house, she acted like I should have known about it.

"That was their old family place," Mama said. "I believe it belonged to Walter, Jean's brother, who died last year. He was a merchant seaman, only came home once every few years."

"Call her," I begged Mama. "I've got to have that house. I'll die if I don't buy that house."

So I put on my most conservative dress, and heels and pantyhose—even my wedding pearls—and Mama and I went and paid a call on Miss Jean.

She gave us hot tea with lemon, even though it was August and stifling in her little brick bungalow, and she quizzed me about my plans for the MacCready home place.

"You wouldn't be tearing it down, would you?" she asked suspiciously. "My grandpapa built that house. My mama was born in that house."

My look of shock was authentic. "I would never tear that house down, Miss Jean," I said, raising my hand in an oath.

"And what about children?" she asked, staring directly at my empty, so far barren, belly. "That house has always had children. That's why Walter never would sell it. All those pansies who live downtown wanted to buy my grandpapa's house, but Walter said he would roll over in his grave if queers got hold of our house."

Mama raised an eyebrow. I wondered if she had coached Miss Jean.

"Oh, we want children," I said. "But the apartment on Jones Street is so tiny, and the landlord doesn't allow children. If we could get your grandpapa's house, we would fill it up with children."

Both Mama's eyebrows shot up, so I avoided looking at her. Tal and I hadn't really discussed children, but he'd never said he didn't want any, and I guess I always, at the back of my mind, assumed we would get around to having them—as soon as we had a house of our own.

"You'd raise the children Catholic, of course," Miss Jean said, leaning over to pat my hands.

We were so close to making a deal, I would have agreed to raise my children as cannibals if it would have pleased the old lady.

"Yes," I said. "Catholic. Of course."

Mother Evans would have a double hissy, I thought evilly.

Miss Jean took a sip of tea. "I never did like the idea of all kinds of people trampling through Grandpapa's house, looking at it, talking about it, touching things," she told Mama, ignoring me now. "But the taxes on this house keep going up, and with Walter gone, I have to think about my future."

"Certainly," Mama said. And then she did the unexpected. She went out on a limb for me, even though I knew full well she thought the house was too old and too decrepit.

"Jean," Mama said, leaning close to her godmother, "Weezie really loves old houses. She's crazy about them. She's a wonderful homemaker, much better than I ever was. Tal is a very talented young architect. But he's just starting out. The children don't have a lot of money."

Mama let Miss Jean take it all in. We sipped our tea and talked about Miss Jean's flowers, and her work with the rosary guild. I was nearly out of my mind with impatience, but I knew what Mama was up to.

Finally, as we picked up our pocketbooks and made ready to leave, Miss Jean pulled me away from Mama's side.

"I want you to have the house," she said. "That real estate man says we should get three hundred thousand dollars for it. But I think he's just telling me a lie to make me happy. I know it's in a state. It would mean a lot to me if my namesake could get my house. Do you think you could pay two hundred thousand dollars?"

My heart raced. It was more money than I dared think about. It was also half what the house was worth, even if it were nothing more than four crumbling walls.

"We'll take it," I said. And she kissed me on the cheek to seal the deal.

Out in the car, Mama had been incredulous. "You agreed to buy that—that wreck—without even consulting your husband?"

Mama didn't buy a tube of toothpaste without my daddy approving it. After forty years of marriage she never even had her name on their checking account. Every Sunday night, Daddy just counted out a modest little stack of ten-dollar bills, and that was her allowance for the week.

"I know what I'm doing," I said blithely. "Tal will love the house. You know how he is about the historic district. And I couldn't pass it up—not at that price. Mama, it's my dream come true. Thank you so much for talking to Miss Jean for me."

Mama folded her arms on her chest and gave a tight little smile that let me know she would have the upper hand over me at last.

It was a Friday afternoon, and just before three o'clock. "Can you take me to the bank?" I asked. We were in her car.

"Why?" she asked.

"I want to go to the bank, move money out of savings into checking," I said.

The truth was, we didn't have a savings account, and God knows we didn't have enough to cover the check I'd just written to Miss Jean. Living the good life took every cent Tal and I made. I wanted to get to my safe-deposit box and raid my stash of savings bonds. The Foleys had been great ones for savings bonds. Every Christmas and birthday, for as long as I could remember, I'd been given fifty-dollar savings bonds—for my college education.

My three-month stab at college hadn't made a dent in the bonds. With Mama sitting outside in the car, I went into the bank, emptied out my safe-deposit box, and cashed them in. When the endorsing was all said and done, I skipped out of the bank with a song in my heart. I raced home as fast as I could to tell Tal the news. I'd bought a house. Our house.

He didn't believe me when I told him.

"You bought a house? For two hundred thousand dollars? Are you out of your mind? Where would we get that kind of money?"

His face was pale, and his lips squinched up at the corners in a way I'd never seen on him before—although I'd seen it plenty of times on Mother Evans.

"It's Charlton Street, Tal," I said, pulling him toward the door. "The three-hundred block. You've always said that's one of your favorite blocks in town."

"I've also said a Jaguar is one of my favorite cars. But you don't see me going out and buying one without telling you, right?"

"Just come and look at it," I said, waving the key under his nose. "I'm sorry I didn't discuss it with you, baby, but there wasn't time. Mama took up for me—for me! And Miss Jean wants us to have it. She really does. It's never been out of her family. And Tal—you won't believe it. She's going to hold the mortgage. Five percent! Can you believe it? The monthly note won't be that much more than our rent here. And think of the tax break."

"Think what it'll cost to make it livable," Tal grumbled. "Have you even seen the inside of this place?"

"I don't have to," I said. "It's wonderful. I just know it. And if it's not wonderful right this minute, you and I will fix it."

"And die broke," he said.

But I was wearing him down. In those days, Tal loved what I loved. We took a flashlight and a bottle of wine and walked the five blocks over to Charlton Street.

"Look at the bricks," I prompted, standing on the sidewalk in front of the house. "Savannah grays. Even if we only knocked the house down and sold it for the bricks, it would be worth what we're paying for it."

"Good-looking brick," Tal said, running his hand over the front wall. He craned his neck to look up toward the third floor. "Decent wrought iron too. Not as nice as some I've seen. But nice."

"Come on," I said, giving him a tiny shove. "Let's go inside."

As he fumbled with the lock, I was already making a list of things to do. The heavy brass doorknob and kickplate hadn't been polished in years. I had a can of Brasso under the sink back at the apartment. All the ground-floor windows were thick with grime. But the wrought-iron window grilles had space for window boxes. Mentally, I planted them with pale pink impatiens, variegated Swedish ivy, with cast-iron urns holding potted palms on either side of the wide front stoop.

Tal opened the door, stepped inside, then stepped out just as quickly. "Christ!" He held his arm across his nose and mouth. "There's something dead in there."

Several somethings were dead inside my dream house. Closer investigation revealed that many generations of pigeons and squirrels had taken up residence in the chimney, and a family of bats had moved into the third-floor bedroom.

"We'll have it fumigated," I said, after we'd made a quick trip to Home Depot for paper face masks and heavy-duty room deodorizers. "But did you see those cove moldings in the living room? Twelve inches wide. And the plaster ceiling medallions? And that darling little sink in the downstairs powder room? And think of the kitchen we could fit in that space where the servant's room is now. There'll even be space for a laundry room. God, I can quit going to the Washateria."

"Did you see the plaster falling off the wall in shreds?" Tal countered. "Did you see the color of the water coming out of your darling little sink? Liquid mud. That means we've got cast-iron pipes. All the plumbing will have to be replaced. Do you know what plumbers charge in this town?"

I felt my upper lip tremble. Here I had cashed in all my college bonds, begged my mother to intercede on our behalf with Miss Jean, and all he could do was complain about a few squirrel skeletons and some bad pipes.

In an instant, he was hugging me and apologizing. "I'm sorry, Weezer," he said, kissing the top of my head. "You're right. It's an incredible house. This is one of my favorite blocks downtown. And you forgot to mention the carriage house. We can move into the carriage house and stay there while we work on the big house. Then, after it's done, we can rent out the carriage house. I'll bet we could get a thousand a month, easy. Income property! Think of it, we'll be landlords."

He started sketching plans for the carriage house layout on the back of the paper sack I'd carried the wine in.

I had thought a lot about the carriage house. And I had my own little sketches—in my head, of course, and not nearly so professionally executed. But my plans weren't for a rental apartment. A little shop was what I had in mind. A tiny, perfect antique shop, a place where I could play store, maybe even set up a playpen in the back. But I kept all that to myself. Tal was right, the income from renting the carriage house would be a godsend. A shop could come later.

Right now, I wanted to celebrate our good fortune. We uncorked the wine, then wandered hand in hand through the house, sketching and planning our future on Charlton Street.

Looking up at Tal now, his face a mask of despair and misery, it was hard to believe how much everything had changed in so little time.

When had the sweetness turned so sour? Why had I given up so easily on my marriage, if it had meant that much to me? I had never thought of myself as a quitter. Maybe, I thought, I should have given Tal another chance, instead of digging in and starting World War III.

I turned the wineglass around and around in my hands, watching Tal, finding myself wanting to go to him, hold him, offer some comfort.

Poor wretch.

Poor sap! I slammed the glass down on the table. Goddamn him for betraying me. Goddamn him for being so careless with what we had together. Goddamn him for loving Caroline DeSantos instead of me.

I drank down the rest of my wine and tossed the remains of my omelette over the back garden wall for the alley cats who kept the lane clear of rats. I'd lost my appetite, but I was suddenly very thirsty.

Back in the carriage house, I drank the rest of the bottle of wine and traipsed woozily up the stairs to my bed. Alone. I shut the French doors to block out the view of Tal, but I needn't have bothered. The upstairs light was out. The house was dark.

CHAPTER *18*

On the Monday morning after my arrest, I had a stinking hangover. I sat in the kitchen and sipped coffee and shot dirty looks at the answering machine. Finally, at nine o'clock, I made myself pick up the phone. If I call her, I told myself, I'll be the one in charge. I'll be the one calling the shots.

What a joke.

"Mama?"

"Where have you been?" she demanded. "I have been calling and calling you for twenty-four hours straight. Your daddy and I have been out of our minds with worry."

"I know. I'm sorry. There were reporters camped out at my place, so I spent the night at BeBe's. Then, when I finally got home last night, it was so late, I didn't want to call and wake you up."

"As if we'd slept a wink since all this happened," she snapped.

"I'm sorry," I said again, making two hatch marks on the back of an envelope on the kitchen counter. It was a habit I'd developed, talking to Mama. Keeping track of the apologies per conversation. My goal was to keep it under a dozen for each ten minutes. Didn't look like I was gonna make goal this time.

"Are you all right? You didn't, I mean, those people at the jail didn't touch you—or anything?"

"I'm fine," I said. "I watched television and read. Didn't Uncle James call and let you know what was going on?"

"He did," Mama admitted, "but I still don't understand why you called him instead of us."

"James is a lawyer," I pointed out unnecessarily. "I just figured he'd know what to do. About getting me bailed out and all."

"Bailed out," she wailed. "I still can't believe this has happened."

"It's not that bad," I said. "Criminal trespass. Hardly even a real crime."

"But they think you murdered that woman," Mama said sharply. "It was on the news, and all over the papers. Even the Atlanta paper. I saw Sarah Donnellen at ten-o'clock mass yesterday. Daddy lit two candles for you, by the way. Sarah's daughter-in-law is a lawyer in Atlanta. She called Sarah because she knew we're friends. And Sarah says her daughter-in-law says they could still charge you with murder."

I bit my lip. Sarah Donnellen's son Ricky had been in my class at Blessed Sacrament School. He was famous for hanging around the jungle gym on the playground, hoping to get a glimpse of a girl's underpants. Any woman who'd married that pervert couldn't have too much on the ball, lawyer or not.

"Mama," I said quietly, "they are not going to charge me with murder, because I did not kill Caroline DeSantos. I never touched her. I went in that house to use the bathroom, and that's the truth."

She gave a prolonged sigh. "How many times have I told you not to use public bathrooms? And I still don't understand what you were doing out there at that time of night."

"I wanted to get into the estate sale as early as possible," I said, trying to be patient.

"It surely doesn't look very good," Mama said. "Everybody was staring at us in mass yesterday. I could hardly hold my head up. Even Father Morrison looked at me funny, when I went up for Communion."

"Father Morrison looks at everybody funny," I said, starting to lose it. "He's cross-eyed, for Christ's sake."

"Don't you take the Lord's name in vain to me, young lady," Mama said. "I have to go now. I'm getting one of my migraines. But your daddy would like to speak to you."

I rolled my eyes to the heavens.

"Eloise?" Daddy grunted.

"I'm sorry, Daddy," I said, getting it out of the way.

"You need any money?"

Good old Daddy.

"No. I'm fine."

"Your mother's pretty upset," he said.

"I know. But Uncle James is going to get it all straightened out. It was just a misunderstanding, that's all."

"What about that dead gal?"

"I didn't kill her," I said.

"Good," he said, as though that settled it. "You be sweet, you hear?"

The phone rang as soon as I put it down. I looked at the caller ID screen and didn't recognize the number, so I let the machine pick up. Good thinking. It was Ira Stein, the police reporter for the *Morning News*. "Please call me immediately," he said. "I understand the police have found your fingerprints on the gun believed to be the murder weapon in the Caroline DeSantos homicide. And I also understand Ms. DeSantos was engaged to be married to your ex-husband, and that you'd been over-heard making threats against her."

God. I found the ibuprofen bottle and swallowed four capsules with another cup of coffee.

The phone rang off and on for the next hour. The doorbell rang too. Instead of answering, I ran upstairs and looked out and saw two different television satellite trucks set up in the lane behind the carriage house.

I was massaging my temples and wishing for a straight shot of mor-phine when there was another rap at the front door. Jethro ran to the hall and started barking. He'd been racing up and down the stairs all morning, barking like crazy with all the phones and doorbells ringing. He was as stressed as I was. I started wondering if they made doggy Valium.

"Good," I muttered, setting the coffee cup down. "Sic 'em, boy."

"Don't sic that dog on me," called a voice from the other side of the door. BeBe.

"Tie him up or something, would you? I'm wearing white and you know how he loves to jump up on me."

I took Jethro by the collar and coaxed him into the kitchen. "Good boy," I said. "Stay here and I'll let you jump up on the very next reporter."

BeBe was in rare form. She was, as advertised, dressed in a simple white linen sheath, with white sling-back sandals. Her hair was glossy and twisted on top of her head in something like a chignon. She was clutching a tote bag full of groceries.

"You look like death," she said, holding me at arm's length. "What have you done to yourself?"

"I got drunk on cheap chardonnay last night," I said. "People have been calling all morning. My father has started making novenas for me. "

BeBe shook her head in disapproval. "How many times do I have to tell you, life is too short to drink bad wine."

"Easy for you to say. You never pay retail."

"True," she said, sitting down in an armchair near the window. "But it's not like you to go get drunk all by yourself. Why the toot?"

"I was depressed," I said. "You know, just getting out of jail, all that." BeBe pursed her lips. "Uh-uh.

"What else?" she asked, leaning closer. "Come on, tell Dr. Babes."

"It was Tal."

She looked shocked. "He came over here? What did he say?"

"He didn't come over here," I said. "I haven't talked to him. I was sitting out in the courtyard, and I happened to look up, and he was upstairs, sitting at his desk, looking out the window. The look on his face, BeBe, the anguish. It was so pathetic. I felt so sorry for him. He looked so brokenhearted. And it all came back in a rush. How we fell in love, what we had together. It was all I could do to keep from running over there and asking him to take me back."

Her eyes widened. "Tell me you didn't do anything stupid."

I snorted. "Yeah, I went over there and fucked his brains out."

"Which means you drank yourself into a stupor feeling all sorry for the scumbag and his slutty little girlfriend."

"Getting drunk seemed smarter than getting laid by my ex," I said.

"True again," BeBe said. "But look, I brought you some provisions."

She started pulling packages out of her tote bag, inventorying the contents. "Chocolate. Much more satisfying than shitty chardonnay. Croissants. Coke. Fruity Pebbles cereal—oh yes, I know your little shameful secret, Eloise Foley. Skim milk, even some doggy treats for Jethro."

"You're the best," I said, getting up to take the groceries into the kitchen.

"Down, Jethro," BeBe said, following right behind me. She took the box of treats, opened it, and tossed him one. "See how nice Aunt BeBe is?"

She reached back into the tote bag again, then paused. "I brought something else, besides food. The papers. Want to see?"

"I think I'll pass. Mama already gave me the rundown."

"Well, now what?" BeBe asked, pouring herself a cup of coffee. "Are you just going to hide out here the rest of your life?"

"No. Maybe. Hell, I don't know."

"What does your uncle say?"

"He says his friend who's a criminal lawyer thinks the security guards screwed up everything out at Beaulieu by messing around inside the house and seizing my bag without my permission. This friend says it's doubtful that any of that evidence—including the pistols—would be admissible as evidence in court."

She took a sip of her coffee. "Who is this hotshot lawyer friend?"

"I don't know. James is being very mysterious about that."

She grinned. "Do you think he's got a girlfriend? Good for him!"

"I don't know who this person is," I said truthfully. I hadn't told BeBe yet that James was gay. He was still very hesitant to let people know about his personal life.

"I think we need to get you out of this house," BeBe said, eyeing the empty two-liter wine bottle in the trash can, "before you start drinking gin out of a steam iron."

"What did you have in mind?" I asked. I was starting to feel a little claustrophobic.

She brought out the newspaper.

"Not interested," I said.

"Not so fast," she said, tapping the page. "These are the classifieds. Remember the Little Sisters of Charity school—out in Sandfly?"

"Sure," I said. "It was the all-black parochial school before the arch-diocese integrated all the schools. But it's been closed since the eighties."

"Right," BeBe said. "And the last of the Little Sisters has retired. Gone back to the mother house in Philadelphia, according to a story in today's paper. They're getting ready to tear down the school and the convent, to build a shopping center. Can you say liquidation sale?"

I slid my bare feet into the flip-flops by the back door and grabbed for my purse. "Let's go."

CHAPTER *19*

*J*ames parked his car beside the navy blue sedan, in the shade of a spreading old live oak a dozen yards from the front door to the old plantation house.

Jay Bradley, the detective he'd met the night Weezie was arrested, leaned against the hood of his county-issue vehicle, smoking a cigarette, which he flipped to the ground at James's arrival. He wore a short-sleeved white dress shirt, wrinkled dark slacks, and a bored expression.

"How ya doin' there, Father?"

"Just James. Remember?"

"Sorry. Old habits die hard, you know."

"So," James said briskly, "we're all clear to take a look around the house?"

He had hated to ask Jonathan for the favor, but he really did need to get an idea of what kind of evidence the police might have against Weezie.

And Jonathan had been uneasy about it too. "It's a defense attorney's right to see the crime scene," he'd pointed out. "Of course, Weezie hasn't really been charged with the homicide."

"But you think she will be," James said.

"You know I can't talk about that," Jonathan said.

So Jonathan had told him whom to call, and this morning Bradley had called back to set up the walk-through, not sounding exactly thrilled with the idea.

James could already feel the sweat soaking through his shirt. It must be close to a hundred degrees already, and not even ten o'clock yet. He hated to think about what that musty old house would feel like in this heat and humidity.

Bradley strode toward the east side of the house. He put his hand on the trunk of a huge old magnolia tree that nearly dwarfed the house. "This here's how your niece says she got in the house," he said.

"If she says she climbed the tree, she did," James said.

"We lifted her fingerprints off the doorknobs, kitchen and front door," Bradley said.

"She tried the doors first, of course, but they were all locked. She needed to use the bathroom."

"Right," Bradley said, doubt dripping from his voice. He dug a key from the pocket of his pants. "We'll go in the kitchen."

James followed Bradley inside. A narrow path had been cleared through the old-fashioned room, but otherwise the place was stacked to the ceiling with dust-covered furniture, dishes, and boxes and boxes of miscellaneous stuff.

"Whole house is like this," Bradley said, clucking his disapproval. "Packed with crap."

"Beauty is in the eye of the beholder," James said, remembering Weezie's insistence that the house was a treasure trove of valuable antiques. Although he himself could not picture anybody wanting any of this stuff.

James followed Bradley into the hallway, and Bradley pointed again, with his radio, toward the stairway.

"The body was found up there, in a bathroom closet. According to your niece, anyway."

"Have your people found any evidence to indicate the body had been moved?" James asked. "The DeSantos woman was much taller than Weezie. Even if she had killed her, which she didn't, I doubt she could have stuffed the woman into a closet."

Bradley volunteered nothing. Instead, he started up the stairs. His labored footsteps echoed on the splintered wooden steps, and the handrail groaned as he pulled his bearlike body upward. James said a small silent prayer that the staircase wouldn't collapse beneath the weight of the both of them.

Upstairs the heat was even more oppressive, if that was possible.

Bradley mopped his steaming forehead with a handkerchief, and James did the same.

"Closet's right in that bathroom," Bradley gasped, lunging toward a bedroom doorway. "I gotta get a window open, get some air in here before I pass out."

"Right," James said. He waited until he heard the wooden window creak open, then whipped out the small camera he'd tucked in his pocket.

He slipped into the bathroom and with the toe of his shoe, James pushed the closet door open, bracing himself for a ghastly sight.

There was actually very little blood. It was an ordinary closet. Empty, save some old wooden coat hangers littering the bottom of the closet.

James clicked away as rapidly as he could, changing the angle with each shot. When he was done, he tucked the camera back in his pocket and stepped back into the hall.

He heard Bradley approaching, his breath labored. The cop's face was an alarming shade of pasty gray.

"Detective Bradley?" James said, reaching for the detective's arm just as the younger man swayed, his eyes rolling upward in his head.

The cop slumped to the floor.

"Sweet Jesus," James said, kneeling down beside Bradley. He put his fingertips at the base of the cop's throat. His breathing was shallow, his color unearthly, and despite the suffocating heat, Bradley's flesh felt clammy to the touch.

James ran back into the bathroom He grabbed an old rag from a towel bar, shoved it under the tap, and turned it on. The pipes groaned, and after what seemed like an eternity, a thin trickle of brown water began to drip from the faucet. He soaked the rag in the water, than ran back to Bradley's outstretched form, squeezing the water onto the detective's face and neck, then dabbing at his wrists and the back of his neck.

He struggled to unbutton Bradley's shirt collar, which bulged under the bulk of his fleshy neck. But his hands were sweaty, his fingers clumsy. He tore at the collar until he'd ripped the buttons off, then went to the man's waist, loosening the cinched leather belt.

"Jay?" James said, keeping his fingers on the man's pulse. It was rapid, fluttery even. The detective couldn't have been much older than forty, but he was at least fifty pounds overweight, and a smoker. Could he have had a heart attack?

Should he raise the detective's head? Try CPR? Years ago, at his first parish in Thunderbolt, he'd sat in the church social hall while the Boy Scout troop went over the basics of CPR. But James had paid scant attention, being more intent on keeping the boys from disturbing a group of parishioners attending the Overeaters Anonymous meeting in the adjacent library.

He needed help, James thought. Was there a working phone in this godforsaken place? Surely not. Then he remembered the detective's radio. It was there, clipped to his belt. James reached over and unclipped it. He held the radio to his face, pushed what he prayed was the send button.

"Er, uh, this is a civilian. My name is James Foley, and one of your detectives is in need of medical attention. He appears to have had an attack of some kind. He's breathing, but his pulse seems erratic. We're at Beaulieu Plantation, near the Skidaway River, on the second floor of the house. Please send an ambulance immediately."

The radio squawked and a woman's voice floated out. "Ten-four that, Mr. Foley. We have a rescue unit on the way."

"Thank God," James said.

CHAPTER 20

When I was just a little kid, we'd go out to Sandfly to buy boiled peanuts from the peanut man. Back then, Sandfly was just a barely paved crossroads, with the peanut stand and a gas station and lots of little children playing ball in the middle of the sandy road. Sandfly had been like that just about forever, according to my daddy, who said he understood the neighborhood was started by freed slaves who moved off Beaulieu and Wymberly and Wormsloe, the big plantations on Isle of Hope, which was just up the marsh road from Sandfly.

Today though, there's an honest-to-goodness shopping center, and a couple of gas stations, and even a four-way traffic signal, and most traces of the old-timey black community have vanished—although the peanut man is still there. The Little Sisters of Charity school was slated to be the next to go.

A neatly lettered banner was strung across the squat two-story brick schoolhouse on Skidaway Road. "Sale Today," it said.

I pulled the truck into the crushed-shell parking lot, alongside a lot of trucks and vans. "What time does the sale start?" I asked BeBe.

"Not 'til noon, according to the paper," she said.

"Looks like they might have opened their doors early," I said, gathering my largest tote bag, the one with wheels and a pop-up handle.

I was hustling toward the school's entrance when BeBe stopped cold in front of a four-foot-tall statue of a nun that had been placed in a sheltered corner of the parking lot.

"Look," she squealed, pointing at it. "Fabulous. I love it."

"That?" I said doubtfully. It was a plain concrete statue, painted many times over, of one of the early Little Sisters of Charity, or the gray nuns, as everybody in Savannah called them. This one wore the old-fashioned white wimple and long gray habit. Her hands were clasped together, a rosary clutched between the broken concrete fingertips. She'd been installed in a shell-shaped grotto that had been covered with a tile mosaic, and a concrete pot held a faded plastic philodendron and some washed-out yellow plastic chrysanthemums.

"Do you think they'll sell it to me?" BeBe asked, kneeling down beside it to get a better look.

"What would you do with a statue of a nun? You're not even Catholic."

"Put it in the restaurant," BeBe said, her eyes sparkling with excitement. "Did I tell you? That hideous tattoo parlor next door is closing at the end of the week. The landlord is dying to unload the building. I'll knock through our adjoining wall and double my space. Finally have a real lounge. Hey, what if I called it Little Sisters Lounge? Wouldn't that be wild? I could fill it with all this funky Catholic stuff. You know, statues, candelabras, the whole deal. And the waitresses could wear short little nun's outfits, but like, with fishnet stockings."

"Sort of the neonun hooker look?" I asked.

"Exactly," she said. "I've gotta have this statue."

Something in the parking lot caught her eye. "Look," she said, pointing at a big black pickup truck parked in the row nearest the door. It had a Marine Corps bumper sticker. "Look who's here. Daniel."

I turned on my heel and started marching toward my own truck.

"Weezie," she ran after me. "What's wrong?"

"If this is your idea of a fix-up, you truly do have the worst sense of timing in the world," I said, feeling my face get red.

"What?" She seemed offended by the suggestion. "I swear to God. I had no idea Daniel would be here today. It's Monday, Weeze. His only day off. He probably read the paper, saw the story about the convent closing, and decided to come over here and check it out—just like we did."

I was not in the mood to deal with Daniel Stipanek.

Still, this was not a sale I wanted to miss. All my life I'd heard my mother tell stories about the little gray nuns. They'd come to Savannah from their mother house in Philadelphia shortly after the Civil War, to minister to the South's underprivileged black children. The convent and the school had been built in the 1930s, with money donated by a wealthy Pennsylvania industrialist.

It stood to reason that the place should be full of good old stuff. And I had never been one to let a mere man—even an annoying man like Daniel Stipanek—stand between me and my junk.

"All right," I relented. "We'll go in. If we see him, we'll be polite. But in no way will you give him any idea that I might be interested in him. Understand?"

"Understood," BeBe said.

We pushed open the heavy carved-oak front door and I was instantly transported back to my own parochial-school days. Institutional green linoleum lined the floors of the hall, and the walls were dotted with faded pictures of saints and popes. The smell of disinfectant mingled with the smell of crayons and chalk dust, mixed with that peculiarly Catholic smell— was it the candles and the incense? Or maybe just eau de holy water?

The hallway itself was lined with scarred old oak pews, each one four feet long. The backs were carved with scrollwork, each side held a slot for hymnals. The sign on the wall said "Pews. $25. As Is."

I felt my neck tingle. This was very, very good junk.

"I'm buying four of these," I said quickly, digging in my tote bag for the roll of masking tape with the "Sold—Foley" lettering. "And if you really are going to do a lounge in the restaurant, wouldn't these make great booths, facing each other with a table in between?"

"Great," BeBe said. "Now what?"

"I'll put the sold stickers on 'em. You go inside and find the cash register. Tell the person in charge you want to start a tab for Weezie Foley. Tell them you've already marked the pews. How many do you want?"

She did some quick math. "Six booths, down the wall opposite the bar. Make it twelve pews."

I gave them a cursory glance. "Better get some spares," I said. "The sign says 'as is,' so some of them probably have broken seats or something."

"Sure, fine," she said.

"And ask them if they have somebody who can start loading them for us."

"Already? We haven't even started really looking around yet."

"I recognize a lot of dealers I know here," I said, lowering my voice. "That big panel truck outside, that's Zeke Payne. He's a great big fat guy, always wears red sweats, summer and winter. He'd steal the gold fillings off his grandma's corpse. Last year, at the church bazaar at Isle of Hope Methodist church? I'd found a stack of old Limoges plates, marked two bucks apiece. I'd stashed them in a laundry basket full of smalls. I put the basket down to look at something, and when I turned back around, Zeke was walking away with my stack of dishes. I went after him and told him he'd taken the dishes out of my basket, but he just ignored me. Finally, one of the church ladies saw what was going on, and made him give 'em back. He's been pissed at me ever since."

"Geez," BeBe said. "You could get hurt doing this."

"Don't remind me," I said.

I was putting the last of the sold stickers on the pews when BeBe raced back. "It's taken care of," she said. "Give me the keys to the truck so I can back it up to the front of the school. I paid a kid ten bucks to load us up."

"Excellent," I said, handing her the keys. "How's the sale look?"

"Pretty good," she said, holding up a beautifully filigreed silver orb hanging from a long silver chain. "Look. Isn't this a gorgeous lamp?"

"Gorgeous," I agreed. "But it's not a lamp. It's a censer."

"What's that?" she asked.

I took the chain from her and held the censer with my right hand. "You burn incense in it, and the priest walks up and down the aisles, swinging the censer and smoking the place up with it."

She took the censer back. "For fifty dollars, it's a hanging lamp. I'll put it in the hallway between the bathrooms. It'll be great."

"According to the cashier, everything else for sale is all piled in the cafeteria," BeBe said. "There's a mob of people in there. And I saw your buddy Zeke. He was shoving a little old lady out of the way to get to a pile of folding wooden chairs."

"That's Zeke."

The cafeteria, as promised, was packed. It had been a small room to start with. Little Sisters of Charity School had probably never had more than two hundred pupils. Now the lunchroom was serving as warehouse.

BeBe spied a group of statues up near the stage. "Look, Christ on a cross."

I looked. "Those are stations of the cross," I told her. "I really don't think you want those in a restaurant."

"Let's split up," she said. "I'll meet you outside in an hour, all right?"

"Fine," I told her.

One corner of the room was taken up with piles of scarred desks being sold for ten dollars apiece. I wasn't interested in desks, but I did find a good-looking old solid brass gooseneck lamp with the original green glass shade. The thing weighed about ten pounds, but it had that great 1940s machine-age look young collectors are paying big money for. I put it in the bottom of my tote bag. Next I grabbed a tabletop-sized set of card catalogue drawers, priced at a buck apiece. Nobody uses card catalogues these days, now that everything's inventoried on computers, but I esti- mated the drawers would make ideal CD holders. There were twelve of them, and I managed to fit ten in my wheeled bag.

A woman I knew slightly from Saturday-morning garage sales was reaching for the other two when she saw me. I had never known her name, just the nickname all the dealers knew her by: "Early Bird." She drove a bat- tered 1970s era brown Mercedes and was notorious for showing up at sales two hours early—even for Saturday-morning sales that started at 7 A.M.

Early Bird's face got a little pale when she saw me. "Oh. Hello there. I didn't know you were out of jail."

I felt like I'd been slapped across the face.

"Yes," I said. "It was all a misunderstanding."

"Of course," she said. She gestured at the card catalogue boxes. "You can take those two. I don't really want them."

I knew what she was thinking. There's that Weezie Foley. She killed a woman. Don't mess with her.

Early Bird scuttled away as fast as she could, glancing back over her shoulder to make sure I wasn't following. I tried to shrug it off. Early Bird was a weirdo. Talked to herself, always bought canned goods at estate sales. Who buys dead people's canned goods? I started flipping through the books. After some judicious digging, I found a nice reading primer from the 1950s. It was the same Dick and Jane series my mother had used in elementary school—the same one she had taught me to read out of before turning me over to Blessed Sacrament School. It had a price of fifty cents penciled on the inner cover.

I stashed it in my tote bag. One of the shops on Whitaker Street did a nice business in framed and matted pages from old books. I could get an easy thirty bucks for this one.

It was just past noon, and the lunchroom was really starting to get crowded. There was no air-conditioning, of course, just a series of ceiling fans trying ineffectively to move the stifling air around. I grabbed my tote bag and wheeled my way toward the checkout table.

An older black lady wearing a bib apron sat at the table, manning an adding machine like she meant it. I called out my purchases and she tallied them up. "I've got a tab started, with four pews at twenty-five dollars apiece," I said. "The name's Eloise Foley."

She looked up, startled, with a wide smile. "I know you."

"You do?"

"I seen you on the TV. In the paper too. You the gal killed her husband's girlfriend. And I say, you go girl! Teach that woman to mess with another gal's man."

"I didn't kill her," I said quietly.

"Oughta give you a medal," the woman said, shaking her head. Suddenly, I didn't feel like junking anymore. Other people behind me in line were starting to whisper. I put my money on the table, then walked away, craning my neck to look for BeBe, but all I saw was a sea of sweaty faces.

The hallway was cooler, and blissfully empty. At the far end I saw a set of carved doors, opening inward. The school's chapel. At one time, I remembered, there had been wonderful stained-glass windows in that chapel, salvaged out of an old church in Augusta that had burned down.

Most of the pews had already been removed from the simple white-painted chapel. I found an old metal folding chair over near the confessional box and sat down. The windows were there, hanging from hooks in front of simple white window frames.

My favorite one was shaped in a gothic arch, with a simple rose fashioned out of colored glass, inset with sparkling prisms that caught the afternoon sunlight and refracted it into a hundred shards of light on the worn wooden chapel floor.

I stood in front of the window and looked up at it. A piece of masking tape was stretched across the bottom of the window. It had writing on it, but it was just above my eye level. So I dragged the chair over to the window and climbed up to get a better look.

A hand touched the back of my knee.

"Christ!" I nearly fell off the chair, but then two hands circled my waist and steadied me.

"Haven't you learned your lesson about crawling out of windows?" Daniel Stipanek was laughing up at me.

I scowled down into his smiling face. "You can let go of me now."

aniel let go. I climbed down off the chair.

"I wasn't trying to climb in or out of the window," I said. "I was trying to see the price tag on the stained glass, until you grabbed me and scared me shitless."

"Oh," he said. "Sorry. How much is it?"

"I can't see," I said.

He stepped up to the window and looked. "Hundred bucks."

I chewed my lip and thought about it. The gothic shape to the window gave it a lot of appeal. It was in good condition, not missing any glass. It wasn't all that old, maybe seventy years or so, but it had a certain appeal.

"I'll buy it if you don't," Daniel said.

"What would you do with it?"

"I'll find a place for it," he said. "Maybe in a bathroom."

"In a rented apartment?"

"I have a house," he said with a touch of smugness. "At Tybee. Near the North End."

"Chefs can afford Tybee prices?"

Tybee Island was Savannah's beach community. Used to be, it was the tackiest beach community on the whole East Coast, with a grimy little street carnival, cheap T-shirt shops, and an abundance of cheesy mom-and-pop motels and all-you-can-eat family restaurants. The houses were hit-or-miss affairs. Along the ocean side you did have some turn-of-the-century beauties, but the rest of Tybee was mostly ramshackle wood frame cottages or concrete block bungalows straight out of the fifties.

When I was a kid, Tybee got so bedraggled that lots of people from Savannah preferred to drive an hour north to the classier Hilton Head Island, or an hour south to St. Simons or Jekyll Island for a beach weekend.

But in the last six or seven years, Tybee had gone and gotten chic. Those ramshackle shacks were now "period Tybee cottages" going for over two hundred thousand, even as much as two blocks away from the ocean, and as for the fifties concrete block babies, those were now "midcentury modern" and red-hot with the retro rehab crowd.

Daniel saw my jealousy. I'd always secretly pined for one of those cute little beach shacks.

"Chefs can afford more than you might expect," he said. "But I'll let you in on a secret. This place has been in my family for thirty years."

"What street?" I asked, curiosity getting the better of me.

"Gladys," he said.

"Right on the water?"

"Right over the dunes," he said.

"Concrete or wood?"

"Wood," he said. "Of course, the only reason it's still standing is 'cause all the termites got together and started holding hands. It's in pretty rough shape."

I nodded. A lot of the cottages on that end of the beach had seen better days. Still, Gladys was a good street. And he did have waterfront property.

"Are you good with your hands?" I asked.

His eyes swept me up and down. "You tell me."

I felt myself going beet red. "Are you going to start that again? For God's sake, it was a long time ago. Can't you just forget about it?"

"Why would I want to do that?" His blue eyes were serious now. "That wasn't just a one-night stand for me, you know. I was crazy about you."

"You were just horny," I retorted. "You would have humped anything that got in that boat with you."

"Not true," he said. "Well, yeah, I was horny. But it was your fault. You made me nuts in those tight little T-shirts and shorts. And my God, that bikini. How was I supposed to act?"

I felt myself blushing again. "We're in a church, you know. This is not the place to have this discussion. In fact, there is no place to have this discussion."

"You dumped me," he said, like he still couldn't believe it, even after all these years. "I called and called your house, first time I got home on leave, and your mother acted like I was some kind of poison."

I sighed. "Look. It was a mistake, OK? I drank too much and got crazy. Anyway, that fall I met somebody else."

"Talmadge Evans? That's the asshole who left you for the woman who got murdered?" He certainly didn't pull any punches.

"Yes," I said. "Tal. My ex."

"BeBe says he's a shit. She says he screwed this woman in your bed, in your house. She says he got everything in the divorce, left you living in the garage or something."

"BeBe should keep her mouth shut," I said, choking back sudden tears. It had all been too much. People staring at me, whispering, talking about me behind my back. And now even Daniel Stipanek knew my life story. I wanted to slink back home and hide under the sofa with Jethro.

"Hey," he said, touching my shoulder. "I'm sorry. Really, Weezie. I didn't have any right to say all that stuff about your ex. I don't usually gossip about people, you know. It's just that, after I found out BeBe was your best friend, I kinda wanted to find out what had happened with you after all these years."

"My life went to shit. Now will you please excuse me?"

"What about the window?" he said, pointing up at it.

"Offer them seventy-five dollars."

I started out of the chapel, wheeling my cart behind me, but he was right beside me.

"Hey," he said. "I was supposed to let you know. BeBe had to go."

"What do you mean she had to go?" I asked, alarmed. "She doesn't have a car. We came in my truck."

"Yeah," he said. "She has the keys, remember? Sylvia, the manager at the restaurant, beeped her ten minutes ago. Our linen supplier showed up with the wrong tablecloths, and on top of that, we've got a backed-up commode in the men's room. She took your truck. I'm supposed to give you a ride home."

↤

I sat, stony-faced, on the far side of the passenger seat while Daniel loaded the truck.

It took him three trips to get it all in. Finally, my curiosity got the better of me. I climbed out and peeked over the edge of the truck bed. "What all did you get?" I inquired.

"Bunch of stuff," he said. He pointed at the stained glass. "The window you picked out. They settled on eighty dollars. Plus another smaller one I can use as a transom over the front door. They only wanted forty for it."

A steal.

"And a bunch of old slat-back wooden folding chairs." He prodded one with the toe of his shoe. They were adorable, almost like vintage French bistro chairs.

"How much?"

"Buck apiece. But I could only get ten. The rest were all in pieces."

"Not bad." I was green with envy.

"That," he said, kicking the side of a huge wooden wine crate, "is full of old dishes."

"What kind of dishes?"

"I dunno," he said. He squatted down and pried the top off the box, handing over a heavy white vitreous china soup plate with a thick blue ribbon around the rim and a circular "C of G" monogram in the middle.

"Oh my God," I said. "Railroad china. Where did you find this?"

"In the kitchen. Off the lunchroom," Daniel said. "What's railroad china?"

"China they used to use in railroad dining cars," I said, turning the soup bowl over to see the manufacturer's mark.

"See," I showed him. "It's Shawnee."

"That's good?"

"It's great," I said enviously. "The C of G was the Coastal of Georgia Railroad. They had a line that ran from St. Augustine all the way up to Baltimore. My meemaw used to ride that train to Maryland to see her sister every summer. They had pink damask tablecloths and fresh flowers in cut crystal on every table. And fried soft-shell crabs."

"I've never heard of that railroad, and I've lived in Savannah as long as you have," Daniel said.

"They closed it down in the late fifties or early sixties. I think they got bought out by one of the bigger railroads. So that's what makes anything with the C of G mark so collectible. Railroad buffs love this stuff."

He nodded. "So, if I had silverware with the same mark—that would be good?"

"You're kidding me. C of G silver? Let me see."

He dragged another box over to the edge of the truck's tailgate. I sat down and reached into the box. Came up with a fistful of gleaming silver-plated flatware.

I turned a hefty serving spoon over, but I didn't really need to check for the hallmark. I'd seen two or three pieces of Coastal's distinctive serving pieces, at antique shows. The handle was narrow at the neck, fanning out at the end to form a stylized palm frond with the C of G monogram marked on the back. The pieces were quadruple silver plated, and altogether a design triumph.

"How much of this did you buy?"

"All of it," he said matter-of-factly. "Maybe . . . what? Four or five dozen place settings. Plus a slew of serving pieces. I even got fish forks and salad tongs and all kinds of wacky serving pieces."

"And for how much?"

"Fifty bucks."

I narrowed my eyes. "Fifty bucks a place setting?"

He shook his head. "For all of it. What's wrong? Did I pay too much?"

"No," I said, laughing. "As my daddy says, even a blind hog finds an acorn now and again. You fell into it, Danny. It's the deal of the day. I'd have to check, but the latest book value I know of for this stuff is seventy-five—for a single place setting."

"For real?"

He jammed his hands in the hip pockets of his jeans, and the boyish grin lit up his deeply tanned face.

"For real," I assured him.

"Well, damn, Sam. I just wanted something cheap to eat off of."

I ran my hand through my sweat-soaked hair. What a morning.

"Looks like you scooped up all the really good deals of the day," I said ruefully. "While I dragged around feeling sorry for myself."

He nudged me. "Don't beat yourself up. You've had a bad couple of days."

"Right," I said briskly, fighting off the urge to wallow a little longer in my own self-pity. "What else did you get? There's still a lot of other stuff in this truck."

"Aw, nothing much."

"Come on," I said, nudging him back. "Show me. I mean if you want to. So far I'm really impressed. I never expected a straight guy to be this interested in antiques."

He bristled. "What's that supposed to mean?"

"Oh stop it," I said. "We both know you're straight."

"Damn straight," he said. "And don't you forget it."

"As if you'd let me. So show me, OK?"

The rest of Daniel's haul was decent, but not remarkable. It looked like he'd cleaned out the school's kitchen—heavy cast-iron skillets, commercial-sized five- and ten-gallon kettles, saucepans, even a wooden box that held two gross of white votive candles.

"What are you going to do with all of this?" I asked. "I mean, don't get me wrong. It's great, but why does a single guy, living alone, need all this china and silver and candles—not to mention a ten-gallon soup kettle?"

He looked uneasy. "If I tell you, you'll keep it to yourself?"

"Yeah."

"And not even tell BeBe? She's my boss, don't forget."

"I don't tell her everything."

"Well," he said eagerly, "some of it's for the Tybee house. But the rest, I guess, you know, every chef wants to open his own restaurant."

"Including you?"

"Sure," he said. "I mean, Guale is great. BeBe's kind of a flake when you first meet her, but she's fantastic in the front of the house. People love being around her. But it's just . . . I want my own place. Does that make sense to you?"

It made perfect sense to me. My whole life I'd gone along with somebody else's plans. Not wanting to rock the boat and put myself first. After all, most of the time I didn't know what my own plans were. But the need for my own dream was screaming to get out of me.

"Yeah," I said, smiling up at him. "Your own restaurant. Your own menu. Your own place. Makes a lot of sense."

We were in the truck, back on Skidaway Road, when he made an elaborate show of looking at his watch. "It's almost two. Way past lunch. You hungry?"

My first impulse was to say no. After all, this was Danny Stipanek. Icky Danny Stipanek. Take me home, I thought.

"I'm starved," I said. "Where should we go? Carey Hilliard's is probably still serving lunch."

"I know a better place," Daniel said, glancing over at me.

"OK," I said. "Where is it?"

"Tybee," he said. "My place."

He saw the hesitation on my face.

"Come on," he coaxed. "The food's great, and you can't beat the price. And I swear—no humping."

"As if," I said, trying to sound haughty.

aniel had the radio in his truck turned to a station I'd never listened to before—an all-oldies station called SURF-101.

I'd never heard this particular song before either, but it was obviously a favorite of his. He sang along with gusto, tapping his fingers on the steering wheel, not the least bit shy about singing in front of me—although his voice was awful, loud, off-key, nowhere close to being able to hit any of the high notes.

The whole song was full of sexual innuendo, sixty minutes of teasing and sixty minutes of pleasing, etc. I looked out the window and tried to act like I was somewhere else.

When the song was over, he nodded his head in appreciation.

"Want some free advice?" I asked.

"Depends."

"Don't quit your day job," I said.

"You don't like Boxcar Willy?" He looked hurt.

"I never heard of Boxcar Willy."

"Man," he said. "I guess that means you're not a beach music fan, huh?"

"You mean, like, the Beach Boys and Jan and Dean? That kind of thing? I guess they're all right, just not really my generation. Not yours either, come to think of it."

"I'm not talking about the Beach Boys," Daniel said. "Although I like their early stuff. No, I mean real beach music, you know, the Drifters, the Tams, the Platters, the Swinging Medallions. Some people call it Carolina beach music, some people call it shag music, 'cause it's music you can shag to."

By now we were on Highway 80, crossing the last bridge over Lazaretto Creek before you came onto Tybee Island proper. The water below was calm, and half a dozen shrimp boats were dotted about the surface.

"Oldies," I said, wrinkling my nose a little. I liked classic rock, myself. "Aren't you a little young for sixties music?"

"Never," he said. "My older brother, Richard, he's the one who turned me onto beach music. He had a hell of a record collection. Still got it too. Vintage vinyl. Beach music is young music, you know, 'be young, be foolish, be happy.' That kind of stuff."

"Well, I like that one," I said. When was the last time somebody had urged me to be foolish, let alone happy?

Traffic was backed up on the other side of the bridge, a line of cars making the right-hand turn into Chu's convenience store. It was Monday, but still, the traffic was heavy. Tybee gets like that in the summer, when all of south Georgia shows up for a day at the beach.

"Look at that," Daniel said, shaking his head and pointing to a billboard on the right side of the street.

"Coming Soon—Exclusive Community of Riverfront Townhomes. From the $200s."

"You should see those things," he said, disgust dripping from his voice. "Prefab shoe boxes, crowded right up on the edge of the marsh, all of 'em painted a different color. Really fruity looking."

"With striped awnings over the front doors, and lots of tacky pseudo-Victorian gingerbread trim," I added.

"You've seen 'em?" he asked. "Don't tell me you're looking to buy one of those pieces of crap."

I laughed. "Not hardly. My ex designed them." And I pointed back at the sign, at the bottom, where it said: "Designed by Evans & Associates, Architects."

"Sorry," Daniel said.

"Don't be. They are pieces of crap. There was a time when Tal would have laughed at anybody who'd suggest he'd design something like those.

But after the divorce, he needed money. Caroline is—I mean—was pretty high maintenance. The firm took one of the end units in trade, instead of a fee. I think he and Caroline planned to make it their little beach love nest. Until . . ."

I looked away.

"You want to talk about it?" Daniel asked. "I, uh, I'm really not a blabbermouth, despite what I said to you before, about knowing about your divorce and all."

"I believe you," I said. "I am just really sick of talking about this right now. No offense. OK?"

"OK."

He drove down Butler Avenue to the far end, past Tybee City Hall and the new DeSoto Motel, a drab concrete cartoon that came nowhere near the funky grace of the place that had been bulldozed for its successor, and then he made a left onto Delores Street, and another quick left onto Gladys.

Cars were double-parked all along the street, most of the tags from out of town, beachgoers too cheap to feed the meters in the public lots.

Half a block down, he pulled into a yard that was more sand than weeds.

He cut the truck's engine. "Here it is. The tiltin' Hilton."

Daniel had called the house a cottage, but it was, to be accurate, more a shack on steroids. It had probably been painted once, but time had combined with windblown sand and salt to scrape away all but the faintest vestiges of pale blue paint.

Low-slung and single story at the front, with a two-story wing at the back, it was built of cedar shingles, with a tattered screened porch that appeared to run all the way around the house. No two windows in the front were of the same size or configuration, and the porch's brick underpinnings had a definite sag.

The yard was littered with the markings of a total remodel—rusted-out harvest gold refrigerator, stacks of cheap fiberboard paneling, a pile of moldy gold shag carpeting, and stacks of lumber, new brick, even a small cement mixer.

"That carpet's the first thing I tore up," Daniel said, climbing out of the truck. "And right after that, the paneling came out."

"Good move," I said. Cheap paneling was the bane of my existence. I had torn a mountain of it out of the Charlton Street house.

"Is it safe to go inside?" I asked. The front door, with three or four jalousies missing, was standing ajar.

"It's OK," Daniel said, walking in ahead of me. "My brother Derek was out here this morning. He's a plumber. He put in a new water heater for me."

"You've got a brother who's a plumber?" I was pea green with envy. Tal was a whiz with plans and design, but anything like plumbing, and especially wiring, he considered beneath him. I had mastered the basics of electricity, but I was absolutely helpless when it came to plumbing.

Daniel took my question all wrong. Like it was an insult.

"Yeah, I got a brother who's a plumber. And I'm a cook, and Richard drives a long-haul truck. Is that a problem for you? Do you have a problem with decent, hardworking people who maybe don't wear a pin-striped suit and call their stockbroker from their cell phone?"

"No," I said, trying to unscramble things. "Daniel, I didn't mean it like that."

He stood in the doorway, his face hard. "Sure sounded like you meant it that way. You know what I think, Eloise Foley? I think you're a fuckin' snob. Who thinks maybe you're just a little bit better than everybody else."

"No," I said, my voice weak. "Really."

"Really what?"

The sun was beating down on my neck, and I could feel my pale freckled skin sizzle, feel the blisters starting to form.

"God," I moaned. "I didn't mean that at all. What I meant was, a plumber? You've got a brother who can install a hot-water heater? Can I adopt him? Borrow him, is he married?"

Daniel's eyes crinkled a little bit. The blue was so bright against his dark skin. I found myself wondering if he worked outside a lot. If he took his shirt off, if he was that tan all over. And what would he look like without a shirt? The gangly teenager I remembered was long gone. Daniel was maybe a foot taller than I was, but he was compact, muscular, with arms that looked like they could easily heft a stack of lumber. His threadbare jeans were baggy, except in the seat. And what a sweet seat he had, I thought, remembering BeBe's praise of Daniel's behind. God, what was wrong with me?

"Richard would like you," Daniel was saying. "But he's big-time married. And Rochelle would tear you a new asshole if you as much as looked at her husband."

"I won't. I swear," I said. "So, are we all right?"

He sighed. "Yeah. You know, this isn't going like I planned it."

That stopped me dead in my tracks. "Wait a minute. Oh shit. Oh no. I'm gonna kill BeBe. I swear to God, she is a dead woman. Could you please take me home?"

Daniel was shaking his head, back and forth. "Damn. Damn. Damn."

"A setup," I said. "A stinking setup. And she swore it was all an accident, us meeting at the sale. Just an innocent coincidence."

"Hey," he said, grabbing my arm. "That part of it was just a coincidence."

I jerked my arm away. "Right. Like I'm going to believe you."

"I had no idea you were going to be there," Daniel said, tight-lipped. "First I knew of it was when I ran into BeBe. She was paying for her stuff, and she told me you were there too."

"And that's when you set it up."

"Christ, Weezie," Daniel pleaded. "It's hot as hell out here. Will you just come inside and we can talk about this without making a scene for the whole neighborhood?"

"And then you'll take me home?"

"I'll call you a cab," he muttered. "What a pain in the ass you are."

It was twenty degrees cooler on the porch of the house.

"In here," he said stiffly, opening the door into the house proper.

The inside looked like a big blank box, but had a smell I adored: sawdust. And fresh nails. And paint. I inhaled deeply and sat down on a pile of two-by-fours.

"Tell me about your plan," I said.

"I just wanted to show you the house," he said, pleading. "Maybe fix you some lunch. Let you see I'm not a horny teenager looking to climb your frame. Is that a federal crime?"

"Not if you tell me that's the plan," I said.

"I told you I wanted to fix you lunch and show you the house."

"You told me BeBe had to go to the restaurant because there was an emergency," I corrected him.

"It *was* an emergency," Daniel said. "There was no other way I could get you to give me the time of day. So we fibbed a little. Is that so awful?"

"Whose idea was it to have BeBe take the truck and leave me stranded?"

"Hers," he admitted. "You know how she is."

"I know."

He stared down at his shoes for a while. Tattered, paint-splattered black high-tops. "You want lunch?"

"All right."

He gave me a hand up and took me on a quick tour of the house. "We tore down most of the interior walls," he said. "There were about a dozen tiny rooms in here. I'm just gonna have a few. The living and dining room, the kitchen, my bedroom and bath, and in the second floor, at the back, eventually I'll have a couple guest bedrooms and a bath."

"Nice floors," I said, looking down at the stripped floorboards.

"Heart pine," he said proudly. "I must have pulled about a million carpet tacks out of 'em. I've still gotta do a final sand yet."

The living and dining room consisted of a big rectangle. New windows, with the manufacturer's label still attached, made up the back wall of the room.

"Can you believe it?" he asked. "This wall was solid, except for one little dinky window. Derek and I put in these windows ourselves. Got 'em at a salvage yard on the Westside, and I bet they still cost more than this whole house cost in sixty-eight when my uncles built the place."

"Wow," I said, looking out the windows. Through the screened porch, which was currently minus screens, you could see two huge sand dunes, and in a valley between the dunes, an emerald slice of Atlantic.

"And this," he said, pointing to the left, toward the entrance into the two-story wing of the house, "is gonna be my favorite spot in the whole house. My kitchen. Or, it will be when it's done."

Right now his kitchen seemed to consist of a bronze Hotpoint range sitting beside an old round-shouldered Frigidaire refrigerator. He'd fashioned a counter from an old door laid across a couple of sawhorses, and an unpainted pegboard on a back wall bristled with cooking utensils.

"Where'd you get this?" I asked, running my hand over the 1940s fridge.

"It was out in the shed," he said, liking that I liked it. "My uncle used it to keep crab bait and beer. Still works great too, although I have to defrost the freezer if I ever want to use it for more than a couple trays of ice."

"It's adorable," I said, and he winced.

"Handsome," I corrected myself. I opened the door, expecting to see typical bachelor fare, beer, maybe some hot dogs. Instead, the thing was packed. Fresh fruit, white wine, vegetables, half a dozen kinds of mustard, neatly labeled plastic containers, and a six-pack of beer, yes, but imported beer.

"You really do like to cook," I said.

"The lunch part was no joke," he said. "You like soup?"

"Soup? Isn't it kind of hot to make soup? I was expecting maybe peanut butter and jelly, or grilled cheese."

"Sit," he said, pointing to a battered wooden step stool in the corner. "You want some wine?"

"No thanks," I said, shuddering at the memory of this morning's hang-over.

"Water, then." He took a pitcher from the fridge and poured me a glass.

I sat on the stool and watched. BeBe was right. People would pay money to watch Daniel cook.

His movements were quick, economical. He pulled a container from the fridge, opened it, and showed me the shell pink contents.

"Chilled seafood bisque," he said. "You like seafood, right?"

"Absolutely," I said.

In seconds, he'd chopped a handful of herbs and dropped them into the soup, then whisked in some white wine from an open bottle in the fridge.

From a basket under the makeshift countertop he pulled a long loaf of French bread, which he quickly sliced into six-inch segments. From another basket he produced two huge tomatoes, which he cut into thick slices, which were in turn topped with some kind of creamy white cheese that was stored in a water-filled dish in the fridge.

"Buffalo-milk mozzarella," he told me, seeing my look of interest. "We get it flown in from Atlanta."

Once he'd built the sandwiches to his liking, he brought out a paper-towel-wrapped packet of herbs and placed a few leaves on top of each sandwich.

"Basil," he said. "I grew it in pots in town. I'm hoping it'll do well out here too." Over the basil he poured a quick slick of olive oil from a half-gallon tin he kept on the countertop.

He ladled soup into two mismatched bowls, which he placed on a tray with the sandwiches and two bottles of the Amstel beer.

"Let's eat on the porch," he said.

We sat on upended Sheetrock paste buckets, and I ate the finest picnic I'd ever tasted in my life.

When we were done, I washed the dishes while Daniel unloaded his treasures from the truck.

"Want to go for a swim?" he asked, coming back into the kitchen.

"No suit," I said apologetically.

"Hmm." He said, running his hands through his hair.

"Never mind that," I said. "This has been wonderful, Daniel, but I really need to get home."

"OK," he said. "But the ocean will still be here. And the invitation stands."

"Maybe another time. When I have a bathing suit," I said.

"Whatever," he said.

CHAPTER *23*

 could hear the phone ringing as I unlocked the back door to the carriage house. I didn't hurry because I knew who the caller was. I unclipped the leash from Jethro's collar before picking up.

"Eloise?" It was Mama. She'd started calling me that again, probably because she knows it makes me nuts.

"Yes, Mama," I said, taking gulps of cold water from the jug I keep in the fridge.

"I prayed for you last night."

"Thank you, Mama."

"Did I tell you I've had to stop going to regular morning mass at Blessed Sacrament?"

"No, ma'am," I said. I scanned the headlines in the *Morning News*, hoping my name wouldn't be in any of them. A story had run nearly every day since Caroline's body was discovered, and of course, they used the worst photo of me they could find—the one taken as I was coming out of jail in the sailor dress.

"Yes. People were looking at me funny. Especially Father Morrison.

I've been getting your daddy to take me to six-o'clock mass out at the Church of the Nativity in Thunderbolt."

I yawned. "That's nice." It was Thursday. I'd picked up the *Pennysaver* paper on the way home from the park. It has the best classified ads for yard sales. Sometimes I can hit a good one on Fridays, although in Savannah, sales mostly just run on Saturday mornings.

"But your daddy is threatening to quit taking me out there," Mama was saying, her voice suddenly all quavery.

"Why's that?" I was marking up the *Pennysaver* with a felt-tip pen, circling the ads that looked promising. I was only half-listening to her. There was an estate sale in the Victorian district, East Gwinnett right near the park. I tried to picture that block in my mind, but Mama kept going on.

"Your daddy doesn't like that evening mass at Nativity. It's the folk mass, you know. And everybody stands up and sings the whole mass, and they have banjos and drums and I don't know what all. Your daddy calls it karaoke church, and he says if he wanted to go to a honky-tonk he'd go down to River Street and get him a cold beer instead of standing around with a bunch of hippie types at Nativity."

I tried to picture my father's idea of a hippie type. Probably anybody who didn't have a flattop crew cut and wear short-sleeved sport shirts, neatly pressed chinos, and well-polished tie-up shoes like my daddy.

"Mama," I said, pushing the paper aside, "I'm sorry you feel like you can't go to your own church. Maybe you should have a chat with Father Morrison. Ask him why he's giving you the evil eye all of a sudden."

"I know why," she said, going quavery again, like a ninety-year-old stroke victim, instead of the perfectly healthy seventy-year-old scratch bowler she is.

"Why's that?"

"Don't get mad at me," Mama said. "It's because of you. Eloise, I can't believe you've gotten our family mixed up in this sordid mess. Now everybody thinks you killed Tal's girlfriend. Because they know you went to jail, and you threatened to kill her out at that Beaulieu place."

"Mama," I said, my voice getting stern. "I can't help what people think. It's not my fault Tal had an affair. It's not my fault we got divorced, and he got engaged to that woman. It's not my fault she got killed, and I cannot control what people are saying about me, or how some mental defect priest looks at you, or what kind of songs they sing at Nativity. Now

I suggest you just hold your head up high and ignore all this mess. That's what I'm trying to do."

A little sob came over the phone. "I told your daddy you'd get mad and yell at me. He wants to talk to you."

There was a silence, and then I heard the distant sound of change jingling and throat clearing. Daddy was on the line.

"Weezie?"

"Yes, Daddy?"

"You got enough money?"

"Yes, Daddy. I'm fine for money."

"Your mama tell you about church?"

"She mentioned it."

"They have church in the lunchroom out there at Nativity this summer. Did she tell you that?"

"No. Just about the music."

"Damned odd, I call it. Going to mass in a school lunchroom. Place smells like stewed rutabaga. I never could abide rutabaga. You know what George Finnegan calls that church, don't you?"

"What does he call it?"

"Our Lady of the Cafeteria."

"Very funny, Daddy."

"Well, that's all I wanted to tell you. When you coming over here? I got a big old basket of zucchini for you, and some banana peppers too. The garden's really coming in good this year."

Good thing Daddy couldn't see the face I was making. Every year he planted a big garden, and every year he had a bumper crop of zucchini. Mama and I made zucchini bread and zucchini fritters and zucchini stir-fry. I even tried a chocolate zucchini cake recipe I clipped out of the newspaper. Jethro was the only one who would eat it.

Mama came back on the line then.

"Eloise?"

"I thought you said Daddy wasn't going to plant zucchini this year," I said accusingly.

"He didn't," she said, lowering her voice to a whisper. "Last year, I started taking the zucchini out and burying them in the backyard. I just couldn't look another zucchini in the face. I guess they just reseeded themselves this year."

"Somebody's got to put a stop to this," I muttered. "Have you thought about pouring Clorox or something on the plants?"

"I might," she said. "Listen, Sarah Donnellen called me last night, and she said—"

"I don't care what Sarah Donnellen said," I shouted. Mama hung up the phone on me.

"Damn," I said, looking down at Jethro, who seemed alarmed that I had raised my voice. "If I'd known she'd hang up on me like that, I would have yelled at her ten minutes ago."

I was circling estate sale ads in the *Morning News* when I heard the familiar rumble of a tour bus—but in an unfamiliar place—it sounded like it was coming not from the street in front of the house, but from the lane behind it.

From the lane? Impossible. The city council had finally enacted tough restrictions on local tour operators, making it illegal for the buses to stop on residential streets, and they were banned altogether from the lanes. Anyway, why would tourists care about seeing a bunch of trash cans and carports? I stuck my head out the door to check for myself.

Sure enough, a bulky diesel-spewing "Scenic Savannah" double-decker tour bus was idling right outside my door. People were hanging out the windows, pointing video cameras in my direction. The tour guide, a spindly middle-aged woman wearing a ridiculous-looking antebellum ball-gown and flowered sunhat, was standing at the front of the bus, speaking into a microphone.

The sound blared around me. "Notorious local murder case," I heard the woman say, followed by the click of camera shutters. "Ex-husband's new lover found shot to death in historic Savannah plantation house . . . Police believe antique dealer stalked prominent young woman architect and killed her out of revenge."

My face burning, I fled back inside the house. I felt nauseous, dizzy. I felt furious. It was the last straw. First a murder suspect, now a damn tourist spectacle. My fingers shook as I dialed the police.

"Savannah Police?" I said, when the dispatcher answered the phone. "I want to report a tour bus. It's parked illegally in the lane behind my house. On Chariton Street. The three hundred block." I was choking back tears. "I want the damn bus impounded. I want the driver and the tour guide arrested. And I want the damn tourists deported," I shouted, and then slammed down the phone.

After I calmed down, I took a shower and got ready to go to the grocery store. I was unlocking the truck when I heard a commotion at the trash cans in the lane. Charles Hsu, my eighty-year-old neighbor, was stuffing a bag of garbage in the city-issued green plastic bin next to mine.

"Hey, Mr. Hsu," I called. "How are your tomatoes coming along?"

Every year Mr. Hsu and I have a friendly competition to see whose tomato plants produce the most fruit. It was never a real contest because Mr. Hsu's plants were some top-secret variety he'd grown all his life.

Now, though, Mr. Hsu turned and glanced over at me, but didn't speak. He shoved the trash in the bin and scurried back toward his side of the fence.

I sighed. Mr. Hsu wasn't the only neighbor shunning me. The day before, as Jethro and I were crossing Charlton Street on the way to the park, I spotted Cheryl Richter pushing the baby jog stroller with little Eddie in it on the opposite side of the street. Lots of mornings we walked in the park together. Eddie loved Jethro, and for him the feeling was mutual.

"Hey, Cheryl," I called. But she kept on her side of the park and at the corner of Abercorn made a point of turning away from the park.

All right, I told myself. Maybe my neighbors had suddenly developed acute hearing loss, or maybe they had a vision problem—they couldn't see themselves consorting with an accused murderer.

Notorious. Jean Eloise Foley, I told myself, cruising toward the Kroger on Habersham. You are notorious.

When I got to the Kroger, I decided to keep my sunglasses perched firmly on my nose. Incognito, I thought. I'll do the Kroger incognito.

Once I was inside the store the dark glasses got me thoroughly disoriented. I'd left my shopping list at home, and the morning's distractions had scrambled my brains in a bad way.

I was standing in the produce aisle, staring down at a display of lettuce, trying to decide what kind to buy, when I heard a high-pitched, excitable voice.

"Eloise? Eloise Foley, is that you, honey?" I looked around. Everything was a murky, underwater green. But even green, I recognized Merijoy Rucker.

Damn. First Mama. Now Merijoy. I was doing penance for a sin I hadn't even committed.

Merijoy had a big bag of red bell peppers in her hand. She dropped them into a shopping cart loaded with children, and enveloped me in a bony, Dior-scented hug.

"Sugar," she gushed. "How awful for you. I have been beside myself with worry. Are you all right?"

Before I could answer, she turned to her shopping cart full of kids. All of them had white-blond hair and huge brown eyes.

"Renee," she cooed. "Sweetheart. Don't give Rodney jalapeño peppers, darlin'. They'll burn his little mouth."

Renee looked to be preschool age, maybe five. Her long, tanned legs were jammed into the compartment of the cart where I usually set my purse. Her face was smeared with what appeared to be either blood or the filling of the raspberry doughnut she was waving with one hand.

The lower section of the cart housed a slightly younger, boy-type version of Renee, who looked to be about four. Rodney, I assumed, since he was holding a partially chewed jalapeño pepper in his hand and howling loud enough to wake the dead.

There were two more children in the cart too, a pair of twin toddlers, a boy and girl, clad in look-alike yellow sunsuits. "Mommy, we're hungry," they chirped.

In one smooth motion, Merijoy snatched the pepper out of the screaming child's hand and flung it to the ground. She reached down into the cart and twisted the top off a plastic jug of Hawaiian Punch and held it to the child's lips. He stopped screaming and gurgled it down. In the next second, she'd opened a box of animal crackers and handed them to all the children.

"All set?" she asked. The children, who strongly resembled a nestful of baby starlings, sucked contentedly on their cookies.

"I am *so* glad I ran into you," Merijoy said, clutching my arm for emphasis. "I told Randy last night, after they ran that awful story about you on channel twenty-two, I said, 'Randy, poor old Eloise is being railroaded for this thing.'"

I tried to say something, but she went rushing on. "Of course, all my neighbors have been asking if I know you—from St. Vincent's and all. And I told them, 'Eloise Foley would not hurt a fly.' But honey, that's not what I wanted to tell you. What I wanted to say is, I've got the most marvelous idea. And it's so nice I ran into you like this. Because I was planning on calling you just as soon as I dropped Renee at tennis lessons, and Rodney at play group, and get Rachel and Ross down for their naps. This is just *too* perfect. Eloise, Randy and I would just adore it if you would be our guest for dinner tomorrow."

"Well," I started to say.

"It's our turn to host supper club. And the host gets to invite another couple. Just a few people, really. And you're to bring a date, of course. Unless you would like for me to invite somebody for you."

"No," I finally managed. "I don't think I can make it. Thank you, Merijoy, for thinking about me, but really, I'm not very good company these days."

"Nonsense," she said. "You'll be with friends. Dear, sweet, wonderful friends. Now, I won't take no for an answer. You'll come, and that's all there is to it. Seven-thirty sharp, and you know where we live, don't you, sugar?"

At that moment, one of the twins started making choking noises. I looked down. Little Rachel seemed to be going blue around her lips.

Merijoy frowned, reached down with one hand, and thumped the child on the back, at the same time cupping her other hand under Rachel's little rosebud lips.

"Spit, sweetheart," Merijoy said urgently. "Spit out the nasty cookie."

She was rewarded with a handful of regurgitated animal cracker.

"Wonderful," Merijoy said, beaming as though the kid had presented her with a bouquet of roses instead of a handful of hurl. She deftly deposited the fistful of baby puke in a plastic produce bag, which she knotted and tucked into her pocketbook.

"Rachel, darlin', remember what Mommy told you? Chew and then swallow. It's not a real lion, darlin', so it won't really hurt him when you bite his little head off."

"Now," she said, wiping her hands on a premoistened towelette that seemed to materialize from nowhere, "let's see. You know our house, don't you? It's the third house in from Habersham, at Forty-fifth Street. Ardsley Park, of course. I know, not the historic district, which Randy and I *adore*, but with five little ones, we really needed more room."

"Five?"

"Oh," she said, seeing my confusion. "That's right, you don't know about the baby. Little Randall is at home with Hattie Mae. I can't get anything accomplished with him along." She sighed heavily. "Sixteen months old and he'd nurse all day long if I let him."

I had a mental picture of tiny, perfectly groomed Merijoy Rucker with five writhing children climbing over her, barfing in her hands, sucking at her breast. I shuddered and was again speechless, which Merijoy took to be an acceptance to her dinner invitation.

"Wonderful," she said. "We'll see you Friday then. And Eloise, it really is seven-thirty, not Savannah time at all."

That, at least, I understood. In Savannah time, if you're invited somewhere at eight, it's bad manners to show up before nine. Savannahians have a deep-seated dread of arriving early for any social function.

"The boys get quite cross if we stretch cocktails past eight-thirty," Merijoy was saying. She patted me on the shoulder, and I could swear she left a trail of cookie spit on my skin.

"All righty then," she said, moving her cart toward the fruit aisle. "We'll see you tomorrow night. Everybody will be just so *thrilled* to get to know you!"

CHAPTER 24

*I* was just taking the last of the cheesecakes out of the oven when BeBe came breezing in the kitchen door.

She looked at the lineup on the counter—two praline turtle cakes, two mocha swirls, two peach melbas.

"How's it going?" she asked, pulling a bar stool up to the counter.

"Not so good," I told her. "Mama had to change churches because I'm so notorious. My neighbors cross the street to avoid having to talk to me. I'm a tour bus stop for Scenic Savannah Tours. Daddy's got another bumper crop of zucchini. You think we could sell zucchini cheesecake?"

She shuddered. "Not at my restaurant, we couldn't."

"I've started shopping incognito at the Kroger. And people still turn around and point at me and whisper. Like I'm a damn outlaw or something."

"You're not an outlaw, you're a folk hero," BeBe said. "Just yesterday, when I was at the beauty parlor, getting my hair foiled, you'll never guess what they had up at the front desk, where the receptionist sits."

"Plastic rain hats," I guessed.

"No, sweetie, this was my hairdresser's, not your mama's. I'll tell you. They had an empty coffee can. And somebody had clipped your picture out of the paper, and it was pasted on the can, along with a sign that said 'Free Weezie Foley.' Can you believe that?"

I shook my head.

"I told KiKi, that's the owner, that you're my best friend. And look—" Now she was pulling an envelope stuffed with twenties out of her purse. "She sent all of this along for you."

BeBe fanned the bills out on the counter. There were at least twenty of them.

"Money? For me? Why?"

"It's the Weezie Foley Defense Fund," BeBe said. "You're a cause. Every woman in Savannah wants to give you a medal for putting a bullet in Caroline DeSantos. You're the patron saint of ex-wives everywhere. You're a Lifetime channel movie of the week."

"I feel like an outcast," I said. "Except for one thing. When I was at the Kroger earlier, Merijoy Rucker stopped me. She invited me to her supper club tomorrow night."

BeBe's ears perked right up. "The Ruckers? They invited you to the Ardsley Park Supper Club? That's great. I've been dying to go to one of their dinners."

"What's the big deal?" I asked.

"Honey," she said, "the Ardsley Park Supper Club is ultraexclusive. Nobody, but nobody, gets invited unless they all agree on it. And they never have any more than twelve guests at the parties, because that's all the room they have in their dining rooms. People who belong to the Ardsley Park Supper Club *do not* believe in folding chairs and card tables. And the food is supposed to be fabulous. It's really a big deal to be invited. You should feel honored."

"You go," I said, easing a cheesecake out of the springform pan and onto a cooling rack. "I'm staying home tomorrow."

"What? No. Absolutely not. Weezie, why did you accept her invitation if you had no intention of going?"

"I didn't accept. Not exactly. Merijoy Rucker just sort of assumed. She has that effect on people. She just runs right over you. I kept telling her no, and she kept hearing yes."

"I've dated men like that," BeBe said, running her finger around the batter bowl sitting in the sink.

"And that's another reason I'm not going," I added. "Merijoy says I have to bring a date. And if I don't bring one, she'll fix me up with one.

And you know what I think about fix-ups." I glared meaningfully at her.

"Now don't start," BeBe said. "It worked out fine, didn't it? I don't get what you've got against Daniel Stipanek. He is absolutely yummy. Can you honestly sit there and tell me with a straight face that you don't find him devastatingly attractive?"

"I don't find him attractive. Not at all."

"You lie like a rug," BeBe said. She stuck the tip of her acrylic nail into one of the cooled cheesecakes. "Oh darn. This one has a crack in it. Why don't we just go ahead and cut it into slices?"

"That's fifty dollars' worth of profit for me," I protested.

She reached into her purse, slapped two twenties and a ten on the counter. "Here. Are you gonna cut me a slice of that damned cake or not? I'm famished."

I cut her a slice of cheesecake and poured her a glass of milk.

"What don't you like about Daniel?" she demanded. "And be specific."

"I don't know," I said, helping myself to a forkful of her cheesecake. It was the peach melba, a new recipe I'd been experimenting with, peach topping with a fresh raspberry glaze. "He's not my type. He's too dark, for one thing."

"You've been wondering about that tan line of his," BeBe said, waggling her eyebrows. "Naughty, naughty."

"Shut up. I've just never been attracted to his type. Men with dark hair. Never have been."

"Tal is totally beige," BeBe observed. "And we know how well that worked out. Don't we?"

"Daniel's eyes are so blue. It's unnatural for a man to have eyes that color."

"They're not contacts," BeBe said. "I checked."

"He's built wrong."

She pretended to choke on her cheesecake. "No, Weezie. He is built all *right*. My God. He is so buff. What's not to like about a body like that?"

"I'm just not used to somebody like him," I said, struggling to put it into words. "Tal is, was, tall; sort of architectural, you know. All smooth planes and straight hair. Pale skin and sharp angles. I used to love to look at his fingers. So long and tapered."

"Unlike the rest of his anatomy," BeBe cracked.

"No comment," I said primly. "Now, Daniel is nothing like Tal. He's shorter. And those muscles. There's such a thing as being too muscular, you know. I never have been one to go for that kind of thing."

I helped myself to another bite of BeBe's cheesecake. Strictly for research purposes.

"What about that behind?" BeBe asked. "Are you going to sit there and tell me that Daniel does not have the most gorgeous set of buns you have ever seen on a man?"

"I've never noticed," I said, crossing my toes.

"Liar, liar, pants on fire," BeBe taunted. "Most of the waiters and bus-boys at Guale are gay. And, honey, they've noticed. They practically fight to get into that kitchen when Daniel's working back there."

"What about that tattoo of his? Very unsanitary. And sort of white-trashy, don't you think?"

"It's just a little bitty old Marine Corps eagle," BeBe said. "He told me all about it. He got drunk on his first leave from Parris Island and had it done. And no, I do not think he is the least bit white trash. That's the trouble with you, Eloise. You were mixed up with that snotty Evans crowd for so long you started buying into that blueblood bullshit of theirs."

She took a swig of milk and patted her lips with the napkin I offered.

"I'll take Daniel Stipanek's tattoo over that so-called pedigree of Tal-madge Evans in a New York minute. I can't stand that family and all their pretensions. They'd like the world to think they're hot snot on a gold plat-ter. But really, they're just cold boogers on a paper plate."

I laughed so hard when she said that that I nearly spit out the bite of cheesecake I'd just snitched off her plate.

She gave me an exasperated look. "Damn it, get your own slice of cake. At least you can afford the calories." She picked up my wrist and dropped it quickly. "My God. How much weight have you lost since this whole thing started?"

"Hardly any."

It was a lie and we both knew it. I'd stayed clear of the scales, but I could tell from the way my underwear sagged that I'd probably dropped close to ten pounds since the night Caroline's body fell from that closet out at Beaulieu.

BeBe got a plate from the cupboard and cut me a slab of cheesecake. She got a Coke out of the fridge and set it by my plate. "Now eat," she ordered. "And tell me some more lies about how you are not attracted to Daniel Stipanek."

I chewed and thought about it.

"We don't have anything in common. We don't even like the same kind of music. I like classic rock and roll. He likes beach music. I didn't even know what that was until he told me."

BeBe shook her head at my ignorance. "You mean you've never made out to 'Under the Boardwalk'?"

"I got groped by Chuck Manetti once at a Van Halen concert at the civic center," I offered.

She clucked her sympathy. "Poor deprived child."

"Look," I said, "I'll concede that Daniel is mildly attractive. I'll even concede that his personality is not nearly as repulsive as I originally thought."

"You must have liked him once," BeBe said. "You admitted to me that you dated years ago, in high school."

Suddenly, unbidden, I flashed back to that naked romp under the live oaks at Beaulieu. I felt my face flush, and I got up to rinse my plate off at the sink to keep my hawkeyed friend from noticing my discomfort.

I would die before I would admit it to BeBe, or anyone else, but the main problem with Daniel was that he was different. And he was dangerous. And right now, I had enough danger in my life.

"It just won't work," I told BeBe, keeping my back turned to her. "I'm not ready for a relationship yet. Daniel can be sweet. I'll say that for him. When he took me home for lunch, he fixed me soup. Chilled seafood bisque. He's a wonderful cook. I can see why you want to keep him happy at Guale."

"Soup?" BeBe stood up and walked over to the sink, took me by the shoulders, and turned me so I was facing her. "He made you soup? Sweet Jesus in heaven. Why didn't you say so in the first place?"

"What's the big deal? He fixed me a sandwich too. With fresh basil. I never knew a man who grew his own herbs before."

"The big deal," BeBe said, "is this. A man who makes soup for you has got to be fantastic in the sack. On second thought, if you don't want him, I'll take him. Although, you know, I have a policy. Never fuck the help."

"Why?" I wanted to know.

"Because it's a bad idea to mix business with pleasure. And besides, it's more fun to fuck the competition. You know?"

"No," I said. "I mean, what has soup got to do with being a great lover?" Now I was flashing back to my boat date at Beaulieu again. The only thing memorable about that encounter was the variety of places I'd been bitten by bugs. I'd used a whole bottle of calamine lotion when I got home that night.

"Weezie, Weezie, Weezie," BeBe said, in the manner of a tutor with a mildly retarded student. "You're a great cook yourself. Think about it. Soup takes time. It takes patience. It takes attention to detail. A man who makes soup knows how to take his own sweet time with things. He uses just the right ingredients. And he whisks in the seasonings with just the right flick of the wrists. Then, and only then, he turns up the heat to finish things off. Bring matters to a simmer. And you know about good soup, right? The longer it takes, the better it tastes."

I picked up a piece of junk mail from the counter and fanned myself with it.

"Lawsy me," I drawled. "I think all this talk about soup and sex is gettin' me aroused."

BeBe gave me a broad wink. "Think about how much better the real thing will be."

"Absolutely not."

"We'll see."

CHAPTER 25

*T*ime was running short. Half a dozen times Friday morning I reached for the phone—to call Merijoy and beg off the dinner invitation. And each time I chickened out.

It wasn't that I wanted to go to her party. I just didn't want to be the pathetic soul who couldn't scare up a date for a stupid little dinner party.

But it was true. My date prospects were nil. Most of the men I know in Savannah were either married or gay. I did have one bona fide single straight male friend—Tony Fields. We'd been friends since grade school. He and his second wife, Bonnie, had split up six months before my divorce from Tal. We'd had lunch together a couple of times, but mostly just to commiserate about the trials of being suddenly single.

The trouble with inviting Tony was that I knew he ran in Merijoy's crowd. He even played golf with Randy Rucker. I didn't want people to start thinking we were an item—because realistically, we never would be.

To get my mind off my troubles I decided to check out an alleged estate sale in Baldwin Park.

Did I say estate sale? The ad in the *Pennysaver* promised antiques, but the offerings consisted mostly of a garageful of ugly outsized polyester frocks, a broken riding lawn mower, and a mound of mismatched plastic giveaway cups from fast-food restaurants. I knew there were people who collected things like NASCAR cups or Star Wars action figures, but frankly, I'm not into plastic.

The morning wasn't a complete loss, though; on the way home I stopped off at the Goodwill, where I picked up four green Depression-glass sherbet cups in the Horseshoe pattern, which is a fairly unusual pattern, for fifty cents apiece. I didn't have to look at my price guide to know that the cups booked out at fifteen dollars apiece.

The phone was ringing.

"Weezie?"

A man's voice, one I didn't recognize.

"This is she," I said warily.

"It's Daniel," he said. Funny, he sounded different over the phone. His voice was low, the Savannah accent not as pronounced. He sounded like a college professor, if you want the truth.

"Oh." I was stumped for something to say. "How are you?"

"I'm fine. You all right?"

"Pretty good," I said. "Think we'll get any rain?" Truly, this was the most inane conversation I'd ever participated in. Pretty soon I'd be asking him how much mileage his truck got, or for his opinions on term life insurance.

"Look here," he said. "I hate this kind of thing. BeBe was by the restaurant this morning. She happened to mention that you need a date for something you have to go to tonight. And here's the thing . . ."

"I do not need a date," I said, my voice dripping ice.

"Suit yourself," he said, sounding annoyed. "Sorry to bother you. Guess I misunderstood. See you around."

He was about to hang up. It was after one o'clock. There was no way I could scrounge up anybody with a pulse and a penis this late in the day. And Merijoy would be furious if I showed up alone and messed up her seating chart. My already sullied reputation would be worse than mud.

"Daniel. Wait."

"Something wrong?"

"I, um, well, look. I'm in a situation. I let myself get talked into going to this dinner party tonight. The hostess is an old classmate of mine, and she wouldn't take no for an answer. And it's a couples thing, and it's such late notice . . ."

"The Ruckers," Daniel said. "BeBe told me all about it. They come into the restaurant all the time. What time?"

"Seven-thirty. Sharp."

"Coat and tie?"

I hadn't thought to ask. But it was deep summer. Usually in Savannah a golf shirt would suffice, but then again, if this supper club was as fancy as BeBe claimed, that would be all wrong. Again I was wracked with indecision.

Daniel had no such problem.

"I'll wear a sport coat and bring a tie. That all right?"

"Yes," I said gratefully.

"You sure now?" he drawled. The old Daniel was back. "Your rich friends ain't gonna think you're slummin'—taking a short-order cook to a fancy house in Ardsley Park?"

He was laying it on thick. And I probably deserved it. "They'll be lucky to meet you," I said. And I was surprised to find that I meant it.

With my date dilemma solved, I spent the rest of the afternoon sitting at the computer, listing merchandise on eBay.

Not all the stuff I buy is suitable for selling at an on-line auction site like eBay. Furniture, for instance, which most people like to see before buying, not to mention the prohibitive cost of shipping. I rarely sell fine crystal on-line either.

But in the past year, I'd starting selling lots of smalls on the Internet. I did really well with things like silver, linens, china, pottery, jewelry, and even a few small oil paintings and water colors. I'd bought myself a good digital camera, and after only a few false starts, I'd gotten pretty good at photographing my antiques to their best advantage.

I didn't make a ton of money on the Internet, but I'd discovered it was a great way to find a market on a much larger scale than I could ever have dreamed of reaching otherwise.

Generally, I spend one day a week cataloging merchandise, updating my Web site, and checking auctions in progress, and another day packing and shipping items to be sent, literally, all over the world.

I had mostly odds and ends to add to the site today. Some funky fifties costume jewelry, a peacock-pattern chenille bedspread, and a gorgeous banquet-sized damask tablecloth and twelve matching hemstitched napkins, which would, I hoped, bring around a hundred dollars.

I'd picked the bedspread and table linens up with a five-dollar box lot of linens at an auction in Pooler, but it had taken time to get them ready to sell.

Like a lot of vintage linens, my tablecloth had been packed away for decades and had yellowed with age, with several prominent brown stains on the cloth and the napkins.

I used my meemaw's favorite stain-removal method to clean them, making a paste of equal parts automatic dishwashing powder, an old-fashioned powdered detergent called Biz, and baking soda. You launder the linens, and then, while the cloth is still damp, you put the moistened paste on any stains and let the paste dry, preferably outside.

The outside drying had been another bone of contention with Caroline. She was horrified the first time I hung laundry to dry on the little clothesline I rigged on my side of the courtyard fence. Tal had even called his lawyer, who had called Uncle James, to make me take the clothesline down.

Needless to say, I hung my linens out whenever I felt the urge.

The tablecloth and napkins had pressed up beautifully, using Meemaw's method of sprinkling the linens until just damp, then rolling them, placing them in a plastic bag, and chilling them overnight in the fridge. I took a weird pleasure in setting aside a morning to iron, sipping a glass of iced tea and watching the steam rise as the iron hit the cool, damp fabric. Maybe it was a way to connect with my long-dead meemaw, who had made such an art out of domestic science. Or maybe it was just my own perverted need to rebel against permanent press and drip dry, which, along with takeout and Lean Cuisine dinners, were such a staple of life with Mama.

I logged off the Internet at four o'clock and started obsessing about what to wear to Merijoy's.

There weren't that many choices. Although I love the look and feel of beautiful vintage clothes, the reality of my postdivorce life is that I rarely need anything more than a pair of jeans, a T-shirt, and flip-flops.

Three choices emerged from the walk-in closet I'd carved from the loft level of the carriage house. A hot-pink-and-white sleeveless Lily Pulitzer print shift straight out of the sixties, a floaty ankle-length white lawn Victorian slip that I wear as a summer dress, and a black cap-sleeved silk shantung sheath that, surprise of surprises, had actually once been Mama's.

I tried all three outfits on at least twice. The Lily Pulitzer was fun, cool, and definitely back in vogue. But the pink was questionable with the current hue of my red hair. The Victorian slip was too waifish; I'd lost so much weight, it gave me the look of the poor little match girl.

The black, I thought, turning around and around in front of the full-length mirror. Definitely the black. Hard to believe Mama had ever worn anything this racy, but when I'd dug it out of the cedar closet in her room, she'd gotten a faraway look in her eyes and told me about her first date with Daddy, when he'd taken her out dancing at Barbee's Pavilion, at Isle of Hope.

"I bought that dress with my first paycheck from the telephone company," Mama said. "It cost almost forty dollars at Adler's on Broughton Street, and your meemaw had a fit when she found out what I'd spent. I had black ankle-strap spike heels I wore with it, but I don't know what ever happened to them."

I'd never tried the dress on before. Tal never liked me in black. Even ten pounds lighter than usual, I had to suck in to zip up Mama's dress. It had a low scoop neck and a cinched-in waist and a tight skirt, and when I looked in the mirror I hardly recognized myself. It was, to my mind, an exact copy of my favorite Barbie doll dress as a kid.

The only problem with the dress was that Mama was four inches taller than I am. The hem hovered down around the middle of my calves, giving me the appearance of a little kid dressing up in her mama's cocktail dress.

I sat on the edge of the bed and hastily turned the hem up so that it touched four inches above the knee—sexy but not slutty. There was no time for sewing, so I resorted to the Catholic schoolgirl's favorite device—Scotch tape. As I taped I prayed the dress would hold together. It was well made, with beautifully finished seams, but the forty-year-old silk seemed a little on the fragile side.

Barbie had a pair of black plastic mules she wore with her dress, but the closest I could come was a pair of high-heeled black sling-back sandals.

Panty hose were out of the question. For one thing, it was too hot. And for another, after my divorce, I'd done my version of the Scarlett O'Hara vow, clenching a fistful of the hated hose and swearing "As God is my witness, I will never wear panty hose again." And while we were on the subject of undergarments, a bra was also impossible because of the way the neckline was cut.

So there I was, at 7:15 P.M., dressed in a dress that was older than I was, wearing nothing underneath but a pair of skimpy black lace panties. The high-heeled sandals made me teeter to begin with, but to calm my nerves I fixed myself a double vodka and tonic and slugged it down like ice water. My first date. My first date after ten years of marriage and the divorce from hell, and the datee was a man with a tattoo.

The doorbell rang. My pulse raced. I seriously considered passing out. Or running out the back door. Instead, I took a deep breath and tried not to exhale, for fear of having my breasts explode out the front of my dress.

I opened the door.

He was standing there, one hand resting on the doorjamb. He wore a crisp red-and-white striped dress shirt, khaki slacks, loafers with no socks, and a navy blazer with a tie poked in the breast pocket. The bright blue eyes swept me up and down. He grinned. "Damn, Sam. You look good enough to eat."

Under the circumstances, I don't think slamming the door in his face was such an unreasonable reaction.

CHAPTER 26

Amazingly, he was still standing there when I opened the door again a few seconds later. "It's just an expression," he said. But I had the distinct impression he'd already done a detailed inventory of what I was—and wasn't—wearing.

"That's some dress," Daniel said, helping me into the truck—no mean feat considering the strictures of the aforementioned dress.

I tugged at the shoulder seams, hoping to reposition my cleavage, but the matter was pretty hopeless. I would just have to remember my mother's lifelong directions and try to "sit up straight" all night.

"Is it too much?" I asked anxiously.

"Not for me," he said.

"But for the Ardsley Park Supper Club? I don't want them to think I'm some kind of tart or something."

He started the truck's engine. "You said you didn't even want to go to this thing tonight. So why do you care what these people think?"

"Because," I said, "I care. You probably won't understand this, because you've traveled and moved away before coming back, but I've lived in Savannah my whole life. My parents and grandparents lived here their whole lives. It matters, what people think. Anyway, it's different for a man. You can say or do anything you want, within reason, and people will admire you for being ballsy. But if you're a woman, just try and get away with anything in this town."

"Ignore it," Daniel said. "I would."

I shook my head and stared out the window. "This whole thing at Beaulieu is a nightmare. You have no idea how it feels, having people gossiping about you. Total strangers are convinced I'm some kind of homicidal maniac. You want to know why I'm going tonight? I'll tell you just how pathetic I am. Merijoy Rucker is the first person in two weeks who has gone out of her way to be nice to me. So yes, I'll admit it. I want people to like me. That's what everybody wants."

"Not me," Daniel said, his jaw tightening. "I don't give a damn what people think about me." He winked. "Or about you."

"Easy for you to say," I retorted. "You're the hottest chef at the hottest restaurant in town. BeBe says every woman who comes in Guale wants to jump you. You don't have a clue what it's like—being a pariah."

"I don't?"

"No," I said, wriggling around in the seat while trying to pull my skirt down. "And quit looking at me like that. I'm already nervous. You're making it worse."

"I'm not looking at you," Daniel said. "I'm looking at the Ruckers' house. Not too shabby."

Merijoy and Randy Rucker lived in the swellest house on the swellest block in Ardsley Park, a huge redbrick Tudor Revival mansion.

The neighborhood was developed around the turn of the century as the city's first true suburb—a new address for the city's emerging class of captains of industry and their families.

Unlike the narrow eighteenth- and nineteenth-century townhouses in the downtown historic district, homes in Ardsley Park were built as big sprawling affairs on roomy lots, complete with large gardens and verandas and terraces—and garages and driveways to accommodate the biggest fad of the new century: the automobile.

Daniel parked the truck at the curb, skillfully piloting it into a slot between a maroon Jaguar and a silver Mercedes.

"All set?" he asked.

I swallowed hard. "Will you do something for me?"

"Maybe."

I bit my lip. "I told you I'm nervous. I think I might throw up or something."

"Not in my truck, you're not."

I opened the passenger door. "I'll try not to splatter." Another deep breath of that soupy evening air and I felt a bit better. I kept my back turned away from him.

"Look," I said. "This is my first, sort of, well, it's the first time I've been out. Since Tal. I know this is not a real date, and you're only doing this because BeBe's your boss. But if you could, just, I don't know. Act like you like me. Could you?"

He slid across the seat of the truck and put his lips so close to my ear it tickled. And he whispered, very softly, "I do like you, Weezie Foley. I always have."

"Eloise!" Merijoy said, beaming and handing me an ice-beaded glass of what looked like gin and tonic. "You're here. I'm so delighted. I was afraid you might cancel on me."

"I wouldn't dream of it," I said. I turned to Daniel. "And I understand you already know my friend Daniel Stipanek."

"Know him?" Merijoy laughed. "Randy and I would starve to death if it wasn't for Daniel. We eat at Guale at least once a week, and lots of times Randy stops on the way home to get a take-out order of that divine salmon tartare of his."

Merijoy handed Daniel a glass too. "Randy," she called. "Look who's here, darlin', it's our celebrity of the evening."

I took a gulp of the gin and tonic. It was icy cold, tart and sweet at the same time. If the Ruckers kept it coming, I thought I might just make it through this evening.

"Well, hello there," Randy Rucker said, wrapping an arm around Merijoy's shoulders. I had to look up, way up, to see his face.

He towered over his wife. He was gangly, with thinning brown hair and thick horn-rimmed glasses, and a smile that seemed to radiate genuine gladness to see me.

"It's nice to meet you, Eloise," Randy said. "Merijoy's been talking a blue streak about you ever since you two met up out there at Beaulieu. I hear you're one of these hysterical preservation types like my bride here."

Merijoy gave him a playful little punch on the arm. "Don't let him tease you, Eloise. He's as interested in preservation as I am. You know, he's the one who stopped his daddy from tearing down the freight company's original building over on West Broad, I mean, excuse me, Martin Luther King Boulevard."

"I didn't know that," I said, impressed. I'd seen the Rucker Freight building. It was a Savannah landmark, a huge, Spanish colonial–style stucco garage with four ornate bays and a façade dripping with black wrought-iron lacework.

"Oh yes," Merijoy said. "Randy's daddy was ready to bulldoze the place. He had an option on some cheap land over on the South Carolina side of the bridge, where he was going to relocate the company. But Randy did some research and showed him how the family could get development authority money to fix up the old building, and even buy some land behind the original plot, so they could expand."

"Pretty darn smart," Daniel said.

"We saved a ton of money in the long run," Randy said modestly. "And that's the only reason my daddy agreed to go along with it. He was not the sentimental type. Bricks are bricks as far as he was concerned."

"But the point is, you saved an important building," I said.

"Yes," Merijoy said with a sigh. "We've already lost so many wonderful homes and businesses around here. I'm just sick with worry, wondering what's going to happen to Beaulieu."

A tiny white-haired woman in a smart blue brocade cocktail suit joined us just then. Her eyes were the same shade of turquoise as the dress, and she wore a single strand of pearls around her neck, and perched in her hair she wore a little scooped-out beaded and feathered cocktail hat. She looked like something out of a 1950s movie.

"Merijoy," she said, putting a birdlike hand on Merijoy's own. "What is going to happen to Beaulieu? Can't the Savannah Preservation League do anything to stop them from putting a paper mill out there?"

"No, Miss Sudie," Merijoy said sadly. "The plantation's not in the city limits. It's completely out of our jurisdiction."

"Somebody has to put a stop to it," the older woman said. "It's sacrilege to even think about touching that wonderful old house, or the land. Why, my mother and grandmother went to school with the Mullinax girls. Mother used to take us out to Miss Anna Ruby's Christmas tea every year, before she got so feeble. Her cook used to make the most wonderful pecan divinity—the pecans were from Beaulieu's own trees, of course."

"It's a scandal," Merijoy agreed. "I'm convinced that man, Phipps

Mayhew—he's the president of Coastal Paper Products—I'm convinced there's something funny about how he managed to get old Miss Anna Ruby to agree to sell. I spent months and months talking to her about deeding the house to the league for a house museum, and then, before you know it—"

"Honey," Randy interrupted. "Before you go off on a tear about Beaulieu, don't you want to introduce our guests to these other folks?"

Merijoy looked embarrassed. "Eloise and Daniel, I am so sorry. I just get so mad about this whole thing, I completely forgot my manners."

She beamed at the old lady. "Miss Sudie McDowell, I'd like for you to meet my old friend Eloise Foley. And her friend, Daniel Stipanek. Did I say that last name right, sugar?"

"Exactly right," Daniel said, shaking hands with Sudie McDowell.

"Miss Sudie," Merijoy continued, "Eloise and I were at St. Vincent's together. She's in the antiques business. And Daniel here is the chef at Guale. You have eaten there, haven't you, Sudie?"

"Several times," Mrs. McDowell said. "I don't suppose you ever share recipes, do you? My son Jonathan raves about that chilled seafood bisque of yours. He's addicted, I think."

"I'd be honored to share it with you," Daniel said, making a courtly little bow.

"Sudie was the first neighbor I met after we moved to Ardsley Park," Merijoy said. "The night we moved in she brought over a bowl of rasp-berry trifle and a bottle of wine, and we've been fast friends ever since. She and her son Jonathan are charter members of the supper club. You'll meet the other members in a little bit."

"I love your hat, Miss Sudie," I said. "Is it vintage?"

"Why yes." She was beaming. "The suit too. I've never thrown any of Mother's old things away. I get a lot of pleasure wearing them. And to tell you the truth, I never feel really dressed unless I'm wearing a hat."

"It's her trademark, Eloise," Merijoy said. "Sudie, Eloise likes vintage clothes too. She had on a darling dress a couple weeks ago."

"Jonathan," Mrs. McDowell called, spotting her son in deep conver-sation with a woman I'd never seen before. "Come over here, will you, dear? I want you to meet Merijoy's friends."

Jonathan McDowell hurried over. He had that young Jack Kennedy look—sailor's tan, tousled sun-bleached hair, button nose, and his mother's turquoise eyes. He wore the summer Savannah uniform—men's division—of khaki slacks, navy sport coat and yellow dress shirt. No socks.

"Eloise Foley," Mrs. McDowell said, "meet my son Jonathan."

"Foley?" Jonathan said. He had a funny look on his face. "Are you kin to James Foley?"

"He's my uncle," I said. "I'm his godchild. How do you know James?"

"Oh," he waved his hand in a vague gesture. "From around. You know, we lawyers are thick as thieves in this town."

"Jonathan is chief assistant district attorney," Mrs. McDowell said.

"Oh." The word was left hanging there.

Now Jonathan seemed distinctly uncomfortable. No doubt he knew my arrest record. Why shouldn't he? Everybody else did.

"Jonathan," Merijoy said, giving him a peck on the cheek. "Good. You've met Eloise and Daniel."

"Weezie," I said.

"I want Jonathan to do something about this awful situation you're in Weezie," Merijoy said. "He practically runs the district attorney's office."

"Don't believe her," Jonathan said quickly. "If you know Merijoy, you know she's prone to exaggeration. Especially where old friends are concerned."

"Be serious, Jon," Merijoy said. "Did you know the police arrested Weezie just because she was the one who found that woman's body out at Beaulieu? She even had to spend the night in jail. And they still might charge her with murder."

"Good heavens," Sudie McDowell said. "Jonathan, do you know anything about this?"

Jonathan tugged at his shirt collar and cleared his throat. "Mother, you know I can't discuss active cases," he said gently.

"Well, I can," Merijoy said.

Randy Rucker came to the rescue. "Listen y'all," he said. "I think we better get this show on the road if we expect to have dessert before midnight. Now, who brought the starter?"

"I did," Jonathan said quickly. "Or, rather, Mother and I did."

"He did all the work," Sudie said. "I never knew a man so crazy about cooking. He certainly doesn't take after his father. Why, Hudson McDowell couldn't even boil water for tea. The man was completely helpless in the kitchen."

Randy picked up a crystal goblet from a group of them massed on a silver tray atop a mahogany sideboard. He tapped the goblet with a tea-spoon.

"All right, everybody, let's head into the garden. That's right, isn't it, Jon?"

Jonathan McDowell was hurrying toward the kitchen, his mother in tow.

"I hope y'all came hungry," he called over his shoulder. "I've got craw-fish cakes with remoulade sauce, on a bed of watercress."

"And I've brought the wine," Sudie added. "A pinot gris. Jonathan said we needed something buttery to stand up to all that spicy stuff he put in the crawfish cakes."

"Honey, did you put the dishes of Rolaids on the table?" Randy joked, poking his wife in the side. "You know how crazy Jon goes with that hot sauce of his."

"Randy, you're awful," Merijoy said. But she stood on her tiptoes and planted a kiss on his chin.

*T*he Ruckers' garden reminded me of a painting I'd seen once at a museum in Atlanta. Huge old live oaks ringed a velvety green lawn, which in turn was bordered with shoulder-high hedges of azaleas, camellias, and gardenias. One gardenia bush was as tall as the roof of the porte cochere. There was a small swimming pool with a fountain in the middle, and a buffet table had been set up on the brick patio, under the shade of a towering sweet-gum tree.

I took a glass plate and helped myself to a crawfish cake. Before I knew it, Daniel had spooned a puddle of remoulade sauce onto my plate.

"Hey," I said. "I can serve myself."

"Just trying to be helpful. You know—acting like I like you," he said.

He poured me a glass of wine, then leaned over and nibbled on my ear.

"Enough already," I said, pushing him away. But he smelled wonderful, and that particular ear had been woefully neglected for a very long time.

We wandered over toward what looked like a pool house, a one-story brick structure with a green-and-white striped awning. Merijoy was chatting with two women I'd never seen before.

"Weezie," she said. "Have you met Anna and Emily Flanders?"

The two women were in their early to mid-forties, striking, but not exactly pretty, with shining chin-length bobs of dark hair, olive skin, and lively brown eyes. They were unmistakably sisters.

"Anna and Emily are the most successful real estate agents in town," Merijoy said. She winked at Daniel. "Be careful, Daniel, or they'll sell you a house you didn't even know you needed. Randy and I weren't even thinking of moving from downtown until these two shanghaied me on the pretense of taking me to lunch at the Chatham Club."

One of the sisters was slightly taller than the other, with a more pro-nounced squareness around the jaw.

"Emily was driving that day, and she insisted all she wanted to do was run by this new listing in Ardsley Park to drop off the lockbox," the tall sis-ter said. "Of course, I wanted to see the inside too. It was Emily's listing, and so we dragged Merijoy along."

"And the next thing you know, Randy Rucker's got himself a three-car garage and a half-acre lawn to mow," Emily said.

She leaned in closer to me. "I hope you don't mind, Weezie, but Meri-joy mentioned on the phone about the, uh, situation out at Beaulieu. I just wanted to tell you how sorry I am for your troubles."

Daniel took my hand and kissed the back of it. "She's been a rock, haven't you, darling?"

I took my hand back. "It was all a misunderstanding."

Anna Flanders nodded sympathetically. "We knew Caroline DeSan-tos, of course."

"You want my opinion?" Emily chimed in. "She was a real piece of work, that gal was. Shrewd."

"Oh for God's sake, Em," her sister said. "Let's call a spade a spade. She was ruthless. A real bitch. She knew what she wanted and she didn't care who she had to step on to get it."

"That's right," Merijoy said. "Anna, tell Weezie that story you told me."

Anna stared down at her shoes. She wore sandals and her toenails were painted hot pink.

"Oh, come on." Emily nudged her sister. "The woman's dead and buried. You don't owe her anything. Especially after the way she tried to cheat us."

Daniel took a sip of his wine. "You did business with Caroline?"

"Not really," Anna said. "But I guess it won't hurt to tell now. We met Caroline about six months ago. She called the office to ask about one of our listings."

"A double row house on Gaston. The Sheehan-Poligny house. It was on the garden tour a couple years ago."

"Caroline was house hunting?" It was news to me. "Why? She'd just moved in with Tal."

The sisters exchanged a look.

"You," Anna said. "Caroline DeSantos was not your biggest fan."

"She hated your guts," Emily added. "Said some awful things about you. And your dog. I should have known she was evil. I never trust anybody who hates animals. It bugged the daylights out of her that you were living in her backyard."

"My backyard," I said firmly. "Anyway, I was there first."

"We showed her the Gaston Street house," Emily said. "Not once, mind you, twice. She went over the place with a fine-tooth comb. Wanted to see the blueprints and property survey. Everything. The house needed some work; the kitchen in particular was a disaster. But that's how all these old houses are. She's an architect, she should have known that. After a week of nit-picking, she finally called and said she'd decided to pass."

"Two months went by," Anna said. "And by that time, the owner had about decided to take it off the market and do the renovations himself. Our listing agreement still had a month to run, but we took the sign down so people wouldn't keep calling about it."

"Right after we took the sign down, it just happened that we were both out of town on the same Sunday. And in the meantime, wouldn't you know it, the owner gets a call from somebody who wants to see the house right away. Now the owner is having second thoughts again. What the hell, he decides to show the house himself, since he can't reach either of us. And guess who the prospective buyer is?"

"Not Caroline?"

Anna nodded so emphatically it set her long earrings swinging back and forth like crazed chandeliers.

"Caroline tells the owner she loves the house. But the kitchen's so awful, it'll cost at least one hundred thousand dollars to fix—which is a complete exaggeration. You could do a very nice kitchen in that space for under fifty thousand. But that's Caroline for you. She makes a lowball offer right there."

"The owner refuses," Emily said, taking over the narrative. "Now Caroline asks if she can bring somebody else over to get a second opinion.

The owner agrees. Says he'll wait right there. Half an hour later, Caroline comes back, with a man she introduces as 'her friend.'"

"Was it Tal?" I asked, confused.

"Wait," Merijoy said. "It gets better."

"They go through the house again. Hand in hand, and he's calling her honey, and she's calling him baby, and it's all very lovey-dovey. After an hour, the man gets in his car and leaves. Alone. And Caroline makes the owner another offer. She says her friend has advised her to offer ten thousand dollars more."

"By this time, the owner is fed up," Anna said. "He suggests if she wants to make a legitimate offer, she should present it to his real estate agent."

"The bitch," Emily said, her nostrils flaring, "tells him very sweetly that he doesn't need a real estate agent. If he sells it by owner, he won't have to pay those silly Flanders girls a seven percent commission. He can keep all the money himself, and since he's saving so much money on the commission, he can afford to negotiate on the price."

"Ha," Anna said. "Unbeknownst to Miss Caroline, the owner happens to be an old family friend of ours. He tells her it's impossible, that he'd signed a listing agreement with us, and even if he hadn't, he wouldn't cheat us like that."

"He laughed in her face," Emily said. "Then he called me and told me what had happened. You can imagine my reaction."

"Did you call her on it?" I asked.

Merijoy put her wineglass down on the buffet table. "Weezie, you're missing the whole point."

"What? That Caroline was a lying, conniving cheat? That's not news."

"The man," Merijoy said. "What about the man she was playing kissy-face with?"

"Tal?"

"Uh-uh," Anna said. "I fussed and fumed about it, and threatened to have a showdown with her, but I never got around to it. Then, maybe a month ago, I saw Tal at the golf club. We've known each other forever. He was by himself, getting takeout from the dining room, and I just lit into him. I told him I didn't appreciate the fact that he and his fiancée tried to stiff us on the Gaston Street deal."

"Tell her what he said," Merijoy prompted.

"He was flabbergasted," Anna said. "He insisted he had no idea what I was talking about. He said Caroline was not in the market for a house, and neither was he. And he insisted neither one of them had ever talked to our client, or stepped foot in his house. Tal got pretty hot under the collar about it. He suggested I check my facts before I went around slandering people, and then he went stomping off with his takeout."

"Now," Merijoy said triumphantly. "Do you get the picture?"

I didn't, actually. "Did you double-check with the owner?"

"Hell yes," Emily said. "He described her perfectly, down to that silly yellow car of hers. Besides, she gave him her business card. He showed it to me. It was her, all right."

Now it was dawning on me, dim bulb that I am. "You mean the boyfriend she showed the house to wasn't Tal."

"Not even close," Anna said. "The guy who looked at the house was only about five ten. Stocky. A good bit older than Caroline. Maybe early fifties. He wore a baseball cap, so our guy didn't see his face or hair, but the build is definitely not Talmadge Evans III."

"Definitely not," Merijoy crowed. "She was running around on Tal. Don't you just love it?"

But there wasn't time for me to think about that.

Randy Rucker stood in the middle of the garden and tapped his goblet again with the silver spoon.

"If everybody's all set here, we're gonna adjourn to the dining room," he said. "Who's got the next course?"

"We do." A ruddy-faced guy in a white sport coat with rumpled seersucker slacks called. "And y'all better get moving. 'Cause Judy doesn't want her soup getting warm."

"You got it all wrong, Doug," Randy said. "Soup's supposed to be warm."

"Tell my wife," Doug retorted. "I don't fix this stuff, I just pay for the groceries."

Merijoy herded us all back into the house. "Do you know Douglas and Judy Hunter?" she asked.

"I know the name," I said. "Didn't he used to be on city council?"

"Oh yes," Merijoy said. "But this last election, Judy put her foot down and told him if he ran for reelection she'd file papers on him. She's tired of politics."

"He looks familiar," Daniel said. "I think they've been in the restaurant."

"They come with us all the time," Merijoy said. "Now scoot on into the house. Judy's a wonderful cook. I can't wait to get the recipe for this soup of hers."

Merijoy's dining room was immense, with fourteen-foot ceilings, chinoiserie wallpaper, and a crystal chandelier that I was pretty sure was Waterford.

A long oval mahogany table was polished to mirror brightness and set with white cutwork placemats, rose medallion china, and heavy Sheffield silver. Three different crystal goblets at each place setting. Just a casual little summertime clambake. Ha. I looked around and surreptitiously tugged my neckline up.

"I saw that," Daniel murmured. "You're not wearing a bra, are you?"

"Behave," I whispered.

A row of silver vases bursting with all white flowers marched down the middle of the table, and their sweet perfume filled the room.

"This is lovely," I told Merijoy.

She smiled. "Hattie Mae liked to have killed herself getting these linens starched and ironed and all this silver polished."

She lowered her voice. "I slipped in here while everybody else was outside and switched place cards so you'd be between Daniel and Jonathan. That Daniel is divine. How on earth did you hook up with him, Weezie?"

"We, uh, have a mutual friend," I said.

Doug Hunter stood in the dining-room doorway, beside his wife. She was pretty, with honey-blond hair and dimples that made her look like a little girl at a grown-up party.

"Y'all shut up now, so Judy can tell you about this soup. She's been slaving over a cold stove all day," he said, drawing laughs from the faces around the table.

I looked down at my plate. An engraved menu card sat atop the carefully fanned and folded damask napkin.

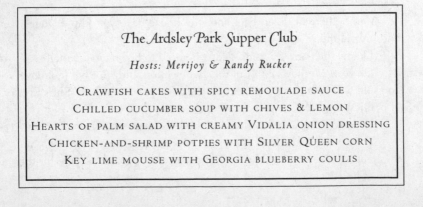

The Ardsley Park Supper Club

Hosts: Merijoy & Randy Rucker

CRAWFISH CAKES WITH SPICY REMOULADE SAUCE
CHILLED CUCUMBER SOUP WITH CHIVES & LEMON
HEARTS OF PALM SALAD WITH CREAMY VIDALIA ONION DRESSING
CHICKEN-AND-SHRIMP POTPIES WITH SILVER QUEEN CORN
KEY LIME MOUSSE WITH GEORGIA BLUEBERRY COULIS

"Wow," I said, holding up the menu for Daniel to read.

"I'm out of my league here tonight," he said. "If these folks decided to cook every night I'd be out of a job."

"Don't worry about that," Randy said, clapping a hand on both our shoulders. "This little shindig is about the only serious cooking we do around here. The rest of the time, Merijoy's got us eating Happy Meals and Pop-Tarts."

"Not true," Jonathan said, smiling over at me. "We all love to cook. We just don't get the time to do it as often as we'd like."

Judy Hunter came into the dining room carrying a silver tray full of soup bowls. She handed the tray to Doug, who went around the room placing a bowl at each setting.

"As you can tell by the menu card," Judy said, "I've made a cold cucumber soup tonight, with cucumbers out of Doug's garden. It's garnished with chives from Merijoy's garden, and lemons . . ."

"Which I picked up at the Kroger on the way home from work," Doug added.

"And that's his sole contribution to this dinner," Judy said.

"And the wine," her husband said. "I paid for the wine."

"What is it?" Jonathan McDowell asked. "Mogen David? King Cotton Peach Wine?"

"It's a New Zealand chardonnay, wise guy," Doug said, brandishing the bottle so everyone could read the label.

After a few bites of soup and a good bit of wine, I felt myself starting to relax. I even slipped my feet out of the killer sandals. Much better.

I was scraping up the last of the soup when I felt something on my foot. I jerked my head up and looked around. Jonathan McDowell had gotten up to pour more wine. A bare foot ran up my ankle, then up my calf, then up my thigh.

"Stop it," I whispered.

"Stop what?" Daniel asked.

"Stop groping me with your toes."

"Is that what you think I'm doing?"

He moved his foot, and not in a bad way. I felt my face turn crimson, and tried to reach down and push it away.

"Hey," he whispered, "do that again. I can almost see your nipples when you bend over like that."

I jerked myself upright and yanked at the shoulders of the dress. Immediately I heard a tiny little tearing sound.

I looked down. The center seam at the scoop neck of my dress was coming unraveled, thread by thread.

"Oh my God," I said, plastering my hand over the slowly growing tear.

"Oh yeah," Daniel said appreciatively.

Nobody else was looking. Doug Hunter was taking up the soup bowls, and Randy Rucker was announcing the entrée, a potpie featuring shrimp he'd netted himself off his dock at Bluffton.

"Do something," I whispered. "Or I'll be arrested for public indecency."

"Are you cold, darling?" he asked solicitously, and a little too loudly.

I nodded miserably.

Daniel got up and slipped out of his sport coat. He draped it over my shoulders and kissed my neck again.

"You've got to get me out of here," I told him.

"What—and miss the key lime mousse?"

CHAPTER 28

*H*ow's the potpie, Weezie?" Randy boomed from his end of the table.

"Delicious," I said, keeping my hand poised delicately at my bosom.

"You gotta give me this recipe, Randy," Daniel said. "I'll call it Bluffton potpie. Put it on the menu for nineteen ninety-five, and those tourists will lap it up."

"No deal unless you call it Rucker's Bluffton Potpie," Randy said. He was passing around another bottle of wine. By now I'd lost track of how much wine I'd had, but it was a lot. It seemed like every time my glass got close to being empty somebody would come around and refill it.

"Is it an old family recipe?" I asked.

"Maybe in Martha Stewart's family," he said. "Merijoy copied it out of that magazine of hers."

"But Martha Stewart doesn't have access to Bluffton shrimp," Daniel pointed out.

"Or Silver Queen corn from Merijoy's daddy's farm," Randy said. "So hers can't possibly be as good as this."

"We have to go," I said to Daniel under my breath. "Before this dress splits completely in two."

"I know you can't wait to get me alone so you can perform unspeakable acts on my body, but it's rude to leave in the middle of dinner." Daniel didn't even move his lips as he said it.

"Hurry up and eat then, damn it," I said.

"Calm down, or you'll pop another stitch," he whispered.

"Listen, y'all," Merijoy was saying. "You know I am not one to engage in idle gossip—"

"Ha!" Jonathan McDowell shouted. "We love you, Merijoy, but face it: you're the gossip queen of Ardsley Park."

"I'm just an amateur," Merijoy said, protesting. "But this whole thing with Caroline DeSantos is so fascinating. I mean, I'm sorry, Weezie, that you accidentally got mixed up in it, but really, it's all so juicy. What I want to know is what was Caroline doing out there at the plantation house at that time of night anyway?"

She looked around the table for agreement. I hoped nobody would ask what I was doing inside the house when I found her. Especially with the chief assistant district attorney sitting right next to me.

"Wasn't she supposed to be the architect for the new paper plant?" Doug asked.

"Supposed to be," Merijoy said sarcastically. "I just find it hard to believe some little scrap of a girl got a huge commission like that, only a few months after she moves to Savannah and starts shacking up with Talmadge Evans."

I winced, but it was another matter I'd wondered about.

"Sorry, Weezie," Merijoy said. "But honestly. Didn't Tal's firm do mostly residential work?"

"They did a lot of residential," I said, "and some commercial stuff. A few banks, a couple of churches, and some multifamily housing. I don't think he'd ever done much industrial design."

"How do you think a hot little number like her got that job?" Doug asked.

"Look at who hired her," Merijoy said.

"The paper company? Phipps Mayhew?" Judy Hunter said.

"Phipps would have done the hiring," Randy said. "But he probably just went on the recommendation of somebody locally."

"Gerry Blankenship," Merijoy said. "He's Miss Anna Ruby's attorney.

And he's the one Caroline was with at the memorial service. The old fart couldn't take his eyes off her."

"You gotta admit she was easy on the eyes," Doug said. His wife shot him a dirty look.

"Gerry Blankenship," Miss Sudie said, tsk-tsking. "I had him in my six-year-old Sunday-school class. What a rascal. He seems to have his finger in a lot of pies, doesn't he?"

"It's called being well connected," Doug said. "And old Gerry is hooked up in ways I'll never understand."

"His mother's people were Cargills," Miss Sudie said. "Wonderful old Savannah family. I don't know much about the Blankenships. I believe his daddy was a salesman or something."

"The guy doesn't even have a real law degree," Doug griped.

"He doesn't?" Merijoy said breathlessly. "Maybe Miss Anna Ruby's will isn't legal then."

"Nah," Doug said. "I guess it's real. He didn't go to Emory or Mercer or University of Georgia, though."

"Doug thinks anybody who isn't a Bulldog is a card-carrying shyster." Judy laughed.

"Guess that makes me a shyster," Jonathan said. "I went to Emory."

"You know what I mean," Doug said. "Blankenship got his degree from the old Ben Franklin University. That diploma mill that used to operate downtown. The state ran 'em out of business in the early seventies, but there's quite a few fellas around town who got their law degrees there."

"Perfectly capable fellas," Jonathan pointed out. "We've got a couple Ben Franklin grads in our office. They don't advertise the fact, of course."

"I'd like to know what's going to become of the furnishings, if they tear the old house down," Miss Sudie said. "I remember Miss Anna Ruby had beautiful things. There was an Aubusson rug in the dining room. It was shades of rose and cream and peach. A beautiful rug."

"Weezie's the one to ask about the furniture," Merijoy said. "The place was full of antiques when we were there for the memorial service. But then the sale was cancelled after, you know."

All eyes seemed to turn in my direction. I had borrowed Daniel's jacket, but I could feel a definite draft on my chest.

"Will they reschedule the sale?" Emily Flanders asked, looking at me.

"I haven't heard," I said, trying to negotiate a bite of potpie with one hand while clutching at the jacket with the other hand.

"I'll tell you what I heard," Judy Hunter volunteered. "Supposedly whoever is in charge out there at Beaulieu has started selling off the really good furniture."

My fork froze in midair. "To who? I mean, whom?"

Judy made a face. "Do you know Lewis Hargreaves?"

"Yes." I said a little silent prayer. Please don't let them sell him the Moses Weed cupboard. Not that.

"I was at the hairdresser's last Saturday, and Vivian Chambers was sitting under the dryer next to where I was getting my hair cut. She was talking on her cell phone—you know how bad reception is downtown, so she was talking real loud. I gather she was talking to her interior decorator. Because she was saying she'd had a call from Lewis Hargreaves about a Sheraton sideboard that came out of Beaulieu. She was asking the decorator to meet her at Lewis's shop, to look at the piece and tell her if she should buy it. And I heard her say the price too—eighteen thousand dollars. Can you imagine? For one piece of furniture?"

"Don't even think about ever goin' in that guy's shop," Doug told Judy, pointing an accusing finger.

"Who? Me?" Judy batted her eyelashes. "Don't worry. I think he's kind of creepy. And his prices are absurd."

Merijoy put her elbows on the table and leaned forward. "Jonathan, doesn't this all sound mighty strange to you?"

Jonathan thought about it. "Murder's always strange, Merijoy."

"Seriously," she said. "This whole business of a paper plant coming in out at Beaulieu. I knew Miss Anna Ruby. I talked to her several times this year before she died, about leaving the house to the preservation league for a museum. She didn't say yes, but she didn't flat out say no either. And she certainly never hinted that she'd sell it for a paper plant. She loved that place, and she was the last of the line, so it wasn't as though she were planning on leaving the money to her relatives or anything."

Sudie McDowell was shaking her head. "Another paper plant. Just as we're finally getting the air and water cleaned up after all those years of pollution from the paper-bag plant."

Doug cleared his throat. "Now, none of this is for publication," he cautioned. "But what I'm hearing around the courthouse is that this Mayhew character may have run into a roadblock with the state environmental folks."

"What kind of a roadblock?" Merijoy asked.

"Something about an environmental impact statement," Doug said. "I'm not up on all these state environmental regulations, but I've heard their proposal calls for dredging out all those old rice canals out there. And you know how these bureaucrats are when it comes to anybody messing around with wetlands."

"Maybe this is one time the bureaucrats are on the right track," Randy said. "That's beautiful marsh-front property out there. I hate to think about some factory mucking up the water out there. When I was a kid, the best crabbing spot on the river was that old dock at Beaulieu. Good fishing out there, hunting too. Miss Anna Ruby used to let my daddy keep a duck blind there."

"Yes," Daniel said gravely, again running his bare foot up and down my leg. "There was some wonderful wildlife out there when we were kids, isn't that right, Weezie?"

I started to slap at his foot, but when I leaned forward I heard another stitch popping.

Everybody was looking at me now. I took a large gulp of wine.

"I am so sorry," I said, blushing again. "What were we talking about?"

"Daniel was just agreeing that it would be a shame to lose such a historical landmark as Beaulieu," Merijoy said.

She got up from her chair. "Everybody ready for dessert? The Otwells fixed it, but their babysitter canceled at the last minute, so Sally Ann brought it over earlier. They send their regrets. Now, I thought we'd have dessert and after-dinner drinks in the library," Merijoy said. "And I imagine Randy has some of those nasty old cigars of his, if anybody feels like poisoning their lungs."

Now was my chance to escape. Everybody was getting up from the table and helping to clear the dishes.

"Let's go," I said, grabbing Daniel's arm as he walked toward the doorway.

"So soon?" he said, staring right down into my rapidly expanding cleavage. "But things are just starting to get interesting."

Ignoring him, I caught up with Merijoy.

"Thank you so much for inviting us, Merijoy," I said. "It's been a lovely evening. But we're going to have to bow out early. Daniel's pager just went off. Some little emergency at the restaurant."

"Oh no," Merijoy said, pulling a pouty face. "That's no fun. But you stay. Randy can run you home after dessert."

"No, no," I said hastily. "I've had a long day, and I have to get up at five in the morning. It's estate sale day, you know."

"All right," Merijoy said, "but you have to promise to come to supper again."

"I promise."

Daniel came up and kissed Merijoy's hand. I thought she would swoon. "Sorry to have to go," he said, "but Weezie's dog got out, and we've got to rush home and look for him."

I could have kicked him.

Merijoy got a funny look, and then she smiled. "Stop with the silly stories," she said. "I remember what it was like to be young and in love. And I can tell you two want to be alone. So just run along."

He draped his arm over my shoulder. "Can I have my jacket back now, sugar? I'm feeling kind of chilled myself."

CHAPTER *29*

*A*re you mad at me?" Daniel asked after I threw his sport coat at him and stomped off to the truck.

I could hear more stitches popping after I hoisted myself up to the seat. I looked down and saw the right side seam had ripped halfway up to my thigh. I was past caring. Daniel had already seen my nipples. Too late for modesty now.

"Just take me home, please," I said, crossing my arms over my chest.

"It's not even ten o'clock yet," he protested. "What's your hurry?"

"In case you haven't noticed, my dress is disintegrating," I said.

"Well, hell, I don't mind if you don't mind."

"I mind."

"You gotta admit, Weezie, that dress of yours made for a pretty exciting night. Did you ever see that Alfred Hitchcock movie where the guy is dangling off the torch that's being held by the Statue of Liberty? And another guy is hanging onto the falling guy, just by the sleeve of his jacket. And all of a sudden, the camera focuses in on the sleeve, coming apart, thread by thead. Pop. Pop. Pop. And there're maybe three little stitches that're the only thing keeping him from falling to his death. Your dress is kind of like that, you know? Real suspenseful."

"I'm glad you enjoyed the peep show," I said. "But then, you weren't the one whose boobs were about to fall out on the dining-room table in front of God and the chief assistant district attorney and his sweet little white-haired mama."

"I gave you my jacket," he said. "What else could I do?"

"Nothing. You've been a real sport. Except when you were looking down my dress or feeling up my crotch with your toes."

"You liked it. Admit it."

"Swine."

"OK," he said, turning the corner onto Abercorn Street. "So now I know what turns you on. Want to know what turns me on?"

"I know what turns you on," I said. "Almost everything. Including groping women in public."

He sighed. "And here I thought I was just doing what you asked me to do. 'Act like you like me, Daniel,' she says. 'Be my friend.' I was being friendly."

"It was embarrassing," I said. "Now Merijoy thinks we're rushing off to go jump in the sack together." I buried my face in my hands. "God."

"I just said we had to go home because your dog got out," he protested.

"I'd already told her a different lie, about an emergency at the restaurant."

"I like my lie better," Daniel said.

"Doesn't matter now," I said glumly. "You heard what her friends say about Merijoy. She's the gossip queen of Ardsley Park. She knew we were both lying. Now by tomorrow morning it'll be all over town. Weezie Foley is sleeping with that hunky chef at Guale."

"She thinks I'm hunky? Really?" He checked himself out in the rearview mirror, finger-combed his hair. Looked really pleased with himself. "Hunky. I like that. Probably be good for business too. BeBe will love that."

"Yeah," I said. "You'll be the hottest stud muffin in town. And I'll be that jailbird slut junk-picker. Mama and Daddy will be so proud."

"Hey," he said, reaching for my hand. "Don't take it so seriously. You worry too much. You know that?"

His hand was warm. He stroked mine with his fingertips. I yanked it away.

"I've got a lot to worry about," I said. "My life is crap. But up until now, people thought I was a nice respectable nobody."

"Those people at the Ruckers' thought you were nice. I'll tell you the truth. I thought this was gonna be just a bunch of stuck-up snobs. But everybody acted real friendly."

"It wasn't so bad," I admitted. "Until they started talking about Caroline. And Tal."

"You handled that pretty cool," Daniel said. "Very classy. Grace under fire."

"Really?"

"Damn straight."

"Thanks. That helps. A little."

"So. What about finishing our dinner?"

"I'm sorry," I said, "I can't face those people again, not in this dress. It really is about to fall to pieces."

"I didn't mean at the Ruckers'. I thought maybe I'd run over to the restaurant, get some dessert to go."

"Well . . ."

"You're not one of those women who won't eat sweets, are you?" he asked, looking worried.

"Hell no," I said. "I love desserts. That's one of the reasons I bake those cheesecakes for BeBe. Tal had a monster sweet tooth. Now that I'm single, I don't have an excuse to do much real baking."

"So," he said, pulling into the lane behind the restaurant, "what do you want for dessert, Weezie Foley?"

"Chocolate. Definitely chocolate."

Jethro sniffed Daniel's pants leg. Then he sniffed the bag from the restaurant. Then he got around to sniffing me. Satisfied, he lay down under the coffee table and gave us his best woeful dog stare.

"Absolutely not," I said, when Daniel started to open the dessert bag. "Chocolate is bad for dogs. He can have a beef jerky treat. They're in the kitchen, in the cookie jar. Could you get him one, please? I have to get out of this dress."

"Need any help?"

"Don't start," I warned.

Upstairs, I pulled the dress off and let it fall on the floor. It felt so good to be free of its viselike grip that I hated to put clothes on again.

I stood in my dressing room staring at the clothes rack, trying to decide what to put on. My usual sweats and T-shirts didn't seem quite right for the occasion.

But I had a gorgeous old yellow silk kimono embroidered with dragons that Mama's brother had brought back to her from Japan. It might work, I thought. Long, loose, yet glamorous. And the yellow was good with my skin and hair. I belted it loosely around my waist, did a turn in front of the mirror, and was satisfied.

I had a date. It was such a funny feeling. Maybe it was the wine. A new man, waiting downstairs in my house—with chocolate, even. This could be good.

"Is that a bathrobe?" Daniel asked.

"No," I said, "it's a kimono."

"Very nice. Although I was getting attached to that dress of yours."

"That dress is history," I said.

He'd set the dessert out on glass plates. It was two thick hunks of something chocolate, covered with whipped cream and topped with chocolate sauce and chopped nuts.

"Yum," I said, dipping my fingertip in the whipped cream. "What do you call this?"

He had a bottle of champagne and two crystal flutes. He popped the cork and poured the wine. Daniel handed me a glass and picked up his own. "It's called chocolate seduction," he said. "Shall we toast to that?"

I raised an eyebrow, but we toasted.

"Let's take this into the living room," I suggested.

We sat down on the sofa in front of my tiny coal-burning fireplace. Jethro was still stationed under the coffee table, staring balefully out at us.

I took a bite of chocolate. It was smooth and slightly bittersweet, with a hint of coffee and some kind of liqueur. "Mmm," I said.

"I like your place," Daniel said, looking around. "It's got a lot of character. Not too girly either. Did you do all this yourself?"

"Pretty much," I said, washing the seduction down with a gulp of champagne. "This was basically a two-car garage when we bought the place. I always figured I'd make it my own someday. For an antique shop. Never in my wildest imagination did I think I'd end up living here. Alone."

He stood up and walked around the room, stopping to look at my artwork, reading the titles of the books on the shelves, even opening the powder room door to get a peek in there.

"Where'd you get all this neat stuff?" he asked.

"Everywhere," I said. "That's what pickers do. This sofa was my grandmother's. I had it re-covered with a bolt of old fabric I found when a dry goods store in Statesboro closed down. The wrought-iron coffee table top was an old window grate I bought for five bucks at a demolition yard on President Street. That chest under the windows there, I bought at St. Michael's Thrift Shop, out at the beach. It only cost twenty dollars, but it had about ninety coats of Pepto-Bismol pink paint on it. Took forever to strip, but I knew there would be pretty old pine underneath, and there was."

He came over and sat down right beside me. "Know what?" he said. "You amaze me." He put his arm around my shoulder. I flinched, just a bit. Jethro made a growling noise deep in his throat.

Daniel looked hurt. He took his arm away.

"I'm sorry," I blurted.

"It's all right," he said, shaking his head. "I guess you've made it pretty clear tonight that you're not attracted to me." He sat up and looked around for his jacket.

"This stuff with Tal still shakes you up, doesn't it? I saw your face tonight when that woman talked about Caroline shacking up with Tal. You looked like you'd been slapped. I guess you're not really over him."

He leaned over and patted Jethro on the head. "I'll go," he said, standing up. "Maybe you'll give me a call sometime. We could just be friends, I guess."

"No." I wanted to shout, but it came out as a whisper. "No. I don't want you to leave."

Daniel eased back onto the sofa.

"Could you be patient with me?" I asked. "It's been a long time since I was with another man. I don't really know how to act. But I am over Tal. Really and truly I am."

He put his arm around my shoulders again and pulled me closer.

"How about if I took things really slow? Would that make you feel safer?" I took a deep breath and nodded.

"No sudden moves," Daniel said. He nuzzled his chin in the top of my hair. "Is this all right?"

"OK," I said. He smelled wonderful. Like fresh-mown grass, and aftershave. And chocolate.

"Now I thought I'd kiss your neck." A series of featherlight kisses landed at the nape of my neck. I closed my eyes and felt his warm sweet breath on my skin. I was a little dizzy from all the wine. Or maybe the newness of it all.

"Do we need these earrings?" he asked, nibbling on my earlobe.

"Not necessarily." I took them off and put them on the coffee table.

He pulled me back to him.

"Now for the good stuff," he said, working his way from my shoulders down to my breasts, then up again toward my lips.

"Feel free to kiss back at any time," he said. "It's customary, you know."

Daniel Stipanek had learned quite a lot of good stuff since our last encounter. I couldn't decide if he'd picked up his moves in the Marines or chef's school, but I didn't care. He was wonderful.

He pushed me gently back on the sofa. His hands found the small of my back and kneaded it while he pushed me closer. He kissed my shoulder and then a lonely spot in the hollow of my throat, and then he was working on the knotted belt of my kimono, with agonizing slowness.

I heard Jethro growling deep in his throat.

"Go away, Ro-Ro," I gasped, in between kisses.

Now Jethro was barking. And someone was knocking at the front door.

"Weezie?"

It was Tal. I jumped up from the sofa, smoothing the kimono back in place.

"That's him, isn't it?" Daniel said, getting up, tucking in his shirt.

I nodded.

"Tell him to drop dead," Daniel suggested.

I just shook my head, tears in my eyes.

"Weezie? Baby, I need to talk to you."

I froze.

"Never mind," Daniel said, grabbing his jacket. "I'm outta here."

He pulled the front door open and stalked past my ex-husband, who was slumped in the doorway with a bottle of wine and two glasses in his hands.

aniel screeched off in the truck, laying rubber, not an easy thing to accomplish in a brick-paved lane.

"Who was that?" Tal asked. "Was that a guy?"

Tal looked like he'd been rode hard and put away wet. His hair was mussed. Talmadge Evans never has mussed hair. He wakes up in the morning and looks like he just came from the barber. His eyes were bloodshot. He wore a white button-down dress shirt that looked like he'd slept in it, baggy Bermuda shorts, and his shiny black penny loafers.

I ignored his question about Daniel. "What do you want?"

Tal ran a finger around the neck of my kimono. "Pretty," he said, almost absentmindedly. "Are you sleeping with that guy? Who is he?"

"None of your business." I went to close the door, but he put his hand on the door to stop me.

"Please, Weezie," he said. His breath smelled like Scotch. "I need to talk to you."

"Call me when you're sober," I said. "I'm going to bed."

"You hate me, don't you?" He swayed a little as he said it.

"I have a right to hate you, don't I?"

"I've been a jerk. I want to apologize. Can't I come in?"

Jethro's breath was hot on my ankles. He poked his head between my legs and growled menacingly.

"Hey, Jethro, buddy," Tal said, stooping down to pat Jethro's head.

Jethro growled and snapped at Tal, who jerked his hand back just in time to avoid getting his fingertips shortened.

"He hates me too," Tal said sadly.

"Come on in." I sighed, opening the door.

He walked unsteadily into the living room and collapsed onto the sofa. The wine from the bottle sloshed on the floor, and the glasses he'd been holding rolled onto the carpet.

"Shit," he mumbled.

"I've got them," I said, rescuing them moments before he crunched them into sand with his penny loafers.

"Want some wine?" he asked, gesturing toward the bottle.

"No thanks. I've had plenty already. Looks like you have too."

"I've been drinking alone," he said. "You had company."

He picked up a fork and helped himself to a bite of Daniel's chocolate seduction, but the fork missed and he smeared chocolate and whipped cream all over his face.

It didn't seem to faze him. He wolfed down all the cake on both plates. "This is good," he said. "Did you make this, Weezie?"

"No."

"I miss your cooking," Tal said, apparently not hearing me. "Caroline can't cook for shit. Did you know that?"

Of course I'd seen all the take-out cartons and frozen-food wrappers in the trash. "That's what I understand," I said.

"You know what's Caroline's favorite thing to make for dinner?"

"Get to the point," I said, picking up the dishes to stack them in the kitchen sink.

"Reservations," he called, laughing at his own incredibly lame joke.

"You know what we eat over there most nights?" he asked. He didn't wait for an answer. "Takeout. I call Mrs. Wilkes's Boarding House at lunchtime and go get us two take-out dinners and we warm 'em up in the microwave. Or Lean Cuisine. Lean Fuck-king Cuisine." He laid his head back among the sofa cushions and shut his eyes.

This was really getting tedious.

Moments later, he was snoring, with his mouth open. I wished for a camera. Anal-retentive Talmadge Evans III passed out on his ex-wife's sofa, with a two-day's growth of beard and a chocolate whipped-cream mustache.

I shook his shoulder. "Tal. Wake up."

His eyes fluttered open.

"Weezie." He grabbed my hand and kissed the palm. He turned it over and kissed the back of it. He got chocolate all over me.

"Go home, Tal," I said. "You're drunk. If you want to talk, call me tomorrow. I'll be home after noon."

"No," he said quickly. "Don't kick me out. I'm not that drunk. I just need to talk to you. About things. All right? Just a couple things."

"Like what?" I pulled a wooden chair up and sat opposite him. I studied his face. He'd always had a thin face, but now he looked positively gaunt. For the first time I noticed that his pale blond hair had started thinning on top, and he was going gray around the temples.

He clasped my hands between his again and closed his eyes.

"Tal," I said sharply. "What did you want to tell me?"

"Huh?"

"This is hopeless." I pushed away from him so he'd let my hands loose.

"Caroline is dead," he said.

"I know," I said. "I'm sorry."

"Mother thinks you killed her. She thinks you're a dangerous criminal."

"Your mother never liked me. But I didn't kill Caroline, Tal. I swear to God, on my grandmother's grave, I didn't kill her."

His blue eyes searched my face.

"I know," he said. A tear trickled down his cheek.

"I didn't like her," I said, "but I'm sorry she's dead. I'm sorry you've been so hurt." I gulped. "I know you miss her terribly. I wanted to come over and tell you how sorry I am, but I felt awkward. I'm not very proud of how I've behaved since the divorce. But that's over. I don't want to fight anymore."

He sniffed, then wiped his face with the tail of his shirt and blew his nose while he was at it.

I nearly gagged. Just how much Scotch had he had?

"Listen," I said. "How about I make you some coffee?"

"Sure," he said, his face lighting up. "Coffee. Like you used to make. Do you still keep the beans in the refrigerator?"

"Yeah."

"The good imported beans, from Kenya?"

"Still Kenyan," I said. He was really weirding me out now.

"And do you grind them on that little electric grinder of yours? The cute little red one?"

"You got the red grinder in the divorce settlement," I reminded him, unable to resist just a teensy little stab.

"I could go get it. You can have it back. Caroline makes instant coffee."

"I bought a new grinder," I said. "Wait right here. I'll go put a pot on."

But he followed me into the kitchen and propped himself up at the counter, watching while I measured the whole beans into the electric grinder and ran it for a minute. He sniffed deeply. "I love that smell of fresh-ground coffee. That's another thing I miss about you, Weezie."

Whatever. I got the coffee perking and took two jadeite mugs out of the cupboard, and then got the jug of cream from the fridge.

"I remember those," he said, picking up one of the mugs. "They keep the coffee nice and hot. The perfect thickness. That's what I love about you, Weezie. You care about the aesthetics. About how the coffee smells, and how the cups feel with your hands wrapped around them. I'll bet that's real cream in the pitcher too. And that's another thing. You pour the cream out of the carton, into that very same pitcher."

It was just an ordinary little pressed-glass cream pitcher. "I always use cream," I said evenly. "It tastes better when you pour it out of a pitcher."

"Caroline buys that powdered nonfat nondairy stuff," Tal said. "She says it's not worth the expense, buying cream for just the two of us."

It was creepy, the way he kept referring to Caroline in the present tense. Like she was still alive. I wondered if he was in some kind of stage of denial.

When the coffee was done I poured out two mugs. I automatically put two teaspoons of sugar into his mug, along with a generous splash of cream.

He smiled. "Thanks. You remembered."

"Some stuff you don't forget."

"I blew it," Tal said suddenly. He set his mug down on the counter. "Christ. This last year. It's like a nightmare. The way I treated you. The things I put you through. I should have been the one who was shot, instead of her."

What did he want me to do—agree? Was he looking for absolution?

"You were the best thing that ever happened in my life," Tal said. "Remember how we met in that club? You flirted outrageously with me."

"My girlfriend dared me to," I said, "and you didn't seem to mind."

"You were so different from all the other girls I'd ever known. An original. So young and adorable . . ."

"And naive," I finished. "I was so impressed that a big society wheel like Talmadge Evans III would be interested in little old Weezie Foley."

He drank his coffee and fiddled with the spoons on the counter, lining them up, then stacking them, then rearranging.

"She didn't love me, you know," he said, playing with the spoons.

I raised an eyebrow.

"It's true. These last couple months, she was different. Bitchy. Impossible to please. You want to know a secret?"

"No. Drink your coffee."

"I think she had a lover. Yep. The other woman had another man. Pretty damn cute, don't you think?"

I wondered just how much he'd heard on the Savannah grapevine.

"She lied about where she was going. Had all these phony appointments with clients. I checked up on her once. She wasn't where she said she'd be. At first I was pretty pissed off. Then, hell, I didn't care. It was too late. I'd fucked things up big-time. There's another secret too. Want to hear?"

"It's too late for secrets," I said. "My head hurts."

"Just one more." He picked up a spoon, turned it, and looked at his reflection in the mirrored bowl. "The night she was killed? She got a phone call. I heard her pick up the phone. And then she left. I followed her."

"Is this true?" I asked. "Where was she going?"

"I dunno. I followed her down Victory Drive, then she ran through a yellow light. I got caught on the red light. A cop was on my tail. I didn't dare run it too."

"Which light at Victory?"

"Right there at the Bee Road," Tal said. "Not that it matters. She was probably going to meet him."

"Him. Who was it, do you know?"

He smiled and wagged a finger at me. "Uh, uh, uh. You said you didn't want to hear any more secrets."

"That one I'm interested in."

"Why?"

"Because she might have been meeting the person who killed her, you idiot. And right now, the police think that's me."

"I don't know who it was."

"But you have an idea."

"No. You know, I don't even know why Caroline went after me in the first place like that. Or why I fell so hard for her. She was prettier than you, sure, and younger. But she wasn't very nice."

"Gee. Thanks for the compliment."

"I think maybe she just enjoyed the challenge. Seeing if she could wreck our marriage."

"It worked," I said.

"After the first time, I felt awful. I told her the next day that I was sorry I'd done it. It was a mistake. Because I loved my wife."

I felt my face flush. I didn't want to hear any of this. True confessions at this point. Why? I was tired of poking and prodding at old hurts.

"Shut up now, Tal," I said dully. "Drink your coffee and go home."

He reached for my hand. "What's done is done," I said. "We can't go back." I took my hand away.

"Why not? I told you, it was all a mistake."

"Because I don't want to," I said. "I've got a new life. It's not much, but it's mine."

"I still love you," he said quietly. "That's a hell of a thing, isn't it?"

"You've got a funny way of showing it," I said.

"We could try again," he said. "I'm crazy about you, Weezie. That's the stupid thing. We never fought. We got along great. I must be insane. I must have been going through some midlife crisis when I cheated on you. The first time—that woman in Atlanta? Afterward, I wanted to die, I was so ashamed. And I swore I wouldn't slip again. And for two years I didn't. I was the most faithful husband in the world. Until Caroline."

"That first time? A woman in Atlanta? Three years ago?" I heard a buzzing in my ears, and the blood rushed to my face and it felt like my head would explode. "You fucked around on me three years ago?" I screamed. "Caroline wasn't the first? You shit! You fucking, lying, slime-sucking dog turd, son of a bitch prick shit bastard, dickhead."

I picked up my jadeite coffee mug, the one that fit so neatly in the palm of my hand, the one with the fresh-ground coffee and the aesthetically pleasing fresh cream, and I threw it in his smug son-of-a-bitching face.

"Jethro," I called, "get him!"

CHAPTER *31*

Saturday. Six A.M. I struggled out of bed and into my work clothes: baggy shorts, baggy shirt, sneakers. Swallowed four aspirin and washed them down with a Coke. My head was pounding from all the gin, wine, champagne, and self-pity I'd swallowed the night before.

It was just barely dawn, but a jaybird was already putting up a fuss at the bird feeder I'd set out on my side of the courtyard. As I was getting in the truck I flipped my own version of a bird in the general direction of the townhouse. "Die yuppie scum," I muttered.

I'd circled only five ads in the *Pennysaver*. It was August and Africa-hot in Savannah. Nobody wanted to fool around with a yard sale unless it was absolutely necessary. The first three sales were in and around Ardsley Park, downtown, and the historic district. My first stop of the day, at a cottage on St. Julian Street, yielded a couple good finds: a heart-pine kitchen table for sixty dollars, and a box of old brass wall sconces for five dollars. I saw two or three dealers I knew there, including Early Bird, who dropped what she was holding and scuttled away when I walked into the parlor where the cash-out had been set up. Everybody agreed it was too hot to work and prices were insane. Then we all paid up and headed out for the next sale.

I rode past the sale on Victory Drive that was supposed to open at seven o'clock, but the people were just starting to set up tables in their carport.

"Amateurs," I sneered, driving past to the next sale, on Forty-fourth, where half a dozen people milled around several tables heaped with stuff. I leaned out the window to take a look. Lots of racks of clothes, laundry baskets full of pots and pans, Tupperware, bad lamps. I drove on.

I almost didn't stop at the last sale I'd circled, a plain-Jane 1940s concrete block cottage on the 500 block of East Fifty-eighth street. The tables set up in the yard had piles of kids' toys, paperback books, and of course, the obligatory piece of exercise equipment—this time a NordicTrack exerciser.

I was about to give up and head over to Mr. B's on Waters for some grits and eggs when something caught my eye. I pulled the truck over to the curb to get a better look. There, in the shade of a crape myrtle, stood two lonely peely paint metal tulip chairs, in my favorite shade of turquoise.

The chairs hadn't been priced. I walked over to the knot of people pawing through the children's clothes and spotted the woman running the sale. You can always tell—they wear a fanny pack. She was in her mid-thirties, her face red and glistening from perspiration, and she was trying to coax a little girl into removing her bare tushy from a wooden potty chair.

The child had white-blond hair, a Mickey Mouse T-shirt, and her shorts down around her ankles.

"But Krystal, you're a big girl now," the woman was saying. "You make tee-tee in the big potty in the house. Let Mommy sell the potty chair, and we'll go to the store and buy you a new toy."

"No!" the child, who looked to be about four, screamed. "My potty."

"Excuse me," I said, tapping the woman on the shoulder. "How much for the yard chairs over there?"

"Krystal!" the woman snapped. "Give Mommy the potty. Right now."

"Noooo!" the child screamed.

"The chairs?" I repeated, a little louder.

"What?" the woman said. She was tugging at the child's hand. "Come on, Krystal. Somebody wants to buy the potty chair. Be a good girl and get up."

This was getting tiresome. I dug in the pocket of my shorts. Took out a dollar bill, and found half a bag of M&M's too.

"Hey, Krystal," I said, dangling the money and the candy in front of her tear-streaked eyes, "do you like M&M's?"

She sniffed. "Yes."

"Do you want some M&M's? And some money?"

Another sniff. "OK."

"Give Mommy the potty chair and I'll give you the candy and the money," I said, holding them about a foot away.

She stood, pulled up her pants. I gave her the money and the candy.

"Thank you," the mother said, grabbing up the potty chair.

"Eew," said the prospective buyer.

I turned around. Krystal had left one last souvenir in the potty.

"About the yard chairs," I repeated.

The woman glanced over at them. "Oh those. I guess you can have 'em for five dollars for the pair. But you'll have to load them yourself. My rat-fink husband took off to go get change an hour ago and he hasn't been heard from since."

Five bucks was a steal. I have a dealer in Atlanta who specializes in shabby chic "garden furnishings," and who pays me thirty dollars for anything with original paint.

"I'll load them myself," I promised, handing her five ones. I walked around the tables, just to make sure I wasn't overlooking anything. I wasn't.

But I went back to the woman, who was now hosing out the potty chair. "Do you have anything else old, like those chairs?"

"It's all out here in the yard," she said, straightening up. "Unless . . ."

"Yes?"

"There's a whole shed full of old crap in the carport," she said. "We put my husband's grandmother in a nursing home two years ago, and it's all just sitting there rotting, taking up room. The chairs wouldn't fit in there, so they've been out in the rain all these months. What an eyesore."

I peered over at the carport, which had one of those prefab aluminum toolsheds attached to it.

"Would you be interested in selling some of that old crap?"

"I'd be interested in pouring gasoline over the whole mess and taking a match to it," she grumbled. "But my husband might object."

"Well. If you're not interested." I picked up one of the chairs and started toward the truck.

"Wait a minute," she said. "Tell you what. I'll make you a deal. You take everything out of that shed, get it off my property before my husband gets back, and you can have it for, say, a hundred bucks."

She was walking toward the shed, standing in front of the door.

"Can I see what's in there first?" I asked.

"Nope," she said. "All or nothing."

Hmm. This was good. It reminded me of *Let's Make a Deal*. Let's see what's behind that door, Monty. Could be tripe. Could be treasure. I already had at least a hundred bucks of profit from the morning. I decided to go with door number one.

"I'll do it," I said.

She threw open the door. "Screw him," she said triumphantly.

I waded in headfirst. The shed was maybe ten by six feet. It smelled of mildew and cat piss. Not a bad sign when you're looking for old stuff.

"One more thing," the woman said, poking her head in the doorway. "If he comes back and you're still here, I'll tell him you're a looter."

Excellent. Now I was on *Mission Impossible*.

It was eight o'clock. I pulled the truck into the carport and started loading boxes. I didn't want to take the time to go through the loot right there, but there were encouraging signs, a pair of little 1940s mahogany end tables, a boxful of old pictures, some with decent carved gilt frames, a pair of matching crocodile-leather suitcases, with a matching crocodile train case, and a box whose open flaps revealed what looked like several sets of blue-and-white toile drapes with silk fringe. My mouth was watering. On the other hand, I also loaded an aluminum walker, an oxygen tank, and at least a case each of adult diapers and liquid nutritional supplement.

After forty-five minutes of intense lifting and lugging, I was done. I slammed the shed door, peeled five twenties off, and leaned out the window of the truck and handed it to the woman as I backed out of the driveway.

"You better go." She jerked her head toward a black Jeep pulling up at the curb. "That's my husband."

I gave the Jeep guy a friendly wave and boogied on down the road.

My first stop was at the St. Francis of Assisi thrift shop, where my mother helps out on Saturday mornings, pricing donations for resale.

I pulled the truck around back and rang the bell. Mama answered. She was wearing her flowered pink apron and a pin that said "May I Help You?"

"What's all this?" she asked, instantly suspicious.

"A donation," I said, handing her the walker. "Just a minute while I get the other stuff. It's a bunch of sickroom supplies. How about getting me a tax receipt while I unload?"

She disappeared inside the thrift shop. I unloaded some boxes of paperbacks, old clothes, the diapers, nutritional supplement, and, as an act of charity, a wooden rocker which I actually could have sold for cash money.

She handed me the tax receipt. "I've been calling you for three days."

"Sorry," I said. "I've been really busy."

"Your cousin Lucy died Wednesday. Didn't you see it in Thursday's paper?"

The only part of the paper I read on Thursdays is the classified ads. "No," I said. "Do I really have a cousin Lucy?"

"You remember Lucy," Mama insisted. "Eighty-six years old. She's on the McKuen side. You missed the wake. It was very nice."

"Sorry again," I said.

"Cousin Lucy had a house at Thunderbolt. The family wants to know if you'd like to buy her things. I'm in charge of cleaning it out so the house can be sold. Lucy was quite a collector, you know."

The only Cousin Lucy I remembered was a shrunken old gnome who chain-smoked Virginia Slims and terrorized everybody in the family so they'd buy Avon products from her. I'd never seen her house.

"I'll let you know," I promised, giving her a quick kiss. "I'll call."

After I'd dumped the excess cargo, I decided to run by Lester Dobie's shop. The heart pine table and brass sconces were right up his alley, and besides, I wanted to pick his brains a little.

Lester was at the front counter, rewiring a chandelier. Wires and bolts and pieces of crystal were strewn all over the counter. A pole fan was pointed at him, but it did little to stir up the hot, still air.

He looked up when I set the box of light fixtures on the counter.

"Hey, shug," he said. "What you got there?"

"Four pairs of brass wall sconces," I said.

He peered down into the box and frowned. "Dime a dozen," he grunted.

"Fifteen a pair, sixty bucks even," I said. It was a game we played. He ran down my merchandise, I ran up the prices.

"Give you fifty and you ought to be ashamed of yourself for taking advantage of a blind old man."

"Got a heart-pine kitchen table out in the truck," I said.

He pushed his sweat-soaked captain's hat to the back of his head. "Let's take a look."

"Not too bad," he admitted, running his hand over the smooth burnt-orange surface of the wood. He ran his hand on the underside of the table and down the legs. "Hand-pegged. What'd you give for it?"

"I'll take a hundred fifty," I said, ignoring his question.

"Hundred twenty. What else you got in there?"

"I'm not really sure," I said. I told him the story of how I'd cleaned out the storage shed on Fifty-eighth Street.

"Hand me that box of frames and stuff," Lester said. "Let's get inside out of this heat and take a look."

We took the box of pictures into his office and went through them one by one. Several were yellowed old religious prints: the Sermon on the Mount, the Last Supper, Jesus and the lost lamb.

"Junk," he said, setting them aside.

There was a pair of decent watercolor floral still lifes, probably the work of a talented amateur, a framed black-and-white photograph of what looked like a high school class reunion, and an oil painting of slaves picking cotton.

"Hey," I said, lifting it up for a better look. The frame, heavily carved gilt, was by itself worth the hundred bucks I'd given for all the contents. But the painting was intriguing.

Roughly eight-by-eleven, it portrayed a group of workers, white and black, stooped over, picking cotton in a field framed by moss-draped live oaks. The brushwork was skillful, with richly textured nuances, giving it a somehow wistful, somber look.

"Let's take it out of the frame, get a look at the signature," Lester said.

With a pair of needle-nose pliers he deftly removed the brads holding the painting in the frame. He handed me the frame and picked up a lighted magnifying glass.

"I'll be damned," he said, motioning for me to look.

"T. Eugene White" was the signature, in carefully looped letters.

"You've heard of him?" I asked.

"Just a minute," Lester said. He turned around in his swivel chair and plucked a book from the shelf behind his desk. He looked in the index, found what he wanted, turned to a page near the end of the book.

"T. Eugene White," the book said. "Edgefield County, S.C. 1872–1949. Exhibited at Southern Beaux Arts Society, Member American Society of Painters and Illustrators."

I picked up the book and looked at the title. *Twentieth-Century American Painters.*

"T. Eugene White is a listed painter," I said, a silly grin plastered on my face. "What else do you know?"

"Southern vernacular subject matter, very popular right now," Lester said. "I got the catalog for an exhibit they did at the Valentine Museum in Richmond; there's a T. Eugene White listed in it, and I think the Telfair, right here in town, has a White in its collection."

"Bottom line," I urged. "What's it worth?"

He scratched his chin. "Hard to say. Oil on board, very good condition, popular size, very popular subject matter. He's a low-country painter, and he's been dead for fifty years. You could probably sell it to any interior designer here in town for, say, two thousand."

"Which makes it worth at least three thousand, and that's just based on aesthetics," I said. "Could I do better? A lot better?"

"Sure," he said. "Take time, though. Might have to call around to some art dealers, see what's happening on the market right now. It could use a good cleaning. That'd up the value right away. I was you, I'd list it with a dealer in Atlanta or Charlotte, get 'em to take it on contingency."

"Oh jeez," I said, hugging the painting to my chest. "Oh jeez."

"You done good, Weezie," he said, patting me on the back. "Old T. Eugene White ought to bring you a nice little nest egg."

"Better than that," I said dreamily. "Maybe he'll bring me the Moses Weed cupboard."

"Moses Weed? You still scheming over that thing?"

"I am," I said, leaning closer. "Lester, have you heard anything about furniture from Beaulieu being sold around town? Anything about Lewis Hargreaves? I was at a dinner party last night and a woman there said she overheard somebody talking about Lewis selling a sideboard out of Beaulieu. But they haven't announced another sale yet."

"Haven't heard anything," Lester said. "But I can check in a hurry."

He picked up the phone.

"Lewis? Lester Dobie here. How you doin'? Look here, I got a client, a lady out at the Landings, got it in her head she needs some real Southern plantation furniture. I know you handle that sort of thing, and I was wondering if you had anything she might be interested in."

He listened and nodded. "Yeah, I know it's hard to come by. Damn shame about that sale out at Beaulieu being canceled. You hear anything about when they're gonna reschedule?"

Lester smiled. "Well that's good to hear. Take care, hear?"

He hung up the phone. "Lewis says he don't have any plantation stock right now. But he did say the sale's been rescheduled. For next Saturday."

I jumped up and down and hugged him. "Perfect. Now all I have to do is sell the painting before next Saturday. And hope Lewis hasn't already gotten his grimy mitts on my cupboard."

CHAPTER 32

*I* was unloading the truck when BeBe pulled into the lane behind the carriage house.

"Park in Caroline's spot," I said defiantly. "It's not like she's gonna need it."

"Won't that piss Tal off?"

"Fuck him," I said, glaring in the direction of the townhouse.

"Ooh, intrigue," she said. "Tell."

"First, help me get the rest of this stuff in the house."

When we'd unloaded, and I'd finally washed all the cobwebs and grime from my hair and body, I put on clean clothes and went downstairs. BeBe had gin and tonics waiting. Dogs are great, but very few of them will fix you a drink.

"You're smiling," she said. "So last night couldn't have been all that bad."

"Last night was a disaster," I said. "But I hit a good sale today, and I think maybe I can raise enough money to buy the Moses Weed cupboard."

She made a face. "Not that again."

"Yes, that again." I told her the story of the toolshed and the T. Eugene White painting. "I should clear a couple thousand, at least."

"Money is good," BeBe said solemnly. "But sex is better. What happened last night?"

I took a long hit of gin and tonic. It was icy and cleared my sinuses. Yum.

"It's the damnedest thing," I said. "Here I've been living like a nun the past year, and last night, I had not one but two men trying to put the moves on me."

"Daniel?"

"And Tal," I said grimly.

"Give me the good stuff first," she begged. "How did it go with Daniel?"

"All right."

"Weezie!" she yelled. "Don't play coy with me. Did you do the deed?"

I tried to look indignant. "Do I look that easy to you?"

She sighed. "Tell me you at least fooled around a little."

"Define fooling around."

She scrunched up her face and gave it her best consideration.

"Let's see. Tongue."

"Check," I said.

"Horizontal position."

"Check."

"Clothes removal."

I frowned. "Sort of."

"Whose?"

"Mine."

"Define 'sort of,'" she said.

"He was in the process. But my belt got kind of tangled. And then Jethro started barking, and it was Tal at the door, and Daniel peeled off in his truck."

"God." She giggled. "Just like in high school. Your boyfriend peeled off."

"Your high school maybe, not mine. And I would hardly call Daniel my boyfriend."

"You almost let him undress you," BeBe said. "If he's not your boyfriend, what is he?"

"Point taken."

"Back to Tal. What did he want?"

"He wanted me to share his pain," I said. "Asshole."

"What did he say to make you so mad?" BeBe asked. "Just the other night you were ready to rush over there and soothe his fevered brow. I thought you were thinking about a reconciliation."

"Never," I said. "Talmadge Evans is a contemptible, low-life, subhuman sack of crap."

"I could have told you that," BeBe said. "But what the hell did he do?"

"For one thing, he ate my dessert. I was planning on having that for breakfast."

"I thought you were planning on having Daniel for breakfast."

"Not just yet. But after last night, I will admit, there are possibilities there."

"Get a room next time," she advised.

"There may not be a next time. He looked pretty mad."

"He'll get over it. They always do. But let's get back to Tal."

"Oh yeah. He had the nerve to tell me that even though Caroline was prettier than me, and smarter than me, he'd come to the conclusion that it was me he loved—not her."

"Nice," she drawled.

"I haven't told you the absolute worst yet," I said. I'd been trying not to think about it since I'd thrown Tal out the night before, but it was like a canker sore, one you can't quit poking at. It hurt to think about, but I couldn't let it go.

"Caroline wasn't the first time," I said. "He'd cheated on me before. Three years ago. Some chick in Atlanta."

BeBe got up and took my glass and fixed me another drink.

"Men are such shits," she said.

"The worst of it is, right up until the moment he spilled his guts about that, I had this sort of secret deep-down feeling that maybe it could work out again. Is that sick or what?"

BeBe squeezed her lemon into her drink.

"Sweetie," she said. "Listen to me. I've been married three times, divorced three times. You may not want to believe this right now, but here's the sad news: You and Tal aren't done yet. Divorce is like a virus. You think you're over the shithead, then a couple months later, wham! You're flat on your back again, and you're not wearing your panties. It's called a stealth fuck. I wouldn't want this to get around, but yeah, I slept with all my ex-husbands after the divorce. It's kind of kinky, you know? Especially the feeling that you're making him cheat on the other woman—with his ex-wife."

"No way," I said flatly. "Even the thought of kissing him makes my flesh crawl. And don't forget—in my case the other woman is dead. And everybody thinks I killed her. That's past kinky. That's macabre."

BeBe raised her hands, palm out. "I'm just saying. OK? Don't be shocked if it happens. And think about this: how pissed off would Mother Evans be if she found out her baby boy went crawling back to bad old Weezie's bed?"

I laughed. "She'd probably castrate him with a dull butter knife."

"Hold that thought. It's gotta be a turn-on. But just remember, that's all this is gonna be. A little meaningless but therapeutic sex. And do me a favor, will you? Make him beg for it. I never did like Tal."

"Not gonna happen," I repeated.

I rooted around in the refrigerator and found a container of pimento cheese spread I'd made earlier in the week. There were some Waverly crackers too. "Hey, Babe," I said, spreading some cheese on a cracker. "You really slept with all of them? Even Howie?"

Howie was the ex-husband she caught ordering ladies' lingerie for his girlfriend off the Internet, and charging it to her American Express card.

"Especially Howie," she said firmly. "And afterward I made sure I left a pair of *my* panties in the glove box of his truck. Something to remember me by."

CHAPTER 33

*J*ames caught up with Jonathan near the Spanish-American War monument in Forsyth Park.

Jonathan slowed to a walk as James pedaled alongside him.

"I've already done three miles," Jonathan said. "Where have you been?"

"The bike had a flat tire," James said. "I had to stop at that gas station on Victory to pump it up, and I saw somebody I used to know, and they wanted to know why I quit the priesthood, and all that." He threw up his hands. "The usual chat. Sometimes I think I should write down the reasons on a business card and hand it out to people."

"You could just tell them you quit because you're gay."

"But that's not the reason," James said.

"No, but it would certainly stall the other questions," Jonathan said.

They circled Forsyth Park twice more, Jonathan running at a slow steady pace to allow James to keep up with him.

"I had dinner with Weezie last night," Jonathan said as they were halfway down the Drayton Street side of the park.

"Where?"

"At Merijoy and Randy Rucker's house, at supper club. Mother and I met Weezie, and her friend."

"Which friend is that?" James asked.

"His name is Daniel Stipanek," Jonathan said. "They seemed very taken with one another. Really a cute couple, was the consensus."

"This is the first I've heard of a boyfriend," James said. "But that's good. She needs to get on with her life. What's he like?"

"Nice," Jonathan said. "He's a chef at Guale, that restaurant Weezie's friend BeBe owns. He's well spoken, intelligent, and"—he grinned,—"he couldn't keep his hands off her all night. They left before dessert. Merijoy had the impression they wanted to be alone."

"They can't have been dating very long. Weezie's never even mentioned him to me."

"That doesn't mean anything," Jonathan said. "We've been dating for months now, and she doesn't know anything about me, does she?"

"No," James admitted. "She knows I'm seeing somebody. And she said she was glad. But she doesn't know who you are."

"For now, I think you'd better keep it that way," Jonathan said. He slowed again, put his hands on his hips, and bent forward. "Let's go get a drink," he said, pointing to the drinking fountain near the Confederate memorial.

James walked the bike to the fountain and they both took long drinks of the lukewarm water.

"There was some interesting talk at dinner last night. About Caroline DeSantos," Jonathan said. "None of it flattering."

"Was any of it useful—I mean, to Weezie?"

"Could be," Jonathan said. He told James about the real estate agents who'd shown the Gaston Street house to Caroline, and about her anonymous friend.

"You know I can't get involved in any of this," Jonathan said. "I've already told the DA that I have a conflict of interest. But I would suggest you talk to Weezie as soon as possible. Get her to tell you the story Anna and Emily Flanders told us."

"And then what?" James asked. "Do you think I should talk to the owner of that house on Gaston Street?"

"Yes," Jonathan said. "See if you can get a better description of this mystery man. And find out what kind of car he was driving."

James nodded. "I've been thinking about why Caroline was killed. If Weezie didn't kill her, who did?"

"That's what the cops want to know too," Jonathan said. "And by the way, I hear you've been promoted to saint status by Detective Bradley."

James made a dismissing motion. "All I did was try to cool him down, and call the EMTs. It really isn't that big a deal."

"It's a big deal to Jay Bradley," Jonathan said. "Don't underestimate the importance of having the lead detective in this case thinking he's indebted to you. It can only help Weezie's cause."

James got back on the bike. "If it helps Weezie, I guess I can let Jay Bradley think he owes me."

"What are you going to do next?" Jonathan asked.

"Next? I'm going to go home and take a long shower and then collapse," James said. "Then I'm going to take a look at Anna Ruby Mullinax's will."

"You got a copy? So soon? How did you swing that?"

"Simple," James said, pleased with himself. "One of the women in the probate clerk's office used to be in my parish here. I baptized her first child."

"Very good," Jonathan said. "I think you're finally figuring out how Savannah works."

James ran a comb through his wet hair. It was still thick and wiry, but the deep ginger color of his youth was a memory. Now there was more gray than red. With his glasses, he looked like what he was, a middle-aged lawyer, fast approaching the far side of his fifties.

He went into the study and pulled out the file containing the Mullinax will.

It was ponderous reading. He'd studied wills and estates what, twenty-five years ago? When he'd gone to law school following the seminary, he'd never really intended to practice law. Canon law had been his specialty, although he'd not had much use for it in his career as a parish priest.

After an hour he set the will aside. It was a seemingly clear-cut document, executed only two months earlier. In it, Miss Mullinax, being without any surviving relatives, left the bulk of her estate to a nonprofit entity called the Willis J. Mullinax Foundation. She also directed that her real property, Beaulieu Plantation, and all its contents be disposed of, with the proceeds from the sale to be distributed to the foundation. The will named Gerry Blankenship executor of the estate, and also director of the Mullinax Foundation.

Odd, James thought. But not strictly illegal. He'd also gone over the legal papers setting up the foundation. Its purpose seemed extremely vague. Although the documents provided that the foundation's funds were to be used "to provide vocational training and community leadership assistance to local youth and young adults," there were no directions about how this should be accomplished.

The sale of Beaulieu to the paper company should generate millions in revenue for the foundation, James knew. But how would that money be used for vocational training?

What James did not find odd or vague was the provision that the foundation be run by its director, Gerald Blankenship, at a salary "commensurate with his duties and responsibilities."

In other words, Gerry Blankenship could raid the foundation's coffers at will. Nice work if you can get it, James thought.

When he was through reading the file, he looked over the page of notes he'd scrawled on a yellow legal pad.

There was more research to be done. He wanted to find out when the Coastal Paper Products sale had taken place, and what the sale price had been.

He'd also made a note about the people who'd witnessed Anna Ruby's will. Grady and Juanita Traylor. He knew those names—but why?

He doodled on the notepad, drew arrows and dots, even a church steeple, hoping that the aimless sketching would free up his subconscious.

The phone rang. He picked it up.

"James?" It was his sister-in-law, Marian. She was breathless, excited.

"Hello, Marian," he said, sketching a bourbon bottle. "How are you?"

"I'm blessed, James. Really blessed."

"How nice," he said. Marian had always been something of a religious zealot. "So few of us these days stop to realize how fortunate we are."

"No, James, not fortunate. Blessed. I've had a vision, James."

He put down his pen.

"What kind of a vision? Where are you, Marian?"

"I'm at my cousin Lucy's house. She died last week, you know."

"God rest her soul." He said it automatically. "Did I know this cousin?" Marian's side of the family, the Brannens, was a huge, sprawling tangle of aunts, uncles, cousins, etc. Marian herself was one of eleven children.

"Lucy Sullivan McKuen, she was. On my mother's side," Marian said. "You remember Lucy. She was the Avon lady."

"Oh yes." He had a cabinet full of evil-smelling potions the old lady had badgered him into purchasing. Horrible person, with pink powdered cheeks and green-tinted eyelids.

"I've been out here at Lucy's house in Thunderbolt, sorting things out," Marian said. "So that the house can be sold. Lucy was a maiden lady, you know, so the cousins will inherit."

He was sketching again. "Uh-huh. Yes. How nice."

"James, Lucy had this statue. It was in the hallway, in a little niche, right near the phone. The Infant of Prague. I was sweeping up in there, and I accidentally knocked the statue over. Onto the floor."

He tsk-tsked. "I'm sure it was an accident. I hear they have some lovely statues over at the gift shop at St. Joseph's."

"It didn't break," she whispered.

"Thank heavens," he said. He started sketching the Infant of Prague, whom he remembered as a chubby-cheeked child dressed in a long robe with a high wimple sort of collar—and a halo, of course. He tried to remember the legend behind the Infant of Prague. He did know that the Infant was regarded as some sort of household mascot by old-line Catholics. His two sisters had Infant of Prague statues in their homes, and his own mother had had one prominently displayed on a windowsill in the kitchen—in this very house. He'd packed away most of his mother's trinkets when he'd taken possession of the house, but somehow he hadn't wanted to displace the Infant.

"James," Marian was saying, "I set the Infant on the kitchen counter so that I could wipe it down with Pine Sol. Lucy wasn't much of a house-keeper, God rest her soul. And then after I'd cleaned it and dried it off, I put it back in the hallway niche. I went back to my cleaning and sorting, and ten minutes later, I was back in that hall. I glanced over and the Infant was crying. The Infant wept!"

"My goodness." James did not know what to say.

"It's a miracle, don't you think?" she went on. "I got right down on my knees in the hallway. Well, first, I ran the sweeper. It's really shocking how dirty the house was. But after I ran the sweeper, I got down on my knees and said two decades of my rosary. Was that the right thing to do, James?"

He sketched faster. Now he was drawing Marian, and a set of rosary beads, and a crucifix, around the bottle of Four Roses. Marian had been a closet lush for as long as he'd known her. But having visions was a new development.

"Well, Marian," he said finally. "I'm sure it never hurts to spend some quiet time in prayer and reflection."

"I know why the Infant was crying, James. And that's why I called you. The Infant weeps for sins."

He put the pen down again. How much bourbon had she had? And how much did she know about his private life? He'd been so discreet. So circumspect.

"What sins? Why is the Infant weeping?"

"Weezie," Marian said. "He's weeping for Weezie."

"And what sin is Weezie supposed to have committed?" James was really perplexed. Weezie and Marian had never had a close relationship. Marian just didn't understand her daughter. But he knew she loved Weezie deeply.

"The divorce, of course," Marian said. "The church doesn't recognize divorce. It's an abomination. And what about that woman she killed? That's why the Infant weeps."

"Marian," he said sternly. "Weezie did not kill that woman. Your daughter is a kind, loving person. She is not a sinner. That divorce was not her idea. Tal was the adulterer, not Weezie."

"No," Marian said. "The Infant wants Weezie to repent. I prayed for an hour about this, James, and that's what the Infant wants. Talk to Weezie, James. She trusts you. You're her godfather. She'll listen to you. You're a priest."

"I'm not a priest anymore, Marian," James said, sighing. "And I can't ask Weezie to repent for a sin she didn't commit."

"I'll just have to keep praying then," she said serenely. And she disconnected.

CHAPTER 34

Weezie? Pick up the phone, Eloise. I know you're there."

I put aside the silver candlesticks I'd been polishing and did as I was told. Mama had been leaving messages since Saturday afternoon.

In my own defense, I'd been busy dealing with my toolshed treasures.

A phone call to a vintage luggage dealer in Dania, Florida, netted me two hundred dollars for the three pieces of crocodile luggage. The blue-and-white toile drapes had been a nice moneymaker too. They were French, beautifully made with silk linings and silk fringe. In all, there were eight panels and four shaped cornices. I got five hundred dollars for the lot from Mallery David, a high-end antique dealer whose shop is on Whitaker Street.

"Eloise!" Mama repeated sharply.

"Yes, ma'am," I said, picking up the phone. "I was just fixing to call you. How's Daddy?"

"He's fine," she said. "Did your uncle James speak to you?"

"About what?"

"Penance," she said. "For your sins. I asked him to talk to you, but I guess he's chosen to overlook your shortcomings."

Uh-oh. It was Sunday, and only eleven o'clock. Had she gotten into the Four Roses this early?

"Mama, I am sorry for all my sins," I said. "And I promise, I'll call you more often. OK? We'll talk soon. Love you." I made kissing noises and hung up.

She called right back. "Eloise, I wasn't finished talking to you. Daddy and I want you to come over for dinner. I'm making your favorite pot roast."

I was barely able to suppress my gag reflex. Mama had discovered a recipe on the back of an onion soup mix box. I'd actually had this pot roast recipe at other people's houses and liked it. But in Mama's hands, the roast came out dry as sawdust, with a bizarre sulfurous aftertaste.

"I don't think I can make it today," I said. "I've got a lot of work to do. I bought a whole shedful of stuff yesterday and I've got to get it all ready to sell."

"You can go back to work after lunch," Mama said, as if that settled it. "And after we eat, you can come over to Cousin Lucy's house to decide what you want to buy. The cousins have agreed to let you have first pick. Isn't that nice?"

"Terrific," I said.

"One o'clock," Mama said. "Don't be late. I don't want my roast to dry out."

I disconnected. Wouldn't want that yummy roast to get ruined. Yeech.

I finished with the candlesticks. They were sterling, with square bases and three arms, probably from the twenties. Silver sells really well in Savannah, and I knew a couple dealers who would be happy to pay me $150 for the pair.

There were a few other pieces of silver that still needed polishing, but they'd have to wait 'til later. Right now I needed to clean up for the command performance at my parents' house.

But first, I called Uncle James.

"I understand my mother wants you to talk to me about repenting my sins."

"Oh jeez. She talked to you, huh?"

"I'd sort've been avoiding her, but she nailed me a few minutes ago. Now I've got to go over there for lunch in a little while. I thought maybe you could fill me in on what's going on. She sounded really strange."

He laughed.

"No," I said, "stranger than usual. What's with the sin stuff? I knew she'd been going to that karaoke church, but this is a whole new approach."

"She's having visions," James said. "At your cousin Lucy's house. There's a statue of the Infant of Prague. She says it's crying real tears. So she prayed about it, and the Infant told her he's crying for you. Because of your sins. You know, the divorce, and the homicide."

I felt sick to my stomach. "My own mother believes I'm capable of murder?"

"Maybe it's the change of life," James suggested.

"She went through that ages ago, remember? When she dyed her hair black and bought that Subaru?"

"Well, something strange is going on with her. A plaster statue is telling her this stuff, if it makes you feel any better."

"I guess I better go see if I can settle her down. I don't suppose you'd like to join us for a lovely family meal, would you?"

"Oh jeez. I'd love to. But my stomach's been acting up."

"It's pot roast," I said.

"I think I feel a cramp coming on," he said.

"Coward."

Mama had the dining-room table set with her good microwave dishes. The pot roast *smelled* delicious, surrounded by canned peas and watery instant mashed potatoes.

We said the blessing and Daddy hacked valiantly away at the roast with a carving knife, eventually slapping two cinderlike slices on my plate.

"Gravy?" Mama passed the sauceboat to me. I spooned the greasy-looking glop over my meat, hoping to moisten it enough to chew.

Mama and Daddy exchanged looks. I knew I was in for it.

"Uh, Eloise, uh," Daddy started.

"Joseph, talk to her," Mama said.

Daddy stared down at his plate. "I was wondering, uh, what kind of tires you're running on that truck of yours?"

"Tires?" I was drawing a blank. "I don't know. Round. Black. Rubber, I suppose. Do they still use rubber to make tires?"

"Hell no," Daddy said, getting worked up. "It's all synthetics now. Come out of who knows where. China or Korea or someplace. I was noticing those tires of yours are looking pretty bald. What you need is a good set of steel-belted radials. American-made."

"OK," I said. Maybe dinner wouldn't be so bad. Maybe we were just going to talk about tires. "I guess I am due for new tires, now that you mention it."

"Joseph!" Mama said sharply.

"We'll, uh, talk about that later," Daddy said. "Right now your mama is very concerned. Uh, when was the last time you went to church?"

They both know the only time I go to mass is with them, to Midnight Mass on Christmas Eve. I decided to head the discussion off at the pass.

"What's this all about, anyway?" I asked, looking directly at Mama. "Uncle James said you've been having visions. Is that true?"

"The Infant of Prague is weeping. For your sins," she said.

"A statue? A statue thinks I committed murder? Mama, it's impossible."

"It's not impossible," she snapped. "Not for a believer. Now finish your food. We'll go over to Lucy's and you can see for yourself."

"I didn't kill her," I said, reaching for a roll. These, at least, I knew would be edible, since they came directly out of a Pepperidge Farm carton.

We ate in silence. Mama's hand rested silently on her tea glass. Twice she went to the kitchen for refills. She was looking extremely glassy-eyed.

"I'll clear," I said, jumping up from the table as soon as I'd pushed the food around my plate for a sufficient amount of time.

Mama looked up, surprised.

"Your daddy always does Sunday dishes."

"Not today," I said. "You two go on in the den and put your feet up. I'll have the dishes done in a jiffy, and then we can take a ride over to Lucy's."

After I heard the television switch on in the den, I closed the kitchen door and went to work. It took only a few minutes to rinse the dishes, load them in the dishwasher, and wipe down the counters and stove.

I went through the cupboards, one by one, and the drawers too. I finally found the bottle of Four Roses in the bottom of Mama's ironing basket. It was only about half full. I dumped most of the bourbon into the sink, leaving about an inch in the bottom of the bottle. I added water until the bourbon was at its original level, then went looking for something to add for color.

Vanilla would make it smell wrong. Mama's bottle of Gravy Magic was on the counter, but it would make the bourbon taste wrong. Then I spotted the pitcher of iced tea on the counter. Perfect. I added the tea to the water. It was a dead ringer for Four Roses.

"All set," I said, standing in the door of the den.

↤

Cousin Lucy's house was a neat redbrick box on a narrow street in Thunderbolt, which used to be a fishing village on the edge of the Wilmington River, but the shrimp mostly played out in the 1980s, and now Thunderbolt is just a suburb of Savannah.

Mama unlocked Lucy's front door. I stepped inside and nearly passed out. The place smelled like the bottom of an ashtray.

"Whew!" I said, fanning my face. "Now I know why that statue's crying."

"Blasphemer. Let me just air it out a little," Mama said, bustling around drawing the drapes and opening windows.

The air helped, but not much. I looked around the living room. Everything was a dull yellow; walls, floors, drapes, and even the frayed and spotted wall-to-wall carpet. Everything had a thin nicotine-tinged sheen to it.

"Isn't this nice?" Mama said, running her hands over the arm of a sofa. "Cousin Lucy spent a lot of money on this furniture, you know."

The sofa was an overstuffed roll-arm number from the forties, with maroon cut-plush upholstery. There were two matching armchairs too. I'd have snapped them up in a minute at another house, but here they had that sick yellow tobacco sheen. To be usable, they'd have to be stripped down to muslin and re-covered. Not an inexpensive proposition.

"Look at this dining-room set," Mama said, moving through the arched doorway into the next room.

It was a good solid Grand Rapids, Michigan–made mahogany dining suite, again from the 1940s. There was a table, six chairs, a sideboard, and a china cabinet. I saw sets like this in every other estate sale in Savannah.

"Real antique," Mama said. "We were thinking maybe a thousand dollars for the whole set. A bargain, right?"

"Very nice," I said, trying to sound noncommittal. The varnish on all the furniture had blackened with age and would probably need to be stripped. Again, not too profitable.

"The bedrooms are back this way," Mama said. I followed her into the hallway. She stopped in front of a small niche in the wall and fell to her knees.

"It's the Infant of Prague," she whispered, gesturing toward the niche.

The Infant of Prague looked like every other statue I'd seen in every other little old Catholic lady's house I'd ever been in. Painted plaster, with a bemused look on its face. But no tears, that I could see.

"I don't see anything," I said.

"Because he knows you're not a believer," she said.

"Whatever."

I poked my head into what must have been the master bedroom. It had the usual assortment of religious pictures, plaques, and shrines. The furniture wasn't too bad. Lucy's bed was a high-backed carved Victorian piece, and there was a matching oak bowfront dresser with mirror, a washstand, and a nightstand. The cigarette smell, however, drove me back into the hallway.

"We've gotta get some air in here," I said, coughing.

Mama and I managed to get some windows open, and I found an old box fan in a closet, which I set up in the hallway to create cross-ventilation.

She stood in the doorway of Lucy's room. "This oak stuff is junky, I know, but I think maybe Lucy's mother passed it along to her."

The "spare" bedroom had a set of badly scarred mahogany furniture consisting of twin four-poster beds, a highboy, a lowboy, a dressing table, and two nightstands. It was of the same era as the dining-room furniture, good, solid, respectable, boring brown furniture.

The bedspreads were pink chenille, with large rose medallions. If I could ever get the essence of Virginia Slims washed out of them, I could sell them on the Internet for a hundred dollars for the pair.

"Well?"

"Let me think about it."

Her face fell. "I told the cousins you'd probably buy everything."

"I know," I said apologetically. "But I just took on a bunch of inventory yesterday. All my money is tied up in it, and until I sell it all, I just don't have any cash ready to lay out for more stuff."

"We could wait," Mama said.

"No," I said. "Tell you what. I'll take the stuff in the two bedrooms. Would three hundred be enough?"

"For that trashy stuff? But what about that beautiful antique dining-room set? Surely you'd rather have that. It's real mahogany, you know."

"It's lovely," I lied. "But I don't have the room to store furniture. I think you and the cousins should have an estate sale. Wouldn't that be nice?"

"I suppose," she said, wavering a little.

"Good," I said, picking up my purse. "If you give me the key, I'll come back after I drop you off at home, and I'll load the bedroom furniture in the truck."

"You can't lift that heavy stuff," Mama said. "And you know your daddy's back."

"I'll get a helper," I said. And I had a very good idea of the sort of helper I needed. I got my checkbook out. "Who do I make the check out to?"

She pressed her lips together. "Well, the cousins said they'd prefer cash. You know, what with your arrest record and all."

CHAPTER 35

*I* really did need help moving all that heavy furniture, I told myself while driving over the bridge to Tybee. I circled past his house twice. His truck was there. It was his day off. A little heavy lifting, I told myself. That's all I wanted.

Right.

I knocked, but there was no answer. From inside the house I heard the high-pitched whine of a power saw. Go home, I told myself. Call Karl. Karl is my handyman. He does odd jobs for me. Like moving furniture. Karl is fifty and bald, and he doesn't believe in deodorant. But he has his own moving dolly and a ramp for his pickup truck. Call Karl, I told myself, opening Daniel's front door and stepping over a pile of lumber.

But Daniel was standing with his bare back to me, bending over a board laid across a sawhorse, moving a power saw smoothly across the board. His shoulder muscles rippled as he worked, and I instantly forgot about Karl.

Daniel was sweaty and half naked, and his jeans hung just right on his hips, which were narrower than his shoulders, and I could see the waistband of his Jockey underwear. And I wondered, since when did I get turned on by seeing a man's underwear, and I told myself, since right now.

"Daniel!" I called loudly.

He finished the cut, and the end of the board clattered to the linoleum floor.

"Daniel!" I called again. He turned around, with the saw still in his hands. His eyes widened in surprise. He cut the power switch.

"Hey," he said. "What are you doing here?"

Good question. What was I doing? He had sawdust in his chest hair. I wanted to wipe it off. Start there. No. Bad. Very bad. I closed my eyes to try to rid myself of the mental image I had, of the two of us, rolling around in a bed of sawdust.

"I, uh." My voice came out a squeak, like Minnie Mouse inhaling helium. "I sort of need a favor."

He put the saw down on the floor and grabbed a T-shirt from the back of a chair and pulled it over his head. Good. Much better. I could think clearer without looking at his chest, not to mention the washboard belly.

"Yeah?" he said casually. "What kind of a favor?"

Daniel walked over to a red Igloo cooler and pulled out a bottle of Rolling Rock. He held it up toward me. "Want a beer?"

Yes. A beer. Very good for clearing up voice problems. No. I had work to do.

"No thanks," I said. "I just bought a load of furniture, and I want to move it out of the house it's in. Just up the road in Thunderbolt."

"In Thunderbolt," he repeated.

"The guy who usually helps me move stuff is out of town," I said. Technically, this was true, since Karl technically lives in Port Wentworth, which is, technically speaking, an incorporated city, not a part of Savannah per se, thusly, out of town.

"The furniture is actually in my mother's cousin's house. I guess that would make her my cousin too," I nattered on. "She died last week, and I'm buying some of the furniture, sort of as a favor to my mother. But I need to move the stuff so they can get the house ready to sell."

Daniel took a swig of beer. He sat on the edge of the sawhorse. "And when you think of manual labor, you think of good old Daniel."

I frowned. "No. Well, yes. I mean, you're strong. You work out. I can't move the dressers by myself. They're big and heavy. Not to mention the beds."

Beds. I groaned inwardly. Dumb. Now I was blushing beet red.

"Beds, huh?" Daniel said. "Why don't you ask your ex-husband to give you a hand with those? He looks like he'd be the handy type."

"I wanted to talk to you about that," I said, not looking up. "I want to apologize. It's not what you think. He was drunk. I've never seen him like that before."

"What did he want?" Daniel's voice was light. No big deal.

"Pity," I said. "He wanted me to know things hadn't worked out with Caroline. He wanted me to know that he misses me."

I looked up at him, hoping for some glimmer of understanding. He just nodded, like he'd heard it all before.

"Actually," I said, correcting myself, "I think he made it pretty clear it isn't really me he misses, as much as my cooking. And my coffee mugs."

"Coffee mugs?"

"He's a WASP," I said. "Very repressed. His mother still buys most of his clothes."

"It's not just your cooking he misses," Daniel said, watching me. "He's still in love with you."

"You think?"

"He was practically baying at the moon last night," Daniel said.

"He ate my chocolate seduction and spilled wine on the carpet. I was afraid he'd yak all over my sofa," I said. "I kicked him out."

"This time," Daniel said. He took another long swig of beer.

"What's that supposed to mean?"

"You kicked him out because he was drunk and acting out. But if he showed up at your door sober, all pressed and showered, it'd be a different story. You'd go running right back to him."

"No," I said, lifting my chin. "It's over. I'm over him. That's what I was trying to show you last night. On the sofa."

Daniel sighed. "Were you trying to show me—or were you trying to show him? Trying to make your ex-husband jealous, so he'd realize what a good thing he was missing out on? You had to know he'd see my truck parked out there. Hell, Tal was probably looking in the windows at us. Is that some kind of turn-on for you? Some sort of sick O. J. Simpson deal?"

"No," I shouted. "God. Is that what you think of me? You think I'm playing games with you?"

He crossed his arms over his chest. "You tell me. One minute you're telling me not to touch you or look at you, the next thing I know you come downstairs wearing nothing but a bathrobe."

"It was a *kimono*," I said. "And I was covered from my neck to my ankles."

"And you were naked underneath," he shot back. "Talk about your mixed messages."

"OK," I said, choking back the tears, determined not to let him see me being a crybaby. "Never mind. If you think I'm a big tease, if you think I'm playing games with you, never mind. I'm going now. Sorry to have insulted you."

With great dignity and deliberation, I turned around to leave.

"Shit," I heard him mutter.

"You're making me crazy, you know that?" he called after me. "I move back to Savannah, think I'm gonna have a nice, uncomplicated life. Cook a little, fish a little, fix me up a beach shack, maybe sleep with a waitress or two. Nice and slow and simple. And then you walk in and screw everything all to hell."

"Sorry to inconvenience you," I said, not bothering to turn around, my hand on the front door.

"Wait a minute," he said. "Just let me lock the place up and I'll help you move the damn furniture. But I'm not moving any pianos, and I'm not doing any second-story stuff. You understand?"

I sniffed. "I understand."

CHAPTER 36

"Whew," Daniel said as he stepped into the living room at Cousin Lucy's house.

"I warned you."

He looked around the living room, ran a finger over an end table coated with nicotine sheen. "Just think what the woman's lungs must have looked like," he marveled. "How old was she when she died?"

"Ninety-three," I said. "The tar was probably the only thing keeping her alive." I pointed toward the hallway. "The bedrooms are back that way."

He poked his head into the guest room. "Start here?"

"Why not?"

I stripped the chenille spreads off both beds, followed by the sheets and the rest of the linens.

"Almost looks like somebody's been staying here," Daniel said, pointing toward the open closet door.

A row of blouses and slacks hung neatly from the clothes rod. "Hey," I said, pulling out a familiar pink flowered number, "this is my mother's."

I picked up a pillow and sniffed it. Aqua Net hair spray and Four Roses. Marian Foley's signature scent.

"I'll be damned," I said. "She's been sleeping in this bed."

"So?"

"So, I wonder why she didn't mention it," I said.

"Maybe she stayed here when your cousin was sick," Daniel suggested.

"I guess," I said, walking around the room, looking for other signs of occupancy. The dresser drawers were empty. I walked into the pink and gray tiled bathroom and opened the medicine cabinet.

It was like opening the door to a time machine. There was a box of Dorothy Gray dusting powder. A tube of "Naughty Nude" Flame-Glo lipstick, a midnight blue bottle of Evening in Paris cologne. Doan's pills. A bottle of Lydia Pinkham's Female Tonic. St. Joseph's cough syrup, a brown bottle of tincture of Merthiolate. The only thing in the cabinet that didn't look like it hailed from the Eisenhower administration was a squat plastic pill bottle on the top shelf.

I picked it up and read the label. "Lucy McKuen. Take 1 tablet as needed for anxiety. Xanax." The bottle was half full.

The Infant of Prague statue was in its niche in the hallway, next to the telephone table. It wasn't weeping, but I could swear it almost winked at me.

I went out to the kitchen. Mama had started sorting things out there. The cupboards had been half emptied, and boxes on the countertop were loaded with pots and pans and bits of kitchenware. I rummaged around in the cabinets and drawers and found the bottle of Four Roses in the pull-out ironing-board cupboard. At least Mama was consistent.

"Weezie?" Daniel stood in the doorway, holding the headboard for one of the guest-room beds. "What's going on?"

I showed him the bottle of Four Roses and the Xanax. "My mother's been having visions. She says that statue in the hallway is crying real tears and giving her revelations. Now I think I understand."

He took the pill bottle and read the label. "Xanax. Some kind of tranquilizer?"

"Yeah," I said. "Heavy-duty tranquilizers. The prescription was filled on Friday, according to the label on the bottle."

"So?"

"Cousin Lucy died last Wednesday," I said. "And this bottle had thirty tablets when it was filled, according to the label. There aren't that many in here now. It's half empty."

"Your mother?" A look of concern crossed his face.

I nodded. "She's been dosing herself with Cousin Lucy's tranquilizers. And washing down the Xanax with a bourbon chaser. Sleeping here too. I had no idea."

"What are you going to do?"

"I don't know," I said. "She's been a closet drinker since I was in high school." I looked at Daniel and felt shame and dread wash over me. It was the first time I had ever admitted to anybody anything about Mama's drinking.

"It's a big secret, you know?" I said, my voice breaking. "She always has a glass of iced tea in her hand. But we all know it's not really tea. It's really pretty subtle. She starts sipping around noon, and then she takes a long nap, and then she wakes up and burns dinner."

I heard my voice trailing off. "Poor Daddy. He's had to live with it all these years, and he's never said a word against her. I got out when I was eighteen, moved out and married Tal. But he's stayed there and put up with Mama. She starts dinner, then forgets about it, and everything's ruined. Daddy just goes out and gets a pizza or Chinese. Cook's night out, he calls it, like it's a big joke."

Daniel slipped his arm around my shoulder. As if it were the most natural thing in the world. He gave me a comforting squeeze.

"Has anybody ever suggested she get help?"

I managed a choked-sounding laugh. "One time she passed out. Right in the middle of Thanksgiving dinner. She went to the kitchen to get the cranberry sauce and just sort of fell out on the floor. Uncle James and Daddy had a long serious talk that day. And the next day, they told me Mama was going in the hospital. Because of some vague female problem. I was only fourteen or fifteen, but I figured out it was some kind of alcohol rehab. Mama hated the place. She called every night, crying and begging Daddy to bring her home. And after a week, he did."

"Was she sober?"

"For a couple months," I said. "And then the iced-tea glass was back."

He held the pill bottle up to the light. "Probably not a good idea to mix these babies with booze—right?"

"Probably not," I said. "Thank God she's apparently been sleeping over here." I shuddered. "I don't want to think about the havoc she could wreak trying to drive home after taking Xanax with a Four Roses shooter."

"Shouldn't you talk to your dad about this?" Daniel asked. "This is pretty serious, Weezie."

"I know. But I can't talk to him. I love my dad. He's a great guy. But we don't talk about problems in my family."

"What do you talk about?" Daniel asked.

"Tires. Religion. Hillary Clinton. He thinks Hillary Clinton is Satan. We just don't talk about anything personal. I never even told them about the divorce."

"You're kidding."

"I told James. He broke the news to them. They were devastated. They thought Tal was the greatest thing since sliced bread. I guess what I'll do is talk to James about this. But I can't leave these pills here. She could kill herself with these things. Or kill somebody else."

I went back into the bathroom and opened up the other pill bottles in the medicine cabinet. The Doan's pills weren't an exact match, but Mama is nearsighted anyway and rarely wears her glasses. They would do. I poured the Xanax out on the top of the toilet tank and put the Doan's pills in the Xanax bottle. I scooped the Xanax up and put them in the Doan's pill bottle, which I stuffed in the pocket of my jeans.

Daniel was waiting for me in the kitchen, where I poured out half of the Four Roses and diluted the rest with water from the tap. "I switched pills," I told him. "She won't be having any problems with menstrual cramps, and hopefully, the Infant of Prague will quit tattling on me to her."

"Weird," Daniel said. He took my hand and kissed the back of it. He put his hands on my shoulders and turned me so that I was facing him. With his thumb he wiped away a tear that had somehow escaped.

"Families suck," he said.

He kissed me. Gently at first, and then more insistently. His tongue slipped into my mouth, and he moved his hands slowly up my back, and I arched forward to get closer to him. I heard the faint sound of my bra snap popping, and then his hands were cradling my breasts, and I gasped a little, and then he had me backed up against Cousin Lucy's yellow Formica countertop, and I heard something fall in the sink and break, but there were other things to think about.

Like that sawdust on Daniel's chest. I pulled his T-shirt off, and he returned the favor, and we were half-naked, chest to chest, and it was so lovely. He worked his knee in between my thighs, and I dug my fingernails into the small of his back, and then he was bent over, doing something interesting with his tongue on my left nipple when there was a sudden sharp rap at the kitchen door.

"Jesus Christ," Daniel muttered.

I jumped backward and knocked a stack of jelly glasses to the floor, where they smashed into a million pieces.

"Anybody home?" a woman's voice called from the other side of the door. "Marian? Is that you?"

I scrambled around on the floor until I found my shirt. I pulled it over my head, sending bits of broken glass raining into my hair.

"No," I called back, trying to catch my breath. "It's Eloise. Marian's daughter. Who's that?"

Daniel found his shirt and put it on. I motioned for him to get out of the kitchen.

"It's Alice. Your mother's cousin. I just came by to pick up a few things. Your mama said it would be all right. I thought maybe that truck was hers."

"Oh sure, Alice," I said, picking bits of glass out of my hair. "Just give me a minute. Mama's got this door dead-bolted and double locked."

Thank God, I thought.

I was opening the door when I saw a bit of hot pink lace out of the corner of my eye. My Victoria's Secret Miracle Bra—it was dangling from the knob of the cabinet under the sink.

Alice rushed into the kitchen and folded me into a hug. I backed up to the sink, hoping to block her view of my missing bra.

"Well, Weezie," Alice gushed, "it's been ages since I've seen you. You weren't at the wake, were you?"

Alice was a tall woman, Mama's age, but she looked nothing like my mother. She wore paint-spattered blue jeans and a tie-dyed T-shirt and Birkenstock sandals, and her wiry gray hair was in a braid that hung down past her shoulder blades.

"I feel awful about missing the wake," I lied, "but I was away on a buying trip and didn't find out until I got back."

Alice wasn't really listening. She looked around the kitchen at the mess. "What happened in here?" she asked, pointing at the broken glass.

"Just stupid old me," I said. "I was trying to help Mama out by packing up the stuff on that top shelf and my foot slipped and I knocked over the whole stack of glasses on the top of the counter."

"You weren't cut, were you?" she asked, stepping closer.

"I'm fine," I said, backing away so that she wouldn't notice my braless state. "You just go on ahead and get what you want out of the house. I want to sweep up this mess before somebody steps in it and gets hurt." I smiled and made a little shooing motion with my hand.

"Well," Alice said tentatively, "if you're sure. There's a cordial set and glasses that I've always liked. It's in the dining room. I'll just step in there and see about packing it up."

"Good idea," I said brightly. "You do that."

As soon as she was out of the room I grabbed the bra and threw it inside the cupboard under the sink.

"Oh," I heard Alice say from the dining room. "Hello. I didn't know Weezie had company."

Daniel came out of the hallway with the footboard of one of the maghogany beds. "Hello," he said, and he walked toward the front door without stopping.

"Alice," I said, walking into the dining room with an empty cardboard box and some newspaper for wrapping, "that's my friend Daniel. He's helping me move the bedroom sets. I bought them." And then I added. "For cash."

"How nice," she said, studying Daniel's broad shoulders as he hoisted the footboard into the truck. I bit my lip. His shirt was on backward. Alice gave me a broad wink. "How very, very nice."

"Here," I said, wanting to look busy, "let me help you wrap those glasses."

She had the china cabinet open and was setting the cordial glasses on the sideboard. "Oh no. Don't let me interrupt you. Go right on with what you were doing before I got here."

My mind flashed wistfully on what we'd been doing before she interrupted. If only, I thought. BeBe was right. Next time, we get a room.

After she'd packed the decanter and cordial glasses, Alice flitted around the house, picking up a few more odds and ends to take home.

"Sure I can't help you pack that stuff?" I asked, watching Daniel plod past with the bed rails.

"Absolutely not," she said. "You go help your friend. I'll just take one last look around out in the kitchen, and then I'll be on my way."

I went into the guest bedroom and started taking drawers out of the dresser. It occurred to me to wonder where Mama would sleep after we'd moved the beds. The sofa probably. Once she'd mixed Xanax and bourbon, she probably didn't care where she slept. Although that would change a little, now that she'd be taking forty-year-old Doan's pills with half-strength Four Roses.

I took the stack of drawers out to the driveway and handed them up to Daniel, who was standing in the bed of the pickup, arranging some old blankets around the headboards.

"Is she leaving anytime soon?" he asked, staring toward the door.

"One more look around and she's out of our hair," I said, secretly enjoying his look of disappointment.

"Hey," I said, watching to see if Alice was watching. "Come here. I've got a secret to tell you."

"What?" He looked wary, but he leaned over the bed of the pickup truck. I put my lips to his ear and quickly flicked my tongue in, then whispered, "Your shirt's on backward, lover boy."

I turned and walked quickly back toward the house, giving my behind what I hoped was a sexy little swish.

I was rewarded with a low but appreciative wolf whistle.

Alice was in the kitchen, strapping tape around a large cardboard box.

"Found a few other little odds and ends," she said, patting the box. "It will be a comfort, having some of Lucy's things to remember her by."

"I'm glad," I said. Alice kissed me on the cheek, hefted her box onto her hip, and went out the back door to load her treasures in the trunk of her car.

Daniel stood in the driveway and watched Alice back her Plymouth into the street.

"What was that you were saying about families—back there in the kitchen?" I asked.

"They suck," he said, scowling. "Just how many more cousins does your mother have?"

"No more than a dozen," I said.

"And are they all coming over here today to root around in this house?"

"Knowing Mama, I'd say there's a good possibility. It's a pretty close family. And Lucy never married, so all her stuff is up for grabs."

"OK." He started back for the house. "Might as well get those beds moved. Since we won't be using them."

He stood in the master bedroom and stared at the high-backed bed.

"This is nice," he said, running his fingers over the carved frieze of oak leaves and acorns.

I took a closer look. "Yeah, it really is, now that you mention it. Are you in the market for a bed?"

"I've got a waterbed still in storage. Haven't had time to set it up yet."

I wrinkled my nose. Waterbeds. I put them in the same category as crushed velvet Nehru jackets. "What do you sleep on?"

"There was an old sofa in the house when I moved in. It works."

"It's a nice bed," I said. "And the dressers are good too. Not too girly."

He looked around the room. "You like this stuff?"

"Sure," I said. "I can sell bedroom furniture like this just about anywhere. The stuff in the other room, that beat-up mahogany, that'll take a little work. I'm gonna slap some white paint on it, sand the corners down, beat it up a little more, put some glass knobs on it, and sell it as shabby chic."

"How would this oak stuff look in my house?"

"It would look great," I said. "Do you like old stuff?"

"I guess. I like the stuff at your place. I like the way you put things together."

"Thanks," I said, smiling.

"I think I'll hire you," Daniel said.

"To do what?"

"Put my place together," he said. "That crap in storage is worthless. I've never really had anything good. Maybe now is the time. You could do that, couldn't you? Buy stuff. Make it look right. How about it?"

"I'm not an interior designer," I said. "I just buy and sell junk. And I keep the junk I like. That's all. What makes you think I could put your place together for you? I don't even know you all that well."

He came very close. Put his arms around my waist. "I like you. I like the stuff you like. Come on, what do you say? Wanna play house?"

"You really want me to?" I was feeling suddenly shy. An hour ago I'd been nearly naked with Daniel, but playing house? That was something different. And speaking of different, something was missing. I looked down at my T-shirt and saw my erect nipples. He saw them too.

"Hello," he said, kissing my neck.

"My bra," I yelped. "I almost left it in the kitchen. God forbid Mama finds it when she goes looking for her bourbon."

He followed me into the kitchen. I knelt down and opened the cupboard under the sink. There was a can of Comet, a roach motel, and a box of Brillo pads. No pink lace.

"Crap," I said, remembering Alice's cardboard box. "Mama's cousin stole my Miracle Bra."

"I told you," Daniel said, pulling me to my feet. "Families suck."

CHAPTER **37**

e left the oak stuff in Daniel's truck in Thunderbolt and took the mahogany furniture back to the carriage house. I parked the truck in my slot in the lane. Daniel grimaced at the sight of Tal's car parked there.

"I don't like this."

"It's where I live," I said.

"It's where your ex-husband lives too."

"I'm not moving," I said, gripping the steering wheel with both hands. "The carriage house is mine. I found it, I fixed it up, and I'm staying here."

"Doesn't it bother you, him living maybe fifty yards away? Knowing he's watching you coming and going? Staring out the window at you?"

"A little," I admitted. I couldn't find the words to tell him how wretched it made me feel, moving out of the townhouse, or how it felt to see Caroline standing in what had been my kitchen, knowing she was carpeting over the hardwood floors I'd stripped, tearing down the wallpaper I'd pasted up, painting over the colors I'd lovingly picked for every room in the house.

"It's freakin' sick, is what it is," Daniel said. "There's a whole town here, Weezie. Savannah is loaded with old houses you could live in—and none of them have *him* living in the front yard. What's so special about this place?"

How could I explain it to him when I couldn't really explain it to myself? It was irrational, but it was there.

"You don't have to come over here, if it bothers you that much," I said.

"Is that what you want?"

"I want to get on with my own life," I said, feeling my voice tighten. "I'm tired of worrying about what Tal thinks or what Mama wants. Just once, I'd like to do what feels good for me."

"So do it," he said. "That's what I've been trying to tell you. Quit worrying about what other people think."

"Including you?"

He laughed. "I was hoping we could work out a compromise there."

"What kind of compromise?" I said, sliding out from under the steering wheel and snuggling up against him.

"Not here," he said quickly. "Not with Tal hanging around."

I moved back to my side of the seat. "Tell me something," I said. "All this talk of yours about not worrying about what other people think . . ."

"Yeah?"

"Don't you have a family? Don't you worry about how what you do will affect them?"

"No."

"No, you don't have a family, or no, you don't care what they think?"

"I have a family," he said cautiously.

"I know you have two brothers. That's all. Where do they live? Are they still here in Savannah?"

"They're around" was all he would say. "They live their life and I live mine. And they don't get in my business," he said fiercely. "Now, where do you want this furniture unloaded?"

Obviously, the subject was closed as far as he was concerned.

"Let's put it under the carport," I said. "I want to get it sanded and painted this afternoon."

"Today? Right now?" He seemed disappointed.

"The sooner I get it done the sooner I can turn it around," I said.

"What's the big hurry?"

"They've rescheduled the Beaulieu sale. For next Saturday. There's a really wonderful piece there. The Moses Weed cupboard. If I can buy it, it would be a major score. I could maybe make enough money to open my own shop. So I need to raise all the cash I can before Saturday."

"A big deal," Daniel said.

"A very big deal."

He helped me unload the furniture and then glanced furtively around before giving me a chaste little kiss.

"You don't want to stay and help me paint?" I asked, knowing the answer without hearing it.

"Not here," Daniel said. So I took him home. Reluctantly.

The message light was flashing on my answering machine when I got home. "It's Lester Dobie," the voice said. "Why don't you come on by and see me this afternoon?"

I glanced at my watch. It was after three o'clock. If I hustled, I could get the dressers sanded and painted in an hour, and then go see what was up with Lester before he closed the shop.

The paint got slapped on the furniture with mad abandon. That's the good thing about this shabby chic look that's so popular right now. It's supposed to look old and cruddy.

When I went back inside the house, Jethro looked up expectantly.

"Come on, boy," I told him. "Let's go see Lester."

He bounded out to the truck and jumped in the open window. Jethro loves riding in the truck, and he loves Lester even more.

"Hey, shug," Lester said when we walked in the shop. He got up from his stool behind the counter and tossed a dog biscuit to Jethro.

"What's up, Lester?" I asked.

He tugged at the bill of his fishing cap, a sure sign that he was excited. "Come on back in the office," he said.

I followed him through the maze of clutter to his even more cluttered office. He closed the door and sat down at the old kneehole oak desk.

"What?"

"Shh," he said. Then he ducked under the desk and brought out a brown-paper wrapped parcel. He handed it across the desk to me.

"Take a look at that," he said.

I ripped the paper off and stared down at my cotton-picking painting. The T. Eugene White.

"It's gorgeous," I breathed.

The canvas fairly glowed with life now, the formerly muddy colors were transformed to emerald greens and sunflower yellows and rich crimsons and browns. Details that had been invisible before now stood out perfectly; a small dog near a fence that hadn't been there before, puffy clouds rising in the bluest imaginable sky, even a red tractor was now visible in the foreground.

"Cleaned up pretty good, wouldn't you say?"

Even the frame had been transformed. Dirt caked in the crevices of the carved molding had been painstakingly removed, and chips and cracks smoothed over and regilded.

"How did you do this?" I asked.

"I know a fella. Ron Ransome. He used to do all the Telfair Museum's restoration work. He's officially retired. Carves Santa Clauses for a living these days. But I thought he might be interested in working on this, since it's a Southern artist. I didn't expect to get it back for at least a month, but once Ron got working on it, he said he couldn't stop. Had to see what was under all that grime."

I propped the painting up in the windowsill and backed away to get another view of it. "Fantastic. I never dreamed it would look anything like this."

Lester tugged at his cap again. "Ron got pretty excited when he was all done. Took some Polaroids of the painting and sent 'em overnight to a lady he knows in Charleston."

"A decorator?"

He grinned. "Better. This lady works at the Gailliard Museum. She's the director. Ron knew her because she hired him to clean up another T. Eugene White for their museum. Turns out your painting even has a name. *Cotton Time.* It's a companion piece to the one they've got in their front parlor, which is called *Planting Season.*"

I was holding my breath, waiting for the other shoe to drop.

"And?"

"Weezie, they want to buy *Cotton Time.*"

"How much?" It came out with a strangled sound.

"The figure she mentioned to Ron was fifteen thousand."

"Oh. My. God."

"You won't clear that much," he said cautiously. "I already gave Ron a thousand for the restoration work, out of my own pocket, and it seems like he ought to get some consideration for setting you up with the Gailliard folks."

"That's fine," I breathed. "What about your commission?"

"I wasn't figuring on charging you a commission. We're friends."

"We're business associates," I insisted. "Lester, if you hadn't spotted the T. Eugene White signature, I probably would have sold the painting for a couple hundred bucks. So let's say a ten percent commission. Fifteen hundred for you, and fifteen hundred for Ron. Does that work for you?"

"I reckon," he said, and a slow grin spread over his weathered face.

"Shame to have to take it up there to Charleston," he said. "That's one beautiful painting. Too bad it can't stay right here in Savannah."

"I know," I said, tilting my head to get another look at it. I handed him the brown paper that had fallen to the floor. "Let's wrap it back up quick, before I change my mind."

"No time to change your mind," Lester said. He handed me an envelope. "The Gailliard lady is driving down today to pick it up. But she sent the check down yesterday."

I opened the envelope. It was a cashier's check, made out to Eloise Foley, and it was for fifteen thousand dollars. Suddenly, my luck was starting to change. Except for the murder rap hanging over my head.

CHAPTER 38

*T*wo point five million dollars," James said, taking off his glasses and wiping them on the hem of his golf shirt. His glasses fogged up every time he walked out of the air-conditioned house on Washington Avenue and into the broiling late-day sun. "That's what the paper company paid for Beaulieu."

Jonathan whistled. "What did Miss Anna Ruby do with all that money?"

"She endowed the Willis J. Mullinax Foundation."

"And what does the foundation do?"

"Vocational training and community leadership assistance," James said. "Don't ask me what that's supposed to mean. I'm just quoting from the legal documents, which seem to suggest that Gerry Blankenship, as executor of the will *and* director of the foundation, can spend the money as he wishes."

"Gerry Blankenship," Jon said, drawing out the name. "I smell a rat."

"So you know Gerry," James said. "Now, if I were assigning him to a rodent family, I'd be more likely to call him a weasel than a rat."

"Good point," Jon said.

James turned up the air-conditioning in the Mercedes to the setting he thought of as arctic blast, and backed out of the driveway.

"Did you ever talk to the Flanders girls about Caroline's mystery boyfriend?" Jonathan asked.

"I did," James said. "And I've called the owner of the house on Gaston Street. Unfortunately, he's up in Highlands, North Carolina, and he's one of those throwbacks who don't believe in having telephones while they're vacationing."

"Were Anna and Emily any help?"

"Some," James said. "Unfortunately, their description of the fella doesn't fit Gerry Blankenship. He's a big lard-ass of a guy, hard to miss. The Flanders sisters described Caroline's friend as average-sized and middle-aged, but with a baseball cap pulled down over his face. And the friend drove some kind of a silver sedan. Gerry drives a fire-engine red Corvette."

"Doesn't Blankensip just have red Corvette written all over him?" Jon asked, and they both laughed.

"So the mystery man is middle-aged and drives a silver sedan. That certainly narrows it down," Jonathan said.

"Piece of cake," James agreed.

"What else have you learned?" Jonathan asked.

"The sale was finalized a week before Miss Mullinax's death. And the clock is ticking. Coastal Paper Products, as of Friday, has a permit to clear Beaulieu."

"Clear—as in tear down the house?" Jon asked, stunned. "How can that be?" he asked. "Beaulieu is the last intact antebellum plantation house on the Georgia coast. The Savannah Preservation League wouldn't stand for it being bulldozed. If Merijoy Rucker finds out, she'll personally have a world-class hissy fit."

"There's nothing SPL can do about it," James said. "And your friend can have all the hissy fits she wants. Beaulieu isn't in the historic district. It isn't even in the city of Savannah. It's in unincorporated Chatham County. And they're the ones who issued the permit."

"So they're free to just knock down a historic landmark?"

"For now," James said. "The state environmental folks and the Army Corps of Engineers still have to rule on the issue of the paper company's request to dredge on the marsh, and that really is questionable, thank God. And there are some other serious roadblocks they'll have to clear before they can start building. But I took a ride out to Beaulieu yesterday and saw a surveying crew at work. The foreman said he was told tree-clearing work could start immediately."

"All those beautiful old oak trees," Jonathan said. "Some of them are at least two hundred years old. So why are we going back there? What do you hope to accomplish?"

"I want to take a look around the house," James said. "Remember, I didn't get much done the last time I was out there. And I thought it would be helpful to have your perspective on things."

"And Detective Bradley agreed to this?" Jonathan looked dubious.

"He still thinks he owes me," James said, a little sheepishly. "I had a long talk with him and filled him in on what we've learned about Caroline's mysterious friend, and the odd way Miss Mullinax's will was set up. I think he's beginning to have his doubts about Weezie's guilt."

"There's something else you're not telling me," Jonathan said.

"Detective Bradley took me into his confidence," James said. "No matter what I say, he still thinks of me as a priest."

"But you're not a priest, and you don't take confessions anymore," Jonathan pointed out. "And I'm trying to help."

"It could get him into a lot of trouble, professionally."

"What about me?" Jon asked. "If the DA finds out I've been poking around out at Beaulieu, my career could be finished."

"True," James said. "Fair enough. Bradley is in the process of applying for a medical disability discharge. That episode at Beaulieu really frightened him. He has a happy second marriage and children, and he doesn't want to die on the job.

"I think he's a good cop," James continued. "He doesn't want to leave the job thinking he arrested the wrong person for this homicide. And he admitted to me that his instincts tell him Weezie didn't do it. Despite the circumstantial evidence to the contrary."

They were driving out on Skidaway Road now, past the Bacon Park golf course and the city tennis facility. It was nearly eight o'clock. The brilliant summer sky had faded to a pale blue, with pinkish strands of clouds shot through with orange and gold. They drove along the marsh, where shorebirds picked through tide-exposed expanses of reeds and mud, and closer to the road the live oaks stretched moss-draped branches across the narrow pavement.

The wrought-iron gates to Beaulieu were chained and locked. A large white billboard proclaimed the property to be the future site of Coastal Paper Products' Plant Mullinax. A yellow hard hat was painted on the sign, beside the cheery slogan "Watch Us Grow!"

"Hideous," Jonathan said, sighing.

James put the Mercedes in park, got out, and fit a key in the padlock. Jonathan slid across the seat and drove the Mercedes through the open gates, and James closed and locked the gate behind them.

"Does the paper company know anything about Bradley giving you a key?" Jon asked, when James got back in the car.

"Don't ask," James said.

The Mercedes rolled slowly down the now-darkening oak alley, the tires crunching the crushed-oyster-shell roadway.

"Beautiful," Jonathan said, his voice reverent—the cool green arches reminded him of a cathedral, its stillness marred only by the pink ribbons fluttering from survey stakes along the way. "It's got to be saved."

"You can worry about saving Beaulieu," James said. "My job is to save Weezie."

By the time he pulled the Mercedes to a stop in front of the old house, it was full dusk. Fireflies blinked in the softening haze, and a whippoorwill called out in the darkness.

James handed Jonathan a flashlight.

"Isn't there any power in the house?" Jonathan looked alarmed.

"It's an old house. And it seemed pretty dark the last time I was here."

"The last time you were here a man nearly died," Jon reminded him.

James held up a knapsack. "I brought bottled water and a cell phone. I'm not taking any chances this time."

He took out the key ring Bradley had given him, and opened the front door, ignoring the sign posted on a porch column, proclaiming the house to be the private property of Coastal Paper Products.

Jonathan stepped inside and snapped on his flashlight, searching for a light switch. He found one, and a single naked bulb lit up the foyer's cracked plaster walls.

"Sad," he murmured, walking into one of the twin parlors. His footsteps echoed in the empty rooms.

"Didn't you say this place was full of antiques?"

"It was," James said. "It was packed when I was here a week ago. I wonder where everything went? There was supposed to be a sale. And there's a piece of furniture Weezie wants to buy."

"I know what happened," Jonathan said, snapping his fingers. "They've moved the sale. I got a flyer in the mail yesterday. It's going to be held in a warehouse over on East Broad Street. I suppose they're emptying the house to get it ready to raze."

"Not much to see now," James said, playing the beam of his flashlight around the empty parlor walls. "Just a falling-down old house."

Jonathan walked slowly around the perimeter of the room, looking up at the ceiling and down at the floors.

"I'm surprised," he said. "All the moldings, light fixtures, baseboards, everything you'd expect to see in a grand old house of this vintage, none of it's here. It's really pretty unremarkable, at least on the inside."

James looked up to where Jonathan's light was pointed. The plaster ceiling was crumbled and showing gaping holes. He frowned. "There was some kind of stuff up there before, I think."

"Stuff? What do you mean?"

"You know. Doodads. There was a fancy light fixture. Like a chandelier. And sort of decorations, I don't know what you call them. Like frosting on a wedding cake. But they were there before."

"A plaster rosette?" Jon asked. "What about the outside of these walls? Were there other kinds of doodads, as you call them?"

"Some," James said. "Painted white. Along the floors too, and there were carved things around the doorways and on top of the doorways."

Jonathan walked through the hall into the twin of the first parlor. "James. Were there any fancy mantels or fireplace surrounds?"

James followed his friend across the hall. "I think so. But so much furniture was piled everywhere, it was hard to see. Not that I paid that much attention."

"You're hopeless," Jonathan said. He pointed at a fireplace that was little more than a square hole in the wall. "Son of a bitch," he exclaimed. "They stripped the place."

"How do you mean?" James asked.

"That's how they got past the county's historic preservation review board," Jonathan said, pointing at the firebox. "Somebody came in here and took down all the old moldings, the cornices, overdoors, mantels, everything. Even the period lighting fixtures."

"To sell?"

"Well, yes, the stuff probably could be sold after it was salvaged,"

Jonathan said. "Somebody stripped it so the house wouldn't be certified as a historically significant landmark."

"So the house could be torn down," James said.

"Were all the moldings gone when you were here with Bradley?"

"I didn't notice," James said. "Bradley collapsed upstairs. I just don't know."

"Let's go upstairs," Jonathan suggested. "See what they did up there."

The box fan was still in the upstairs hallway where James had pulled it out to cool Detective Bradley down. Another naked bulb's dim wattage threw little in the way of light, but enough to convince Jonathan that the upstairs, too, had been stripped of its architectural detailing.

Still, they walked from room to room, Jonathan bemoaning the loss of Beaulieu's trappings, James wondering aloud what evidence might have been destroyed.

The two of them stood in front of the bathroom closet where Caroline DeSantos's body had been found. It was just a closet.

"Let's go," James said. "This place is depressing."

"It's haunting," Jonathan said.

James looked at him with an expression of surprise. "You're the last person in the world I would have expected to talk like that."

"Not supernaturally haunting," Jonathan said. "Nothing like that. No ghosts or wee things that go bump in the night. All these years, through the Civil War, and the stock market crash, through hurricanes and tornadoes, one family made a living here, and other families lived off the land. And after a hundred and fifty years, poof, it's all gone. The Mullinaxes, a great old Georgia family, vanished. And the house will be gone soon too. Not to fires or floods. Just greed. Good old American greed."

CHAPTER 39

By Tuesday, I'd sold Cousin Lucy's furniture for seven hundred dollars, and in two days of frantic wheeling and dealing I'd raised a total of five thousand dollars in cash, most of it from my one-hundred-dollar toolshed investment. It was the biggest score I'd ever made in my picking career. I felt light-headed with my own power and success.

When my phone rang I sang out, "Hellooo."

"Aren't we in a happy mood," BeBe said.

"Actually, we are," I said. "I've got a seventeen-thousand-dollar stash, and I still have four or five more boxes of stuff to sell from the toolshed. I'm in the money, Babe."

"Perfect," she said. "What are you doing right now?"

"Getting ready to take a box of sterling silver out to a dealer at Tybee. He refuses to come into town, so I'm going out there to meet him."

"The silver can wait," BeBe said. "Meet me at the restaurant in half an hour."

"I can't," I started to say, but she'd already hung up the phone.

I looked down at my ensemble. Cutoff army fatigue pants, a white ribbed tank top, and green flip-flops. If I went to the restaurant, I might see Daniel. I got a nice little tingling feeling thinking about Daniel.

I jumped in the shower, then, while toweling off, I tried to decide what to wear. Nothing too fancy. After all, this was just a casual drop-by. But nothing too sloppy either. No raggedy-ass shirts or threadbare cutoffs. I pulled on a pair of black Capris. Fine. Just fine. The hot pink sleeveless top would go good, but damn, my pink bra was missing in action. Black, I decided. Black would be right. I picked out a cropped black boat-neck top with three-quarter sleeves. I slid into a pair of cork-soled black slides. Dangly silver shell earrings. Nice, casual, not too horny.

It was after noon when I pulled up to Guale. I found an open space at the curb. Odd. The restaurant is usually packed at lunch.

I walked to the front door. There was a handwritten sign on the door. "Closed for Remodeling."

Since when?

The lights were on inside, but the venetian blind on the door was pulled down. Through the slats of the blind I could see BeBe inside, standing at the reception desk, talking on the phone. I tried the door, but it was locked. I rapped on the glass.

"We're closed," she hollered.

"It's me, you fool," I hollered back. "Open up."

She was still talking on the cell phone as she unlocked the door and waved me inside.

"All right," she was saying. "But you understand this: if he shows up here drunk again tomorrow, I'll cut off his balls with an oyster knife. You tell him that for me."

I raised an eyebrow.

"Painters," she said, clicking off the phone. "Find me one sober painter in south Georgia and I'll pay anything he asks."

"What's going on?" I asked. "What's this about redecorating?"

"I've lost my mind," she agreed, running her hands through her already tousled blond hair. "But yes, it's true. Come on now, I've got something I want to show you."

She went to the maître d' stand and picked up a ring bristling with keys. I followed her outside and waited while she locked the door to Guale. Seven paces to the right, and we were standing in front of the Rose Tattoo Parlor.

There was a sign on the window: "Closed. Lost Our Fucking Lease."

"They didn't take it well," BeBe said. "I've got to take that sign down before our customers get the wrong idea."

"What is the idea?" I asked as she unlocked the door.

"My lounge," she said excitedly. "Remember? Little Sisters Lounge? Isn't it dreamy?"

She stepped inside and gestured around. "Incredible."

"Gross," I said. It smelled like backed-up sewage. "You can't put a lounge in here."

Her face fell. "I thought you, of all people, could see the possibilities."

The floors were gummy linoleum. The dropped ceiling was water-stained and sagging. A cockroach scuttled across the floor, probably eager to make a quick escape.

"I see the possibility of multiple forms of airborne disease, starting with hepatitis A," I said. "This place is a disaster."

"You wait," BeBe said. "It'll be divine. I've had a vision."

She locked up the tattoo parlor and we went back to the restaurant, where she fixed me a glass of iced tea.

"Oh." BeBe whipped a piece of paper out of the pocket of her dress. "I'd almost forgotten. Look. This came in the mail." It was a flyer. For the Beaulieu estate sale.

"I didn't get one of these," I said.

"Can you really blame them for taking you off the mailing list?" she asked. "You kind of put a damper on the last sale they tried to have."

I read the flyer. It listed all the stuff the original advertisements listed. But not the cupboard, which hadn't been listed the first time around.

"The cupboard might not even be there," I told BeBe. "There are rumors floating around town. I heard Lewis Hargreaves might have already bought the best pieces."

"Who cares?" BeBe said breezily. "If the cupboard's there, you buy it, and make a killing on it. If it's not, you've still got your stash. That's more than enough to get your shop going."

"But I don't have any inventory. I've sold everything, even some of my own furniture, to raise money to buy the cupboard. I'd have to go out of town, maybe down to Florida, for a buying trip."

"Stop with the gloom and doom," she ordered, putting her hands over her ears. "I don't want to hear another word."

"Where's Daniel?" I asked, looking around the darkened restaurant.

"You little minx!" BeBe said, looking me up and down. "I should have known you didn't put mousse in your hair just for me. I bet you douched too. Well, you're out of luck. He's not here."

"Where is he?"

"On vacation," she said, shrugging. "It's our slow time anyway, and I've got to get this place painted and recarpeted, and the wall knocked down for the new lounge. So we've shut down for two weeks. Assuming, that is, that my painters sober up sometime soon."

"He didn't mention going on vacation the other day," I said.

"I didn't really decide to go ahead and close down until Sunday night," BeBe said. "And what other day did you see him, may I ask?"

"Sunday," I said, smiling at the memory of our kitchen encounter.

"Details," she said, snapping her fingers impatiently. "I need details."

"He bought my cousin's bed. And now he wants me to play house," I said dreamily.

"Horizontal?" she asked. "Was there any horizontality?"

"We were vertical," I said. "But in a good way."

CHAPTER 40

*J*ethro was hiding under the kitchen table when I got home, his dark eyes rebuking me for leaving him behind.

I got a dog treat from the cookie jar and tried to coax him out.

"Come on, Ro-Ro," I crooned. "Come get a treat, boy. Come and get it."

But he stayed put. "Stubborn mutt," I said, standing up.

That's when I noticed it—a potted yellow orchid in a gorgeous blue-and-white Chinese porcelain ginger jar. I picked the pot up for a closer look, peered at the jar's crackled glaze and the Chinese markings stamped on the bottom. It was the real thing.

A tiny envelope fell to the floor. I picked it up and opened it.

Tal's business card was inside. On the blank side he'd written "Come back to me."

I put the orchid back on the table. Jethro hadn't moved.

"Did you let him in, Ro-Ro? Did the bad man scare you?"

But Jethro was taking the fifth. And I was feeling nauseous.

I fixed myself a glass of iced tea, and that reminded me of the situation with Mama. So I did what I always do when I have a problem. I called James.

"Weezie!" he said, after Janet told him I was on the line. "I've got good news. Detective Bradley just called. He's advised the district attorney's office that he doesn't have enough evidence to get an indictment against you for Caroline's murder."

"That's great," I said. The orchid was really an obnoxious shade of yellow, with an almost obscene meaty red tint to its phallic-looking throat. I got the kitchen shears out of the drawer and cut off one of the cascading blossoms. I felt better immediately.

"You don't sound very excited," James said. "They've dismissed the criminal trespass charge too. Your record is clear."

"That ought to make Mama happy," I said. "It's wonderful. Really, Uncle James, I'm so grateful for all you've done. I can't thank you enough."

"You're family," he said simply. "I kind of enjoyed dabbling in criminal work, to tell you the truth. But something else is wrong. Are you going to tell me or are you just going to sit there and brood about it?"

"I'm not brooding," I said. "It's just that strange stuff happens to me. And I'm not being paranoid either. I seem to give off some kind of energy that invites bizarre behavior."

"Give me an example," he said. "Not counting the fact that you discovered your ex-husband's fiancée's body in a closet."

"It's Mama," I said. "And the weeping Infant of Prague. I've been meaning to ask you about that, James. What's the Infant of Prague supposed to represent?"

"I've always thought of it as the baby Jesus in drag," James said. "But I don't have any documentation for that."

"Well, I've got documentation about Mama," I said. And I told him about finding her bottle of Four Roses at Lucy's house.

"Oh dear," James said. "I was hoping maybe she was tapering off on the drinking. Your dad hasn't said anything about it."

"You know Daddy. I also found a bottle of Xanax at the house. The prescription was Lucy's, but according to the label on the pill bottle, the prescription was refilled two days after Lucy died. Half a dozen pills were missing. Mama's been taking Lucy's tranquilizers and washing them down with bourbon."

"Good heavens," James said. "She could kill herself. Or somebody else, zonked out on pills and booze."

"The good news is she's apparently sleeping at Lucy's house. I think that's when she has these little chatfests with the statue."

"We've got to get her help," James said. "Poor soul. I had no idea. Your father hasn't mentioned anything about her sleeping over there, or acting funny?"

"Not a word. What can we do?"

"I'll have to talk to Joe," James said. "Make him see that Marian needs help desperately. He probably has no idea about the pills, although we both know he just ignores the drinking."

"Then you'll talk to them?"

"I'll talk to my brother," James said. "But I think you need to talk to your mother, Weezie."

"No," I said, feeling panicky. "I can't. You have to do it, James. You're good at that stuff. She adores you. She'll listen to you."

"She's your mother. It's time the two of you had a good talk."

"But what will I say?" I wailed. "It's not like we're pals. We've never had that kind of a relationship."

"Start now," he said calmly. "Invite her out to a nice lunch. Someplace quiet, nonthreatening. And just let her know that you found the tranquilizers. Tell her how dangerous it is, mixing pills and alcohol. Try not to sound judgmental. But let her know that you and your dad want her to get help with the drinking."

"I don't know," I said. "I'll try. But you'll talk to Daddy? Promise?"

"I promise. Feeling better now?"

"A little," I said, still eyeing the orchid. It looked malevolent, with its long reaching spray of blossoms. I took the scissors and cut off two more flowers.

"It's Tal," I said, grinding the flowers under the heel of my shoe. "He's acting weird. The other night, he barged into the carriage house, drunk as a coot, begging me to take him back. Can you believe that?"

"Tal did that?"

"Yes. I told him to leave, but he was so pathetic, I was actually starting to feel sorry for him. James, Tal says Caroline was having an affair with another man, right before she was killed."

"Really?" James didn't sound all that surprised.

"Yes. And Tal said he thinks Caroline was going to meet her lover the night she was killed. He was already suspicious, and that night, she got a mysterious phone call. So he tried to follow her when she left the house, but he lost her at the red light at Victory and Bee Road."

"Do you believe him?" James said. "Or was he just trying to get you to feel sorry for him so you'll take him back?"

"I believe she was screwing around on him," I said. "The other night at a dinner party I was at, everybody was gossiping about Caroline."

"Yes. I've heard some of the same gossip from a friend," James said.

"What friend? You don't hang around with gossips."

"I hear things," James said. "Do you have any idea who the other man could be?"

"Gerry Blankenship was the first name that came to my mind."

"No other candidates?"

"She could have been sleeping with just about anybody," I said maliciously. "I just don't know. It's Tal's behavior that's worrying me. He's been acting bizarre. After all those months, when he was so hurtful and cruel, now he comes crawling back. He was slobbering all over me the other night. Revolting."

"I would think you'd be flattered by the attention," James said.

"I'm not," I shot back. "Look, I've started seeing somebody. A man. And he doesn't want to come over to my place, because Tal's always hanging around."

"You knew when you kept the carriage house that he'd be living right next door," James said.

"I didn't know he'd scare off my first date. Or that he'd spy on me. Or break into my house and leave ugly orchid plants."

Silence. "He actually broke in? When? That's a whole different matter."

I went over and looked at the kitchen door. The lock hadn't been tampered with, and the doorjamb's paint was undisturbed. I'd left in a hurry that morning. Had I forgotten to lock up? Had Tal been watching, seen my slipup?"

"It happened today," I said. "Maybe he didn't actually break in. But he definitely was in here, and he didn't have my permission. He left these flowers with a note saying 'Come back to me.' And he scared Jethro."

"I'm going to call Tal's lawyer," James said. "I'll tell him we're going to get a restraining order against Tal unless he stays away from you."

"Really?" I felt my resolve faltering. "I don't want to make a scene or get Tal arrested or anything. I just want him to leave me alone."

"I'll take care of it," James said. "Now you call your mother and take care of your end of the deal."

"I will," I said.

I hung up the phone. The orchid still had one more cluster of blooms. Snip.

I dumped the potting soil in the trash and went to get on-line to see what kind of prices antique Chinese ginger jars bring on eBay these days.

CHAPTER 41

*C*onvincing Mama to let me take her to lunch took some doing.

"Oh, I couldn't," she said when I invited her. "I have so much to do at Lucy's. And what about your daddy's lunch?"

"I'll help you finish packing and pricing stuff at Lucy's," I said. "And I'll bring Daddy a sack lunch when I come pick you up. Tomato sandwich on white bread with Blue Plate mayonnaise. Right?"

"And chips," she said, giving in. "He likes the potato chips with ridges. And maybe some cookies. You know his sweet tooth."

After I picked her up I parked the truck across from the restaurant, a quiet little place called Arabella's that BeBe had recommended. It was only a short walk, but we'd had a brief rainfall in midmorning and now the air was like a steam bath. Mama's face was pink and dripping with perspiration by the time we pushed open the heavy red door at Arabella's.

Cool air welcomed us into the foyer, which was painted a restful dark green. The floors were polished wood, and chintz drapes at the windows looked out on Monterey Square. Charming. Just the place for a little family intervention.

Mama smiled apprehensively, looking around.

"Isn't this nice?" I asked, tucking my hand in the crook of her arm. "Just us girls. BeBe says the seafood is especially good."

"It's not spicy, is it? You know my diverticulitis."

"We'll ask them to leave off the garlic and onions," I said, patting her arm.

The maître d' walked quickly across the room toward us. He was tall and model thin, with razor-cut hair, apostrophe-mark sideburns, tortoise-shell spectacles, and hips I'd die for. He was wearing clogs.

"Ladies?" He looked a little puzzled. "Can I help you?"

"Yes," I said. "We have reservations. The name is Foley."

He looked down at his book on the maître d' stand, leafing through the pages. "For dinner?"

"No," I said. "Lunch. One o'clock. We're just a little early. Is that all right?"

"Whatever," he said, pursing his lips. He ran a finger down the page until he found what he was looking for. "Foley. Here we are."

He picked up two menus, then looked at me, and at Mama. He slid his bifocals down onto the end of his nose. "Don't tell me," he said. "Sisters. You're sisters—right? The resemblance between you two girls is really startling."

Mama giggled a little. "Oh, you're sweet. But this is my daughter. Eloise."

He wagged a playful finger at her. "You must have been just a child bride when you had Eloise here."

Mama didn't get it, and it wasn't just because of old age. I doubt if she'd ever had a flirt gear.

"No," she said seriously. "I was forty when I had her."

He pretended to look shocked. "Come right this way. I've got a cozy little table by the window that I think you'll like."

We followed his swaying hips through the restaurant. The place was full, but there was something different about the clientele. They were all men. And not your usual downtown courthouse crowd of loud shirtsleeve-clad lawyers or salesmen chatting on their cell phones.

These were nicely dressed men. The room was hushed. It dawned on me. Arabella's might have been a fun couples place for dinner, but at lunchtime, at least on Wednesdays, Mama and I were a distinct minority, and not just because we were women. Not even the wallpaper was straight at Arabella's.

Mama, thankfully, was oblivious.

"This is so fancy," she whispered, tugging at my arm. "I hope it isn't too expensive. I don't want you spending a lot of money on me."

"It's fine, Mama," I reassured her. "I feel like giving you a little treat."

"You don't have a husband to support you anymore," Mama fussed. "You need to be saving your money instead of frittering it away on fancy lunches."

She really knows how to set my teeth on edge, Mama does.

"I want to buy you lunch. OK? I can afford it."

"Well, all right," she said, her voice going all quavery. "But we're not having a salad if it's extra. Do they have a senior-citizen discount?"

It was a good thing Mama was busy giving me financial counseling. Because the last booth we passed was occupied by a familiar face.

Uncle James. And he wasn't alone. Sitting across the table from him, gazing fondly at my uncle, was Jonathan McDowell, the chief assistant district attorney I'd had dinner with at Merijoy Rucker's house.

In a flash I knew who James's special friend was. And I knew who was feeding him all the local gossip too.

"Mama," I said, stopping and turning her around so that her back was toward James. "You've got lipstick smeared all over your upper lip."

"I do?" She put her hand to her face. "I checked before I left the house."

"It's all smudged now," I said sympathetically. "You go on back to the ladies' room. I'll order us something to drink. Is iced tea all right?"

"No lemon," she said quickly, and she hurried off to fix her lipstick.

I grabbed the arm of the maître d'. "I think it would be better if you gave us a table up front."

"There isn't another table," he said, his tone turning icy. "We're all booked. Wednesdays are our busy day."

"So I see," I said dryly. All the couples in the room looked like they'd come directly to Arabella's from a discreet little nooner.

I glanced over at Uncle James's table. He chose that moment to turn around. Our eyes met. I gave him a little finger wave. His face went white. He looked like he might faint. Jonathan McDowell noticed the look on James's face and swiveled to see what was giving James such a fright. Now Jonathan was looking pale too.

They had a hurried conversation. James motioned the maître d' over to his table. Two half-full plates were at each setting, but it appeared they'd had a sudden, drastic loss of appetite.

James scanned the check and put money on the table. Both men stood up. Jonathan scurried toward the door, deliberately skirting the room to avoid passing me.

As James started to follow him, Mama chose that moment to reappear.

"Why, James," she said, spotting him and stepping into his path. "Are you having lunch with us too? I thought Weezie said it was just the girls."

I had to bite my lip to keep from laughing out loud.

Mama planted a happy lipsticky kiss on James's cheek. "This is so nice. And it's not even my birthday. Is Joe coming too?"

"Well, no," James said. "I had a business lunch. With another lawyer. But I've got to get back to the office now. Clients to see, and all."

"Can't you stay a little while?" I asked, pleading in my voice.

But the rat was swimming for shore. "I'd love to, another time. But Janet will skin me alive if I keep this client waiting."

Mama sat down in her chair and unfolded her napkin in her lap. "All right," she said placidly. "Bye, James."

"You go ahead and order for us, Mama," I said. "I'll just walk Uncle James to the door."

I waited until we were out of her earshot. "You could have told me about Jonathan, you know."

"I couldn't, actually," he said. "He asked me not to."

"He seems nice."

"He is. Very nice. And he likes you too. Also, he likes your friend. Who *you* haven't chosen to tell me anything about."

"I get your point," I said. "I guess we both like to play things close to the vest."

He draped an arm around my shoulder. "I want to see you happy, Weezie. Does this Daniel fella make you smile?"

"Yeah. He makes me smile, and he makes me laugh, and he makes me so mad sometimes I think I could happily choke him to death."

"He sounds great."

We were at the front door. I could see Jonathan standing outside, a worried expression on his face.

"Did you talk to Daddy?"

"Right before I got here. You were right. He had no idea things had gotten so bad with your mother. He's worried."

"But he agrees? That she needs to get help?"

"Reluctantly. He still remembers that last time she was in the, uh, hospital. How unhappy she was."

"But that was fifteen years ago," I said. "They have all kinds of programs now. She might not even have to stay in a hospital."

"I mentioned that. I have a friend, a priest, who runs a program at Candler-St. Joseph's. I'm supposed to talk to him this afternoon. See if that would be a good fit for your mother."

"I'd better go," I said, squeezing his hand. "She'll think I've disappeared."

"Go easy," he said.

"James? Don't worry about Mama. She doesn't have a clue about you and Jonathan. Tell him I said bye. Maybe the two of you could have dinner with Daniel and me. If things work out."

"A double date?" He grimaced. "Don't think I'm quite ready for that yet. Arabella's took enough nerve."

"The shrimp salad is the special today," Mama said when I sat back down. "It's five ninety-five. For shrimp. Can you believe that? But it was the cheapest thing on the menu. I'll leave the tip."

"That sounds fine," I said, taking a sip of iced tea.

"This is very nice," Mama said, looking around the room. "I wonder if this would be a nice place for our altar guild luncheon?"

I put the tea glass down. "Maybe dinner would be better," I pointed out, thinking about the altar guild ladies mingling with the Wednesday lunch crowd at Arabella's.

"Oh no," Mama said. "A lot of the girls don't like to drive downtown at night. The crime, you know."

I'd rehearsed my little speech over and over the night before. I'd even tried to write it down. Now I didn't know how to bring up the subject. We talked about the weather, and family stuff, and Daddy's garden until the waiter brought our shrimp salad.

Mama was just buttering a yeast roll. And I just blurted it out.

"Mama? I know about the Four Roses. I know you don't really drink iced tea all day. I know you have a bottle hidden over at Cousin Lucy's. I know you've been taking her Xanax. And I know you've been sleeping over there."

She went on buttering her roll, tearing off little chunks of bread, spreading butter on each tiny piece, then sitting the chunks around the edge of her plate. She didn't say anything. Didn't look up. A tear rolled down her face and splashed on the front of her blouse.

"Mama," I whispered. "It's all right. Don't cry. We're going to get you help."

She looked up, frightened. "No," she whispered. "I won't go back to that place. Never, never, never. I won't go."

"Not that place," I said, reaching for her hand. She jerked it away.

"They have other places. You can come home at night. They don't lock you up. But they'll help you. And Mama—you need help. You know you do. Taking those pills, you could kill yourself."

"Does your daddy know?" She looked at me pleadingly.

"He knows," I said. "And he wants you to get help too."

"You told him?" Her face twisted into a tight white mask of anger. "You had no right!"

"He already knew about the drinking. We all knew."

Her face crumpled. "Even James?"

"Yes."

"I hate you!" she cried. "You've been going around, talking about me behind my back. To my own family. Telling them lies. I don't need you. And I don't need to go to a hospital. I can take care of myself."

"But you can't," I said, leaning forward. "Those pills you were taking are a powerful tranquilizer. And you were taking them with liquor. That's why that statue was talking to you. You were having hallucinations, Mama."

She sat up straight in her chair, outraged. "I was having a *religious vision*." Her eyes were blazing. "And it's your fault. Because you are a sinner. An adulterer. That's why I drink. Because of you. All because of you!"

She started weeping loudly and pushed back her chair to stand up, and the chair tipped over onto the floor.

The maître d' came rushing over, oozing concern. "Is there a problem?"

"No," I said, digging in my pocketbook for my billfold. "We won't be staying for lunch. My mother's not feeling well."

"I am not *drunk*," Mama hollered. "And I do not have *hallucinations*." She snatched up her purse and bolted for the door.

Our waiter appeared just then too, holding a tray of pastries.

"No dessert?" he asked.

"Not this time," I said. "We're trying to quit."

CHAPTER 42

After a fruitless half hour of searching for Mama, I called Daddy. "Did Mama come home?"

"I thought she was with you," he said. "James said you two were going to have a talk. About the drinking."

"We did," I said. "She's furious at me. She went running out of the restaurant. I can't find her, Daddy. And I've looked everywhere."

He sighed heavily. "Don't feel bad. It's not your fault. I should have been the one to confront her. I'm her husband."

"And I'm her daughter. Do you think she's all right?"

"She didn't have anything to drink at lunch, did she?"

"Nothing," I said.

"That's a relief. You go on home. I'll ride around, see if I can find her."

"Where would she go?" I asked. "She doesn't have her car."

"She has cash, though," he said. "She always carries fifty dollars in cash in her pocketbook. In case of an emergency. And there's half a dozen places I can think of she might have gone. Don't worry, now. I'll call you when I find her."

"Let me come with you to look," I begged.

"Better not," he said. "Let me get her settled down some."

I'd only been home for forty-five minutes when Daddy called.

"I found her." He sounded exhausted.

"Where? Is she all right?"

"She took a cab to Cousin Lucy's house. She's locked herself up inside there. I knocked and knocked, but she won't come out. Do you think she's all right in there? You don't think she'd hurt herself, do you?"

"She can't get drunk," I said. "I dumped out most of her booze. And I switched the Xanax. I doubt she'd do anything else to herself. What did she say? Does she still hate me?"

"She told me to go away," Daddy said. "She said she's never coming home. That we've all been plotting against her."

"Oh, Daddy," I moaned. "I'm so sorry."

"Couldn't be helped," he said in his slow, matter-of-fact way. "James is on his way over there now. He's good with your mama. I'm gonna meet him over there. We got the key to the house from one of the other cousins, so if she won't let us in, we'll just go in with the key. You be sweet, you hear?"

"I will. Call me."

The phone didn't ring again. I sat by it, willing it to ring, but nothing happened. I called the house again, but nobody picked up.

Waiting around was making me nuts. I paced the carriage house, polished more silver, went on the Internet and posted Tal's ginger jar on eBay and checked a couple of other auctions in progress. I felt like I might jump out of my skin. At one point, I even got Lucy's Doan's bottle out of my purse and considered following Mama's lead. It might feel good to zone out with a little Xanax for a while. Maybe the Infant of Prague would have some words of advice for me.

God knows I needed some wisdom. What to do about Tal, about Daniel, about Uncle James, about BeBe's offer to finance a shop for me. What to do about Mama and her drinking.

In the end, I decided on a little retail therapy. When the going gets tough, the tough go shopping. I'd seen an ad in the *Pennysaver* for an estate sale at an address on the Southside, in the Windsor Forest subdivision.

Windsor Forest wasn't on my usual junking route because most of the houses on that side of town were built in the sixties and later, meaning most of their furnishings were too contemporary for my taste.

But I had a bad case of cabin fever. Besides, I rationalized, this was a rare midweek estate sale, which meant less competition for the good stuff.

When I pulled up to the house, a redbrick split-level, I started getting good vibes. A lipstick red Lexus was parked in the driveway. I knew that car. It belonged to Sue Pierson, a downtown interior designer with an uncanny nose for antiques. If she was here, there was good stuff. Guaranteed.

Just as I was walking up the driveway, Sue walked out of the front door, a black-and-gold Hitchcock chair under each arm.

"Am I too late?" I asked.

She laughed. "Darlin', there's enough goodies in there for both of us." I saluted her and she laughed again.

As Sue had promised, the split-level was indeed overflowing with antiques. All of the rooms were packed with tables holding china, silver, crystal, pictures, dishes, and linens.

In the midst of the confusion, an elderly man in a bathrobe sat in a tattered recliner stationed squarely in the middle of the living room, shouting at nobody in particular about the history of each item.

"That radio was a premium my mother got for buying Jewel Tea," he said, seeing me pick up a vintage radio. The price tag said sixty-five dollars, so I put it down.

After glancing at half a dozen price tags, I decided that the owners of the house had hired an appraiser to do the pricing; this meant that most of the stuff was priced at book value—and therefore out of my price range.

The last room I visited was a sunporch on the back side of the house. It was crowded with dusty flowerpots and yard tools. I almost turned around to leave, until I caught sight of the curved arm of a rattan armchair.

I moved a galvanized tin washtub to get a better look at the chair.

The cushion was a hideous orange-and-green floral velvet, but the chair itself was a goodie. It was late 1940s or early 1950s Heywood-Wakefield rattan. Very funky. Very collectible. A price tag for seventy-five dollars dangled from the chair frame.

I went inside the house and found the cashier. "I'm interested in that armchair in the sunroom," I said. "Could you do any better on the price?"

He was a heavyset man with a straggly goatee and greasy gray hair that hung to his collar. I'd seen him around town running other estate sales.

"I might could," he said, sizing me up. "Are you interested in the rest?"

"The rest?" My pulse went giddyap.

"Out in the garage," he said, pointing to a door in the kitchen. "There's a settee, a rocker, two end tables, and a coffee table. Also a split bamboo bar with two stools. Midcentury Heywood-Wakefield. And it's the complete suite."

My pulse settled back down. If he knew what the rattan was, he also knew what it was worth. "How much?" I asked, unwilling to even look at the rest of the set unless I knew it was affordable.

He picked up a small silver penknife and started whittling away at his long yellow thumbnail. "It books at eighteen hundred," he said. "And we can get that if we take it up to Scott's Antique Market next month."

He got no argument from me.

"But the family has sold the house, and it closes Friday. They want the place empty by then. So we'll take a thousand."

"Let me think about it," I said.

I went out to the garage to look at the rest of the Heywood-Wakefield. It was truly wonderful, with big rounded arms and backs and tabletops of varnished blond wood. I could picture it in a beach house, the cushions covered, maybe in a reproduction bark cloth with big palm fronds and caladium leaves. I know a woman who lives out at Spanish Hammock, she calls herself Tacky Jacky, and she does upholstery and slipcovers at the best rates in town.

A beach house. That gave me an idea. The rattan would be too expensive to buy and expect to make a profit on, but it would be perfect for a certain Tybee Island beach shack.

I flipped my cell phone open and called directory assistance for Daniel's number.

"It's Weezie," I said. "Were you serious about having me buy furniture for your beach house?"

"Sure," he said. "Did you find something already?"

"Maybe. A set of rattan furniture. For your living room. You'd have to have the cushions re-covered, but I know somebody who can do that for you. There's even a bar. It's very cool. Very forties-looking."

"Go for it," he said. "If you like it, I'll like it."

"Don't you want to know how much?"

"I trust you," Daniel said. "What are you doing tonight?"

"Worrying about my mother," I said. "She's run away from home."

"Screw that," Daniel said. "I'll pick you up at six. OK? Just casual. Shorts and sneakers."

"I guess," I said.

"See you at six."

The cashier was still paring his nails when I got back to the living room. I'd been mulling over my approach. The rattan was good, and a thousand dollars was a fair price, but I had a gut feeling I could get it cheaper. After all, he only had two days to empty the house, and dealers weren't exactly crawling over the place.

"I like the rattan," I said, flashing the dealer a smile. "But the price is a little steep if I'm going to turn it around."

He shrugged and kept working on his nails.

"How about if I leave a bid?" I asked.

"You could do that," he said. He scrabbled around on the table until he found a green-lined steno pad, and turned to a blank page.

I scribbled away, making a bid of $750 and listing my name and number.

"When will you let me know?" I asked.

"Pretty soon. I'll talk to the family and see what they say."

 stopped at my parents' house on the way back into town. I found my father sitting at the kitchen table, scowling down at a pamphlet.

"Hey, Daddy," I said, landing a kiss on the top of his head. "Did Mama come home with you?"

"No. She says she's not ready to come home yet. But she did let us in the house. And the three of us had a long talk."

"Is she going to get help?"

He put the pamphlet down and took off his glasses and wiped them on the hem of his shirt. The pamphlet was called "Family Response to Alcoholism."

"She says she will," Daddy said. "We'll have to wait and see. We're going to go over and talk to this friend of James's who works at Candler-St. Joe's tomorrow. Marian promised she would go and at least hear what they have to say."

For the first time, I noticed that Daddy had changed recently, and not for the better. His once brown hair had gone to gray while I wasn't looking.

His once cheerful face suddenly looked like unset pudding. And for the first time in my life, I saw that Daddy didn't look taken care of.

His thick-rimmed glasses were held together with a Band-Aid, his short-sleeved sport shirt needed pressing, his pants were faded and shrunken, and most shocking of all, his black lace-up brogans needed polishing.

Once upon a time, Mama would never have let Daddy walk around looking the way he did now. But this was not something my father would talk about. It would seem disloyal to Mama, and he would have no part in criticizing her.

"Mama agreed to go," I said, seizing on the positive. "And she let you in the house. And she admits now that she is an alcoholic?"

Daddy rubbed his eyes again. "No," he said. "She won't admit that at all."

"She doesn't think she has a drinking problem?"

"She says we're picking on her," Daddy said. "The only reason she has agreed to go talk to these people is so that they will tell us that she is not an alcoholic."

"But Daddy, she *is*. She gets drunk near about every day. She has for years now. And it's getting worse."

"I know, sweetheart," he said. "I know it and you know it and James knows it. He says Marian is in denial. But we have to start somewhere. So that's what we'll do."

"She hates me," I said. "This divorce of mine has been her undoing."

"No," he said quickly. "That's the liquor talking. And the denial thing. She loves you more than anything in the world. But she's hurt and upset, and she's scared to death of going back to a hospital. We have to be patient with her."

"Why won't she come home?" I asked.

"She says she's tired of people spying on her. Truth is, I think she's ashamed to face us, now that it's out in the open," Daddy said. "She knows the drinking has gotten out of hand, and she feels bad about letting us down."

I nodded, looking around the kitchen. Like Daddy, the house had seen better days. The café curtains hung limp and greasy at windows that hadn't been washed in months. There were fingerprints on the refrigerator and dirty dishes in the sink, and the floor was feeling gummy. Why hadn't I noticed any of this? Waxy yellow buildup on Marian Foley's kitchen floor? That should have been a red alert that something was bad wrong with Mama.

I put my pocketbook on the kitchen table and went to the sink, getting out the mop bucket and the Spic and Span.

"What are you up to now?" Daddy asked.

"Setting things right," I said, running hot sudsy water in the sink. "So Mama can come home again."

"I'll help," Daddy said, getting up heavily from his chair. I watched speechlessly as he opened the cupboard and got out the broom and dustpan. Never, not once in my entire life, had I ever seen my father do a lick of housework. I couldn't believe he even knew where the broom *was*, let alone how to use it.

He saw my amazed expression and gave me a wink. "Never too late to try something new, is it?"

"No sir," I said.

I had one more stop to make on my way home. It was a little lingerie boutique on Whitaker Street downtown. I'd passed the place hundreds of times before and never stopped. Now I slipped guiltily inside the carved wooden door, hoping nobody passing by would see me.

My excuse was that I really needed a new bra, since Cousin Alice had swiped mine. Really though, I was browsing for more of a new me.

My days of white cotton were over. As soon as I saw it, I knew I had to have it—a black lace over blond bra with matching silk panties that reminded me of the negligee Lana Turner wore in an old pinup poster from the 1940s. My size, my new style, and together it made a ninety-dollar hole in my shop money. I bit my lip and paid cash. The salesgirl took her time wrapping it in peach tissue and then a peach shopping bag tied with peach chiffon ribbon, when all I wanted to do was grab and go.

At home I took a quick shower and dressed in pale yellow linen shorts and a matching linen top. I painted my toenails—just because. It had been a gritty, gruesome day. I was ready for red toenail polish . . . and the most expensive undies I'd ever owned.

Daniel rang the doorbell just as I was coming downstairs. He looked me up and down. "Aren't you kind of dressed up for crabbing?"

"You never said we were going crabbing," I pointed out. "You said shorts."

"Not nice shorts."

"I don't wear grubby clothes when I go out on dates," I said, starting to do a slow burn. Why did he have that effect on me?

"You look great," he relented, "but don't blame me if your clothes get ruined."

I gave him a look and went back upstairs and threw grubby cutoffs and a T-shirt in a tote bag, along with a pair of beat-up sneakers.

"Let's go," he said, yanking me out the door. "We'll miss the tide."

The next thing I knew, we were in the middle of the Talmadge Memorial Bridge, which crosses over the Savannah River and divides Georgia from South Carolina.

"Where are we going?" I asked, slightly alarmed.

"Bluffton." He glanced over to see if I would object. "It's the only way I can pry you away from your family and your dog and your ex-husband."

I looked down at the slow-moving brown water of the Savannah River. "Are you transporting me across state lines for immoral purposes?"

"I sincerely hope so," he said. "A buddy of mine has a house with a dock on the May River, and I've got the use of it while I'm on vacation this week."

"I can't go to Bluffton for a week."

"*I've* got the house for the week, not you," he said. "I just thought you might like to see it. It's kind of junky, like you seem to like. We'll have a little dinner, go crabbing, maybe go for a swim afterward."

"You didn't say anything about a bathing suit," I pointed out.

"Must have slipped my mind," he said, keeping his eyes on the road.

"I'll bet."

It started raining just as we reached the South Carolina side of the bridge. The rain came slow at first, and steam boiled up off the sunbaked pavement. July had been bonedry, but now it was getting to be prime hurricane season. The sky darkened and the rain came down harder, quickly flooding the low-country roadway.

Daniel turned up the volume on the radio to drown out the sound of the rain. He had it tuned to his favorite oldies station again.

They were playing "Summer Rain," an old Johnny Rivers number that I remembered from long years ago, when I'd gone to sleep-away camp and had a counselor who was lonesome for her boyfriend back home, and who played that song over and over at night after lights out.

Daniel hummed along with the music, and I watched the marshland flash by in a rich green streak, punctuated here and there by a fireworks store or a tomato stand.

He slowed the truck as we came into the town limits of Bluffton, and pointed at a small strip shopping center on the right. "Ever been in there?"

I looked where he was pointing. Half the shopping center had been given over to a place called La Juntique. Chairs and tables and dressers lined the sidewalk in front of the place.

"No," I said, craning my neck to get a better look. "Is it any good?"

"I've never been there," he said. "You want to take a look?"

This was something new. A man offering to stop at an antique store instead of speeding by, as Talmadge Evans would have done.

"Is there a catch?" I asked, looking at him suspiciously.

"I'm just trying to be nice," he said. "Can't a guy be nice?"

"You want something."

The grin again. "Yes."

"I'm guessing it's not my cheesecake recipe," I said.

"Maybe later."

CHAPTER 44

*T*rue to its name, La Juntique was mostly junk, with just enough antiques scattered around on the shelves and cabinets to keep me browsing.

Daniel followed me through the narrow aisles of the shop, studying me as I studied the merchandise. "What's that?" he'd ask as I picked up a pressed-glass fruit compote or a Victorian beadwork pillow. "Is it any good?"

He was starting to wear on my nerves. Maybe it had been a good thing that Tal avoided junking with me.

At the back of the shop was a large roped-off area. A cardboard sign taped to the back of a chair said "No Admittance. Employees Only."

A jumble of stuff; furniture, boxes overflowing with packing paper, wooden crates full of dusty books and old record albums, took up most of the space. Standing out like a diamond in a can of tenpenny nails was a small, square table.

It was made of cherry, with neatly tapered legs and a top inlaid with ebony.

I stopped and stared. Daniel was breathing down my neck. "Are you ready to go yet?"

"Not yet," I said, stepping over the rope.

"The sign says No Admittance," Daniel said. "Come on, Weezie. You want to get arrested again?"

I squatted down on the concrete floor and poked my head underneath the table. I ran my fingers over the dusty tabletop.

"What's so special about that table?" Daniel asked, looking around for the armed guards he obviously expected to descend upon us at any minute.

"It's an Empire card table," I said. "The nicest one I've ever seen. That's what I thought the last time I saw it."

"Huh?"

"At Beaulieu," I said, walking slowly around the table to get a look at it from all sides. "This table came out of Beaulieu. I'm positive of it."

I went up to the front of the shop, where a young woman of about eighteen sat concentrating on the latest issue of *People* magazine.

She looked up at me. "Yes, ma'am?"

"There's a table back there that I'm interested in," I said, pointing toward the back of the shop. "But it isn't priced."

She chewed her gum. "You'll have to talk to the owner."

"All right," I said pleasantly. "Where is she?"

"At home."

"Can you call her?"

"I guess."

She put the magazine down and picked up a cell phone.

"Liz? It's Catharine. There's a lady here with a question about a table."

"Tell her it's the Empire card table," I said. "In the employee area."

The girl frowned at that, but repeated it.

She listened and hung up the phone. "The owner says to tell you that table is not for sale." She looked at me accusingly. "You weren't supposed to be back there. It's private."

"Call the owner back, please," I said.

"Weezie," Daniel tugged at my elbow. "She told you it's not for sale."

"I just want to talk to her," I said. "To ask her where it came from."

The cashier rolled her eyes, but she punched in the number again. "I *told* her that table wasn't for sale, but now she wants to talk to you." She handed the phone to me.

"This is Liz Fuller," the woman said, her voice annoyed. "As Catharine explained, the card table is already sold."

"I understand," I said. "But I was wondering where the table came from. It's really an exceptional piece. Do you know anything about the provenance?"

"No. I bought it from one of my pickers because I have a customer who was looking for a piece of that description."

"But it's Empire," I said. "And it's really exquisite. Surely you know something about it. What's the picker's name? I'm a picker myself, and I'd be interested in seeing anything else that might have come out of the same house."

"I never share my resources," Liz Fuller said. And she hung up.

"Anything else?" the girl asked, smirking.

I took a business card out of my pocketbook and scribbled a note on the back, then handed it to the girl. "Give that to the owner when she comes in," I said. And I turned and stomped out of the store.

Daniel caught up with me at the truck. "What's with you?"

I looked down along the shop fronts in the strip center and saw that there was another antique shop at the far end.

"That table came out of Beaulieu. I saw it the night I was there, when I found Caroline. They canceled the estate sale, and supposedly it's been re-scheduled for this weekend. But I've been hearing rumors that the best pieces from the estate have already been sold off."

"So?"

""I told you about that cupboard, the Moses Weed. I need to know who is selling off those pieces from Beaulieu. If I knew that, I could approach them before the sale about buying the Moses Weed cupboard."

"Can't you just wait until Saturday?"

"I'm not the only one interested in the cupboard. There's a big-deal antique dealer, Lewis Hargreaves. He's interested in it too. And the rumor is that he's already bought some pieces from Beaulieu. I want to get to the Moses Weed piece before he does. If it's not too late."

"What did you write on your business card?"

"Just that I'd be willing to pay a finder's fee for information about who sold her the card table."

"Will that work?"

"I don't know," I admitted. "Dealers can be very closemouthed about this kind of stuff. They want to protect their sources, and the names of their pickers, to keep the best stuff for themselves."

"Are you ready to go?" he asked. "The rain's stopped. We can still get some crabbing in before it gets dark."

He saw the direction I was looking in.

"Just one more shop? Just a quick look-see?"

"Fifteen minutes," he said. "I've got to get the coals going for dinner."

"Deal," I said.

The shop was called Annie's Attic. Looking through the window, I could see it was a fussy little place, full of crystal and porcelain, with lots of frilly pseudo-Victorian reproduction pieces mixed in with candles and soaps and high-priced teddy bears and dolls. It was really not my kind of place at all . . . But I wasn't about to give up another fifteen minutes of junking.

The shop smelled like cinnamon potpourri. The displays were the opposite of La Juntique's. Everything in Annie's Attic was organized and displayed on pristine glass shelves lined with paper lace doilies.

I wrinkled my nose.

"Now what's wrong?" Daniel asked.

"Nothing. It's just a little too foo-foo for my taste."

"Foo-foo?"

"You know. Prissy, sissy. Fixed-up. Fancy."

"Not cruddy?"

"Well, yeah," I said. "I like my antiques to show their age. I don't trust anything too gussied-up. I think it smacks of pretense."

"That's why you like me," he said, a little too smugly.

"That and your chocolate seduction."

A display along the front of the store caught my eye. Unlike the shop's other pastel and lace offerings, this was an almost masculine vignette of wicker fishing creels, wooden duck decoys, old leather boxing gloves, and three majolica oyster plates.

The plates were wonderful, glazed in exuberant yellows and blues and greens, each of the oyster depressions glazed pink on the inside to look like a stylized oyster shell. Two of the plates matched. They had a raised seaweed border, with another border of tiny scallop shells along the very edge of the plate.

"This stuff doesn't look too foo-foo," Daniel said, picking up the pair of boxing gloves. "My dad gave my brother and me a set of gloves just like these when we were kids. We used to beat the crap out of each other with them."

I picked up one of the pair of matching plates and turned it over. The marking was what I'd expected. Minton.

"That's the first time I ever heard you mention your father," I said, looking at the other plate to make sure it was also Minton.

"My dad is dead," Daniel said, his voice flat. "He died when I was four. That's why I don't talk about him. There's nothing to say."

I gave him a thoughtful look. My great-grandmother had been dead since I was four. I thought about her and talked about her all the time. Maybe it was different with men.

I held up one of the plates for Daniel to see. "Aren't these great-looking?"

"You like oysters?" he asked, perking right up. "I've got a killer oyster stew I do in the fall, when they get sweet again."

"I love oysters," I said.

He took the plate from me and looked at it. "Cool." But he winced when he saw the price sticker. "Wow. Three hundred fifty dollars for a plate to eat oysters off of?"

"It's three hundred fifty for the pair," I said, picking up the matching plate. "This is English majolica. Minton, which is the manufacturer, is very desirable. I'm not an expert on majolica at all, but these look pretty early, probably 1860s. And I could swear they're the same ones I saw at Beaulieu."

A pained expression crossed his face. "Again?"

"At least these are apparently for sale," I said.

I took both plates up to the front counter, where a white-haired woman was sorting and pricing sterling silver flatware.

She looked up at me and smiled when she saw the plates in my hands. "Aren't those lovely? Do you collect majolica?"

"They're wonderful," I said. "Are you Annie?"

"Yes, I am," she said. "Shall I wrap those up for you?"

"Not just yet," I said. "What can you tell me about them?"

"They're Minton, of course, and really, the color and modeling is exceptional on these plates. Anyplace else you'd buy these, you'd pay double the price I'm asking."

"Where did they come from?" I was smiling too, just a friendly, curious collector.

"England."

"No. I meant, where did you buy them from?"

Her sunny smile suddenly took on a layer of frost. "An estate. I buy things all over the Southeast. And I do a buying trip in New England every summer."

"Did these come out of a local estate? Maybe over in Savannah?"

She picked up a silver soup spoon and pasted a price tag on the handle. "I really don't remember."

"They look exactly like a set of Minton oyster plates I saw at an old plantation house outside of Savannah. Called Beaulieu. Did these plates come from Beaulieu?"

Her blue eyes glittered dangerously. "I've never heard of Beaulieu. I'll have to ask you to leave now, I'm afraid. We close early on Wednesdays."

I looked pointedly at the sign on the wall behind her, which said "Open Weds., Noon–9 P.M."

She saw where I was looking, and didn't blink.

"Summer hours." She walked around the counter and held the shop door open. "Good-bye."

wo strikes," Daniel said. "I think there's another antique store up the road a little bit. Want to try for a third strike there?"

"I'm done," I said ruefully. "Sorry I got us sidetracked. What was that you were saying about dinner?"

He steered the truck onto the main road. "I've had a pork loin marinating all day. Then we've got some new potatoes with rosemary, chives, and sea salt to toss on the grill along with the pork. You like mango?"

I nodded.

"Mango and pineapple salsa, with cilantro and habanero peppers. I went all the way out to Polk's at Sandfly and got some killer Kentucky Wonder pole beans. And for dessert . . ." He glanced over at me. "I think I'll let that be a surprise."

"I think I could get used to this," I said.

"Hope so."

He made a right turn onto a narrow road and we bumped along past a dozen or so houses. Some of the houses were clearly nothing more than river shacks, while others had more uptown aspirations, with brick veneer and fancy decks and patios. All the houses were tucked higgledy-piggledy among thickets of cypress trees, oleander, swamp myrtle, and palmetto.

I smelled the river before I saw it, the tang of mud and salt an unexpected balm to my jangled nerves. And then it was there, green patches visible between houses, with long fingers of dock stretched out to meet deep water.

"Here we are," Daniel said, turning onto a dirt drive. The house was unpainted cedar, worn silvery gray. It had a shed roof made of rusting tin, and a screened porch ran along the front of it. A board nailed to a live oak in the front yard proclaimed it to be the Love Shack.

"Tater's last name is Love," he said. "He's the buddy I told you about."

"You know somebody named Tater Love?"

"His real name's Wesley," Daniel said. "But when he was a kid, the only vegetable he'd eat was potatoes."

"Guess it's no weirder a name than Weezie," I said.

It had started back to raining again. We sat in the truck with the motor running for five minutes, waiting for it to let up. "Guess we won't do any crabbing after all," Daniel said. "Getting late, anyway."

The rain kept coming down. "Want to make a run for it? The front door's unlocked. I'll be right there."

I splashed through the weed-strewn yard and pushed the screened door open with my foot. Daniel came right behind me, lugging a forty-quart Coleman cooler, and I held the door open wide and let him pass by.

Another screened door led into an abbreviated living room. He walked past and set the cooler down on a weather-beaten cedar picnic table.

"Well?" He was like a kid, wanting to please me.

"It's adorable," I said, and it was, in a rough-and-tumble fish camp kind of way. The first floor looked to be all one room. The living room flowed into the dining room, which flowed into a tiny galley kitchen. At the far end was a short hallway and a set of stairs that presumably led to the second floor. The interior was done in weathered cedar planks too, and there was a small rock fireplace at the living-room end of the great room. Big threadbare sofas and chairs faced the fireplace in a U shape, and the table and half a dozen rickety wooden kitchen chairs were set up so that you could look out at the river during mealtime.

"Heaven," I murmured, looking out at the rain-swollen marsh.

Daniel put his arms around my waist and pulled me to him. "Yeah," he said softly, "that's what I was thinking."

He nuzzled my ear. "There's some wine in the cooler. Can I pour you a glass?"

"That would be nice," I said, kissing him. "You mean, you shop for antiques, cook, and serve wine?"

"I'm a full-service kind of guy," Daniel said, demonstrating with his hands just what kind of service he was offering.

I followed him into the kitchen and helped unload the cooler. He uncorked the wine and poured us each a glass. We sipped and cuddled, and eventually the rain let up enough for us to wander outside to look for the grill.

"Tater said it was out on the dock last time he was over here," Daniel said. "But it's a family place, so stuff gets moved around." He led me by the hand out to the dock, which was just as weather-beaten as the house.

The tide was in, and the river lapped gently against the dock's pilings.

We found a rusty kettle grill at the end of the dock. A storage bench next to it had a flip-up lid that revealed a locker full of paddles, boat cushions, tackle boxes, and near the bottom, a bag of charcoal and a can of lighter fluid.

Daniel made the fire and I watched, sipping my wine, enjoying his efficiency of movement. I pulled a couple of the boat cushions out of the dock box and arranged them on top of a plank bench looking out across the river.

The sky was beginning to streak crimson and gold, and the rain had cooled things off considerably.

When he'd arranged the coals to his satisfaction, he sat down beside me on the bench, stretching his arm around my shoulders.

"Nice sky," I said.

"It'll do," he said. "Now what were we talking about before?"

"Something to do with lighting my fire," I said.

"Oh yes," he said, pulling me onto his lap. "You can light my fire."

Sometime after that, the coals burned down to white ash. The sun got set, and most of the bottle of wine got drunk. Daniel and I took our time getting to know each other.

"We should go inside," I said lazily, watching him undo the buttons on my blouse. "Somebody will see us."

"Who?"

"Fishermen. People in the other houses. People out on the docks."

"It's dark," Daniel said. "And nobody pays any attention to anybody else over here. This is Bluffton."

"You have a real thing about lovemaking alfresco, don't you?" I asked. He was busy kissing me, and I didn't get an answer for some time.

"Oh," I said, and he kissed my shoulder blade and went a little lower.

"Oh," I said again, but this time it had an entirely different context. As in, oh yes.

When the sun was entirely gone, a bright yellow light blinked on atop a light pole beside the grill.

Suddenly self-conscious, I tried to pull my blouse together.

"Hey," Daniel said, "you're ruining all my hard work."

"I know," I said, struggling to stand up. "But I really don't feel like putting on a show here. Besides, don't you want to start dinner?"

He tugged my hand until I landed back in his lap. "The hell with dinner. I'm doing just fine with the starter."

He pushed my blouse off my shoulder. "Hey," he said, slipping a finger under the shoulder strap of my black-on-blond bra, "this is nice. Is it a breakaway number like that black dress of yours?"

"No," I said. "It's brand new. It's the most expensive lingerie I've ever bought."

"For me?" He reached both hands around my back. "Here. Let's take it off so it doesn't get all swampy."

He popped the snap with the same wonderful efficiency he'd used in lighting the fire.

"Can't you make that light go away?" I asked.

He reached the lamppost in a single stride. A minute later it was dark, and I heard what I was sure was a lightbulb hit the top of the water.

After that, the only sounds were the gentle lapping of the river against the dock pilings and the even gentler rustling of clothing being removed.

At some point in the proceedings, a long-forgotten concern occurred to me.

"Birth control," I murmured, rolling away from him on the dock.

He trailed a fingertip lightly down my belly. "You're on the pill—right?"

"Wrong," I said, catching his hand with mine.

He groaned, and it wasn't a good groan. "Did you happen to see a drugstore back there in town?"

I had to laugh. "You transport me across the state line for immoral purposes, you pack a cooler with a four-course dinner, including wine, and you forget a thing like that?"

He kissed my shoulder and sat up and started looking for his clothes.

"Don't move," he said. "I'll be right back. Tater probably has something up in the house."

"You're nuts," I said, "if you think I'm waiting out here, naked, alone, on the end of a dock in the middle of nowhere. I've seen all the 'B' movies, and this is the perfect slasher setup. Besides," I said, reaching for my own clothes, "I'm getting splinters in my butt."

Back in the house I sat on the edge of the sofa and giggled while Daniel ransacked the house, opening cupboards and drawers and closets and slamming them all with loud, explosive expletives.

"Goddamn it, Tater," I heard him mutter. "Where do you hide your damned rubbers?"

By now I really was starting to get hungry. I found the loaf of french bread he'd brought, and cut off a slice, which I slathered with what looked like homemade pâté.

Daniel came stomping down the stairs, cursing and muttering.

I held out a piece of bread to him, but he shook his head in refusal.

"Just how old is this Tater person?" I asked, looking around the Love Shack. Now that I thought about it, the place didn't look much like a swinging bachelor's pad. No black leather sofas, no lava light, no CD player, no condoms.

"Tater?" Daniel got a blank look. "I don't know. He's in his late fifties or early sixties, I guess."

"And is he married?"

"Not any more. Why?"

"Give up the search, genius," I said. "If Tater did have any Trojans, the expiration date probably passed twenty years ago. They'd probably fall to pieces as soon as you unwrapped one."

His face fell. "God damned Tater." He picked the car keys off the table by the cooler. "There was a convenience store right before we came into Bluffton. I'll bet they'll have something."

"Good thought," I said. "In the meantime, don't you want me to start dinner? It's past nine, you know."

"Yeah, sure," he said. "There's a grill basket for the potatoes. Pour some olive oil on 'em before you put them in the basket. And put the tenderloin at the side of the grill. I don't want it to get too charred. And the green beans can be heated up; I cooked them earlier in the day . . ."

"Go on," I said, waving him away. "I *do* know how to cook, you know."

"Not as good as me," he said.

"We'll see about that."

I found a canvas tote bag hanging on a hook by the back door, and loaded it up with the pork, the potatoes, and everything else I'd need. Then I took my fixings out to the dock and arranged everything on the coals.

I sat and sipped my wine and listened to the sizzle of the meat and potatoes on the grill. After fifteen minutes, I took the pork off the coals. And after another ten, I added the potatoes and the pork to the platter I'd brought, covered it all with foil, and strolled back to the Love Shack.

Daniel had been gone over half an hour. I set the table for two, fixed myself another slice of bread and pâté, and put the green beans in a saucepan on the stove and turned the heat on low.

I roamed around the house, wineglass in hand, exploring. As I'd expected, there was a small bathroom downstairs. Upstairs, there were only two more rooms. A rustic bathroom with a rust-stained porcelain sink and a claw-foot bathtub, and a single bedroom.

It was not the Ritz. The room was fitted up under the eaves of the house, meaning the bed sat under a sloping ceiling with no more than four feet of headroom above it. The bed itself was an old four-poster whose headposts had been sawed off to allow the bed to fit into the space. A pile of neatly folded sheets sat atop a threadbare cotton quilt covering the bed.

I thought about making the bed, but in some weird way, I couldn't. It seemed to planned. Too hussyish.

I went back downstairs and looked at the clock. Daniel had been gone forty-five minutes. By now he could have gone all the way to Savannah and back.

Looking around the living room reminded me of the bid I'd left earlier in the day for the rattan furniture. I wondered if the dealer had called.

There was a phone on the wall in the kitchen. I picked it up and dialed in my phone card number, and then my house number. I punched in the code to retrieve messages from my answering machine. There were three messages.

The first one was from Uncle James.

"Weezie? Your mother is fine. Don't worry about her. You both took a big step today. I'll talk to you later."

The second message was from the dealer.

"Eloise Foley? This is Gary Wolcott. Your bid for seven hundred fifty dollars for the Heywood-Wakefield has been accepted. Pick it up tomorrow, by five, or it's no deal."

The third caller really didn't need to identify himself.

"Weezie?" His voice was soft, little more than a whisper. "Baby, I'm sorry. I'm sorry about everything. I swear to God," he said, and now his speech was slurring. "I never meant to hurt you. Just believe that I loved you. Only you. Caroline was a mistake. You were the only woman I ever really loved. I always did, and, uh, baby, about the house . . ." His voice trailed off for a moment. "Yeah. The house. I want you to have it. After-ward. So, OK. And I love you. I told you that." His voice trailed off. The tape kept going, but Tal's voice stopped.

I hung up the phone, feeling chilled. What did he mean, afterward? He was drunk again, I told myself. He was trying to make me feel sorry for him. Trying to scare me.

I called Tal's number. My scalp prickled when I heard the voice on the answering machine, a voice from beyond the grave. A clipped, nasal accent. "Hi. You've reached Caroline and Tal. We're busy. So leave a num-ber. OK?"

I almost hung up, but instead I hung on. "Tal? Are you there? Pick up if you're there. It's Weezie, Tal. And I'm tired of your little games. Sober up and pick up the phone, damn you," I shouted.

The kitchen door swung open and Daniel pranced in, holding aloft a large shopping bag in one hand and a tiny brown bag in the other.

"Look what I brought!" he called in a giddy singsong voice. "Big pres-ents and little presents. Who wants a present?"

"Just a minute," I said, covering the receiver with my hand. "Pick up the phone, Tal," I shouted. "Pick it up and quit playing games."

All I heard was the tape spooling. I hung up.

Daniel threw the small paper sack at me. A box of Trojan Ultra Pleasures fell out.

"Here," he said, disgust dripping from his voice. "I don't guess I'll be needing these tonight. You can take 'em to Tal."

"his isn't what you think," I said. "Tal left a message on my machine. He sounded strange. He said something about giving me the house. Afterward. And then he quit talking. I'm afraid he might be suicidal."

"He's drunk," Daniel said, throwing his keys down on the table.

"I'm telling you, something was wrong with him," I said, dialing my own number. I punched in the activation code again and handed the phone to Daniel. "Here. You tell me what you think."

He listened, then hung up. "He knows how to push all your buttons, doesn't he?"

"Are you telling me that was an act?"

"What do you want to do?"

"I don't know. He's never been like this before. He never gets drunk. He's always in control. But his voice . . . I wonder if he took something . . ."

"That's ridiculous, Weezie. Think about it. The voice on the message trailed off. But you called his house, right? And you got the answering machine. Right? So it's not like he collapsed and left the phone off the hook."

"Right," I said, feeling a mixture of anger and relief. "But what if he didn't call me from his house? What if he was at the office or someplace else?"

Daniel ran his fingers through his hair, leaving it standing on end.

"I can't believe this is happening. Are you saying you want to rush back to Savannah, to save him from himself?"

"I don't know," I shouted, pissed that I was on the verge of tears. "I don't know what to do, damn it. But this isn't some kind of popularity contest, Daniel. I'm over Tal. I've told you that. I don't know how to make you believe it."

"I'll believe it when you believe it," Daniel said.

I picked up the phone.

"Now what?"

"I'm calling his office," I said, turning my back on him. "I'd do as much for a casual friend, if I thought he was in trouble. You can't expect me to just act like Tal never happened. Not if you care about me."

"He's playing you," Daniel said. He went into the kitchen and started clattering pots and pans. The phone at Tal's office rang and rang, and then the answering machine picked up.

"Christ," Daniel shouted. As I turned around I saw a cloud of black smoke rising from the saucepan full of green beans. He picked the pan up and threw it in the sink, drowning it under the tap.

"I'm sorry," I said. "I got distracted and I forgot. I'll pay for the pan. I'll buy you more beans. I don't know what else to do."

I dialed another number.

"BeBe?"

"What's up, Weezie?"

"Something's going on with Tal. He left a message on my machine. I don't know, I think he sounded drunk or drugged or something."

"Which is it? And why are you calling me about it?"

"I'm over in Bluffton. With Daniel. Tal doesn't answer at the house, or at his office. I'm worried. He's been depressed. Do you think he could have tried something stupid?"

"He did try something stupid," BeBe drawled. "He left you for that slut Caroline. Forget about him, Weezie. He's not worth it. Tal Evans is your past. Daniel is your future. Now hang up the phone and quit fucking up your life."

"One thing," I pleaded. "Just do me one thing."

"What?"

"Drive over to the townhouse. See if his car is there. There's a key to the back door under the planter on the back steps. Just check to see if he's there."

"You're crazy, you know that?"

"Will you do it?"

"What do you want me to do after that?"

"Call me here."

I looked over at Daniel. "What's the number here?"

I told her the number. "Call me as soon as you know something."

Daniel was scrubbing the layer of burned beans on the bottom of the pan with a piece of steel wool. Then he took a steak knife and started stabbing at the charred food. I watched for a minute or two, then walked over to the sink and took the pan out of his hands.

"I was working on that," he said, his voice cold.

"You'll never get it clean that way," I said. "Believe me, I've watched my mother burn a lifetime's worth of food. Have you got any bleach?"

He rummaged around until he found a small bottle of Clorox.

I put a couple of inches of water in the pan and added about a quarter of a cup of bleach, then I set the pan on the back burner on the lowest heat.

"Bleach fumes," Daniel said. "You'll kill us both. The cops will find Tal's body at his house and ours here. They'll say it was a lovers' triangle." He was trying not to smile, but it wasn't working.

I pointed at all the open windows, and at the screened porch. "We've got plenty of ventilation. And I'm not planning on killing myself. Or you. Not with bleach fumes. Not just yet, anyway."

I picked up the paper bag of condoms, looked at the box. There were twenty-four in the carton. "You had some mighty big plans for tonight, I see."

"Not just for tonight," he said quietly.

The phone rang again. I snatched it up.

"He's home, and he's alive, more's the pity," BeBe said.

"Thank God," I said. "What did he say?"

"Nothing," BeBe said. "He's passed out on the sofa."

"He's not in a coma? You didn't see any pills or anything?"

"Just a half-empty bottle of Scotch," BeBe said. "I slapped him around, and he came to long enough to tell me to get the hell out of his house."

"I owe you, Babe."

"You certainly do," she said, and then she hung up.

"He's not dead," I told Daniel. "Just drunk and passed out. You were right. I guess Tal was just yanking my chain. Again."

"Imagine my relief," he said, his voice dripping with sarcasm.

"What now?" I asked wearily. "Do you want to take me home?"

He had been standing at the kitchen counter, methodically cutting the pork roast into half-inch-thick slices. He put the knife down and came and sat down on the sofa beside me.

"You know what I want?" he said, taking my hand in his. "I want to know why you keep trying to run away from me. Every time we start to get close, something happens. At first I thought it was just circumstances. But now? I don't know. Everything was going fine tonight. Then you decide to call home and wham! We're right back where we were before."

I looked down at the floor, then out the kitchen window. But there were no answers there.

"I want to be with you," I whispered. "I do. But it's no good. I'm terrible at this relationship stuff. I try, but it just doesn't work out."

"What the hell is that supposed to mean?" Daniel asked. He put his hand under my chin and turned my head so I was looking straight at him.

"Look at my track record," I said. "I thought my marriage to Tal was perfect. And look what happened. Tal and I never fought. I mean never. And then one day, it was over. I had no clue he was having an affair. No clue he wasn't happy. And now, look at you and me. It's crazy. I am *so* attracted to you. Half the time I want to get naked with you and the other half I want to beat your brains in. We fight all the time. And I don't like fighting."

"How do you know?" he countered. "I think you never fought with Tal because he never cared enough. And you did whatever he told you to anyway. So he didn't need to fight with you. Me? I've had to fight for everything I've ever gotten in my life. That's OK. It makes it better. It makes it worth having."

He kissed the back of my hand. "You are worth having, Weezie Foley. You're worth fighting for. And fighting with. And making up with."

"How do you know?" I demanded.

"I know," he said. He picked up the carton of Trojans. "Do you think I would have made a major investment like this if I wasn't positive we'd be great together?"

I sniffed a little and smiled. "What's in the big shopping bag? If it's more Trojans, I'm out of here."

"It's a gift," he said. "I thought if this was going to be a special night, you should have something to remember it by."

"You mean something besides splinters in my butt?"

The bag was heavy. The object inside was swaddled in thick layers of tissue, all of them taped together. I tore at the tissue until the bright green and blue glaze became visible.

"The oyster dishes," I said, my voice catching.

"That's what took so long," he said. "That shopkeeper was locking up when I got there. I didn't think she was going to sell them to me, until I whipped out the cash."

"You paid cash?" I asked, incredulous. "But you should have tried to bargain with her. Dealers always come down at least twenty percent, especially when you pay cash."

"Nope," he said. "I wanted you to have them. At full price. No dickering."

"They're wonderful," I said. "But you shouldn't have spent that much money on me."

"On us," he said. And he took the plates and set them carefully down on the coffee table. Then he picked up the carton of Trojans and took me by the hand. And we went upstairs to discuss our investment potential.

CHAPTER 47

When I woke up, Daniel was nibbling on my ear.

"What ever happened to that dinner you promised me?" I asked sleepily.

"Why, are you hungry?"

"Starved," I said, sitting up. "What time is it, anyway?"

He picked his watch up from the nightstand and handed it over to me.

"Seven," I said, sinking back into the pillows. "I've got to get going."

"What's your hurry?" he asked, pointing toward the Trojan carton, which was surrounded by little foil wrappers. "We've barely made a dent in the supply."

"You may be on vacation," I said, planting a kiss on his forehead, "but I've got work to do. Including getting over to that house on the Southside to pick up your new living-room furniture."

"Oh yeah," he said, yawning again. "Furniture."

"Dibs on first shower," I said. I took the quilt and wrapped it around myself and padded toward the bathroom.

"I think we should share," he called after me. "The drought, you know."

"It rained most of yesterday and all night last night," I pointed out. "Anyway, I'm serious. I really do need to get back to Savannah."

By the time I got out of the shower, Daniel had fallen back to sleep. I dressed in the clothes I'd brought to wear crabbing, and was silently grateful that I had something clean to change into, just in case anybody who'd seen me leaving my carriage house yesterday should happen to glance out the window and see me coming back today—in the same clothes.

Downstairs, I made coffee and piddled around in the kitchen, slicing the french bread and toasting it under the broiler with some slices of Havarti cheese Daniel had packed. When my breakfast was ready, I took it out to the dock and watched the early morning sun sparkling on the May River. A blue heron stalked quietly by in the mud, and I tossed it the last bits of my toast.

At eight, I took a cup of coffee and more of the cheese toast upstairs for Daniel. He was still sleeping. I set the dishes down on the nightstand and leaned over to kiss him, but as soon as I got close, an arm snaked around my waist and pulled me down onto the bed.

"None of that." I laughed, trying to push myself away from him. "I've showered and I've dressed, and now I'm ready for business."

"Mmm," he said, running his hands up under my T-shirt. "I'm ready for business too."

"I can tell," I said, patting the covers. "But that's not the kind of business I had in mind. Come on, Daniel, I really need to go to town."

He grinned.

"That's *not* what I meant," I said. "Is everything a double entendre with you?"

"The morning after? Yes. Do you have a problem with that?"

"Not as long as you get up and get dressed and take me home. Are you going to do that, or do I hijack the truck and drive myself back to Savannah?"

"I'll take you," he grumbled. "But this is not what I had in mind."

"Give me a raincheck," I said, tugging him upright.

Tal's BMW was parked in his slot behind the townhouse.

Daniel pointed at it. "Guess he's not feeling up to work this morning."

"Asshole," I said. "I hope he has the king hell hangover of all times, after what he put me through last night."

"What you put yourself through," Daniel said. "I'll call you later."

He put the truck in reverse and started to back out into the lane.

"Hey," I yelled, pounding on the hood of his truck to get his attention. He stuck his head out the window. "What?"

"I'm going to go pick up your furniture this afternoon. Want to give me a check to pay for it?"

He fumbled around in the glove box until he found his checkbook. "You shack up with me for one night and already you're making me write bad checks?"

"It better not be bad," I told him. "I've got a reputation to protect."

"It's good," Daniel said. "Like me." He tore the check out of the book and handed it over.

"And what should I do with the stuff after I pick it up?" I asked. "There's no room to store it here."

He sighed. "What time were you going over there?"

"The guy wants it gone by five o'clock."

"All right," he said. "Guess I'll just spend the rest of the day in town, then go back over to Bluffton tonight. Give me the address of the house and I'll meet you out there. Four o'clock OK?"

"Fine," I said. I gave him the address, and without checking to see whether or not Tal was watching out the window, I leaned in the window and gave Daniel a long wet kiss good-bye.

Inside, I propped my Beaulieu oyster plates up against the living-room mantel and stood back to see how they looked.

"Great," I muttered. "They look great. But two oyster plates aren't enough to fill the space. I need something else. Preferably another piece of majolica."

I took one of the plates over to my desk and got out my magnifying glass. The Minton mark was quite clear under the glass, which made me feel much better about Daniel's paying full price.

For the first time I looked closely at the price tag on the back of the plate. It was the dealer's handwritten tag. Like most dealers, she'd put the store price on the tag, but there was also a series of letters and numbers which I knew was her own code, probably for the amount she'd originally paid for the plate, plus any other pertinent information she would want to remember, such as the date the piece was purchased and, possibly, the source.

Every dealer has his own code, a way of keeping inventory. Most of them allow the dealer to tell, at a glance, a fairly complete history of a piece.

I took the other plate down and checked the back, but it didn't have a price tag, since—duh! The dealer had priced the plates as a set.

The dealer's code was a mystery to me, but if anybody could decode it, I thought, Lester Dobie could.

Lester stared down at the oyster plate through a jeweler's loupe.

"That's an authentic Minton mark," he said. "Where'd it come from?"

"My friend bought it from a shop over in Bluffton. Annie's Attic."

He pursed his lips. "Doesn't ring a bell."

"The dealer code is what I'm interested in," I said. "Does it look familiar?"

He took a pencil and jotted the code down on a piece of scrap paper.

"Part of it's just straight old pricing code, substituting letters for numbers," he said, reading off the scrap of paper. "AEO—that's a hundred and fifty most likely."

"She got them for a steal if that's all she paid. What about the rest?"

"Seven-three-oh-oh-oh," he read off. "Could be the date of purchase. July thirtieth, 2000."

"And the ZK?"

He shrugged. "The initials of the seller?"

"ZK," I repeated. "Sound familiar?"

"Zack?" he said.

I dug in my tote bag until I found my business-card directory. I flipped over to the K page and glanced down at a dozen business cards belonging to antique dealers, interior designers, salvage yard operators, and other pickers. I had plenty of Ks in my directory, but no ZKs.

Lester pulled the big Rolodex from atop a stack of antique reference books on his desk and thumbed through the inch-thick section of Ks.

"No ZKs here," he reported.

I moved papers around on the desktop until I found the Savannah yellow pages. I turned to the section for antique shops.

"Kaplan Fine Antiques. Keyes Kollectibles. King's Ransom Antiques. Kramer & Culkin," I said, moving my fingertip down the alphabetical listings. "Nothing matches here. Think maybe the code is reversed, and the seller is really KZ?"

He shrugged. I flipped to the Z page of my directory. Only one card, for a Ruth Zofchak, a Pennsylvania dealer who specialized in Bohemian glass.

Lester had two Zs in his Rolodex, but not KZs, and there were no Z listings in the yellow pages either.

"Could be anybody," I said. "I buy and sell antiques from Orlando all the way to Wilmington, North Carolina."

"Or it could just be she bought the plates from somebody who happened to have two majolica plates that just looked like the ones you saw out at Beaulieu," Lester said.

"No." I shook my head emphatically. "It couldn't just be a coincidence. That woman at Annie's Attic absolutely clammed up when I started asking questions about where she bought the plates. And the owner at La Juntique, she had the same reaction when I asked where that card table came from. No, Lester. I think they both bought stuff from the same person, who swore them to secrecy, because the stuff came out of Beaulieu, and they don't want anybody finding out about it."

Lester scratched his chin. "How are you gonna prove any of this? And even if you could prove the stuff came out of Beaulieu—so what?"

"It came out of Beaulieu after the memorial service for Anna Ruby Mullinax, but before I found Caroline's body," I said. "Don't you see the connection? Whoever is selling this stuff off probably knows who killed Caroline. Probably killed her himself."

Lester rolled his eyes. "Stick to picking, Weezie," he said. "'Cause as a detective, you're pitiful. You've been in this business long enough, you know how things work. People cut corners. They make shady deals. It's the nature of the business. Just 'cause somebody sells an antique under the table, that don't make 'em a murderer. Hell, if that was so, we'd all be locked up in the jailhouse."

"I know I'm right, Lester," I said. "Can't you think of anybody to call? Somebody else who knows everybody along the coast? Somebody who might know a ZK?"

"Maybe," he said. "She sure enough likes to gossip, and that's a natural fact. Let me give it a try."

He put his hand over his Rolodex, shielding the card so I couldn't see the name; obviously this source was his own version of Deep Throat.

He dialed the number and waited. "Shug? Hey. It's Lester. You been keeping sweet?" He listened, then chuckled. "Got a little puzzle for you. I'm trying to track down somebody who might be doin' a little picking, over there in the Bluffton vicinity. All we know is the initials. Either ZK, or maybe KZ. Can you think of somebody like that?"

He shook his head. "The person's selling off stuff could have come out of Beaulieu. You know? The old plantation house out there at Isle of Hope?"

He waited. Then wrote something quickly on his pad of paper.

"It's a start. Thanks, shug. Tell your daddy hey for me."

He hung up the phone and pushed the pad of paper toward me.

"Zoe Kallenberg," I said, reading it. "You know her?"

"Never heard that name before," he said, picking up the white pages of the phone book. He leafed over to the K listings. "Lives at two-oh-four and a half Liberty. That'd be pretty close to the intersection there at Abercorn. An apartment probably. Most likely a basement apartment."

"Wait a minute," I said. I opened the yellow pages back up to the antique dealer listings. L. Hargreaves was the first listing on the page. Lewis Hargreaves' shop. At 206 Abercorn.

 ames pushed through the door to his office, concentrating on the lateness of the hour and not on the weeping woman who occupied a seat opposite Janet, his secretary.

"James," Janet said. "Mrs. Cahoon has been waiting to see you."

"Oh," he said. "I have another meeting this morning. Out of the office."

It was uncanny how Janet could read his mind.

"I explained that to Mrs. Cahoon," she said smoothly. "That the normal procedure is to make an appointment. But she wanted to see if you could spare her just a moment. Before you leave in five minutes for your appointment."

Denise Cahoon poured herself into the chair opposite his desk. "It's Inky," she said, slapping a file folder on his desk. "He wants a divorce. A man came to the house this morning and gave me these papers. After twenty-two years of marriage."

James scanned the papers. Bradley R. Cahoon Jr. was filing for a divorce from Denise Doheny Cahoon on the grounds of desertion.

"Desertion," he said, handing Denise a tissue. "I thought Inky left you."

"He did," she cried. "While I was living at my sister's house in Waycross."

"You were living in Waycross? With your sister?"

"Just until her nerves settled down. Sheila's always been very high-strung. So I went over to Waycross to help out."

"How long ago was this?" James asked.

She pursed her lips and thought it over. "It was 1996 probably. Yes, 1996 definitely."

James nodded. "You moved to Waycross. In 1996. To stay with your sister. And when did you move back to Savannah?"

"Months ago," Denise said. "It's been months and months I've been back."

"Mrs. Cahoon," James said, "you haven't lived with your husband in five years. Is that what you're telling me?"

"He was never home. Always sneaking around with that whore girlfriend of his," she cried.

"According to the law, Mrs. Cahoon, you are the one who left the marital home. Five years is a long time for a wife to live apart from her husband."

"Sheila needed me," Denise said, her chin trembling.

"I'm sure," James said. He glanced down at his watch. "Well. Sorry to have to rush you along, but I really have to be getting along to my meeting."

"What about my problem?" Denise demanded. "This divorce. I want it stopped. I don't believe in divorce."

He had an idea. He flipped through the cards in his Rolodex, scribbled down a name and phone number, and handed it to Denise Doheny Cahoon.

"Who's this?" she asked.

"A former colleague, Father Gower. He works for the archdiocese."

"Does he do counseling?" she asked eagerly.

"No," James said. "He handles petitions for annulment."

"Annulment," she asked. "Is that legal?"

"Perfectly legal," James said, "and if ever I knew of a candidate for an annulment, it's you and Inky. Good day, Mrs. Cahoon."

Janet was shaking her head when James emerged from his office. She'd been eavesdropping, of course. "Annulment. That's a brilliant idea. Why didn't you think of that before?"

"Don't know," James said. "I really do have a meeting, you know. It's out in the country someplace, near Guyton."

"Fine," Janet said. "I hope it's an appointment that will produce some billable hours. Your sister-in-law called while you were in with Denise Cahoon."

"Did she sound sober?"

"She wasn't talking to any saints or anything. Just said for you to remember you're supposed to go someplace with her this afternoon."

"I know," he said wearily. "We're going to try to get her in a rehab. And move her out of her dead cousin's house again."

"Whatever," Janet said.

It had been on one of his mind-numbingly boring walks around Forsyth Park that he remembered the names of Grady and Juanita Traylor, the witnesses listed on Anna Ruby Mullinax's will.

Grady Traylor had been a deacon at Christ Our Hope, James's first little country church. Grady's wife, Juanita, had been the church's only catechism teacher. They were elderly back then, probably in their sixties. And Grady Traylor, he finally recalled, was a cousin to Clydie Jeffers, who had worked for many years as Anna Ruby Mullinax's housekeeper. Grady, he thought, had worked as a sometime yardman at Beaulieu.

It had taken some digging to find the Traylors. Christ Our Hope had been annexed into another country church, and the priest there, Father Viraj, was new to the parish and uncertain where the old parish records were kept. It had been Karyl Conners, the church secretary, who finally called James back with the news that she had traced the Traylors to their new address in Guyton, Georgia.

With the address in hand, Janet had done a title search on her computer and turned up the deed to the house in Guyton, which, it turned out, was owned by the Willis J. Mullinax Foundation.

Now the white Mercedes hummed over the still-wet pavement of the country road outside Guyton.

Juanita Traylor had been overjoyed to hear from him, although he'd had to shout to make himself heard.

"Father Foley!" she'd exclaimed when he called. "Wait 'til I tell Grady you coming to visit. He'll be fit to be tied. Sure will. And I believe he might recognize you. These days, he don't know me too good, but he sure does remember folks from a long time ago. Doctor says that's called short-term memory loss. You come in time for lunch now, Father, all right? I know you be missing good country cooking living in the city all these years."

James felt bad about not mentioning the purpose of his visit, or the fact that he was no longer Father Foley, but he reasoned that in this case, the ends justified the means.

Juanita had given him directions to turn right after he came to an abandoned feed store, and left when he came to an abandoned school bus yard.

On a quiet road not far from the field full of abandoned yellow buses, he was surprised to find a stout new brick house with the names of Grady & Juanita Traylor painted in two-inch-high letters on the mailbox.

"Father Foley!" Juanita exclaimed, when she opened the front door. Twenty years ago, she had been a plump woman who favored large flowered hats and flowing dresses. Now she resembled a shrunken little doll, her faded dress hanging from skeletally thin shoulders, her head nearly bald except for a few sparse patches of snow white hair.

She ushered him inside the house, clutching him by the arm to keep herself upright.

"This is so nice," she said, beaming up at him through cataract-frosted eyes. "So nice to get some company."

She made him sit at a small Formica table in the kitchen and fed him a plate of home-cooked vegetables. "Them's field peas from my garden, and sweet corn, of course, and stewed tomatoes and okry. My okry didn't make this year, but I put up a mess in the freezer last year," she said, her high-pitched voice trembling with delight.

He held her papery hand in his and they said the blessing together, but Juanita wouldn't eat. "Oh no, Father. I don't eat 'til four o'clock, when I fix supper for me and Grady. He's having his nap right now, but in a little while, I'm gonna get him up and let him have his surprise. That's you. You're his surprise. He'll be so tickled."

The food was magnificent, fresh, simply prepared, with a slab of cornbread on the side, and a jug of iced tea so sweet and cold he could have drunk a gallon of it.

When he'd finally satisfied Juanita that he'd eaten all he could, James took his time about getting down to the reason for his visit.

"Your children," he asked. "Little Grady and Juanette and Boo and Travis, how are they all?"

She beamed again and filled him in on the number of grandchildren and great-grands she and Grady had helped raise.

"And Grady?" he asked. "I take it he's had some health problems?"

"Oh yes," she said, patting his hand. "But the Lord didn't give us nothin' we can't bear. He's real good, Grady is. This house was just a blessin' from the Lord. Air-conditioning so his emphysema don't worry him so much, and a big tile bathroom I can get his wheelchair into real easy. Miss Anna Ruby, she done us a blessin', and that's a natural fact."

James smiled. "Miss Anna Ruby died last month, you know."

Juanita nodded. "Yes, Father, I knowed all about that. Boo, you remember him, he was my youngest, his oldest boy cut the piece about her passin' out of the Savannah paper and brung it over here to read to me. Me and Grady were real sad about that, but happy Miss Anna Ruby went to a better place."

"I understand you and Grady had some dealings with Miss Anna Ruby's lawyer, Gerry Blankenship, a few months before she passed," James said.

Juanita looked down at her hands and studied them. James waited.

"Mister Gerry said we wasn't to speak about that," Juanita said finally. "He been so good to us, I don't like to do him wrong."

"The will is a matter of public record, Juanita," James said, taking some papers from his briefcase. "See here? I got a copy from the courthouse. So you wouldn't be breaking any secrets talking about it now."

"You reckon?" she asked. "I know it's sinful to be fixed on material goods, but this house here, Miss Anna Ruby made that happen, and I don't hardly like to think what we'd do if we had to leave it now. First time in my life I ever had air-conditioning, and I just praise Jesus every day when that cool air comes floating across my face."

"It's a beautiful home," James said, gazing admiringly around the tiny spotless kitchen. "How long have you lived here?"

"First of May, we moved in," Juanita said quickly. "At first, I said, no sir, I can't move to Guyton. That's too far. None of my people be over there. But Mr. Gerry, he was real firm that me and Grady should have this nice brick house. And he put the furniture and everything in it for us, so we didn't have to worry about a single thing."

"That was very kind of Mr. Blankenship," James said. "And he told you that the house was a gift from Miss Anna Ruby?"

"That's right," Juanita said. "And I worried and fussed, thinking I'd get a bill or something in the mail, but I never did. It's been three months, so I reckon the Lord wants us here."

"I'm sure that's right," James agreed. "I wondered if you would talk to me a little bit about how you came to witness Miss Anna Ruby's will?"

He held the papers he'd brought with him out for her to inspect. She looked down at them and back up at him. "That's right. We done signed that paper good and proper, like Mr. Gerry asked us to."

"When did he ask you to sign them?" James asked.

"Hmm," she said. "Well now, I recollect he come over to the house, the old house, that is, one day way back in the spring, and he brung me a box of candy. That was sweet, wasn't it? I didn't like to tell him I can't eat candy 'cause I got the sugar diabetes. And he had some papers he needed me and Grady to sign. As a favor to Miss Anna Ruby. So we done that, and Mr. Gerry he was so pleased. And he said Miss Anna Ruby had a house over here in Guyton she was fixin' to move into, but then she was failin' and decided to stay put, and so we would be doing Miss Anna Ruby a favor if we moved in over here to take care of things."

"That was very kind of Mr. Blankenship," James said. "And did you get the chance to see Miss Anna Ruby when you signed the papers?"

"No, Father," Juanita said. "We never did get to see her sweet face again."

"And you didn't see her the day you signed the papers?"

"No," Juanita said, and then she frowned. "Oh, Lord. I wasn't supposed to say nothing about that, was I?"

"Did Mr. Gerry ask you not to tell anybody about how you signed the papers?" James asked.

She stared down at her hands again. "Mr. Gerry been awful good to us," she repeated.

"You and Grady are good folks," James said. "And I sure did enjoy the lunch you fixed for me."

"You're not gonna leave yet," Juanita exclaimed. "Not before Grady gets a chance to see you."

James looked down at his watch. Marian's appointment at St. Joseph's was at 2:30. "I hate to have you wake him from his rest."

But Juanita was out of her chair and making her way haltingly toward the hallway. "Now you just set right there for a minute or two, Father Foley."

Five minutes later, she pushed a wheelchair into the living room. The man in the chair had once been a bear of a man, short, but powerfully built, so strong he'd single-handedly cut and hauled all the pine trees that had fallen on Christ Our Hope during a bad tornado. Now Grady Traylor slumped over in the wheelchair, a strap around his chest the only thing keeping his frail body from slipping to the floor. An oxygen mask was fastened to his face and his brown eyes seemed unfocused.

"Looky who's here, Grady Traylor," she called loudly. "You remember

Father Foley, Grady. He come to visit with us today. Ain't that grand? Come all the way from Savannah."

Grady Traylor blinked, and James thought he saw a spark of recognition.

Juanita smoothed the worn fabric of Grady's cotton pajama top, her thin hands caressing the shrunken shoulder blade.

"He's just so pleased," she told James. "Now, I was wondering if you would do something for us. Something special. 'Cause to tell the truth, this here house is so far out in the country, we ain't been able to get to Mass."

James nodded. He knelt down on the carpeted floor beside Grady Traylor's wheelchair, and Juanita knelt beside him, clinging to the arm of the wheelchair for support.

"Bless me, Father, for I have sinned," Juanita began, her eyes tightly shut.

"And bless me, Father," James thought, for the sin of wanting to give comfort to these frail but faithful children of God.

CHAPTER 49

*J*ames eased himself into a rocking chair and took a deep sip of gin and tonic.

"Better?" Jonathan asked.

James took another sip and tipped his head back. "Some."

"I'm sure the Traylors were delighted to see you," Jonathan said. "And they didn't really have anything to confess, did they?"

"No," James admitted. "Grady has had a stroke and can't speak. And Juanita, poor old soul, the only thing she could confess was an occasional bout of impatience with the doctors."

"You gave comfort to the afflicted," Jonathan said. "Isn't that what the Bible tells us all to do?"

"It doesn't tell us to masquerade as priests while we're doing it," James said ruefully.

"You didn't wear your collar or your robe and cassock," Jon pointed out.

"Still," James said, "I deliberately went out there on false pretenses."

"And found out what?" Jon asked.

"Gerry Blankenship hoodwinked them into witnessing that will," James said. "I took some meaningless court documents out and showed them to Juanita, acting like it was the will she'd signed. She looked right at them and smiled and nodded that they were the papers they'd signed. She's nearly blind from her diabetes, Jonathan. She can't read a newspaper, and she only finds her way around the house by feel. Grady, of course, is basically a vegetable, and has been for some time now."

"And that's why Blankenship stashed them out in the middle of nowhere in Guyton," Jonathan said.

"The house belongs to the Willis J. Mullinax Foundation," James said. "He told them it belonged to Miss Anna Ruby and that they would be doing him a favor if they moved in and looked after it. Poor old things, they're delighted with the place. A brick house, with air-conditioning and a tiled bath—to Juanita, it's a palace. He told them to keep quiet about everything, and of course, Juanita feels beholden to dear Mr. Gerry."

"Dear Mr. Gerry," Jonathan said, "certainly gets around."

"And gets rich doing it, I imagine," James said.

"Maybe not," Jonathan said. "I've had my ear to the ground lately. Gerry's in debt up to his comb-over."

"Really?"

"This will be news to you, but it costs money to keep up appearances in this town, James. The club memberships, the big house downtown, the donations to the right charities; none of that is cheap. And Gerry likes to do things in a big way, make a big splash. But appearances can only get you so far. Blankenship's billings have been pathetic. He's even started doing divorce work."

James winced, thinking of Inky and Denise Cahoon. Maybe he should have referred Denise to Gerry Blankenship.

"This Coastal Paper Products deal could be his salvation," Jonathan went on. "Putting Phipps Mayhew together with Anna Ruby Mullinax was a stroke of genius. Blankenship makes money on both ends of the deal; representing the estate and Coastal Paper Products."

"Can he do that? Ethically, I mean?"

"Who's going to stop him?" Jonathan asked. "Anna Ruby Mullinax left no heirs. All the money goes to a foundation that Blankenship controls."

"He'll have to file some kind of papers to keep his nonprofit status," James pointed out.

"Gerry's no dummy," Jonathan said. "You watch. The paperwork will make it look like he's handing out money faster than the Rockefellers."

"How much money are we talking about here?" James asked.

"No telling. The property at Beaulieu sold for two point five million. That we know. But we don't know how much Blankenship is making handling Coastal's permitting work. That alone is worth hundreds of thousands."

James rocked back and forth, letting it all sink in.

"A very sweet deal, for nearly everyone involved," he said. "Except Caroline DeSantos, who got killed. And Weezie, who nearly got arrested for it. You know Blankenship, Jonathan. Is he capable of murder?"

"He's capable of a lot," Jon said. "This whole scheme of his, rigging Anna Ruby's will—if he did—shows that."

"We can't prove he rigged the will," James said. "Maybe Anna Ruby did agree to sell Beaulieu to Coastal Paper Products. And maybe Blankenship really does intend to provide vocational training for community youths."

"And maybe pigs can fly," Jonathan retorted. "Blankenship is mixed up in something criminal, that's definite. I just can't figure out what his motive might have been for killing Caroline DeSantos."

"Lover's quarrel?" James asked.

Jonathan sat forward in his rocking chair and smiled. "I think not."

"What's that supposed to mean?"

"The gossip around town was that Caroline was seeing somebody on the side. And of course, since she was working so closely with Blankenship on the paper plant project, that started the gossip."

"We know she had a boyfriend who was considering buying her a house," James said.

"Not Blankenship," Jonathan said. "He's not on that team."

"How do you mean?" James asked.

"I told you Gerry is good at keeping up appearances," Jonathan said. "And that includes his private life, which he likes to keep very, very private."

"He's gay?"

"As a goose," Jon said.

"And you know this how?"

"I'm a criminal attorney. People tell me things. Gerry Blankenship has been living a double life for years. He was married, briefly, years ago, for appearance' sake. No children, and the divorce was very amicable. The former Mrs. Blankenship took her settlement and moved to Florida. And Gerry has, since then, had a series of very discreet, very young, boyfriends."

"You're sure of all this?"

"Positive," Jonathan said. "Gerry wasn't even in town the night Caroline was killed. He was in Charleston, at a coming-out party." He winked subtly at James. "A coming-out-of-the-closet party, that is."

"Oh. That lets Blankenship off the hook, for the murder, anyway. Who else could have done it?" James asked.

"How well do you know Talmadge Evans?"

"That's absurd," James said. "He was in love with the girl."

"What if he found out she was cheating on him?"

"He did find out," James said slowly. "He told Weezie the other night that he knew Caroline was seeing another man."

"And how did he feel about it?"

"Betrayed, I suppose. He's been trying to persuade Weezie to reconcile with him. Sending her flowers, leaving messages on her machine. He showed up drunk at her door one night and made a big scene, begging Weezie to take him back."

"Do the police consider Tal a suspect in Caroline's murder?"

"Detective Bradley questioned Tal," Jonathan said. "I read his report on the interview. Tal claimed he was working late at the office that night. Everyone in the firm was working a lot of overtime on the plans for the new paper plant. Tal told Bradley that Caroline left earlier in the evening, for a business meeting."

"He never called the police to report her missing?"

"No. He told Bradley he was too embarrassed. He had an inkling she was lying about where she was going, but didn't feel ready to force the issue. And of course, the next morning, he got the call that she'd been found. Dead. At Beaulieu."

"Found by Weezie," James said. "Here's another thought. What about Phipps Mayhew? He was working closely with Caroline on the design of the paper plant. He's rich. And married. I met his wife at the memorial service for Anna Ruby. She seems to think Southerners are slightly demented when it comes to their determination to save crummy old plantation houses."

"I'm sure the police questioned Mayhew," Jonathan said. "But I don't remember reading anything in the file on what he may have told them."

"Maybe you should go back and take a look," James suggested.

"I'll do that."

CHAPTER *50*

Mama?" I poked my head around the doorway of my parents' den, where my mother sat staring at the television set.

"What?" Her eyes never left the TV. She was watching a cooking show featuring a Chinese chef demonstrating how to debone a Cornish game hen with the longest, wickedest knife I had ever seen.

I sat on the sofa facing her easy chair. "How did it go this afternoon?"

She had her hair combed nicely and was wearing a pastel pantsuit and her pearl earrings, so I knew she'd made her appointment at the rehab.

"Shh," she said. "I'm trying to see what this man is doing."

"He's deboning a Cornish game hen," I said. "And even if you ever decided to cook a Cornish game hen, which I doubt would ever happen, why would you debone it? Mama, I want to know how it went at the rehab today."

"It went fine," she snapped, holding up the remote control and turning up the sound on the television. "Now could I please have some peace and quiet around here without everybody asking me a lot of snoopy questions?"

"Oooh-kaay," I said, getting up and walking out. I found Daddy in the backyard, under the carport, trying to untangle a knot of monofilament line that was wound around the stem of his beloved Weedwhacker.

"Hey, baby," he said, looking up when I plopped down in an aluminum yard chair next to him.

"Mama seems kind of tense," I said. "Did it go all right at the rehab place this afternoon?"

He took out his pocketknife and started sawing away at the snarled line. "She didn't run off."

"That's a start," I said. "But was she receptive at all?"

"Hand me that trash can, will you, Weezie?" he asked, unfurling the ruined line.

I started gathering up the monofilament and throwing it in the trash.

"It didn't go too good," he said finally. "James says it's gonna take time. But today, well, I'd have to say this first time was a bust."

"What happened?"

"When we first got there the intake person, that's what they call the nurse who asks you all the questions, she took Marian in a room and talked to her and asked her a lot of questions for an hour. And I went off with another person, and they asked me family-type questions. And then we went into a meeting together with the intake people, and they talked about what all they thought your mama needed to do for her treatment."

"When did things go bad?" I asked.

"Right about the time they told us they really thought she should do inpatient treatment. That means stay at the hospital for six weeks."

"Oh no," I said.

"Your mama got hysterical and accused me of trying to trick her into getting locked up again. I told her and told her that wasn't what was gonna happen, but you know how your mama gets."

"I know," I said.

"Finally we got her calmed down, and the intake person said since your mama was so opposed to staying in the hospital, maybe they could just see her on an outpatient basis, which she finally agreed might not be so bad."

"What happened after that?"

"They had her sit in on a group therapy session. And when she came out, she was just like you saw her in the house. Shell-shocked, kinda like."

"And she wouldn't say what upset her so much?"

"Just kept saying those other people in the group were all dope fiends and winos and bums and criminals, and how could I expect her to stay locked up in a room with that kind of element six days a week for three months."

"Did you try to talk to her?"

"James and I both tried our hardest to talk some sense into her. Your mama still doesn't think she has a drinking problem. She doesn't see why she should have to go to rehab with a bunch of dope fiends and winos."

I wondered if any of the dope fiends and winos at rehab had ever thought to mix Xanax with Four Roses, like Mama had.

"Is there anything I can do?" I asked.

"Later on, they want us all to do some group counseling together," Daddy said. "But not until your mama is ready to admit she has a drinking problem."

"All right," I said, getting up from the lawn chair. I started to leave, then I went back and gave him a tight hug. "I love you, Daddy," I said.

"And I love you too," he said, hugging me back. "We'll get through this, Weezie. Just say a prayer for your mama, will you?"

"I will," I said. "And one for you and me too."

Daniel's truck was parked outside the house on the Southside, and he'd already loaded the sofa by the time I got there.

I did a quick walk-through around the house but didn't see much else worth buying, so I grabbed an end table and added it to the pile of stuff in the back of Daniel's truck.

He stopped on the way back into the house and gave me a quick, sweaty kiss.

"Do you like the furniture?" I asked.

"Yeah," he said. "It's cool. Really. I was afraid you meant some of that frilly-looking wicker, but I really like this bamboo kind of look."

When we had both trucks loaded, I followed him out to Tybee.

The last time I'd seen his house, the place had been a shambles. But Daniel had been busy. The walls still smelled of fresh paint, and the floors had been stripped and refinished.

"Wow," I said admiringly. "It looks great. How did you get so much done?"

"My brothers came over and helped out," he said, setting down one of the arm chairs against the far wall.

"Not there," I said, shaking my head and pointing toward the opposite wall. "Here. And the sofa over there, and the end tables between the sofa arms and the chairs. And the bar, over there, near the dining alcove."

"You sure are bossy," Daniel said.

"You hired me to boss you around."

He put down the bar stool he was carrying and wrapped his arms around my waist, pulling me close to his sweaty chest. "I've got a confession to make. I had ulterior motives when I hired you."

"And I had ulterior motives when I took the job," I said. "Let me see where you put everything in the bedroom."

He grinned.

"That's not what I meant," I said. "I just want to make sure you didn't put things in the wrong place."

"I thought you liked where I put things," Daniel said, tagging after me.

"No," I said, standing in the doorway to the bedroom. "This is all wrong."

He'd put the big oak bed blocking the best window in the room, the one with a great view of the sky and the river, and the highboy was right next to the bed.

"Your lovemaking techniques are superb," I told him, "but as an interior designer, you're hopeless. Here. Help me move this bed."

He grabbed my hand and pulled both of us onto the mattress.

"Not that way," I said, struggling to free myself. "I want the bed against the other wall, so you can see the water when you wake up in the morning."

"I hate waking up with the sun in my eyes," he grumbled.

"We'll get you some split bamboo shades you can pull down," I said, "but you really don't want the bed blocking your view. And you don't want to be stumbling over the dresser when you get out of bed in the morning."

He stood up and began shoving the furniture around. "How do you come to know all this stuff?" he asked.

"It's just common sense," I said. "Didn't your mother teach you any of this?"

"My mother worked most of the time," Daniel said. "She didn't spend a lot of time worrying about furniture placement."

The air had suddenly taken on a chill. But I pushed ahead. After all, if we were going to sleep together, I wanted to know something about his family.

"Where did your mom work?" I asked.

"At the sugar plant," he said.

"Who took care of the kids?"

"We took care of ourselves," he said. "We made out all right."

"It sounds like you and your brothers are pretty close," I said. "When can I meet them?"

"Whenever," he said. "Is this like you want it now?"

"Better," I said, standing in the middle of the room. "You need some lamps, and some kind of bedspread. And what about pictures for the walls?"

"Why do I need pictures?"

"So you'll have something to look at when you're lying in bed," I said.

"I know what I want to look at when I'm lying in bed," Daniel said. "And it's not pictures. Are you coming back to Bluffton with me tonight?"

It was a tempting thought. "I can't. The sale at Beaulieu is Saturday morning. And I've still got some stuff I want to do."

"When, then?" he asked.

I knew what he meant, but I asked anyway.

"When, what?"

"When are you going to stop all this running around? When are we going to be together for more than just a night?"

I slouched up against the wall and crossed my hands over my chest. "Now I've heard it all."

"What's that supposed to mean?"

"A guy who wants a commitment after just one night."

His face got red. "I am not asking for a commitment. I just want to know where we stand with each other. Remember, you're the one who was ready to go running back to old lover boy, just last night."

I shook my head. "Oh no. I'm not getting into this again."

"You don't get how weird this is, do you?"

"No," I said. "Why is this weird?"

"You're living in your ex-husband's backyard. He watches you. He's just waiting for you to coming running back across that courtyard to him."

"Are you asking me to move in here with you?"

He looked shocked. "No. I mean, I hadn't thought about it."

"Good," I said. "Don't. I like where I live just fine. And don't get the idea that just because we slept together means you get the right to boss me around."

"You're the one who does all the bossing, is that it?"

I wrenched my hand away from him. "No. I don't want to do all the bossing. Listen to us. Bickering again. It's just the way I told you it would be. All we do is fight. This isn't working."

I turned my back on him and headed out to the yard to my truck.

"Hey." He stood in the doorway and called after me. "That wasn't a fight. That wasn't even a good bicker. There you go, running away again. Come on back, damn it."

When I got to the carriage house, Tal's car was in its parking slot. I could see something on my doorstep. A flower arrangement.

"Shit," I muttered, and I backed out and drove straight to BeBe's house.

She took one look at me and knew what had happened. "You did it, didn't you?"

I stalked past her into the kitchen and opened the door of her big stainless-steel double-door refrigerator. "You got any chocolate in this thing?"

"There's some Godiva fudge sauce in that jar on the door there," she said. I took the sauce and opened the freezer. "Ice cream?"

"Second shelf from the top."

I took the carton of Mayfield Moose Tracks and sat down at the kitchen counter. I took the top off the ice cream container and spooned chocolate sauce in. "Bourbon?"

"You know where I keep it," BeBe said, pointing to the liquor cabinet. I got a double old-fashioned glass and poured two inches of Wild Turkey bourbon over a layer of ice cubes, and I drank it neat, followed by a healthy chaser of ice cream and chocolate sauce.

"Let me get this straight," BeBe said, pouring herself a drink. "At some point last night, presumably after we talked on the phone, you and Daniel made mad passionate mattress music together. And at some point after that you two had your first official fight."

"We had our first official fight the first time you introduced us," I said.

"First official fight as a couple," she said, correcting me.

I took a couple bites of ice cream. "What makes you think we're a couple?"

"You're not? This is just recreational fucking? I mean, Weezie, I am the first person to wholly endorse recreational fucking. It's a concept that far too few contemporary American women embrace. It's just that I didn't think you were that kind of girl."

"Why is everybody so worried about what kind of girl I am?"

"Never mind," BeBe said. "I can see you're in no mood to discuss philosophy. Is there anything else I can do for you tonight, besides provide chocolate and liquor?"

"I couldn't go back home," I said apologetically. "Tal left another flower arrangement on my doorstep."

"At least he didn't leave this one inside the house," she said.

"I had the fucking locks changed," I said. "And James called him and told him to knock it off. But he still doesn't seem to get the fucking message."

"You are in a mood," she said, eyeing me warily.

"It's been that kind of a day," I said. And I told her about my mother's reaction to alcohol rehab, and about the fight Daniel and I had had, and about my sinking feeling that Lewis Hargreaves had already snagged the Moses Weed cupboard.

"You want my opinion on any of this?" she asked.

"Yeah," I said. "I'm sorry I'm being a bitch. Now that I've got a little chocolate and brown liquor in me, I'm ready for some counseling. God knows I could use it."

"First," she said. "About your mother. Face the facts. She's hooked on Xanax and bourbon. She's an addict. You've done what you could for her. You and your dad let her know you think she has a problem. You told her you'll help all you can. Now step back and let her own it."

"Easier said than done," I said.

"Second. Daniel. I hate to say it, Weeze, but I think he's right. You have some kind of aversion to a romantic relationship."

"Are you saying I'm frigid?"

"Christ, I hope not," she said. "He's a great guy. He wants to be with you. It's only natural that he would be creeped out by Tal. Hell, everybody who knows Tal is creeped out by him."

"Are you saying I should move out of the carriage house?" I started to stand up.

She pushed me back down. "Stay seated. Jeez. You are so touchy tonight. Getting laid certainly hasn't improved these mood swings of yours."

"I do *not* have mood swings."

"Fine. Hormonal surges. Did you keep any of that Xanax you stole from your mother?"

"I have the whole bottle in my pocketbook."

"You might consider taking one if these flare-ups of yours continue."

I opened my mouth to protest but then closed it again.

"You said you wanted my opinion," she said.

"Go on."

"Give the guy a chance," BeBe said. "That's all I'm saying. He's sweet, he's funny, he's damn fine-looking. He's obviously nuts about you. And I bet he's good in bed. Am I right?"

I just looked at her.

"Fine. Be discreet. He was great. I can tell just by the way you walked in here tonight."

"What?"

"You had a definite hitch in your getalong, as my grandma Loudermilk would put it," she said.

"You are unbelievably crass," I said.

"And I'm right. Admit it."

I smiled despite myself. "You were right about the soup theory. And that's all I'm saying."

"Okay. Daniel Stipanek is fine in every way. Why are you running away from him?"

"I'm not," I said. "I mean, I don't want to. It just happens. Something about him scares me, BeBe."

"Like what?"

"For one thing, he has a real hang-up about his family."

"Like how?"

"He won't talk about them. He knows all about my whacked-out family, but he won't say anything about his own background. All I know about him is that his father died when he was a little kid, and he has two brothers and they basically raised themselves because his mother was working at the sugar factory."

"That's a lot," BeBe said.

"Uh-uh," I said. "He's angry about something. His mother, I think."

"Honey, we are *all* angry about our mothers."

"We know why I'm pissed at my mother, and why you're pissed at yours," I said, then stopped myself. "By the way, why are you pissed at your mother?"

"How would you like to be named BeBe?"

"Oh yeah. But what's Daniel got to be so pissed about? Here's another thing, BeBe. I knew him in high school. And I never heard him mention a word about his family. It was like he was raised by wolves or something. What do you know about him?"

"I know he's the best chef in Savannah," BeBe said. "That's all I need to know."

"But what about his background? I mean, God forbid I should sound like Mama, but BeBe, who are his *people*?"

"Hey," she said. "This is my office and that's my chair."

She sat in a chair in the corner and sulked.

"Last place of employment was the Huguenot House in Charleston," I said.

"No good calling them," she said. "They went out of business."

"His references don't sound too interesting," I said, reading on. "Here it is; next of kin: Paula Gambrell. And there's an address in Columbia, South Carolina."

"Does he have any sisters?" BeBe asked.

"No," I said. "Just two brothers."

"Maybe it's his mom," she said.

"Or a cousin."

"I know that name," BeBe said. "Gambrell. But I can't think why."

She picked up the phone.

"Who are you calling?" I asked.

"Emery Cooper," she said, winking at me.

"Your funeral director boyfriend?"

"Emery literally knows where all the bodies are buried in this town," she said, winking again. "He's very well connected. And well endowed."

She fluffed up her hair and put on some lipstick while she was waiting for her call to be connected.

"Emery?" she cooed. "Darlin', how in the world are you?"

Her tinkly laugh echoed in the office.

"You are the naughtiest man I have ever known," she said. "And I would do something about that condition of yours if I didn't have other pressing business to attend to right now."

She gave me another broad wink. I considered leaving the room.

"Darlin', what does the name Paula Gambrell mean to you?"

"Yeah. Gambrell, with two 'l's."

"I'm checking on a prospective employee's references," she said. "So the name does mean something to you?"

"Oh," she said, putting her hand to her mouth. "That's right. Hoyt Gambrell. Good heavens, I'd forgotten all about that man. Whatever happened to him?"

"You don't say. And you think he's still in prison?"

I sat up a little straighter at the mention of prison.

She listened a little longer. "Well, that's a sad, tragic story," she said finally. "All right, lover. Yes. Just as soon as I get through with business."

e could check Daniel's personnel file. From the restaurant," BeBe said.

"What would that prove?"

"A lot. His last place of employment, his last address. Next of kin."

"He'd probably list one of his brothers. I know he's got one named Derek, who's a plumber, and one named Richard, who drives a big rig."

BeBe finished the last of her drink. "Do you want to do this or not?"

"Yeah," I said, throwing the ice-cream carton in the trash. "Let's do it."

BeBe's office at Guale was in a tiny room just off the kitchen. She flicked on the overhead light and pointed to a file cabinet. "Personnel records."

BeBe opened the bottom drawer of the file cabinet and thumbed through the contents until she came up with the file she was looking for.

"Here it is," she said. "Stipanek, Daniel F."

"Quick," I said, "what's the F for?"

"Francis," she said, leafing through the papers inside. "What else do you want to know?"

"Give me that," I said, taking the file and sitting behind her desk.

She hung up the phone.

"What did Emery say?"

"Do you remember that thing with Hoyt Gambrell? He was some kind of assistant vice president over at the sugar plant, years ago, back in the eighties, I believe."

"I was in parochial school in the eighties," I reminded her.

"At the time it happened, I was just old enough to know it was the juiciest thing to hit Savannah in years," BeBe recalled. "Mama hid the newspaper so I wouldn't read all the trashy stuff that was going on, but the other kids at school filled me in, because, of course, Gambrell's kids went to school at Country Day with me."

"What was so juicy about Hoyt Gambrell?" I asked.

"He was married to the daughter of one of the company founders, but he had a roving eye. There was a young woman, Paula Stipanek, who worked on the plant floor, in the bag room. She was attractive and raising a passel of little kids by herself. She caught Hoyt Gambrell's eye, and he had her transferred to his office. One thing led to another, and pretty soon they were 'dating.'"

"But you don't get sent to jail for adultery," I said.

"No," BeBe said, "but you do get sent to jail for extorting kickbacks from vendors—if you get caught. Which Gambrell did. The whole thing might have blown over, since he *was* married to the boss's daughter, except that after he got caught, he was quietly invited to leave the company. But Gambrell went berserk when they fired him, called up his former father-in-law and threatened to burn the plant to the ground. That's when the law got involved."

"And when he got sent to jail," I said.

"Yep. He had actually rigged some kind of bomb to go off in the executive dining room, but the thing was a dud. Right before the shit hit the fan over the extortion thing, Gambrell figured out that the company's lawyers might try to get Paula Stipanek to testify against him, since she was his secretary and presumably knew a lot about the kickback scheme. Damn if he didn't get a quickie divorce from Miss Sugar Princess and marry Paula."

"That way she couldn't testify against him."

"From what I remember hearing, she wouldn't have done that anyway," BeBe said. "Hoyt went off to a federal prison in Florida, and Paula followed him down there."

"She left her kids?"

"Yes, ma'am," BeBe said.

"My God," I said. "Daniel wasn't kidding when he said he and his brothers raised themselves. How awful."

I handed Daniel's personnel file back to BeBe. Now I wished I'd never seen it. Families suck, he'd told me, and I'd been sure he hadn't meant it. But now I knew he did mean it, and I knew why, and I wished I didn't.

"Let's go," I told BeBe. "I feel like I need a bath."

CHAPTER 52

On the way home from Guale, I drove by the warehouse on Martin Luther King Boulevard, where they were going to have the Beaulieu estate sale in the morning.

I parked out front and stared at the place. For the first time I realized the old white brick building had once housed Cranman's, my daddy's favorite sporting goods store. My very first fishing pole had come from Cranman's, as had the sleeping bag I took on my first Girl Scout camping trip.

The windows that had once showcased pup tents and racks of shotguns had long since been boarded up, and now the store entrance stood behind a sturdy chain-link fence.

Neon orange posters were attached every six feet along the length of the fence. "Important Estate Sale. Saturday—8 A.M.," the signs said.

Important was an understatement, as far as I was concerned. Urgent was more like it. With the money I'd raised, I should have more than enough cash to buy the Moses Weed cupboard. *If* it was still there, and *if* the price hadn't been hiked up.

When I got home to the carriage house, Tal's flower arrangement was still on my doorstep. I picked it up and dropped it in his garbage can.

Jethro was thrilled to see me. I went in the kitchen and gave him a bowl of fresh water and a doggy treat, and I swear, he had a doggy orgasm right there on the kitchen floor. He followed me upstairs and lay down at the foot of my bed.

The Beaulieu sale was to start at eight. I packed my estate-sale kit: flashlight, measuring tape, magnifying glass, checkbook, and billfold. No thermos of coffee though. I was damned if my bladder would get me in trouble this time.

I set my alarm for 4 A.M. and dropped off to sleep, dreaming about dancing cupboards and singing chifforobes.

A cop, wearing a neon orange reflective safety vest, directed traffic around the old Cranman's store. The curb in front of the building was lined with cars. I cursed but followed the cop's directions and parked in a gas station parking lot a block from the store. I hoofed it back and joined a motley crew of about thirty people lounging or sitting against the chain-link fence in front of Cranman's.

My buddy Nappy was in line four people ahead of me.

"Hey, Weezie," he called, "you going in legally this time?"

I gave him a wan smile. The other people in line around me started whispering and looking at me funny. I sat down with my back against the fence and dozed off. Three hours later I woke up when people started jostling and talking. It was nearly seven-thirty. The line had grown—it stretched down Martin Luther King and around the corner beyond my sight. I stood up, stretched, and yawned.

Nappy caught my eye. "How long has it been like this?" I asked.

"Since about six. You missed the excitement. A dealer from Miami tried to pay somebody up in the front two hundred dollars for his place in line. The guys in back of him nearly lynched the guy."

"I don't need any more excitement," I told Nappy.

"You got something in particular you're looking for in there?" he asked. "I know you got a good look around the last time out."

I bit my lip and motioned him closer. "Hold my place for a minute, will you?" he asked the woman behind of him.

He walked over to me. I put my lips to his ears. "There's a pre–Civil War cupboard. Made at Beaulieu. I saw it last time, and it was marked fifteen thousand. If I could get it, I could set up my own antique shop."

Nappy nodded knowingly. "You want me to tag it if I see it?"

"Absolutely," I said, and I gave him a roll of my masking tape marked "Sold–Foley." "If you grab it before I do, there's a finder's fee," I told him.

"Good deal," he said, winking.

As the line inched forward, a fight broke out in front of us. Normally Savannahians are too well mannered to brawl over an estate sale. But this was not a normal estate sale, and anyway there were people here from all over the East Coast. And for them, business was business.

A burly black man in a white T-shirt that said "SECURITY" threatened to relocate the instigators, and they quieted down. The security man proceeded on down the line handing out cardboard fans with numbers. Mine was number thirty-six.

I clutched it to my chest and said a little prayer and planned my strategy for finding the cupboard. Cranman's had been closed for at least fifteen years, and I could no longer remember what it looked like or how it was laid out inside. All I could do was plan to move very fast through the store, looking for the cupboard's tall profile.

At eight o'clock people started jostling forward. At eight-thirty I was at the door. At eight-forty-five I was inside. The place was jammed with stuff, all of it arranged in rows, on tables, and in glass cabinets.

I raced up and down the rows. I saw the Charm-Glow stove, the rows of McCoy flower pots, the Aubusson rugs, and the oriental rugs, which had been cleaned and unrolled for display. I ran up and down the vast old store, past stuff I would have drooled over any other day.

At 10 A.M. I called it quits. I fought my way to the checkout line, where a bank of women with calculators and credit card machines were ringing up people's purchases.

"Who's in charge?" I asked one of the young women.

She pointed toward the store's old mezzanine level, the stairway to which was now roped off. "Up there. Her name's Stephanie."

I stepped over the rope and climbed the stairs. At the head of the stairs a woman stood with binoculars in one hand and a two-way radio in the other.

"Yes?" She didn't look happy to see me.

"I'm looking for a cupboard," I said. "I saw it when I visited Beaulieu for Anna Ruby Mullinax's memorial service, and I know for a fact it was included in the original sale. But I've been all over the store, and it's not here now."

"If it was part of the estate, it should have been here," she said, shrugging me off.

"It's not here," I said, "and I doubt somebody ahead of me bought it. It was listed last time at fifteen thousand. That's not an impulse buy, and I was number thirty-six in line this morning."

"Describe the cupboard," she said, grabbing a typewritten inventory sheet.

"It's a burled elm cupboard, nineteenth-century, with original glass. Made at Beaulieu. You'd have it listed as the Moses Weed cupboard," I said. "Fifteen thousand," I repeated. "I want to buy that cupboard."

She scanned the sheet and shook her head. "No. Nothing like that."

I lost my cool. "What's your name?" I demanded.

"Stephanie Prevost. Why?"

"Because I want to remember it," I said hotly. "This sale has been picked over. You've sold off the best stuff to a favored few dealers and I resent the hell out of it."

"I don't know what you're talking about," she said, her voice low.

"You do know," I said. "I've already seen three different pieces that I know for a fact came out of Beaulieu for sale in antique shops in Bluffton. A cherry inlaid card table and two majolica oyster dishes. They were in the house before the last sale started. I saw them. But they're gone now, and I know for a fact that you people sold them to Lewis Hargreaves. And now the Moses Weed cupboard is gone too. I don't know who you are, lady, but I'm going outside now, and I'm going to tell every picker, every dealer I know, that you've already skimmed off the best stuff."

"Who do you think you are?" she asked, her eyes blazing. "I've been getting this stuff ready for a month now. I personally did the inventory, and I can tell you unequivocally that nothing, and I repeat nothing, has been skimmed off. I've been fielding phone calls for weeks. I've personally chased dealers away from the house and the warehouse, because my sales start when advertised, where advertised. And I *don't* preview."

"Then how did Lewis Hargreaves get his hands on those pieces?" I asked.

"I don't know," she said grimly. "I was hired by the estate's attorney, Gerry Blankenship, to run this sale after the last one was postponed. If you have any questions, you'll have to ask him."

"Damn straight, I will," I said, turning to go.

She picked up her two-way radio again. "Security," she barked, "there's a woman up here on the mezzanine with me. I want her escorted off the premises."

CHAPTER 53

I drove directly to Uncle James's house on Washington Avenue. As I was signaling to turn into his driveway I saw his white Mercedes approaching from the other direction. I waited and pulled into the drive right behind him.

As I got closer to his car I noticed he had company. Jonathan McDowell. When he got out of the car, James's face was scarlet and dripping with sweat. Jonathan was dressed in running shorts and a T-shirt that was plastered to his chest with sweat. He looked slightly chagrined to see me there.

"Weezie," James said. "I thought your big sale was today."

"It was."

"And the cupboard?"

"Gone," I said. "I don't think it even made it over to the warehouse, Uncle James. I was number thirty-six in the door this morning, and nobody came past me carrying it."

"Weezie had her eye on some fantastic piece of antique furniture from Beaulieu," James explained to Jonathan as we all trooped in the front door.

I sat at the kitchen table. I noticed with amusement that Jonathan seemed to know his way around James's house quite well. Right now he was pouring us all glasses of orange juice from a pitcher he retrieved from the refrigerator.

"What do you think happened to the cupboard?" Jonathan asked, taking a seat at my grandmother's red Formica dinette table.

"I know what happened," I said. "Gerry Blankenship has been skimming the best pieces out of the house and selling them off to Lewis Hargreaves."

"Lewis has a very good eye. Are you sure he has the cupboard?"

I nodded and told them both about the majolica oyster plates I'd traced back to Zoe Kallenberg. "She's his shop assistant, and she lives in an apartment at Lewis's house on Abercorn," I said. "I think she's been selling off some of the smaller items for him. But I can't understand why they're doing this so quietly."

Jonathan and James exchanged a look.

"Blankenship doesn't want to attract any attention to what he's doing out at Beaulieu," James said. "We went out there the other day and had a look around."

I raised an eyebrow.

"Detective Bradley gave Jonathan a key. It's all perfectly legal."

I leaned forward. "Is the house totally empty now?"

"It's more than empty," Jonathan said sadly. "It's been stripped. Every noteworthy bit of any architectural significance has disappeared. Moldings, cornices, mantelpieces, stained glass. All of it's gone."

"But why?" I asked.

"It was the only way the paper company could be sure that the county's historic preservation officer wouldn't certify the house as a historic landmark."

"And it worked," James said. "They've got a demolition permit. We saw it. The earthmoving equipment is out there. They've already started clearing trees for the new road into the property."

"Oh no," I said. "It's bad enough that Lewis Hargreaves got all the best furniture from the house, but now they're going to tear that beautiful old house down? I can't believe they can get away with it. It sucks. This means if they sell everything off and put some hideous paper plant out there, Caroline wins."

"She's dead," James said quietly. "How is that winning?"

"She gets what she wants. Tal's miserable, and he's making me miserable. Beaulieu is gone without a trace. And people like Gerry Blankenship and Phipps and Diane Mayhew end up richer than ever."

"Maybe not," Jonathan said.

"How can we stop them? You just said it's a matter of days until they tear the house down."

"There might be a way," Jonathan repeated. "If there was enough of a public uproar."

"From whom?" James asked. "You can't be involved in anything like that. It's a conflict of interest with your job."

"Not me. Not directly," Jonathan said. "But I know somebody who'd move heaven and earth to save Beaulieu."

Suddenly I knew whom he was talking about.

"Merijoy Rucker. But what can she do?"

"Given the facts we've gathered, she can do a lot," Jonathan pointed out.

"What facts?" I asked.

James sighed and shook his head. "I really don't want to do anything that might put Grady and Juanita Traylor at risk of losing their house."

"What house?" I asked, looking from my uncle to his friend. "What have you guys been up to?"

"Your uncle is quite the detective," Jonathan said. "He figured out that Gerry Blankenship tricked an elderly couple who used to work for Anna Ruby Mullinax into witnessing the will that allows Beaulieu to be sold to the paper company."

"Tricked them, how?"

"The husband has had a stroke and is basically a vegetable," Jonathan said, "and his wife is nearly blind from diabetes. Blankenship had them witness the will without Miss Mullinax present. Heaven knows whether or not she was capable of agreeing to the sale. And then, to ingratiate the couple and keep them quiet, Blankenship moved them into a new house way out in the country, to a house that belongs to the Willis J. Mullinax Foundation—which he runs."

"But that's illegal," I said. "Blankenship engineered the whole thing. The sale of Beaulieu is bogus. We could stop them from tearing it down." I looked over at Jonathan. "You're the chief assistant district attorney. Can't you have Blankenship arrested or something?"

"Maybe," Jonathan said. "The will and the foundation and all of that is probably a matter for a grand jury to look into. The whole thing reeks of fraud. But what interests me even more is the question of how Caroline DeSantos's death ties into all of this. My boss hates the idea of having an unsolved homicide on the books. It's an election year coming up, you know."

Jonathan got up and rinsed his juice glass out, then placed it neatly in the dish drainer.

"Weezie," he said, coming back to the table. "Your uncle tells me Tal knew Caroline was having an affair."

I nodded, feeling my stomach start to knot up.

"How angry was he about that? Angry enough to kill her?"

"No," I blurted. "He was depressed, it's true. He told me he knew it was over between them before she died, but it wasn't that he was angry about that. More like resigned. To the fact that she'd found someone else, and that he'd ruined his own life by divorcing me."

"He says he was alone the night she was killed. But nobody else can verify that," Jonathan said.

"She told him she had a meeting. Tal didn't believe her. He tried to follow her. But he lost her at the light at Victory and Bee Road."

"But nobody else saw him that night," James reminded me.

"Tal wouldn't kill anybody," I said. "That's just not him. The man has no convictions. He—he doesn't feel things deeply enough to kill for. Not love. Not hate. Not jealousy."

"What about money?" Jonathan asked.

"His family has gobs of money," I said. "And the firm was doing well. That new paper plant commission would have been worth hundreds of thousands of dollars."

"Maybe he knew how fragile the deal was," Jonathan said. "He was president of the firm. He had to know what was going on out there. Certainly he knew Blankenship was involved in something sleazy, possibly with Caroline's help."

"No," I said, shaking my head. "He's a rat bastard. But he's no killer."

"He knew his way around Beaulieu," James said quietly. "He had a key to the plantation house. Think about it, Weezie. Tal had motive, and he had access."

"But not the guts," I said. "He didn't even have the guts to make her buy him real cream for his coffee."

Jonathan put his palms flat on the table. "All right. Talmadge Evans is innocent. What does that leave us?"

"I think your idea before was a good one," I said. "Let's go talk to Merijoy. She was at Beaulieu for the memorial service. And you said yourself," I reminded Jonathan, "she's the gossip queen of Ardsley Park."

"I've got a better idea," James said. "You two go see Merijoy. And after I get cleaned up, I'll go pay a call on Gerry Blankenship. It might be interesting to see what he has to say about Anna Ruby's will and the Mullinax Foundation."

CHAPTER 54

As we pulled up into the Ruckers' driveway, Merijoy emerged from the house followed by a gaggle of small children, all of them dressed in snowy white shirts and shorts and clutching the smallest tennis rackets I'd ever seen.

"Hey there, Jonathan. And Weezie!" she said, not bothering to hide her surprise at seeing us together. She opened the doors to her Suburban and started hoisting the children inside.

"Y'all, I would love to sit and visit, but you've caught me at the worst possible time. The children have tennis lessons at the golf club, and we're ten minutes late as it is."

She lowered her voice. "Ross had an upset tummy this morning, and I've changed his little outfit three times. I swear, if he makes poopie one more time, I'm going to put a cork up his little behind."

"We really need to talk to you, Merijoy," Jonathan said. "When could we get together?"

"Oh, Jonny, today is *not* a good day," she said. "I've got to drop the children at the club for their lessons, then I have to race over to the cleaners before they close at noon. And I've got to look at some wallpaper samples for the downstairs powder room, and then I've got to pick up a wedding gift for Randy's niece—the wedding's tonight at St. John's and I've got a nail appointment—"

"It's about Beaulieu," I said, being deliberately rude. "How about if we just ride along with you on your errands? It's really important, Merijoy. You could help us stop Gerry Blankenship and the Mayhews from tearing down Beaulieu."

Her eyes widened. "But I thought it was all settled. The environmental impact statement hasn't been approved. They can't dredge the rice canals without that."

"They've got a demolition permit to raze the house," Jonathan said bluntly. "The bulldozers are already on the premises."

"Good Lord," she said. She poked her head inside the car. "Rodney and Renee, be Mommy's little angels and climb in the way back, will you? Miss Weezie and Mr. Jonathan are going to go for a ride with us. Isn't that exciting?"

Jonathan got to ride shotgun. I got wedged in the backseat between the twins, Rachel and Ross. Ross eyed me suspiciously from behind pale wheat-colored bangs that fell over his eyes.

"Hello," I said, trying to be friendly.

"Go away," he whined, turning his head away from me.

Once we'd unloaded the kids and picked up Randy Rucker's tuxedo at the dry cleaners, we went to the Krispy Chik for a friendly little lunch chat.

"You know, Jonny," Merijoy said, dipping a french fry in some ketchup, "I'd do anything to save Beaulieu. I'm dead serious about that. I know people think that Merijoy Rucker is just a flake, a rich do-gooder with too much time on her hands; but Beaulieu means something to me. It's the last great intact antebellum rice plantation in the low country. I've done my research. There's not another place like it; not in Georgia or Florida or South Carolina. There are a couple in Louisiana, but that's it. What can I do to help, Jonny?"

"Do what you do best," Jonathan said. "Run your mouth."

"Now you sound like Randy Rucker," she said crossly.

"I'm serious," Jonathan said. "You've got the best contacts in town. And I've got some ammunition for you."

"Like what?"

"Remember the day we met at Beaulieu, during Anna Ruby's memorial service?" I said, butting in. "I saw you snooping around that day, taking pictures and samples of wallpaper. Do you still have any of that?"

"Of course," she said. "At the time I was still under the impression that the preservation league might be able to acquire Beaulieu as a living-history museum. I wanted to start documenting things. For the fund-raising campaign."

"Those photos could prove that the house was deliberately stripped," Jonathan said. "And if we could prove that, maybe the preservation league could do something to get the county to withdraw the demolition permit."

"Lord knows, I've tried everything else to stop Phipps Mayhew. Including some things I'm not too proud of," she said, making a wry face.

"Like what?" I asked.

She turned around in her seat so she could face me. "I wasn't ever going to tell anybody about this. Ever. Especially not you, Weezie. After you were arrested, and it looked like they might actually charge you with killing Caroline DeSantos, I nearly died of shame. And guilt.

"You know that day we ran into each other in Kroger?" she asked. "That was no coincidence. I deliberately followed you into the store so that I could act like I'd bumped into you and invite you to dinner. I had the whole thing planned out. I had to do something nice to make it up to you for spending the night in jail."

"Why should you feel guilty about me being arrested?" I asked. "I'm the one who climbed in the window and went in the house."

She lowered her eyes, then cut them over to Jonathan.

"Jonny, if I tell you something, will you keep it just between the three of us? If Randy ever found out what kind of crazy stunt I pulled, I swear he'd have me locked up in the funny farm."

Jonathan laughed easily. "I won't say anything to Randy. Unless you're about to confess you're the one who killed Caroline."

She tucked a strand of her dark hair behind her ear. A nervous gesture, because every hair on Merijoy Rucker's head belonged right where it was.

"I didn't kill her, but honestly, I was so angry at her, at the way she was, that I wanted to. Of all the scheming, conniving Yankee tramps to hit this town, Caroline DeSantos was the worst. That's speaking ill of the dead, but it's true."

"What did you do?" I asked.

"What Jonny said. I used my God-given snooping talents. It wasn't even hard. She was such a trashy thing, she hardly ever bothered to be discreet."

"Discreet about what? Sleeping with Tal and wrecking my marriage?"

Merijoy looked a little uneasy. "No, honey, that she was sleeping with Phipps Mayhew."

"What?" Jonathan and I said it together.

"Oh yes. They were quite the hot item. At one point they even went house hunting together."

"So that's who Anna and Emily's mystery client was," Jonathan said. "Why didn't you say something the night of the supper club?"

"Because I already knew too much," Merijoy said. "I didn't want you asking a lot of questions I couldn't answer."

"What else do you know about Caroline and Phipps Mayhew?" I asked.

"He was wild about her," Merijoy said. "I saw a program about it, on *Oprah*. They were talking about sexual obsession. That's what I think it must have been like for those two. It was indecent. They had sex everywhere, like a couple of animals in heat. In his office, at her office, at his house at Turner's Rock, even at your house, Weezie—I mean, Tal's house. They even did it at Beaulieu, right there in the parlor." Her face was now pink with indignation.

"How do you know all this?" I asked, getting a queasy feeling.

"I followed her," Merijoy said. "That little yellow Triumph of hers was like a big old neon arrow. All I had to do was look for that yellow car. God, a couple of times they nearly spotted me, peeking in windows at the two of them just banging away. In broad daylight!"

Jonathan's lips twitched. "What did you intend to do about them?"

Merijoy nibbled at the cuticle around her thumbnail. "It wasn't really blackmail," she said finally. "I wasn't demanding money or anything. I just wanted to put a stop to that paper plant."

"Tell me what happened," Jonathan said, now straight-faced.

"The day before the sale at Beaulieu, I finally got up the nerve to call Caroline," Merijoy said. "I thought it was my last chance to stop the estate sale. No offense, Weezie, but it killed me to think of all the Mullinax things being carted away from the house. Think of it—all the original furnishings, gone. I called Caroline at her office. And I told her I had a matter we needed to discuss.

"She told me she didn't have time for any of my hysterical historical nonsense. So I just told her she'd better get down off her high horse and meet me, because I knew all about her affair with Phipps Mayhew. That got her attention."

"What happened next?" I asked.

"I told her to meet me out at Beaulieu," Merijoy said. "At first she flat out refused. Then I told her that if she didn't meet me, I'd tell Tal and Diane Mayhew about the affair. That's when Caroline changed her tune."

"Did you actually see her that night?"

"No," Merijoy said. "I got to the house at eight o'clock, like we'd arranged. I went inside and waited. But it was pitch black. I waited and waited. Finally, at nine, I didn't dare stay any later. I went home. And the next morning, I saw on the news that Caroline was dead. And they'd arrested you, Weezie."

"Why didn't you say anything? Why didn't you tell Jonathan right then what you knew?"

Tears welled up in her eyes. "I couldn't. If Randy knew I'd been sneaking around, spying on people, threatening them, he'd have a fit. An absolute fit. Anyway, I didn't know who killed Caroline."

"You knew who had a good motive," I said coldly.

She sniffed a little, and wiped at her eyes with a balled-up paper napkin.

"Honey, please don't be mad at me," she pleaded. "I'll help you now. I'll do whatever it takes to make it up to you. All right?"

CHAPTER *55*

*A*fter we left Merijoy Rucker's house, Jonathan took me back to Uncle James's to pick up my truck. The Mercedes was gone, so we assumed he'd left on his visit to Gerry Blankenship.

"Do you really think we'll be able to save Beaulieu?" I asked Jonathan.

"I do," he said. "Those photos Merijoy gave us, plus the affidavit she'll swear to, will document the fact that Coastal Paper Products, or their agents, deliberately engaged in fraud by stripping the house of elements that contributed to its landmark status. And," he said smugly, "Gerry Blankenship is toast. I'm sure we'll be able to nail him on the matter of the Mullinax will, as well as the foundation. He'll at least be disbarred, and if everything falls into place like it should, I'll be able to pursue criminal charges too."

"How long will all of that take?" I asked. "What's to stop Coastal Paper Products from firing up those bulldozers today and knocking the house down?"

"As soon as I leave here I'm heading in to the office," Jonathan said. "I'll call a judge and ask for a temporary restraining order to keep their demolition permit in abeyance at least until we finish gathering all the facts."

"Can you get a judge to do that?"

He took his glasses off and polished them on the hem of his golf shirt. "Merijoy is at home right now, working the preservation league's phone list. At the top of her list is Bea Gunther, who is a very preservation-minded person. I think Judge Gunther will give us our TRO without batting an eyelash."

"Jonathan," I said, "do you think Phipps Mayhew killed Caroline?"

"It's possible," Jonathan said. "But in light of what we've just heard, I'm more inclined than ever to believe that Tal was involved."

I opened my mouth to defend him, but I could think of nothing to say. What did I really know about my ex-husband after all? He'd cheated on me for years, and I'd been blissfully unaware of his betrayal. He'd gotten involved in the Coastal Paper Products deal too, and it was impossible to believe he hadn't condoned the stripping of Beaulieu.

"Detective Bradley's medical leave doesn't take effect for another couple of weeks," Jonathan said. "I'm going to call him right now to see if we can get together this afternoon so I can bring him up to speed on all I've learned today." He looked suddenly and unexpectedly stern, like the prosecutor he was.

"I can trust you to keep quiet about all this, can't I?"

"Yeah," I said. "I don't suppose you can put one of those TROs on Lewis Hargreaves while you're at it, can you?"

"Only if you can prove he acquired those antiques through a criminal act."

I was halfway back to the carriage house when it struck me; Tal could be a killer. Not just a rat-fink liar and a cheat and a sloppy drunk; he very well could be the one who put a bullet in Caroline DeSantos.

It was ninety-five degrees outside, but the memory of her body sliding out of the closet at Beaulieu sent cold shivers up my spine. What if I had totally underestimated Tal? What if he was the killer? He'd known she was having an affair. He'd admitted to me that he'd followed her halfway out to Beaulieu. By now I knew he was a skilled liar. Maybe he was lying about everything else too.

And if he'd killed Caroline in a jealous rage, what was to stop him from killing a second time? He'd seen me at least once with Daniel. Maybe Daniel was right. Maybe Tal was watching me. Stalking me. I'd changed the locks on the carriage house, but if Tal decided to come after me, a little thing like a lock wouldn't stop him.

I detoured over to BeBe's house.

"What now?" she asked when I barged in the back door.

I went straight to the refrigerator and found the chocolate fudge sauce where I'd left it the night before. The spoon was still in the jar. I dipped in and started finishing it off.

"Don't tell me," BeBe said. "You made up with Daniel after you left here last night, and now you're broken up again? Weezie, sweetie, you need to pace yourself with these things."

"It's not Daniel that's got me stressed out," I said between bites. "It's Tal. Jonathan and James think Tal killed Caroline. Think about it, Babe. Tal, the man I slept beside for ten years, a killer."

"No," BeBe said. "He doesn't have the guts."

"What if that gutless-WASP thing is just an act? I'm serious, BeBe. I could be living right next door to a stone-cold killer."

"Look at the bright side," BeBe said. "Maybe they'll arrest the SOB and throw his ass in prison. And then you can move back into the townhouse."

"Maybe." I put the cap on the fudge sauce and started to put it back in the refrigerator. BeBe took it and handed it back to me. "You keep it," she said. "Since you've basically licked it clean.

"Hey," she said, brightening. "I almost forgot to ask about the estate sale. How did it go? Did you get the cupboard?"

"No," I said. "It wasn't even listed in the sale catalog. Lewis Hargreaves beat me to the punch again."

Her face fell. "Are you sure?"

"Who else?"

She stood up and grabbed her purse and car keys. "Let's go."

"Go where?" I asked. "Not home. Not right now. I'm too spooked."

"Not home," she said. "To L. Hargreaves. My money's as good as anybody else's. If he's got the cupboard, what's to stop me from buying it?"

"Money," I said. "If Hargreaves bought it for fifteen thousand, that's his wholesale price. He'll have it marked up to thirty thousand or even forty-five thousand or more. Retail. If we pay that much for it, there's very little margin for profit left."

"Weezie, Weezie, Weezie," she said, shaking her blond curls. "This is BeBe Loudermilk you're talking to. I never paid retail in my life. And I don't intend to start now."

I looked around the kitchen for my own pocketbook, but I couldn't find it. Panic set in. All my cash—more than seventeen thousand dollars—was in that purse. "Oh my God," I said slowly, and then it hit me. I'd taken it into Uncle James's house. It must still be there.

I called his house, but there was no answer. At least it was locked up safe and sound, I thought. BeBe and I could retrieve it later.

The front window at L. Hargreaves featured a typically spare Hargreaves tableaux: against a backdrop of wrinkly unbleached muslin he'd set a spindly-legged heart-pine huntboard in original paint.

"Ugh," BeBe said, stopping dead in her tracks in front of the window. "I thought you said Hargreaves has exquisite taste."

"I did. He does. That huntboard has the original faux-grained blue paint, and dovetailed drawers. It's definitely Southern, late nineteenth century. He's probably asking around eight thousand dollars for it."

She sniffed. "My granddaddy's got a table just like that out in the hen-house at his farm."

"Tell him I'll give him five hundred bucks for it," I said.

"Let's go in and browse," BeBe said. She pushed against the glass door, but it didn't give. We stood back, and that's when we noticed the Closed sign on the door.

"Since when does an antique shop close down on a Saturday afternoon?" BeBe asked.

"If you're Lewis Hargreaves, you can afford to keep banker's hours," I said. "He's mostly open by appointment. Let's go. This is pointless, anyway. He's probably already sold the Moses Weed."

We were starting to cross the street to get to the car when I happened to turn around. A tall, thin girl with waist-length red hair came out of L. Hargreaves and locked the door.

"Look," I said, clutching BeBe's arm. "That's Zoe Kallenberg. She's Hargreaves's assistant."

She walked quickly down the street until she got to a white van parked at the curb along Liberty Street. She unlocked the van and got in.

"I'll bet she's going back out to Beaulieu to fetch another load of furniture," I griped.

"Come on," BeBe said, quickening her pace until we were both at her car. "Let's follow her and see what she's up to."

"I was kidding," I said, but I got in the car and BeBe fired it up and swung easily into traffic behind the white L. Hargreaves van.

We followed Zoe Kallenberg to a hardware store on DeRenne Avenue. When she got out of the van she had a cell phone clutched to her ear.

BeBe and I trailed along behind her as she pushed a shopping cart up and down the aisles.

Zoe's long tresses swayed slightly as she minced along in tiny little steps, which were necessitated by the three-inch heels on her black mules. Her lacquered fingertips fluttered over the shelves while she consulted with the person at the other end of the phone, who was obviously dictating the shopping list.

Our decoy cart stayed empty, except for a can of spray paint we added for effect, but Zoe's cart was piled high with paint and brushes, steel wool, sandpaper, lacquer, mineral spirits, and other assorted hardware-type goods.

"She doesn't look like Ms. Fix-it to me," I said as we watched her pay for her purchases with a Platinum American Express card.

"Not with those nails and that outfit," BeBe agreed.

We tagged after Zoe to her car.

"Keep going?" BeBe asked as she started her car.

"Yeah," I said. "This is kind of fun."

We followed the van easily through the light Saturday-afternoon traffic toward the east side of Savannah, where the neighborhoods were more run-down, and the look more urban industrial than residential.

"The shipyards?" BeBe asked as we approached the sprawling Port Authority complex.

"Maybe it's the hot new Gen-X stomping grounds," I said.

"Uh-uh," BeBe said. "There aren't any nightclubs over here. Motorcycle clubs, maybe."

But we passed by the shipyards and kept going until Zoe swung the van unexpectedly into the parking lot of a grimy warehouse complex.

BeBe drove on past, pulled into a convenience store, and turned and cruised slowly back past the warehouses.

The white van was now parked next to a loading dock. Zoe stood by the open back doors, talking to two men standing on the dock above her. One of them was Lewis Hargreaves.

I slid down in the seat until my chin was touching the dashboard.

"Keep going," I told BeBe. "I don't want Hargreaves to spot us snooping around here."

"What do you suppose they're up to?" she asked, craning her neck to see in the rearview mirror.

"I don't know," I said, sitting up again. "But I think it bears looking into."

CHAPTER *56*

James sat down at the desk in the house on Washington Avenue. He folded his hands, said a quiet prayer for serenity, and called Gerry Blankenship.

"Gerry. This is James Foley. We met out at Beaulieu the day of Anna Ruby Mullinax's memorial service. I have a matter I'd like to discuss with you."

Blankenship tried to give him the brush-off. "Call me Monday, during office hours," he barked. "Tell my secretary what it's in regard to."

"It's in regard to Miss Mullinax's will," James said calmly. "And the sale of Beaulieu to Coastal Paper Products and the impending demolition of the plantation house."

"Foley?" Blankenship sounded puzzled. "Who are you? What's your interest in this matter?"

James was prepared for the question. Prepared to fib too.

"Grady and Juanita Traylor are old friends of mine," he said smoothly. "I visited them this week. I was shocked at the extent of their impairment."

He heard a quick intake of breath.

"What do you want?" Blankenship repeated.

"I'd like to talk to you in person. Today."

"Right now?"

"Yes," James said. "Events at Beaulieu are happening so quickly, I think it's important that we talk immediately."

"You know where my office is? On Madison Square? I can be there in half an hour," Blankenship said. "But I have a tee time at three."

"That'll give us plenty of time," James said.

It was only after he'd hung up the phone that he realized he was sweating profusely. He mopped his forehead with his handkerchief and decided to get a cold drink of juice from the refrigerator.

As he was taking a glass from the dish drainer he noticed a pocket-book lying on the counter next to the sink. Weezie's purse, he thought. It was a blue canvas affair, and its contents had spilled onto the countertop. There were a billfold, a pair of sunglasses, a lipstick, and an old-fashioned pill bottle. He picked it up. Doan's pills, the label said. But these would be Marian's stolen tranquilizers, which Weezie had retrieved from Cousin Lucy's house. The brand name escaped him, something with an X. Brand X? How appropriate, he thought, tucking everything but the pills back into the pocketbook.

He put the Brand X bottle on the kitchen counter, beside his mother's sugar canister.

It really wouldn't do for Weezie to be running around town with such powerful narcotics, James thought. Weezie had already had one brush with the law this summer. And one was more than enough.

Gerry Blankenship's fleshy cheeks quivered with agitation at the sight of James Foley standing in his outer office.

"I checked up on you," he said flatly. "You're a priest. Why didn't you say so on the phone?"

"Former priest," James said. "It wasn't germane to the matter at hand."

Blankenship pointed toward the inner office. "We can talk in there."

"Fine," James said. He took a seat in a straight-backed leather chair opposite Blankenship's enormous desk.

"Say what you came to say," Blankenship said bluntly.

"Very well," James said. "As you're well aware, Grady and Juanita Traylor are both in their late seventies. Grady's stroke two years ago left him totally incapacitated. Juanita has suffered from diabetes for some years now, and glaucoma has left her virtually blind. You and I both know there is no way either of them was capable of properly witnessing Anna Ruby Mullinax's will."

Blankenship had a silver fountain pen that he was rolling back and forth over his desktop, his thick freckled fingertips caressing the silver at each touch. He kept his gaze on the pen while he spoke.

"The Traylors witnessed the will at Miss Mullinax's request. She was very fond of them because they'd been in her employ for so long. I had no idea they were incapacitated. They were both alert and cognizant of what they were signing at the time."

"No." James clutched the file folder on his lap with both hands. "That's not true. The Traylors were not present when Miss Mullinax signed that will. You brought papers to their home and instructed them that they were to sign them "as a favor" to their old friend. Neither of them had seen your client for many months before her death."

Blankenship kept the pen moving over the desktop.

"A misunderstanding," he said finally. "The Traylors are elderly. Probably it slipped their mind about the day their son drove them out to Beaulieu for a visit with Miss Mullinax."

"I checked with their children," James said. "None of them drove their parents to Beaulieu. And for your information, Juanita's grasp of reality is quite clear. Although she is a little confused about the house you so generously provided for them. She seems to think you told her the house belonged to Miss Mullinax."

Blankenship smiled. "You see? Of course the house belongs to the Willis J. Mullinax Foundation, which Miss Mullinax established before her death."

"I wonder how a foundation whose stated purpose is to provide vocational training for the youth of the community is served by providing housing for an elderly retired couple," James mused aloud.

Now Blankenship looked up. He was frowning, and the purple vein in his nose was throbbing violently.

"I'm not sure the foundation's business is any of your business, Foley. And I'm damn sure we're done here now." He stood up abruptly, scattering papers onto the floor.

James stayed seated. "I think it's probably time for me to put my cards on the table, Blankenship. The last time we met, you'll recall, was at Beaulieu, the day of Miss Mullinax's memorial service, which I attended with my niece Eloise."

"Oh yes," Blankenship sneered. "The woman who killed Caroline DeSantos. Caroline told me that day that your niece had a vendetta against her. Poor woman was terrified of what insane action your niece would take next. I advised her to get a restraining order against your niece. Tragically, Caroline didn't believe her life was at threat."

"Her life was never at threat from Weezie," James said. "But I believe her involvement in your scheme to sell Beaulieu illegally to Coastal Paper Products led to her death."

"Nonsense," Blankenship said. "The sale was perfectly legal. It was Miss Anna Ruby's desire to sell the property for the greater good of the community."

"Weezie and I walked all around Beaulieu the day we were there," James went on, as though he hadn't heard Blankenship. "She was particularly interested in all the architectural details of the house. Historic preservation is a special interest of hers, and she pointed out all the nineteenth-century details to me. I was back out at Beaulieu this week, Gerry, and I've seen what you people did to it."

"You were trespassing on private property," Blankenship said, raising his voice. "We have a demolition permit from the county, and the house is being readied for that."

"No," James said. "You or Phipps Mayhew stripped the house before the county's historic preservation officer did his survey. It's part of a pattern of fraud the two of you have engaged in since you first came up with the idea to put that paper plant out there. Caroline DeSantos was involved in your fraud. And she was romantically involved with Phipps Mayhew."

"I wouldn't know anything about that," Blankenship said.

Now James stood up. "I came to see you today because I want you to know that I've documented everything I've told you, and turned over that material to the Chatham District Attorney's Office. I intend to clear my niece of any involvement in Caroline's death, Blankenship. I don't know why Caroline was killed, but I do know you and Phipps Mayhew were involved in this fraud, and with millions at stake, both of you had a motive to kill her."

James slapped his file folder down on Blankenship's desk, enjoying the solid sound of paper on wood. He turned to go.

"I didn't kill that silly bitch," Blankenship said. "Why would I?"

"I'll leave it up to the police to figure that out," James said. "In the meantime, you should know that the Savannah Preservation League has filed for a temporary restraining order to stop the demolition of Beaulieu."

"I didn't kill Caroline DeSantos," Blankenship repeated. "And it wasn't my idea to tear down the house. We were supposed to save the damn house. That was Mayhew who decided to tear it down, once Caroline was dead. He's the one who had the house stripped. Mayhew. Goddamned Yankee."

James was on a roll. Blankenship had as much as admitted his involvement in the Beaulieu fraud. He decided to take it one step further. He would go see Phipps Mayhew.

Everyone in Savannah knew where Phipps Mayhew lived. The Turner's Rock property had once been part of another plantation, Turnewolde, which had been broken up in the late 1960s.

The house was an imposing pink stucco affair, with rounded windows and patios and stone chimneys that reminded him of pictures he'd seen of French châteaus. James mopped his forehead with his handkerchief and presented himself at the Mayhews' immense carved front door. He rang the doorbell and was surprised to hear a voice, distant and tinny, floating out of a small box by the bell.

"Yes? Who's there?"

"Um, Foley. James Foley. To see Phipps Mayhew."

"What do you want?" It was a woman's voice, and she was being surprisingly rude in that cultured New England accent of hers.

"I'm here to see Phipps Mayhew." He had an idea. The devil put him up to it. "About Caroline DeSantos."

No answer. "Hello," James repeated. "Are you there? Did you hear me?" This was impossible. It was like going through the drive-through at one of those fast-food restaurants.

But now he heard footsteps coming from within. The door swung open. A short middle-aged woman in a flowered silk dress and garden hat stared out at him.

"My husband doesn't want to see you," she snapped, and started to close the door.

"Diane?" a voice boomed from the back of the house. "Is that someone at the door?"

"It's nobody," she called. "Just a salesman."

"It's James Foley, Mr. Mayhew," James hollered, surprising even himself. "I'm here to talk to you about Caroline DeSantos."

That got his attention. More footsteps, quick, agitated ones.

"What the hell?" Phipps Mayhew was, like his wife, dressed for some sort of a garden party, in a blue seersucker suit, red-and-blue striped tie, and buckskin shoes. James tried not to stare at the shoes, but he'd never seen anyone over the age of twenty wearing them.

"I told him you were busy, Phipps," the woman said. "Let me handle this. I'm going to call the police if you don't leave," she said.

"The police are already involved," James said quickly. "The district attorney's office has opened an investigation into the sale of Beaulieu to Coastal Paper Products, and into the way Gerry Blankenship handled Anna Ruby Mullinax's alleged will."

It was quite a mouthful.

"Goddamn," Phipps Mayhew roared. "Who the hell are you?"

"James Foley," James said, glancing meaningfully at Diane Mayhew. "My niece Eloise's ex-husband is Talmadge Evans, whose architectural firm you hired to design your paper plant. Talmadge Evans was engaged to Caroline DeSantos. Now wouldn't you like to go somewhere more private to discuss this matter?"

"I'm calling the police," Mrs. Mayhew whispered, and she leaned hard against the door, trying to close it.

"Never mind, Diane," Phipps said, gently prying his wife's hand from the door. "We'll only be a few minutes. Why don't you go ahead to the party without me? I'll meet you there."

"No," she whispered, her face pale. "I'll wait. I have some things to do upstairs. Just call me when you're ready."

"In a few minutes," Mayhew repeated.

He clamped a strong, tanned hand on James's arm and steered him into a room just off the foyer, a study, outfitted with sets of leather-bound books and mahogany paneling and dark red walls. Even a fireplace.

"What the fuck do you mean coming out here and making wild accusations?" Mayhew asked, slamming the door behind them.

"I'll tell you the fuck what I'm doing. I mean to stop you people from tearing down a Savannah landmark," James said, emboldened by Mayhew's coarse language. "And I mean to clear my niece's name once and for all. I know all about your dealings with Gerry Blankenship. I know that will was fraudulently drawn up so that it would appear Miss Mullinax wanted Beaulieu sold to your company. And I know Blankenship has some sort of sham foundation set up to siphon off the money from the estate to the two of you. And once the police start investigating, I feel sure they'll find that Caroline DeSantos was involved with your scheme, and that's what got her killed."

←

Mayhew's eyes bulged. "Blankenship called me just now. To tell me what you've been saying around town." He stood, inches away from James's face, his fists clenched. "If you repeat these lies one more time, I'll sue you for slander. I'll get a real New York lawyer, not one of these local yokels, and I'll sue you for every fucking dime you own. And I'll win too. And in the meantime, if you want to try and air my personal affairs, I'll make sure yours get aired too, you fucking closet queen."

James blinked.

"Oh yes," Mayhew said. "Gerry told me all about you. About you and your faggot boyfriend in the district attorney's office. A former priest. Disgusting. And I understand your pathetic little law firm does business with the Catholic archdiocese. I wonder how they'll feel once they find out their lawyer is the biggest fucking queer in Savannah."

James smiled. "My sexual orientation changes nothing. But your sexual orientation, and your relationship with Caroline DeSantos, was by no means a secret. You got away with screwing Caroline, Mr. Mayhew, but I'm not going to let you screw me, or my family, or this community. So call your New York lawyer. And tell him to pack a bag. Because this is a fight I'm not walking away from."

"Faggot," Mayhew sneered.

Sticks and stones, James thought as he left Phipps Mayhew's overdecorated study. Diane Mayhew stood by the front door, staring daggers at him.

"Good-bye," James said pleasantly. "Enjoy your party."

CHAPTER *57*

hat do you think they're doing in that warehouse?" I asked, edging a glob of guacamole onto my nacho chip.

BeBe pulled the plate of nachos over toward her side of the kitchen counter and finessed a chip loaded with melted cheese, salsa and sour cream into her rosebudlike mouth.

"Smuggling drugs?"

"Lewis Hargreaves is an antique dealer, not an international drug lord," I said.

"Think about it," BeBe said. "That place is right over near the Port Authority docks. Maybe they drill holes in the antiques and stash drugs in them and ship them overseas to their partners."

"Or it could work the other way around," I said. "Maybe their partners in places like Hong Kong stash the dope in the antiques and ship them over here to Lewis. He takes the drugs out and peddles them, and gets to sell the antiques too. That could be how he can afford to buy the kind of stuff he does."

"But I don't get how the Moses Weed cupboard fits in with any of this," BeBe said.

"Me neither," I admitted. "But they've got to be up to something crooked."

"Why?"

"Because Lewis Hargreaves just looks evil," I said.

BeBe nodded. She gets me.

"You got any more Dos Equis?" I asked. "That salsa of yours is about to burn off the roof of my mouth."

She had a mouthful of chips, so she just waved in the general direction of the undercounter cooler where she keeps beer and Cokes.

I fetched two more bottles of Dos Equis, cut a couple more wedges of lime, and handed BeBe one of each.

"You're big buddies with Jonathan McDowell now, right? Why don't you see if he can get a search warrant so we can get in there and look around?" BeBe asked.

"He's all hung up with ethics and stuff like that. He won't call out the dogs on Hargreaves just because I ask him to."

"Ethics are a pain in the ass," BeBe said. "How about if we just cruise over there after dark and take a look around?"

"How?" I asked. "It's a warehouse. I didn't see any windows."

"Maybe the windows are on the sides, or at the back," BeBe said. "Look. It's Saturday night. We've got no dates, and if we get any more bored we'll end up eating everything in my house. Let's just ride over there."

"All right," I said, finishing off the guacamole, because really, guacamole doesn't keep, and the cost of avocados is criminal. "Maybe we'll come up with a plan once we get situated."

BeBe got up and walked over to her freezer and opened the door. She pulled out a huge cardboard carton. "Fudgsicle?"

"Awesome," I said, taking one. "I haven't had a Fudgsicle since I was twelve."

"I know," she said, biting off the end of her own Fudgsicle. "My ice-cream wholesaler at the restaurant had these on special. I had to buy a box of sixty to get the price, though. Have two, why don't you?"

"Nah," I said, looking around for my truck keys. "If I get too full, I'll fall asleep."

"Where you going?"

The chocolate had given me a macho buzz. "I'm going home to shower and change," I said. "You wanna pick me up in half an hour?"

"You're not afraid? To go home with Tal there?" BeBe asked. "You could shower here. And you've still got clothes left from the last time you stayed over."

"I'll be fine," I said. "Jethro's there, and he hates Tal. Besides, I've decided he really is basically gutless." But just in case, I opened a drawer and pulled out BeBe's sharpest meat cleaver. "Protection," I said.

Tal's car wasn't parked at the townhouse, and I didn't see it on the street either, leaving me to wonder whether Jonathan had hauled him in for questioning.

Not my problem, I decided.

I ran upstairs, showered, and prowled around my dressing room, trying to decide what to wear. Something dark, of course. Sleek, so I wouldn't be catching my shirttail on anything if we decided to do a little climbing.

I finally decided on a pair of black stretch leggings and a zip-front black top, with flat-heeled black crepe-soled loafers. Standing in front of the mirror, I did some poses, crouching, bending, pointing my make-believe pistol. Secretly I thought myself pretty damn hot. Nearly as hot as my television idol, Mrs. Emma Peel, as played by Diana Rigg on *The Avengers*. The outfit needed a little oomph, though, so at the last minute I added a silk leopard-print scarf knotted at my neck.

I was in the kitchen, feeding Jethro a doggy treat and trying to explain why he couldn't come along for the fun, when BeBe knocked at the door, which I'd started locking and dead-bolting, just in case Tal developed a last-minute criminal streak.

I opened the door and let her in. She stood very still and looked at me. I looked at her too. She was wearing a sleeveless black lycra zip-front catsuit with black lace-up running shoes, and a leopard-print belt.

"Nice outfit," I said, laughing.

"You too," she said.

"I was going for the Diana Rigg look."

Her face was a blank.

"You know, from *The Avengers*. Back in the 'sixties."

"Who are you supposed to be?" I asked.

"Honey West," BeBe said, pointing to a mole which she'd eyebrow-penciled just to the right of her lips.

"Who?"

"You never saw the reruns? Weezie, Honey West, as played by Anne

Francis, was who Angie Dickinson wanted to be when she grew up. Talk about hot. She was like a private detective–slash–cat burglar. And she had a pet ocelot named Bruce."

"Are you ready to go?" I asked.

Just then, we heard the kitchen door open behind us. I know I jumped a foot in the air. I grabbed BeBe's butcher knife and whirled around to face my attacker.

Daniel stood in the doorway with a bottle of wine in one hand and a platter of chocolate seduction in the other.

"Jesus," he said, backing away.

"I'm a little nervous," I explained. "The cops think maybe Tal killed Caroline."

"We found out Caroline was having an affair with Phipps Mayhew," BeBe added. "So if Tal found out about that, maybe he killed her in some kind of jealous rage. Although personally, I can't imagine Tal in any kind of rage."

"Could you put the knife down?" Daniel asked.

"Did you come over here to apologize for bossing me around?" I asked. That chocolate buzz of mine was really something.

He set the dessert and the wine on the counter, beside the knife. "Actually I was hoping we could make up and then make out. But from the looks of things, you two must have other plans."

He glanced from me to BeBe, then back to me again.

"What's with the matching outfits? You look like flight attendants for Air Leopard."

BeBe raised an eyebrow, but she left the explaining to me.

"We're going out on a little expedition. To find out what Lewis Hargreaves is up to. He's the antique dealer who bought the Moses Weed cupboard."

"Why don't you just ask him?" Daniel asked.

"He's up to something illegal," BeBe said. "We followed his assistant to this creepy warehouse over near the Port Authority. She was buying all these chains and paint and stuff. Weezie thinks maybe they're smuggling drugs."

"That's absurd," he said.

"We're going anyway," I said. "Just put the dessert in the refrigerator. You can stay here with Jethro if you want."

He shook his head. "I'll drive."

"OK," I said, "but you don't get to boss us around."

✦

The three of us made a snug fit in the front of Daniel's pickup truck. I let him fondle my leg while he drove, and BeBe pretended not to notice.

"Shit," I said when we got to the street where the warehouse was located. It was lit up like a Wal-Mart on Saturday night. There was even a spotlight in the parking lot.

Daniel parked the truck across the street so that we could see the front door of the warehouse. "Seems like a pretty brazen way to be doing drug smuggling," he said.

We rolled the windows down and watched the place for a while.

"Hear that?" I asked. A high-pitched whining sound floated across the street.

"Power tools," Daniel said. "Sounds just like my place."

"They could be cutting the drugs out of the furniture shipped from Hong Kong," BeBe offered.

"That's absurd," Daniel said again.

"We're not gonna just sit here," I said finally, nudging BeBe in the side. "Let me out."

"Hold on," Daniel said, grabbing my arm. "What's the plan?"

"Plan?"

"I've got a plan," BeBe announced. She pointed toward the corner of the warehouse, where a For Lease sign was nailed to the siding.

"We'll tell them I'm a real estate agent, and you're my client, and we want to look at the space to lease."

"Not bad," Daniel said.

"You're just sucking up to her because she's your boss," I said. "Who do I get to be? The interior designer?"

"Nobody," BeBe said. "Hargreaves knows you—right? If he sees you, you'll blow our cover."

"No fair," I said. "This was my idea. Anyway, you two don't know anything about antiques. You've never even seen the Moses Weed cupboard."

"You've described it to me a dozen times," BeBe said. "If it's in there, I'll recognize it. Now come on," she said, nodding at Daniel. "Before I lose my nerve."

I sat in the truck and pouted, watching the warehouse with my hand on the cell phone in case any dangerous-looking drug-smuggling types showed up.

Daniel and BeBe crossed the street, and I had to admit that BeBe looked very cool in her Honey West jumpsuit. BeBe tried the door, then turned around and pantomimed to me that it was locked.

Daniel found a buzzer beside the door and leaned on it for a minute. After a long time, the door opened, and a man, short, Mexican-looking, with thick forearms, came out to talk to them.

I could see BeBe talking and gesturing animatedly, and Daniel talking and nodding in agreement. The Mexican kept shaking his head no, but every time he did that, BeBe took another step forward, followed by Daniel, until they were inside the warehouse and the door swung shut.

Nothing happened for about five minutes, which made me nuts. I tucked the cell phone in the waistband of my pants and got out of the car and crept across the street, trying to stay out of the beam of the parking-lot spotlight.

I crouched down behind a row of Dumpsters at the edge of the lot, out of the light but close enough to keep the doorway in view.

After another five minutes, the door swung open and BeBe and Daniel walked out, followed by the Mexican, who was doing a lot of his own gesturing and talking.

The Mexican stood in the doorway and watched them cross the street to the truck, but I didn't dare move from my hiding space. They got in the truck, and I could see they were wondering where I'd gone. After a moment or two, Daniel started the truck's engine and rolled slowly down the street. The Mexican watched them go, then, finally, let the warehouse door swing shut.

Shit. Were they leaving me? I crouched down next to the Dumpster and tried to decide what to do.

My waist started to buzz, which startled me badly until I realized the buzzing was coming from the cell phone. I flipped it open. "Hello?" I whispered.

"Where the hell are you?" BeBe demanded.

"Hiding between the Dumpsters," I whispered. "Come back and get me. And make it snappy."

When the truck cruised slowly past the parking lot, I did a very un-Diana Rigg run for the truck. BeBe had the passenger door open, and I jumped inside before Daniel could roll to a stop.

"What did you see?" I asked, gasping for breath.

"A warehouse," Daniel said.

"Four thousand square feet, unheated," BeBe added.

"What were they doing in there?" I asked.

"That Mexican kept trying to shoo us back to the front," BeBe said. "But I explained that my client needed to see all of the space. We wandered out to the warehouse for a minute or two, before he hustled us back to the front office area."

"You were right about the building materials," Daniel said. "There were stacks of lumber, power tools. Lots of hand tools too, which I found peculiar. Old bandsaws and chisels and old-timey stuff. They had a paint table set up, and lots of hardware, nails, chains. Like a workshop."

"What about antiques? Did you see any antiques?"

"We saw a couple of tables almost exactly like the one you and I saw in the window at Hargreaves's shop," BeBe said. "Except these were just plain wood. And there was a stack of like, table legs, and doors, like the kind that might go on a cabinet or something. And lots and lots of piles of old-looking wood. The kind that looks like it's been pulled off an old house or something."

"What about the Moses Weed cupboard?" I asked. "Did you see it?"

"No," BeBe said. "But we only got a glimpse of the workshoplike place. There was furniture in there. That's for definite."

"Antique furniture?"

"You know, sort of that primitive, junky stuff like you like," BeBe said. "The guy didn't speak much English, but it was real clear he wanted us out of there, and pronto."

"Primitive furniture," I said. And then I remembered all the sandpaper and steel wool and paint Zoe Kallenberg bought at the hardware store. And I had a very good idea of what Lewis Hargreaves was doing in his warehouse. Really good Southern vernacular antiques were getting harder to find. The market was heating up, but the supply had dwindled to nothing. So Lewis Hargreaves had found a solution. He was making his own.

aturday nights, James had a gin and tonic promptly at 5 P.M. He liked to take it on the back porch, looking out at the garden Bernadette had tended for so many years. Here, more than any other place in the house, he felt close to his mother. Her worn-out cotton mop still hung from a nail by the back door. Her gardening shoes, a pair of rubber-soled boots she'd cut the tops off of, stood companionably in the corner, toes pointing in, and the granite-ware dishpan she'd used to shell white-acre peas was placed upside down on a wobbly table beside his rocking chair.

He rocked and thought about the day's events. Phipps Mayhew was not a man to cross. His anger was volcanic; his pockets deep. Faced with any kind of threat, he would strike back, and viciously.

James winced, thinking of Mayhew's threat to make public his sexual orientation. Money was the least of his worries. He would be forced out of the closet. His family, old friends, would be shocked, disgusted, and feel betrayed. Not Weezie. Weezie knew and apparently accepted that aspect of his life. But the rest, how would they react?

He sipped his drink and weighed the issue. But no matter how he framed the question, the answer stayed the same. He would do what needed to be done. He would take the consequences as they came.

From inside the house he heard the quiet dinging of the doorbell. He picked up his drink and walked through the house to the foyer. He was expecting Weezie to come by to pick up her pocketbook. He opened the door.

Diane Mayhew stood on his porch in a silk party frock. Her flowery hat was gone, but she had a new accessory: a snub-nosed pistol.

"Hello, Father," she said.

He stared down at the barrel of the gun.

"It's a forty-five," Diane said, seeing what he was looking at. "It's loaded, and I know how to use it. May I come in, please?"

Inviting her inside seemed the thing to do.

"Now what?" James asked.

"Could we sit down?" she asked. "I've had these damned heels on all day. My calves are throbbing."

He gestured toward the living room, whose picture windows faced Washington Avenue. The drapes were open. Maybe somebody would drive by and see Diane Mayhew holding him at gunpoint.

"Not here," Diane said, reaching down and kneading the back of one leg. "Don't you have a study or something?"

"Of course," he said, pointing to the dining room. He ate all his meals in the kitchen, so he'd given his mother's furniture to one of the nieces and moved in a desk and some bookshelves.

"This is nice," Diane said, looking around the room. "This house is much bigger than it looks from the street. Did you do the decorating yourself?"

"Some of it," he said, trying not to sound nervous.

"I like this paint color," she said, running her free hand over the wall of the study. "What do you call it?"

"Brown," James said.

Diane Mayhew, James thought, was unhinged. She was pointing a gun at him and asking him for decorating hints. It occurred to James that most of the women in Savannah he had contact with were, on some level, slightly deranged. Look at Marian, his sister-in-law. And Denise Cahoon. And Merijoy Rucker.

It could be hormones, he decided. Or maybe just the humidity.

"Sit right there, Father," Diane was saying, pointing with her gun to one of the straight-backed chairs against the far wall. He did as he was told.

"What's this about, Mrs. Mayhew?" he asked, keeping his voice low and nonconfrontational.

"I heard everything you said to Phipps in his study today," Diane Mayhew said. "If you stand in the master bedroom upstairs, by the heat vent, you can hear every word spoken in the den. It's really uncanny."

James said, "I'm very sorry you had to hear it from me. I apologize."

"I already knew he was cheating on me with that woman, Caroline DeSantos," Diane said. "But you've got it all wrong. Phipps only fucked her." She blushed slightly. "Excuse me, Father, I mean, he had sex with her. He never would have killed her. I'm the one who killed Caroline."

"I'm sure you had your reasons," James said calmly. "It must be devastating to find your husband is attracted to another woman. And Caroline DeSantos was not a nice person. A home wrecker, you might call her."

"Exactly," Diane said. "And to think, things might have gone on until it was too late, if I hadn't been so worried about my boys."

"Your boys?"

"Our sons. Phipps III, we call him Tripp, and Phillip. Flip. They're teenagers, enrolled at Country Day, but I was afraid they were mixing with the wrong element."

James nodded, understanding nothing.

"I found condoms in Tripp's backpack. I begged Phipps to talk to the boys, but he said I was blowing things out of proportion. I decided to find out who the girls were."

"A fine idea," James said. He wondered how this had anything to do with why Diane Mayhew found it necessary to shoot Caroline DeSantos in the chest.

"I bought a taping device," Diane went on. "A bug. And I put it on the boys' phone. And every night I'd listen to their conversations.

"About a week after I bought the device, I heard Phipps. On the boys' phone. I almost died. He was talking to a woman. Dirty talk! On my boys' phone. What if they'd overheard him talking that smut talk?"

"Could be damaging to their self-esteem," James murmured soothingly.

"He was talking to Caroline DeSantos," Diane said, gritting her teeth as she said the name, "setting up meetings. She didn't wear panties. Did you know that? Whenever she was going to meet him—no panties. I heard her telling him that on the phone. And that's when I decided she had to die."

"Very disturbing," James agreed. Disturbed? She was a whack-job.

"Phipps was talking to a divorce lawyer too," Diane said, tears welling up in her pale brown eyes. "I had to stop him from leaving. For the boys' sake."

"Mrs. Mayhew?" James said, leaning forward. "I think you should tell this story to a therapist I know. You've been under such stress."

"No!" Diane screeched, raising the gun and pointing it at him again. "No therapist. You sound like Phipps."

She swallowed. "Don't waste your time trying that therapy crap on me, Father. The point of all this is, I killed Caroline. You figured it out, or came close, and now you'd like to blow the whistle on Phipps. But if you do that, you'll ruin everything. We've spent millions putting this paper plant deal together. The financing is all laid out. But it's all short-term, high interest. Any delay, and we're wiped out. I can't let that happen. I have my boys to think of."

James nodded. "I understand."

"Do you?" she said bitterly. "I doubt it. The planning that went into all this, the thought. It was masterful, if I do say so myself. I kept all the tapes of Phipps and Caroline's phone calls. I got another tape recorder, and I cut bits and pieces of their conversation. And then I called Caroline's office and waited until I got her answering machine. I played back a tape I'd made. It was Phipps's voice, asking her to meet him out at Beaulieu. And that's all it took."

"Very clever," James said.

"She went out to Beaulieu that night, thinking she and Phipps would have one more filthy little sex session," Diane said. "But I got there first. I brought my own gun, but when I got to the house, I found the box with the dueling pistols. It was providence, really. Both pistols were loaded. I took one, fired it once into the wall, and it worked perfectly. After that, I hid in the upstairs bedroom. She came running up the stairs, calling his name. And I came out of the bedroom, and I shot her right in the chest. You should have seen the look on her face," Diane said triumphantly. "You know, if she'd known she was going to die, I'll bet she would have worn panties that night."

"Mrs. Mayhew?" James felt tired. "Isn't there anything I can do to help?"

Diane cocked her head and smiled. "You have to die. The children's college money is at stake. And the Mayhew name. I can't let anything interfere with that. Or with our marriage. You being a priest and all, you understand."

"I'm not a priest anymore," James said. He was fed up. "Your husband betrayed you, Mrs. Mayhew. Why don't you take your anger out on him?"

"He's a husband. And a father," she said. "You're just another gay man. There are thousands of your kind in Savannah. No wife, no kids. No big loss."

"I have family here," James said. "People who love me."

"They don't know you're queer, do they?" she said pityingly.

"Don't do this," James said. "You're a person with morals. Killing is immoral."

She stood up suddenly. "I hate this godforsaken town. The minute the boys are out of high school, I'm packing up and leaving. She laughed. "Actually, 'hate' isn't a strong enough word. I *loathe* this town. My God! The roaches. And the gnats. They gnaw on my skin until I bleed. And this obsession with being from Savannah. Have these people ever heard of Boston? Or Philadelphia? Those are seats of culture. And learning. Not this stinking bug-ridden swamp.

"And the rice!" she moaned, waving the gun around.

"Rice?"

"Rice," she said, shuddering. "If anybody else serves me another dish of rice in this town, I think I'll just die."

She was standing very close to him, and the gun was pointed right at his chest. But James thought of an old joke. It was about how Savannahians are just like the Chinese— they both worship their ancestors and eat a lot of rice.

Diane's breath was coming in short gasps now. Her hair was askew and her face was sheened with perspiration.

"You seem anxious," James said.

"You think I like killing people?" she snapped. "This isn't easy for me. I'm not a serial killer. I'm a woman at the end of my rope."

"Would you like a cool drink?" he asked, crossing his fingers.

"Maybe a quick one. I need to get home before the boys get back from lacrosse practice."

"I'll just go in the kitchen and get you something," James said.

"I'm right behind you, so don't try anything funny," Diane instructed, poking him in the small of the back with the barrel of her pistol.

"Some iced tea?" he asked when they were in the kitchen. "Or juice?"

She stood with her back to the kitchen door, taking shallow breaths. "I'm so tense," she complained. "Really anxious. It wasn't like this with Caroline. I was cool as a cucumber when I shot her. Walked out of the house, saw all those people driving up for the sale, and I just drove off like nothing happened. Maybe I'm anxious because of you being a priest."

James's own nerves were considerably frayed. His hands shook uncontrollably as he fumbled around in the cabinet, looking for a clean glass. And his eyes lit upon the pill bottle. Marian's tranquilizers. Brand X.

"Let me fix you a glass of wine," James said. "I have a nice Bordeaux."

"Maybe just one glass. I have to keep a clear head. Don't want to get pulled over by the cops while we're out for our drive."

"Our drive?" A chill ran down his spine. Reaching for the wineglass, he managed to palm the pill bottle in the same hand. He set the glass on the counter.

"Yes. I can't very well shoot you here. I've been thinking about that swamp out at Beaulieu. There are alligators there. I've seen them sunning on the banks."

"Let me see," James said, squatting down in front of the lower cabinet and thrusting his torso inside. "That bottle is way at the back here." It was actually in the front. But with his body nearly inside the cabinet, he managed to open the pill bottle and spill six tablets into his hand. Would they dissolve in the wine? He stood up, put the tablets on the counter and the bottle on top of them. James took the corkscrew out of the drawer and while lifting the cork, mashed the pills as hard as he could with the bottle bottom.

"I've been saving this wine for something special," he said, trying to keep his voice light. "I guess this is as special as it's going to get for me."

"Oh, don't be so melodramatic. I'm a very good shot," Diane said assuringly. "Don't worry. You won't feel a thing."

He swept the crushed pills into the wineglass, then poured the Bordeaux on top of it. He swirled the glass lightly, watching with relief as the powder dissolved. The wine was still a little cloudy, however. Would she notice?

"Maybe you'd like some crackers?" he asked, ever the good host, tucking a paper napkin around the bowl of the glass in hopes of obscuring the cloudiness.

"Never mind that," she said, snatching the wine out of his hand and taking a deep gulp.

"Would it be all right if I joined you?" James asked. He poured himself a glass, filled it to the rim. Maybe the alcohol would deaden the pain if Diane Mayhew wasn't the shot she boasted of being.

Diane held the glass away from her face and frowned. "Did you say this was a Bordeaux?" she asked.

"Yes," he said.

"Funny," she said. "Usually I don't like a Bordeaux so much. But this isn't bad. What kind is it?"

"Georges DuBoeuf," he said. "They had a special at Johnny Ganem's back in the fall." He handed her the cork. "Here. For your wine log."

She tucked the cork in the pocket of her garden party dress. "Let's go."

"One more for the road?" he suggested, stalling now.

"Not for me. I'm driving."

Still, she allowed him to pour himself another glass. He dawdled, sipping, disposing of the bottle, wiping the kitchen counters down, rinsing her empty glass out and placing it in the dish drainer. He took the damp dishrag and folded it precisely, laying it neatly on Bernadette's towel bar on the back of the kitchen door.

She glanced down at her wristwatch. "OK, let's get the lead out now. I have a lot of work to do tonight."

His mind raced. "Could I have a last request?"

"No," she snapped. "This is not the French Foreign Legion."

"Please? My rosary. It was a gift from my late mother."

"Get it," she said. "And hurry up. My God. I should have just shot you when you opened the door and gotten it over with."

The rosary was in the farthest corner of the house. It was a miracle he remembered where he'd put it. Diane tramped up the stairs behind him, down the hall to his mother's old bedroom. He had to get a stepladder to reach the highest shelf of the closet. James took his own sweet time climbing the ladder, shuffling the cardboard boxes, taking down one, then another. The rosary was, as he knew it would be, in the last box on the shelf.

"Let's go," she screamed as he lifted it out of the box. "The gnats will be coming out of the marsh. I told you how I feel about gnats."

How long? James wondered, dragging himself as slowly as he dared down the stairs. How long? he wondered, locking the back door, switching on the front porch light, locking the front door behind them, with Diane's pistol poked in his side.

Her gleaming white Lincoln was parked in the driveway, behind his Mercedes. "Get in," she said, pointing to the driver's seat. Did he detect a slight slur in her speech?

"You drive. And don't try anything funny, or I'll put a bullet in your brain right here in your driveway."

"All right," James said. She stumbled a little as she rounded the back of the car. But then she opened the passenger-side door and slid inside.

He put the key in the ignition and turned it on. The dashboard lit up and a bell started dinging insistently. He looked over at Diane. Her head was lolled over on her shoulder. Her eyes were closed. She was snoring.

"Mrs. Mayhew?" he said gently. No answer. Her hands were in her lap, her facial muscles relaxed. He reached over and unbent her fingers from the pistol. "Sweet dreams, Diane," he said. And he picked up her cell phone and dialed 911.

CHAPTER *59*

"ell me again how this scam of Hargreaves's works," Daniel said, turning away from BeBe's stove, where he was sautéing garlic and shallots in butter. We'd gone back to BeBe's from the warehouse, still pumped up with excitement.

Daniel couldn't be content with opening a bottle of wine and nuking a celebratory Budget Gourmet. Instead, he'd decided to make a batch of crab cakes. "I can't help it," he said, assembling his ingredients at the counter. "It's all this nervous energy. When I get like this I have to burn it off; work out, go for a run, fix something at the house. Or cook."

"I know better ways to burn off energy," BeBe quipped, "and none of them involve knives or hammers."

She gave me a meaningful glance and I blushed to the roots of my hair. Daniel saw too, and gave me a wink.

"Don't burn that stuff," I warned him. "I'm starved."

I took a sip of pinot noir and went over my theory about Hargreaves. "He buys the very best authentic antique pieces he can find, and he has them copied," I said. "And the beauty of it is, these are really very simple pieces. The Moses Weed cupboard, for instance, is elegant, but not complicated. It doesn't have any inlays or marquetry or veneers, things that would be complicated to reproduce."

"Why don't more people make phonies then?" BeBe wanted to know.

"It isn't all *that* easy," I explained. "For one thing, to make a believable-looking copy you'd have to make the furniture with similar tools to the ones that were used in that period. Antique draw knives, hand-carved pegs, tools that can produce hand-cut mortises and tenons for the drawer joints. It would take a real craftsman, with the right tools."

"Probably have to have old wood too, right?" Daniel suggested.

"Exactly," I agreed. "The Moses Weed cupboard is burled elm, made of boards cut from trees at Beaulieu. But elms in this part of the country were wiped out decades ago by disease. And it's not just the wood that's hard to duplicate. The antique brasses were handmade in the metal shop at Beaulieu. And the glass in the cupboard doors was the old wavy bull's-eye glass. If you look at it closely, it has almost a purplish tint."

"Could Hargreaves find that kind of stuff?" BeBe asked.

"If he knew where to look, which he would," I said. "Uncle James says Phipps Mayhew and Gerry Blankenship had Beaulieu stripped of all its old moldings and cornices and baseboards, anything of architectural significance that would allow the house to be designated as historically significant. My guess is that since Blankenship had already started skimming off the best pieces to Hargreaves, he also let Hargreaves do the stripping, helping himself to whatever he wanted. He could have found old windows or doors in the basement or attic of the house, or in some of the outbuildings on the property."

"That seems like a lot of trouble to go to, just to build a piece of furniture to look old, and risk getting caught," BeBe said. "Lewis Hargreaves is already filthy rich. I mean, have you ever seen that townhouse of his? On Madison Square?"

"I've seen it," I admitted. "He's got a rice-carved poster bed I'd kill for."

"Maybe it's phony too," Daniel cracked. I looked over and flashed him a smile. He'd taken the frying pan off the fire and was stirring in crabmeat and half-and-half and beaten eggs. Now he was patting the mixture into cakes, his touch as gentle as a baby's, then dipping the cakes in a saucerful of crushed saltine crackers. His hands were big yet delicate looking, the pale pink nails standing out in stark relief against the deep tan of his long, slender fingers as he deftly transferred the cakes to a plate covered with a paper towel.

"I don't know why Hargreaves would take the risk," I admitted.

"Maybe he's just goddamn greedy," Daniel said, his face darkening with anger. "Rich people are like that. You see it all the time in the restaurant. Big fat lard-ass millionaires come into Guale, order a hundred-dollar bottle of wine and a big dinner, then stiff the waiter. It's arrogance. They do it because they can."

"And the profit margin's not bad either," I pointed out. "If he has the right customer, Hargreaves can sell the Moses Weed cupboard for as much as a hundred thousand dollars. If he has two cupboards, he doubles his money."

"But won't people find out?" BeBe asked. "I mean, y'all, this is Savannah. It's impossible to keep a secret in this town."

I'd been thinking the same thing. Hargreaves's customers were some of the savviest and richest people in Savannah. These weren't dopes he'd been duping.

"He probably wouldn't sell the phony pieces to anybody around here," I said slowly. "He wouldn't dare. Anyway, he's got an international clientele. He probably sells through the Internet. Maybe even has his own Web site."

BeBe slapped the countertop with the flat of her hand. "We have got to bring this turkey down." She crouched in her Honey West pose. "Bust his sorry ass!"

The doorbell rang and she ran off to answer it. I wandered over to the stove, and Daniel held out his empty wineglass for me to refill.

"Look who the cat dragged in," BeBe called cheerfully as Jonathan McDowell came trailing in behind her. He smiled briefly, and for the first time I noticed dimples on both sides of his face.

"Have you heard?" Jonathan asked, looking straight at me.

"Heard what?" I asked. "Did you get the restraining order?"

"Better than that," Jonathan said. "We got Caroline DeSantos's killer."

"What?" I shrieked. "Not Tal. Tell me it wasn't Tal."

"It wasn't Tal. It was Diane Mayhew. When James went to see Blankenship today, he blamed Mayhew for what happened at Beaulieu. So James decided to confront Phipps too. Diane eavesdropped and overheard their whole conversation. It must have spooked her pretty badly when James told Mayhew he'd contacted our office about criminal charges. She went over to James's house a couple hours ago and calmly told him she'd killed Caroline."

"You're kidding," BeBe said, laughing dismissively. "Diane Mayhew a killer? I don't believe it. That little gray biddy couldn't hurt a fly."

"She was about to put a bullet in James's skull and dump him in the swamp for the gators to finish off," Jonathan said grimly. And now the dimples were gone. "She killed Caroline because Caroline was having an affair with Phipps, and she would have killed James to keep him from spilling the beans about the affair and the crooked deal at Beaulieu."

I felt a buzzing in my own skull. "Is James all right?" I asked, clutching Jonathan's arm. "Where is he?"

"He's fine," Jon said quickly. "Diane Mayhew was completely deranged. While she bragged about how she'd do anything to hold her family together, James remembered his Southern manners and served her a nice glass of Bordeaux. Liberally spiked with your mama's Xanax. Diane passed out just as she was about to force James to drive out to his intended burying ground."

"Jesus, Mary, Joseph, and all the saints," I said, borrowing one of my uncle's favorite sayings. "You're sure he's all right?"

"He's shaken," Jonathan admitted. "Diane had a forty-five stuck right in his face. I wanted him to go to the hospital, just to have his vital signs checked, but you know Jimmy. Damn stoic."

Jimmy? I'd never in my life heard anybody call my uncle anything but James. Maybe I didn't know him as well as I thought I did.

"Anyway," Jonathan said, "I wanted to tell you in person. Before the media started calling. James said you'd probably be here if you weren't home."

"What happens next?" I asked.

"Diane Mayhew is still at Memorial Hospital. The docs say she should recover fully. When she wakes up, Detective Bradley is going to have a long, serious talk with her. I was by there before I came over here. Phipps is in the waiting room, and Fulmer Woodall is sitting right beside him for moral support."

"Who's Fulmer Woodall?" BeBe asked, beating me to the punch.

"Biggest criminal attorney in the Southeast," Jon said, dimpling. "Flew down from Atlanta in his private Gulfstream as soon as he got the call from Phipps. Things are going to get very, very interesting here shortly."

"But you've got her dead to rights, don't you?" I asked. "And Phipps and Blankenship too?"

"Diane told Jimmy the whole story. She was very precise about the details. Especially the one detail only the killer could know."

"What's that?" I asked.

Jonathan ducked his head and colored slightly. "Caroline wasn't wearing any panties the night she was killed. She'd gone out to Beaulieu expecting to have an, er, assignation with Phipps. The police kept that part quiet."

"I should say so," BeBe said. "My Gawd. How trashy can you get? Being killed without panties, that's worse than having a car wreck wearing raggedy drawers. Can you imagine what her mama will think when she finds out?"

"I think her mama's dead," I put in.

"Diane even kept tape recordings of phone conversations between Phipps and Caroline," Jonathan went on. "If we can get hold of those, it'll go directly to motive. Of course, nothing is cut-and-dried."

"What's that supposed to mean?" I demanded.

He ran a hand through his already tousled hair. "First thing, Fulmer Woodall will claim Diane suffered from diminished mental capacity. That's a given. And of course, they'll try to load the jury with middle-aged women who'll sympathize with her plight."

"Her *plight*?" I said, my voice rising. "She's a filthy-rich socialite. The biggest drama in her life is whether to take the Beemer or the Lincoln to the golf club."

"Her marriage was being threatened by a younger woman," Jonathan said, his voice toneless, his face expressionless. "She's menopausal. Her children no longer need her. Her sense of self-esteem was a shambles. Her physician overmedicated her with dangerous psychotropic drugs. She had abandonment issues." He raised an eyebrow. "Pick a plight. Any plight."

I felt my shoulders sag.

"We'll give it our best shot," Jonathan said. "That's all I can tell you."

"What about Lewis Hargreaves?" BeBe demanded. "You guys will at least bust him, won't you?"

"For what?" Jonathan asked.

"He's got a factory set up over near the Port Authority," BeBe said angrily. "He's making phony antiques. That's why he wanted that cupboard of Weezie's. So he could make copies and sell them to out-of-town clients."

Jonathan looked at me. "Is this true?"

I nodded. "I found out Blankenship was skimming the best pieces from the Mullinax estate and selling them to Hargreaves under the table. We went to L. Hargreaves today. BeBe was going to make an offer on the

Moses Weed cupboard. But the shop was closed and his assistant was leaving. So we followed her to that warehouse."

"And Daniel and I bluffed our way inside," BeBe said excitedly. "We saw the whole operation. Now all we need is for you to bust 'em."

Jonathan nodded but said nothing.

"Hargreaves was in cahoots with Blankenship and Phipps Mayhew," I said. "He's a crook, Jonathan."

"So you say," Jon said. "But I need more than that."

Daniel was pouring olive oil into a skillet on the stove. "Like what?"

"Did Hargreaves sell either of you a phony antique?" Jonathan asked pointedly. "Did he make any representations about merchandise that you know to be untrue?"

BeBe and I just looked at each other.

"Are you aware of any persons who bought merchandise from Lewis Hargreaves that you personally know are not what they were represented to be?"

"Give us a break," BeBe protested. "We just figured it out today."

"And you were brilliant to figure it out," Jonathan said soothingly. "But we can't just march into some warehouse and arrest him because he beat Weezie on a business deal."

I started to say something, but Jonathan looked down at his watch and held up his hand.

"Look. I've got to go now. I'm going to pick Jimmy up at the police barracks and take him out for a hot dinner and a cold martini. All I'm saying is this: we need more. What I'd like, Weezie, is for you and BeBe to come down to my office Monday morning. I want you to talk to N'Lida Shearwater. She's one of our assistant DAs. Very sharp. Very aggressive and very good at fraud and white collar crime. The three of you can figure it out, and then we'll nail Hargreaves within an inch of his life. OK?"

"Whatever," I said.

Jonathan put an arm around my shoulder and squeezed me ever so briefly. His facial hair was scratchy against my cheek.

"Hey," he said softly, "I know you want it all tied up in a neat little package. But real life doesn't always work that way. Look at it this way. Jimmy's alive and well. Diane Mayhew is under arrest, and Gerry Blankenship and Phipps Mayhew have their dicks in a wringer, pardon the expression. And for now, at least, Beaulieu is safe from the bulldozers. Life is good. Right?"

"Right," I said. But if life was so peachy, why did I suddenly feel like shit?

CHAPTER *60*

*B*eBe waited until we heard Jonathan's car pull out of her driveway.

"Jimmy?" she said, her hands on her hips. "Jimmy?" She shook her head sadly. "You never said a word. I'm your best friend and you never said a word about this."

"I couldn't," I said. "Anyway, I just found out myself."

"Found out what?" Daniel put the plates of crab cakes on the kitchen counter, along with a platter of sliced tomatoes and cucumbers, over which he'd spooned some homemade vinaigrette.

"Weezie's uncle James has a boyfriend. Jonathan McDowell. Honestly, Weezie, this is the juiciest news I've heard in years, right after the thing about Caroline being killed with no drawers. I mean, I knew he was gay, but I never said anything because you Catholics are so prissy about that kind of thing. But you knew about Jonathan and you never said a word."

I helped myself to a crab cake and some tomatoes. "James never told me in so many words. He's a painfully private person."

I picked at my food, brooding over all the injustices in the world.

From what Jonathan said, it was going to take heaven and earth to bring Lewis Hargreaves to justice. And in the meantime, he'd probably sell the Moses Weed cupboard and who knew what else from Beaulieu, and make a couple hundred thousand in the process.

"This whole thing sucks," I said finally, pushing away a crab cake that I'd picked to pieces with my fork.

"What's wrong?" Daniel asked. "Too much cilantro?"

"It's not the food," I said. "It's this whole deal that gripes my grits. Look at what's happened here. No matter what we do on Monday, Lewis Hargreaves is still going to have his fancy shop and his zillion-dollar townhouse and his big fancy van. And I'll still be an itinerant picker who drives a beat-up turquoise truck. People like Hargreaves don't get arrested for crawling out a second-story window. They don't get booked and fingerprinted and have sweaty grubby hands patting them down. And they sure as hell don't have to wear jail shoes."

"Jail shoes?" BeBe and Daniel said it together.

"Forget it," I said. "I'm lousy company tonight. Sorry to eat and run, but I think I'll eat and run."

"No dessert?" BeBe asked, holding up a box of the Fudgsicles.

"Not this time," I said. "Talk to you tomorrow maybe."

"I'll walk you out," Daniel volunteered.

He held my hand as we walked out to my truck. It made me want to cry. Tal had never held hands with me after we got married.

"You feeling all right?" Daniel asked, glancing over at me.

"Just kind of blue," I admitted. "It's been a long day. I'll get over it."

"Let me come home with you," he said. "I won't stay over. We could just sit on the sofa. Maybe listen to music or something. Hey. I've got it. I'll give you a back rub. I give a killer back rub."

I shook my head. "Not tonight."

"Come on," he coaxed. "I'll even listen to show tunes if you like."

I bristled. "What's that supposed to mean?"

"Nothing," he said. "It was just a little joke."

"Was that a crack about my uncle being gay?"

"No," he said quickly. "I was just trying to cheer you up. Jeez, why are you being so sensitive all of a sudden?"

"Do you have a problem with my uncle being gay?" I demanded.

"No," he said, stammering slightly. "I told you before, I hate all this family stuff. I'm not interested in that kind of thing." He reached to pull me closer. "You and me. That's all I'm interested in, Weezie. Everybody else can go to hell as far as I'm concerned."

"But it's not just you and me," I said sharply. "I'm part of a family, Daniel. A screwed-up, nutty family. The Foleys put the fun in dysfunctional. But as messed up as they are—as I am—I love them. And I know they love me too. Mostly."

"So?" He raised an eyebrow, suddenly tensed.

"You're part of a family too, in case you've forgotten," I said. "But you won't admit it. You won't even talk about it. And that worries me."

"Why should it worry you? You think there's something wrong with my family? What? You think the Stipaneks aren't as good as the Talmadge Evans family? You afraid we're a bunch of inbred freaks or something?"

"Tal's family?" I said, hooting. "They're nothing. I never even took his name when I got married, in case you hadn't noticed. I just think all those secrets of yours are really dangerous, Daniel. They eat at you."

His hand tightened on my shoulder.

"What the hell are you talking about? What secrets?"

I bit my lip. Suddenly I wished BeBe had never talked me into looking at Daniel's personnel file. Maybe Daniel was right about one thing, the past was none of my business. But damn it, his past kept getting in our way.

"I know about your mom," I said, my voice barely a whisper.

His blue eyes seemed to bore a hole through my forehead. It was as though he could see the wormy little secrets stored there.

"What are you talking about? What do you know about my mother?"

There was no graceful way to put it. I'd done something low and sneaky. It was impossible to put a nice spin to this. *Just tell it,* I told myself. *Get it over with. Once it's out in the open, you can talk it out.*

"I know your mother got involved with Hoyt Gambrell, back when you were just a kid. I know there was a terrible scandal. I know she married him, and he went to prison and she abandoned you and your brothers. I know that's why you left Savannah. Because of her."

"Who have you been talking to?" His voice was calm, but his fingers were digging into the flesh of my shoulders.

"Nobody," I stammered. I'd been expecting fire, now he was killing me with coldness.

"Tell me," he said. "That was twenty years ago. Who told you about it?"

I grabbed his hand. "You're hurting me."

He loosened his grip, but his blue eyes were unwavering. "Who's been talking to you about my family?"

"Daniel, that's beside the point," I said pleadingly. "I don't care what your mother did. I swear to God, I'm not judging you because of her."

"Who's been digging around in my family's dirt? I need to know."

"One of BeBe's boyfriends told us," I said finally. "It wasn't his fault. I started it. I couldn't figure out why you were so secretive about your family. It worried me, Daniel. So BeBe and I looked at your personnel file from Guale. We saw the name you'd put down as your next of kin. Paula Gambrell. I knew you didn't have a sister, so I was wondering who she was. And BeBe said she'd heard that name before. So she called her boyfriend. He knows everything that ever happened in Savannah. He'd forgotten your mother's name, but he told us about Hoyt Gambrell . . . and about what happened," I added lamely.

"And you two girls had a good giggle about it, didn't you?" Daniel said. "That BeBe just loves juicy gossip. And you don't mind it either, do you, Weezie?"

"No," I cried. "It wasn't like that. I felt awful once I knew. BeBe felt bad too. We didn't know, Daniel."

"You had no right," he said.

The street lamp at the curb spilled warm yellow light on Daniel's face, but it was absolutely still. Stony. Unrecognizable. He stalked away, out of the pool of yellow light and into the gray-blue darkness.

CHAPTER *61*

After Daniel left, I was in shock. He hadn't yelled, hadn't shouted. He'd simply walked away. I hardly remembered driving home. I rushed inside and tried calling BeBe's, to see if he'd gone back there. I left messages on his answering machine at the beach house. I even considered, briefly, going after him. But the steeliness of his spine as he walked away into the darkness persuaded me that I might drive nonstop to hell in a handcart before Daniel Stipanek would come back to me that night.

Finally, I slumped down on the sofa and did what all tough-minded contemporary women do these days when faced with what beauty-shop magazines call "life challenges."

I bawled like a damned baby. It felt good too. But after fifteen minutes of mewling and sniffing, I started getting thirsty. I was out in the kitchen, making myself a cup of herbal tea, when I heard the front door creak open.

I sucked in my breath. He'd come back. In an instant I scrubbed my red puffy face with a wet dish towel and finger-combed my tear-matted hair back into some semblance of order. Not wanting to seem too eager to make up, I kept my clothes on, although I will admit to having unzipped my black Emma Peel top just the eensiest bit in an attempt to look somewhere this side of provocative.

"Daniel?" I called nonchalantly.

From the front of the house I heard Jethro whine. Not bark. Just whine.

"No baby, it's me."

I dropped the tea tin into the sink and whirled around. Tal stood in the kitchen doorway, stooping because he was too tall to fit completely under the arched door frame.

For a minute, my mind froze. And then it thawed, fast.

"Get out," I told him.

"Daniel?" he said, slurring it, making it sound like a nasty word, like phlegm or uvula. "Is that your fry cook's name?"

The cordless phone was mounted on the kitchen wall. I snatched it up and held it out like a weapon. "Get out or I'll call the cops. I mean it, Tal. I'm not in the mood for any of your shit tonight. Or any other night."

"Oh baby," he said, taking a step closer. "Bet you were in the mood for Daniel though, weren't you?"

"Go away, Tal," I said. "You're drunk and you're disgusting. And from now on, stay away from me. I don't want any more surprise visits, or any messages on my answering machine, or any more flowers. I just want you out of my life. Forever."

He took a step forward and stroked my face. I cringed and batted his hand away.

"Weezie," he whispered, his breath laced with Scotch. "You don't mean that."

"I mean it," I said through clenched teeth.

"No," he said, shaking his head like a dog trying to shed a flea. "You're confused. All this mess with Caroline, it's had you upset. But that's all over. Did you hear? They've arrested Diane Mayhew. She killed Caroline. Remember Diane? She and Phipps came here for dinner one night. You were madder than a wet hen, because the silly bitch wouldn't eat your cooking."

"Go away. Now." My voice sounded eerily calm, but I could feel my knees buckling. I picked up the phone to call 911. Time to send for reinforcements.

"No!" Tal slapped my face with the broad of his palm, sending the phone flying to the floor, where the cheap plastic shattered on impact.

For a moment, I was blinded by the pain. Tears streamed down my face as I clutched both hands to my bruised cheek.

"Weezie," Tal crooned, pulling me to his chest. "I'm sorry, baby. I never meant to hurt you. Damn, Weezie. Why'd you make me do that?"

I was sobbing, gasping for air, trying to comprehend what had just happened. Good old gutless Tal Evans had just whaled the tar out of me. And now he was hugging me and blaming me for what had just happened.

"Let me go," I cried, trying to push him away. "Let me go, Tal."

He folded his arms tighter around my back, crushing me to him.

"Shh," he whispered, stroking my hair. "Be still now. Just be still."

"Tal," I whimpered. "You're hurting me. Please let go."

"Now you just be still and listen," he continued, his grip tightening. "That's the problem with you, Weezie. You never wanted to listen."

"I'm listening now," I said. I felt a warm trickle from my nose. Blood. "Really, Tal. I'm listening."

"Good," he said, and he actually kissed the top of my head, like a father rewarding a recalcitrant kid for good behavior.

"That guy. Daniel. Have you been sleeping with him, Weezie? Have you?" He looked down at me, his face stern. "You don't even know the guy, and you're prancing around over here half-naked with him. That isn't like you."

"I know," I managed to say. What was going on here? My mind reeled with the possibilities. Tal was drunk. He was crazy. His handprint was on my cheek. Men from Mars had invaded his pants and commandeered his penis, transplanting it into his brain. Whatever the cause, he was really giving me a serious case of the heebie-jeebies. If I ever got away from him, I vowed, right before I had him locked up I was going to kick the living shit out of Tal Evans.

"These women," Tal was saying. "My mother was right. There's no shame. No morals among young women anymore. Running around, acting like common street whores. There's no decency anymore."

Could this be happening? Was my faithless, philandering ex-husband really giving me a lecture on morals? Maybe I was the one who was crazy. Maybe that one-time experiment with blotter acid back in junior high was giving me the bad trip of a lifetime.

Holy jeez. If I ever got out of this, right after I kicked the shit out of Tal, I was going to start my own antidrug crusade. "Hey kids, just say no. In fact, say hell no."

"My mother was wrong about Caroline, though." Tal sounded absolutely lucid. "Mother was crazy about Caroline. That's why she gave me Great-grandmother's diamond ring. To give to Caroline. Mother never liked you, Weezie. She thought you were trashy. Caroline had her fooled. She had every-body fooled. Even me, for a while. She acted so refined. So elegant. The fuck-ing slut. Walking around in a two-thousand-dollar dress, wearing my great-grandmother's ring, and underneath that silk dress, she was naked."

I felt myself freeze.

I looked up at Tal. He nodded, his smile twisted. "Shocked you, didn't I?"

"What are you talking about?" My mouth was dry.

"Caroline. The night she went to meet Phipps Mayhew. Out at Beaulieu. That was part of her little game with him. No panties. Classy, huh? She died wearing a two-carat diamond, and no panties."

"How did you know that?" The blood was trickling down into the cor-ner of my mouth. I tasted it with the tip of my tongue. It was hot and salty. Like Caroline DeSantos. But how did Tal know what Caroline wasn't wearing the night she was killed? Jonathan said the cops had kept it a secret. Only the killer knew. And Diane Mayhew was the killer. Wasn't she?

"They had phone sex," Tal was saying. "Caroline and Phipps. Revolt-ing. Diane played me a tape recording she made of it. The silly bitch tapped the kids' phones, but instead of the kids, she caught the old goat."

He laughed. Tal always did love his own jokes.

"You and Diane?" Maybe I had a concussion.

"Diane came to my office one day. Told me about what was going on between Phipps and Caroline. She demanded that I fire Caroline."

"Why didn't you?"

He smiled again. "Phipps Mayhew was the firm's biggest client. Ever. With a commission like that, it was only a matter of time before we started getting other big commercial projects. Sewage treatment plants, schools. Hospitals. And all because of Caroline. Because she couldn't keep her legs together. If I fired Caroline, she would have gone to another firm. Taken the Plant Mullinax project with her. There was no way. No fuckin' way. And I told Diane that too."

He stroked my hair. Out of the corner of my eye I saw a glint of gold. His wedding band. The one I'd given him. Tal's touch was deceptively gentle. It triggered what shrinks call a sense memory. A long time ago, I had lain in bed with this man, the two of us, naked, intertwined. The same touch.

"You and Diane. Together. The two of you killed Caroline."

His hand slid down to my shoulder again. He sighed.

"Diane did it. All by herself. She didn't need any help from me."

"You set it up, didn't you?"

"No." He said it carelessly. "I told Diane she was crazy. It was too risky. But she wouldn't listen. What could I do? How could I stop her? I had a feeling the night I followed Caroline out to Beaulieu. And I was right."

"You were there?"

"I didn't go into the house," Tal said. "I heard the shots. And I saw Diane drive away. There was nothing I could do for Caroline by then."

"But you knew," I said. "You knew she did it. The police thought I killed Caroline. They arrested me. Put me in jail. If it hadn't been for James . . . . They would have tried me for murder."

"Diane would have confessed. Eventually." He frowned and shook his finger in my face. The man really needed killing. "It was your own fault, Weezie. You had to go snooping around out there at Beaulieu. Caroline told me about the way you showed up at the memorial service for Miss Anna Ruby. Shameless, really."

"Me?" It came out as a squeak. "I'm shameless?"

"You've changed," he said, frowning. "Did you do it, Weezie?" He held me at arm's length, and his fingertips dug into my shoulder blades.

"Did I, what?"

"Did. You. Fuck. Him." Each word was a statement.

"No." I said it calmly. I rocked back a little on my heels, brought my knee up with every ounce of strength I had, and issued Tal a direct hit in the balls.

He howled and doubled over from the pain. It was all I needed. I started running toward the front door. I had to get away. But over the din of his screams I heard a voice calling me.

"Weezie? Eloise?"

I stopped in my tracks. It was my mother.

"Mama?" I ran back toward the kitchen. She never came here. She'd said she couldn't stand seeing me living in a garage.

But she was here now. My mama was standing in my kitchen doorway, clutching a white-and-blue Corning Ware casserole dish in both hands. Tal was rolling around on the kitchen floor, howling like a scalded dog, both hands cupped over his privates.

"Weezie? I brought you one of my tuna noodle casseroles. What on earth is going on here? What's wrong with Tal?"

Mama looked nice. She'd had her hair colored and combed out, and she was wearing lipstick and a little pair of pearl earrings. She was clear-eyed and sassy. It was my old mama.

She put one finger under my chin. She sucked in her breath. "My Lord, child, you're bleeding. And you've got a big old knot raising up under your eye."

"It was Tal. He hit me. We've got to get out of here. He's dangerous, Mama. He helped Diane Mayhew kill Caroline." I tugged at her arm. "Come on, Mama. Let's call the police."

She pulled away from me. Looked down at Tal, her eyes narrowing. He was struggling to his feet.

"Marian," he gasped, pulling himself up by grasping one of the cabinet doors. "Thank goodness you're here. Weezie's not herself. We need to get her help. Psychological counseling."

"You hit Weezie?" Mama's voice made shivers run down my spine. I looked up and saw Jethro standing in the doorway. He was positively cowering at the sight of my mama.

"You hit my child?"

"Weezie's lying," Tal said. He was breathing hard, but he was standing upright. "She got drunk with that boyfriend of hers and fell. Either that or he hit her. That's why I ran over here. I heard her screaming for help."

Mama stood very still for just a moment. Then, before I could stop her, she raised the tuna noodle casserole up and slammed it down flat on the top of Tal's head.

He went down like a sack of meal.

"Shame on you, Talmadge Evans," Mama said sternly, shaking a finger at his motionless body, which was now covered in canned tuna, egg noodles, and potato-chip topping. "You better not ever let me catch you hitting my daughter ever again. And don't you go round calling her a liar either. Or I'll tie a knot in your tail you won't soon forget, little mister."

I turned toward Mama and gave her the biggest hug in the world. "Mama," I said, breathing in the smell of her, of Aqua Net and Shalimar and Secret deodorant. "You saved me. But you ruined your nice casserole."

She let me hug her for exactly ten more seconds, then she pushed me gently away. "Don't you worry about that," she said briskly. "I've got two more in the freezer at home. All this sobriety has got me cooking like there's no tomorrow."

CHAPTER 62

*M*ama cocked her head and gave me a coy look. "What's this about a boyfriend?"

"Never mind that," I said, kneeling down beside Tal, who was groaning but keeping fairly still. "I think we better call 911. I think maybe he has a concussion."

"Nonsense," Mama said, wiping her hands on a dish towel. "That little bitty old casserole couldn't have hurt him that bad. He's just lucky I didn't have my cast-iron skillet in my hands when I saw how he'd hurt you."

She was standing at the sink now, running water over a wad of paper towels. "We've got to move him right away though, because I don't want that tuna stuff soaking into your floor. Grease stains are the very worst on hardwood."

This was my old mama, worrying more about tuna stains than the possibility that she'd nearly killed her former son-in-law.

Between the two of us, we managed to get Tal to his feet, and haltingly dragged him out to the living-room sofa.

"He's gonna have a headache to remember me by," Mama said grimly, looking down at Tal, sprawled out on the sheet she'd hastily thrown over the sofa. "The sorry blankety-blank."

This was harsh language for her. I gave her a quick look of surprise.

"I'll never forgive him for the way he did you," Mama said, ducking her head. She reached out and took my hand. "And I'll never forgive myself for the way I did you, acting like the divorce was your fault."

I gave her a quick peck on the cheek, which was the Foley family's version of sloppy sentimentality. The night was turning out to be a regular old lovefest.

"That's why I came over here tonight," Mama said. "In rehab, we call it making amends. Your daddy and I have had some nice long talks." She sighed. "What that poor man has put up with."

"He loves you," I said. "And I love you too. And I'm so glad you are getting help now. That's all that counts. That you're getting help."

I looked back down at Tal. He had a large red egg rising up on his forehead. "I read somewhere that head injuries can be life threatening."

"If he can say his name, he's all right," Mama declared. She jabbed Tal's arm with a long pink lacquered nail.

"Hey!" she said loudly. "What's your name, fella?"

Tal opened his eyes, reached up, and gingerly probed his forehead with his fingertips. "Christ, Marian, you've cracked my skull."

"Better yet," Mama said triumphantly. "He knows my name. He's all right."

But I wasn't looking at Tal anymore, I was looking at Mama's hands. Her nails, to be exact. I'd never seen her wearing polish before, and certainly not long acrylic nails.

"What's this?" I asked, catching one hand in mine.

"Aren't they pretty?" she asked, fluttering her fingertips. "Naomi did them. She says I could be a hand model. I have very nice nail beds, did you know?"

"Who's Naomi?" I asked.

"She's in my Wednesday-night Christian women's recovery group," Mama said. "She used to be a manicurist at the Elizabeth Arden salon in Atlanta, until she started smoking crack so bad they let her go."

"You're friends with a crack head?"

"*Former* crack addict," Mama said firmly. "Naomi is a lovely person. And she's my very first African-American friend. She didn't charge me a penny for this manicure. And you know in Atlanta, they get forty dollars for something like this."

"How nice," I said. Up until very recently my mother always referred to black people as "coloreds." This rehab program she was enrolled in was certainly broadening her horizons in a hurry.

"Christ," Tal moaned again. "Would you two be quiet? My head is splitting in two. Get me some aspirin for God's sake. And some Scotch too."

"No Scotch," Mama said, wrinkling her nose. "You reek of it already. For goodness sake, Talmadge Evans. You are knee-walking drunk. You need to pull yourself together."

"Look who's talking," Tal muttered, closing his eyes again. "Weezie, for God's sake, get me something for my head."

"Don't you talk to her that way," Mama snapped. "She's not your wife anymore, you know."

"Never mind," I said. "I'll get it."

She followed me out to the kitchen. I shook some aspirin out of the bottle I keep in the cabinet by the back door, and picked up the cell phone, which was cracked but still functioning.

"I'm worried about him," I said. "He's a son of a bitch, for sure, but I don't want us to be responsible for him having some kind of life-altering injury."

"All right," Mama said, taking the phone away from me. "If it'll make you feel better, I'll call Dr. Dick. He just lives over on Jones Street. He'll come over and take a look, and if he says so, then we'll cart Tal over to Memorial."

"Who's Dr. Dick?"

"He's my rehab sponsor," Mama said. "Everybody in rehab has a sponsor who has successfully completed treatment. In treatment, they call folks like him an impaired physician. Dr. Dick just says he had a really bitchin' Percodan habit."

"Oh," I said. "You don't think he'll mind taking a peek at Tal?"

"Absolutely not," Mama said. "He says I can call him day or night. For anything I need. And that includes house calls."

While Mama called Dr. Dick, I took Tal a glass of water and three aspirin.

"Here," I said, thrusting the glass at him. "Take your damn aspirin."

He swallowed the pills and handed me the glass. "Thanks a lot," he said.

"Fuck you," I said softly.

He opened one eye, then the other. I guess the sight of the bruise on my cheek and the blood around my nose took him aback.

"I'm sorry," he said softly.

"Fuck you," I repeated.

"Honest to God, Weezie, I never, ever meant to hurt you. I never hit a woman in my life. You know that. I don't know what came over me."

"I do," I said. "Probably a quart of Johnnie Walker black."

"I wasn't drunk," he said.

"No. Just a mean, sick son of a bitch," I said. And I knelt down on the floor beside him.

He turned toward me, grimacing from the effort.

"Listen to me," I said softly. "I could call the police. Have you charged with aggravated assault. But I won't. I could also call that detective who's investigating Caroline's murder, and tell him you knew Diane Mayhew killed your fiancée. That you were there that night. That's at least concealing evidence."

"I wasn't there," he protested. "There was nothing I could do to stop her."

"Save it," I said. "I'm tired of dealing with cops. I'd prefer to deal with you."

"What's that supposed to mean?"

"It means I want you out of the townhouse."

"What?" He lifted himself up by one elbow. "You're out of your mind."

"No," I said. I put my face right up against his. "I don't feel safe here anymore with you right next door. You've harassed me enough. I want you out."

"Tough luck," he said, rolling backward on the sofa. "It's my house."

"Think about it," I said. "Mama saw what you did to me tonight."

"She wasn't there," he said.

"She'll lie," I said. "She'll swear she saw you hit me. And that's why she beaned you with that casserole. To keep you from doing it again. And the cops will believe her. I'll have you charged with aggravated assault. And breaking and entering. And I'll make sure it gets in the *Morning News*."

"You wouldn't," Tal said.

"Believe it," I said. "Uncle James's secretary's nephew is the police reporter. She'll call him as soon as I call her. It'll be all over the news by tomorrow. The Evans name dragged through the mud. I can't wait. Mother Evans's baby boy, a common criminal. A wife beater."

"That's blackmail," he said.

"Call it whatever you want," I said. "But if I don't see you loading your stuff and moving out by tomorrow morning, I'm calling the cops. And aggravated assault will be the least of your worries."

"Where would I go?"

"Go to hell," I said lightly. "Just get out of that house. By nine tomorrow.

I'm going in the kitchen now. Mama wants to take some photographs of my bruises."

Mama was just clicking off the cell phone when I got back to the kitchen. I put the kettle on the stove for a pot of tea. What I really wanted now was a very stiff drink, but I didn't dare with Mama there.

"I'll make us some toast," she said. "Where do you keep the bread?"

She got two slices of bread and popped them into my toaster, a funky chrome fifties model I'd picked up for a quarter at a thrift shop on Waters Avenue.

"Look at this cord," Mama said, pointing to it. "It's all frayed. You could get electrocuted."

"It works fine," I said. "Just a little sparking once in a while."

She frowned but went on making the toast and tea.

"Now tell me about this boyfriend," she said when we sat down at the counter to drink our tea and wait on the doctor.

"Former boyfriend," I said glumly. "We broke up tonight."

"Do I know him?"

"As a matter of fact, you did know him. Do you remember that boy I dated the summer before my senior year of high school? Danny Stipanek?"

She took a sip of tea and squinched up her eyes. "Stipanek. Was that the boy with the loud muffler?"

"That was Danny all right. He went into the Marines at the end of that summer, and he only moved back to town this past year. He's a chef at BeBe's restaurant."

"Do we know his people?" Mama asked, frowning.

"No," I said, dreading the conversation that was sure to come.

"Stipanek," she said, mulling it over. "What church did they go to?"

"I wouldn't know." I busied myself with rinsing out the teacups.

"Was his mama a little bitty brunette? Blue eyed? Wore pointy-toed high heels and always had a matching handbag?"

"Don't know," I said, scrubbing at a nonexistent spot on the countertop. "He didn't talk about his family a lot. Anyway, it's over between us. So it really doesn't matter who his people are, does it?"

"Matter?" Mama looked shocked. "It certainly does matter."

The doorbell rang just then, and I jumped up as an excuse to escape her questioning.

The man at the front door was tall and slightly balding. He had hip-looking wire-rimmed glasses and a pointy goatee.

"Are you Eloise?" he asked.

"Dr. Dick?"

He smiled. "That Marian. I'm Dick Sorensen. I understand you've had a little accident? Somebody with a head injury?"

"Dick!" Mama's voice trilled. I stood aside and she gave him a huge hug. "You are such an old sweetie for coming over like this. Come on in here and take a look at Talmadge, would you?"

She led him over to the sofa. "This is Talmadge," Mama said. "He hit his head going up the staircase there, didn't you, Tal?"

"Whatever," Tal said.

Dick Sorenson produced a small penlight from the breast pocket of his shirt and crouched down beside the sofa.

"Do you feel able to sit up?" he asked Tal.

"My head feels like it's going to split in two," Tal whined.

"Sit up and act like an adult," Mama said sharply.

Tal did as he was told. I think Mama finally had him scared.

The doctor shone the light in both of Tal's eyes, waved his hands around, asked Tal questions about whether or not he was seeing any spots, asked him to count from one to ten, backward and foreward, and gently prodded the impressive knot on Tal's head.

"You can lie back down now," he said after a couple minutes.

Dr. Sorensen motioned for us to follow him toward the front door.

"I think he'll be all right," he said softly. "Maybe a mild concussion. Here's what I want you to do. Stay with him tonight. Let him doze if he wants, but wake him every couple of hours and ask him the same questions I did, have him count, tell you his name, that kind of thing. If he seems disoriented, or is in any more pain, then I would go ahead and contact his own physician for treatment."

"Stay with him?" I said, shocked. "Can't he go home?"

"Not really," Dr. Sorensen said. "He has to be supervised. And he shouldn't be moved tonight. Is that a problem?"

"No," Mama said quickly. "We'll take care of everything." She edged him toward the door. "See you at the meeting tomorrow," she said, closing the door almost in his face.

"Now what?" I demanded, when the coast was clear. "I don't want Tal here. I won't sleep with him under the same roof. We should have gone on and taken Tal to the emergency room."

"Don't you worry about that," Mama said soothingly. "I'll call your daddy. He can come over and spend the night and keep an eye on Tal."

"All night?" I protested. "I don't want to do that. Daddy never even liked Tal."

"He won't mind a bit," Mama said. "He doesn't sleep that well anyway. You just go upstairs and get him a quilt and a pillow and I'll take care of the rest."

CHAPTER *63*

When I came downstairs in the morning, Tal
was gone. Daddy was sitting at the kitchen table, surrounded by various
tools and brushes, plus my chrome toaster, the vacuum cleaner, the VCR,
and an old nonfunctioning kitchen clock I'd hung on the wall for looks.

He had the back off the clock and was frowning down at it over the
tops of his bifocals.

I noticed that his shirt had been freshly pressed. His slacks had a
razor crease and his hair had been trimmed recently. He was even wearing
new glasses—new by his standards, anyway, which meant the 1980s.
Mama was better.

"Hey, shug," he said absentmindedly. "Coffee's made." He nodded in
the direction of the stove, where my meemaw's old West bend percolater
was bubbling away.

"What's going on here?" I asked, gesturing toward all the appliances.
"And where's Tal?"

"Gone," Daddy said. "Said he had some packing to do."

I peeked out the kitchen window. The back door to the townhouse
was open, and I saw Tal walk slowly out with a suitcase in each hand.

"Did he seem all right?" I asked. "Did you wake him up to check?"

"He knew his name and he could count," Daddy said grimly. "And he seemed to understand what I'd do to him if I ever caught him so much as laying a finger on my daughter again."

"Good," I said, kissing the top of Daddy's head and picking up a Baby Ben chrome alarm clock happily ticking away. "I finally slept last night, knowing you were downstairs keeping watch. Is this what you did all night?"

"Some," Daddy said, putting down a screwdriver. "Your TV reception wasn't too good, so I diddled with that a little bit. Then when the John Wayne movie went off, I remembered your mama wanted me to look at your toaster cord. I took a little catnap, then I just piddled around here and there."

"Mama's right," I said, pouring two mugs of coffee. "You are a saint."

He blushed a little and coughed to hide his pleasure. "That vacuum cleaner ought to pick up a little better now. I oiled it and cleaned it out real good."

I took a sip of coffee. "Why can't I find a man like good old Dad?"

"Hush up," he said. He nodded in the direction of the window. "You tell Tal he had to move out?"

"I suggested he might want to," I said.

"Or?"

"You don't want to know," I said.

"Try me."

"I told him Mama would swear to the cops that she saw him hit me. And that I'd have him arrested for aggravated assault."

"Should have done that anyway," Daddy said.

"Even if I got him arrested, they'd let him out on bail. And next time he got liquored up he'd be right back over at my door again," I said. "I want him gone for good. I won't sleep right until I know he's not looking in at my windows."

"How you gonna make him stay away?" Daddy asked. "It's his house. Weezie? Shouldn't you maybe think about moving? You could come home for a while. Mama and I wouldn't bother you. And Tal sure as hell wouldn't either."

I shuddered, both at the thought of moving home and at the thought of Tal.

"No," I said finally. "I'm not running away. But thank you anyway. You were sweet to spend the night and keep me safe. And to fix everything in my house."

He grinned. "How's that truck running?"

"Good," I said. "I got the new tires like you suggested. Now it's my turn to fix something for you. How about some scrambled eggs and grits?"

CHAPTER *64*

*J*ames fidgeted with his collar. He straightened his tie, coughed to clear his throat. Finally, when he could delay no longer, he called Janet into his office.

"Are they here?"

"They've been here for ten minutes. Just get on with it, James. You've got other appointments this morning, including Tal Evans. If you don't see them now, everybody else will get backed up."

"All right," he said, sighing. "It's now or never. Bring them on back."

He folded his hands and put them on the desk in front of him. Then he tilted his head back and looked at the streaming dust motes. He liked the dust motes better than cloud formations, which never looked like much of anything to him. Maybe that was his problem. He'd always been a concrete thinker. Abstraction was lost on him. But the dust motes, those had something to show him. Today they were swirling like the sun in one of Vincent van Gogh's landscapes. It was, he decided, possibly a good portent.

"Ah-hum."

He jerked his head forward, looked at his brother Joe and his sister-in-law, Marian, standing in front of his desk, looking expectant.

"Hey!" he said, a little too cheerfully.

He stood up and shook Joe's hand, gave Marian a sketch of a hug. They both sat down in the chairs Janet brought in, declined her offer of coffee.

"Are you all right?" Marian blurted out, once Janet left the room. "James, you're not sick, are you? Nothing terminal?"

"Oh heavens, no," James said quickly. "Is that what you thought? That I was dying?"

"It occurred to us," Joe said. "You know, calling us to see you here at the office and all. Like it was something official."

"No, that's not it at all," James said. "I'm sorry if I frightened you. It's just that I've been so busy lately, and with all that's happened, with Weezie and all . . . there were some things I wanted to discuss with you."

"She's not in any legal trouble, is she?" Joe asked, his face creased with worry. "She told us all that was over with. They charged that Mayhew woman with murder, that's what we read in the paper."

"It's not Weezie," James said. "She's fine. No problem at all there. In fact, I think she and Tal are going to renegotiate the divorce settlement."

"Why?" Marian asked.

"Tal wants to sell Weezie the townhouse," James said, smiling despite himself. "He's, uh, had some reversals of fortune lately."

"Meaning what?" Joe said bluntly. "Is the son of a bitch broke?"

"Not quite," James said. "But the state has issued a stop-work order at the paper plant out at Beaulieu. Some kind of environmental concerns. There are suits and countersuits. Coastal Paper Products is suing Tal's firm, alleging malfeasance in the firm's management of the project. In the meantime, all the negative publicity has hurt the company. The work isn't coming in. And since he's not currently living in the townhouse, he's decided that's an expense he can trim. He called yesterday and offered to sell the house to Weezie."

"I'll bet he'll try to soak her for it too," Joe said.

"Not necessarily," James said, smiling again. "I think he's had a late-breaking attack of guilt. Considering the fair market value of the house, the offer he's made is extremely reasonable. Favorable, even."

"Can she afford to buy it?" Marian asked, the look of concern on her face matching Joe's now. "On what she makes selling junk?"

"I wouldn't worry about Weezie," James said. "She's really quite a good businesswoman. Now. About why I asked you to meet me here today."

He took a deep breath. Said an abbreviated prayer.

"I'm gay," he said.

"We know," Marian said.

Joe shifted a little in his chair. He looked down at his shoes, which were neatly polished, and tugged at the top of his socks. He straightened the crease in the khakis Marian had pressed early that morning.

James looked down at his own socks. They did not need pulling up, so he looked back at his brother and sister-in-law, who were regarding him with some mild curiosity.

"You know. How long have you known?"

"Always," Joe said. "Since you were a kid. I didn't know what to call it, but I knew you weren't exactly like everybody else in the family."

"You knew I was homosexual?" James could not believe how easily the word slipped from his mouth. He had never, up until now, used it to describe himself. "But how? I didn't know myself. Not until recently."

Joe shrugged. "It was a feeling I had." He glanced over at his wife. "I never talked to anybody about it. Not even you, Marian. I just didn't think it was anybody else's business but yours, James."

Marian patted Joe's hand reassuringly. "You know how he is, James."

James felt his jaw dropping. "What about you, Marian? Did you know?"

"No," Marian admitted. "Not until that day in the restaurant Weezie took me to. I saw you with that other man, and I think at some point, I realized that he was your, um, friend." She blushed. "Even though I was pretty drunk that day, I somehow figured things out. And as soon as I figured it out, I also figured out that I was the last one to know."

She forced a little smile. "That's what alcohol does. It clouds things."

"Oh."

James scooted his chair a little ways from the desk so that he could get a broader picture of his family. They seemed very calm. No hysterics, no accusations. This was not what he had expected.

"What made you decide to tell us?" Marian asked. "If you don't mind my asking."

"Several things," James said. "You're my family. I don't want to have that kind of a secret from you. It's not something I'm ashamed of, you know."

Joe nodded.

"And another thing," James went on quickly. "Phipps Mayhew, the husband of the woman who murdered Caroline DeSantos, has been going around town spreading stories about me. It's revenge. Because I figured out his crooked dealings with Beaulieu. He's told the archbishop that I'm gay. Because he thinks that will hurt me financially."

"Will it?" Joe asked.

"I don't know yet," James said. "If it does, so be it. There's plenty of legal work in this town. I own the house, my car's paid for. I'm not worried about money."

"Good," Marian said. "Listen, James. One of the women in my Christian women's group, I was telling her you're a lawyer. She needs a will. I told her to call you."

"Thank you," James said, touched by her gesture.

"Her name is Naomi," Marian said proudly. "She used to be a crack head."

Since it was full disclosure time, James decided to go all the way. Get everything out in the open. "My friend," James said, suddenly emboldened. "His name is Jonathan. He's a lawyer. He works in the district attorney's office."

"A lawyer! How nice," Marian said, beaming. "Who are his people?"

CHAPTER 65

Merijoy Rucker's face was flushed with excitement.

"Weezie, darlin'," she said, hopping up and down on the doorstep of the carriage house. "I know it's awful of me to drop by this time of the morning without calling first, but I just had to rush over here to show you something."

I had a towel around my wet hair, and another around my still-wet body. It was only 8 A.M.

"Come on in," I told her.

"It's out in the back of my Suburban," she said, grinning. "Hurry up and get dressed. If I don't show it to somebody, I'm just gonna bust."

"Give me a minute," I said, heading upstairs.

I slid into a pair of jeans and a T-shirt, not bothering with a bra.

When I came downstairs, she grabbed me by the hand and fairly dragged me outside to where her car was parked in the lane.

Merijoy flung open the cargo doors to her Suburban. Inside, wrapped in a faded blue quilt, I could see the faint gleam of dark wood.

"What is it?" I asked, pulling at the edge of the quilt to get a better look.

"It's an antique Empire card table," she said, yanking the quilt away. "And it came right out of Beaulieu. Could you die? Could you just die?"

With the quilt gone, I could now see Merijoy's new prize. A cherry-wood card table, with ebony inlay and neatly tapered legs. But it wasn't the first time I'd seen the card table. Its exact twin was in that antique store in Bluffton.

I sucked in my breath.

"What?" Merijoy said, her smile fading. "Is there something wrong with it?"

"No," I said quickly. "Let's take it out so I can get a better look."

Together, we eased the table out of the truck.

It was an exact match of the other table.

"Where'd you buy this?" I asked.

She smiled and showed a dimple. "I'm really not supposed to say."

"Not even to me?" I asked, faking a pout. "I thought we were friends."

"I know," she said, throwing an arm around my shoulder and giving me a fond squeeze. "Anyway, I'm awful at keeping secrets. Just promise me you won't tell Randy Rucker. If he finds out what I spent on this little old table, he will have a conniption fit for sure."

"Where did you buy it?" I repeated. "Bluffton? A shop called La Juntique?"

"No," she said, looking puzzled. "Bluffton? What made you think of there?" She looked around, checking for spies. "I bought it from Lewis Hargreaves," she whispered. "Could you just *die*?"

It took an entire pot of coffee and half of a pan of Sara Lee cheese Danish to pry the whole story out of Merijoy.

"You know I've been busy trying to raise funds to buy Beaulieu back from Coastal Paper Products?" she asked, taking a sip of coffee.

I nodded. I'd seen stories in the newspapers about the historical society's efforts to have Beaulieu declared a historic landmark. I'd even been invited to the fund-raising gala Merijoy chaired. It was held at the Telfair Academy. But at five hundred dollars a plate, the price of admission was a little steep for me. And besides, I didn't have a date. To be truthful, with Daniel out of my life, I barely had a life. Eat. Sleep. Junk. Obsess. The only good development lately had been that Tal had seemingly disappeared off the face of the planet. The townhouse was empty, and I was sleeping a lot better. But alone.

"Lewis Hargreaves contributed a thousand dollars to my fund-raising campaign," Merijoy said excitedly. "So, naturally, I called him up to thank him. And that's when he mentioned that he might have a piece I'd be interested in acquiring. For when we turn Beaulieu into a house museum."

"The card table?" I asked.

"Lewis told me he bought quite a few nice pieces from the estate sale. And I remembered that cupboard you wanted so badly."

I felt my pulse quicken. "The Moses Weed cupboard? Did he offer to sell it to you?"

"No," she said. "I asked about it, and he acted like he didn't know what I was talking about. Which I thought was odd. Because we both saw him that day, at Miss Anna Ruby's memorial, circling around and sniffing at it like a dog in heat."

"Very odd," I said dryly.

"Anyway," she went on, "he sort of hemmed and hawed, and said he had a client ready to buy all the pieces, but he hated to see them go out of Savannah. Because they were made here," she said.

"How noble of Lewis. How preservation-minded," I said.

"I practically had to beg to see this piece," she said. "But he called late last night. Very mysterious. Said if I got over to his shop first thing this morning, he would 'entertain an offer' for this card table. Did you ever?"

"I never."

"I fell in love as soon as I saw it," Merijoy said. "Now tell the truth, Weezie, do you think fifteen thousand was too much to pay?"

I nearly spit out my coffee.

"You paid fifteen thousand for that card table?"

Her face fell. "Was it too much? I thought, since I'm going to donate it to the house museum, it would be tax-deductible and all. And Lewis said it was made on the premises. Before the Civil War. And he had another buyer in the wings, he said. Somebody from Charleston. I just closed my eyes and wrote the check. I took the money out of my little investment account. Randy Rucker will kill me when he finds out."

My mind was racing. Had Hargreaves really sold her the piece I'd seen in Bluffton? Or had he sold Merijoy Rucker one of his own carefully manufactured copies?

"It's a beautiful piece of furniture," I said finally. "And it would be wonderful to have family pieces in the house, once you're able to buy Beaulieu."

"That's what I thought," Merijoy said happily.

"One thing that's important though," I said, hesitating. "A lot of that table's worth is based on its provenance. You have to be able to prove it came out of Beaulieu. Otherwise, it's just another nice piece of nineteenth-century furniture."

"Don't worry about that," Merijoy said. "Lewis told me all about the provenance. He swore me to secrecy, but he finally admitted that horrible Phipps Mayhew let him buy a select few pieces out of Beaulieu before the estate sale. He gave me a copy of the bill of sale and everything."

"Good," I said thoughtfully. "Hang on to that piece of paper, Merijoy. And if I were you, I'd just keep quiet, for now, about where you bought that table. Until the society has the funds raised to buy the house."

"Great idea," she said, beaming. "I knew you'd love that table as much as I do. And nobody else in Savannah could appreciate it as much as we do."

"You're absolutely right," I told her.

Half an hour later I was on the road to Bluffton. It was late September, still summer, really, in Savannah, but in places I could see where the marsh grasses were starting to turn copper and gold, and the usual shroud of humidity had lifted somewhat. I left the truck's windows rolled down, and Jethro hung his head out the window to enjoy the feel of the cool air on his pelt.

La Juntique had a Closed sign on the door. It was just barely ten o'clock, but there was a van parked in the lot behind the shop, and I could see through the front window that a light had been turned on inside.

I bit my lip but pounded on the door.

"Hello?" I called loudly. "Anybody around?"

Another light came on in the front of the shop, and a middle-aged woman came hurrying toward the door. She was dressed in paint-spattered jeans and a blue work shirt and looked annoyed.

"We're closed," she said loudly. "Come back at noon."

"Please?" I asked, smiling prettily. "I saw a piece in here last month and I've just been dying to find out if you still have it. I drove all the way over from Savannah to check on it."

She shook her head but unlocked the door. "Which piece were you interested in?"

"It was an Empire card table. Cherry. With ebony inlay."

I felt her hand close firmly on my arm.

"Were you the woman pestering my niece about that table?"

Her mouth was pressed into a grim line.

"I asked her to call you and let you know I was interested in it. I left my card, but you never called me. And I'm more interested in it now than ever."

She put her hands on her hips. "Why? What's so special about that table?"

"I saw that same table just this morning. In Savannah. A friend told me she paid an antique dealer there quite a lot of money for it. She's even got the original bill of sale."

"No," she said flatly. "That's not possible. I sold it to a couple from California. It was shipped the day after you saw it."

I crossed my fingers and toes. "If it wasn't that exact table, it was a really good copy. But the dealer gave my friend a copy of the original bill of sale. It came out of an old plantation house in Savannah. Beaulieu."

Her lips twitched. "What are you trying to pull? The table I bought came out of Beaulieu. And I have a copy of the original bill of sale too."

"Your name is Liz. Liz Fuller, right?"

"Right. Who are you?"

"I'm a picker. My name is Eloise Foley, but everybody calls me Weezie. And I'll tell you what I think is going on, Liz. I think somebody's making copies and selling them as the real deal. And I think the somebody's name is Lewis Hargreaves. You bought your table from him, didn't you?"

She sighed and ran her hands through her hair. It was short, dark hair, frosted with paint spatters that matched the ones on her jeans.

"Look around here," she said, gesturing to the crowded aisles brimming with knickknacks, crystal, and china. "I'm a junk shop, masquerading as an antique mall. I sell Depression glass, Fiesta ware, discontinued Beanie Babies. Nothing big. I paid the guy five thousand dollars for that table. It's the most expensive piece I've ever handled. A once-in-a-lifetime deal."

She shook her head. "I should have known better. Guess I just got greedy. That couple stopped in here the same day I put it in the shop. The Follachios. They paid nine thousand for it, without batting an eyelash."

"Hargreaves gave you all the provenance?"

"Oh yes," she said bitterly. "I'd never met him before, but I knew his reputation. Big wheeler-dealer. He threw out the bait, and I bit. Hard."

"If you didn't know him, how did he approach you?" I asked.

"He didn't," Liz said. "I was working here late one night. Refinishing an oak dresser. A young gal came in, asked if the owner was around. Then she asked if I ever bought antiques. From estates. She said she had some pieces from an old plantation house in Savannah. She had them in a van, out in the parking lot. I took one look, latched onto the card table. I knew it was something special."

"Did you buy it from her?"

"Not right then," Liz said. "She was being oddly evasive. Finally I told her I could sell it for a lot more if I knew something about the piece's history. I gave her my card and told her to come back when she had something on paper."

"And did she?"

"Hargreaves came. The next day. He showed me the bill of sale from Beaulieu, and a photograph of the table standing in a living room with a lot of other period pieces. He said five thousand dollars was the rock bottom, and that if I didn't take his price, he had other dealers lined up who would."

"So you bit."

"Wouldn't you?"

"Sure," I said. "In a minute. Do you happen to have a phone number or address for that couple in California? The ones who bought the table from you?"

"In the back," she said. "But I'd prefer to call them myself."

I sat in a dusty wing chair while she made the phone call.

When she'd finished, Liz Fuller poked her head around the door of her office. "They definitely haven't sold the piece. They love it."

"One of those tables is a very expensive fake," I pointed out.

"God." She groaned. "I should have stuck to Depression glass."

"If it were me who'd been cheated like that," I said slowly, "I'd be pissed. Really pissed."

She lifted her chin. "What are you suggesting?"

"How pissed are you?"

Liz Fuller chewed her lower lip. "Very. I don't enjoy being cheated. And I hate the idea that I might have accidentally cheated somebody else."

I nodded agreement. "Would you be willing to tell somebody from the district attorney's office about your transaction with Hargreaves?"

"I am *not* looking to get in a pissing match with somebody like Lewis Hargreaves."

"It'll be a royal pain in the ass," I agreed.

"Who'd you say he sold the other table to?"

"She's sort of a socialite, in Savannah. Hargreaves knew she'd be interested in the table, because she's trying to raise money to buy Beaulieu for a museum. My friend paid fifteen thousand for her table."

"The son of a bitch," she said under her breath. "Guess he thought he'd pull one over on a couple of dumb dames."

"How 'bout it, Liz? You feel like rattling Lewis Hargreaves's cage?"

She straightened her shoulders and stood up. "Why not? What have I got to lose? I own this building, my husband's got a great pension plan. And I don't give a pee-diddly what Lewis Hargreaves thinks. Nobody messes with Liz Fuller."

CHAPTER 66

"Absolutely not," Merijoy said, looking from me to Liz Fuller and frowning.

"Please, Merijoy," I said, pushing the photo of Liz's "Beaulieu table" toward her. "If you don't go to the district attorney's office to complain about Lewis Hargreaves, he'll go right on selling phony antiques. Is that what you want?"

"I want my Empire card table sitting in the parlor at Beaulieu," Merijoy said. "If word gets out that I was stupid enough to let Lewis cheat me, nobody will give me a dime for my museum project. I'll be the laughingstock of Savannah. And Randy Rucker will never let me live it down."

We were sitting in the sunroom of Merijoy's Ardsley Park house, sipping iced tea and nibbling on cheese straws. Her housekeeper was keeping most of the children at bay, although Merijoy did have an infant sucking contentedly under the top of her tennis outfit.

"Nobody will think you're stupid," I protested. "Hargreaves is really good at what he does. You weren't the only one he fooled. There's no telling how many fake copies he's made. Or how long he's been at it."

"I'm in the business and he tricked me," Liz Fuller said sympathetically. "But I don't care what people think. This guy has got to be stopped."

Merijoy stroked the top of the baby's head. "Not by me. I'm sorry y'all, but I can't do it. It's too embarrassing. And it would wreck the Beaulieu project. I can't stop you from going to the police, Liz, but I just will not get involved in this."

"What if we left the police out of it?" I asked. "What if it was just between you and Liz and Hargreaves? And me, of course, since I'm the one who figured out what he was up to."

"What good would that do?" Liz asked. "No offense, Weezie, but what makes you think Hargreaves would listen to you? It's not like you're the law."

"He knows I'm in the business," I said. "And if all three of us confront him with what we know, maybe that'll carry some weight."

"And?" Merijoy asked skeptically.

"At best, we'll get him to give you both your money back and own up about whether either of your tables is the real thing. And maybe I'll find out something one way or the other about the Moses Weed cupboard."

"And at worst?"

"He'll laugh his ass off and lie like a rug," I said. "Either way, it's better than nothing. Wouldn't you say?"

"I guess," Liz said.

"You swear Randy Rucker won't hear a word about this?" Merijoy asked.

"Not from me," I promised.

We arranged to meet at L. Hargreaves at four o'clock. Merijoy called and set up an appointment with Hargreaves, telling him that she was interested in looking at more pieces from Beaulieu.

"He couldn't have been sweeter," Merijoy said after she hung up. "He even said he's got a painting I might be interested in. Of Anna Ruby's great-uncle."

"Right," Liz said. "A Mullinax heir. How handy, since there's no living family members around to say whether or not it's legitimate."

"It could be legitimate," I pointed out.

"Or it could be another doggone phony," Merijoy said. "I've got to admit, Weezie, this is all starting to get under my skin. I can't wait to hear what Lewis has to say when we confront him with what we've figured out."

"Now you're talking," I told her.

Liz and I got to L. Hargreaves five minutes before Merijoy. We sat in my van and stared at the showroom window. Hargreaves had it decorated for fall, with a simple plank-top table with original pumpkin-colored paint, six mule-ear chairs and a jelly cupboard with punched tin insets.

Liz sighed. "There's no denying it. The man has an eye. I could search for a year and never find a set of six chairs like that."

"Or a table in original paint," I added. "I hate his guts."

"Me too," Liz said. "Wonder what he paid for the stuff?"

"Maybe they're copies," I said.

"By God, if they are, they're still magnificent."

Merijoy pulled up in her Suburban and parked behind us at the curb. When she got out, I saw she was dressed for bear, wearing a sage-colored raw silk pantsuit, Ferragamo pumps, and gold coin earrings.

We got out of my truck, Liz in her floral cotton jumper and me in my black capri pants and white poplin shirt. We looked like country cousins come to town.

Merijoy gave us a brief hug and a big smile. "I just had me a big old gin and tonic for courage," she said, winking. "Let's go get the bastard."

Zoe, the long-haired assistant, looked up and then, when Merijoy walked into the showroom, stood up.

"Hello," she said. "Mrs. Rucker?"

"That's right," Merijoy said coolly. "Is Lewis around?"

"I'll let him know you're here," she said, reaching for a phone on her desk. She noticed Liz and me for the first time and frowned.

"Yes?"

"We're with Mrs. Rucker," I said, hoping to sound as dismissive as I felt.

"It'll just be a moment," the girl said, after hanging up the phone.

I circled the showroom and looked at the goods while we waited.

A pair of oil portraits in the style of Peale looked down from a spotlit wall above a Chinese Chippendale curio cabinet. The sitters in both were sober-looking men dressed in eighteenth-century garb.

Liz gestured at the portraits. She raised a questioning eyebrow. I shrugged. They looked real to me.

I was running my hand over the front panel of the curio cabinet when Lewis Hargreaves materialized.

"Merijoy!" he said happily, reaching for her hands.

"Lewis," she said, taking a half step backward, neatly avoiding his embrace.

"Hello," he said, nodding curtly at me.

I reached out my hand to shake his. "Eloise Foley," I said. "We met at Anna Ruby Mullinax's memorial service."

"Oh yes," he said, waiting for more of an explanation.

I put my hand on Liz's arm. "This is Liz Fuller. You've met Liz too."

He pursed his lips. "I'm sorry. I don't remember. Perhaps you could arrange with Zoe here to make an appointment. As you can see, I have business this afternoon with Ms. Rucker."

"Lewis," Merijoy said, "Liz and Eloise are here with me. We would like to speak to you. Together."

"I don't understand," Lewis said, nibbling at the cuticle around his thumbnail.

Merijoy laid one hand on his forearm. "Oh, don't worry. You will."

He led the way to the back of the showroom and into a small private office. The room was workmanlike: sisal carpet, a long pine farmhouse table used as a desk, some file cabinets, and three extra chairs. We all sat down and faced Hargreaves.

His face was long and narrow, with a high forehead and wisps of sparse blondish hair covering a balding dome. Hargreaves had thick black-rimmed bifocals balanced at the tip of his nose, the nose he was currently looking down at us from with a worried frown.

"What's this about, Merijoy?" he asked, drumming the desktop with his fingertips. "I don't particularly care for surprises, you know."

Merijoy glanced over at me, and I nodded in silent encouragement.

"We don't like surprises either, Lewis," she said quietly. "And I had a particularly nasty one earlier today, when I showed Weezie the card table I bought from you."

He raised an eyebrow. "She's jealous. The woman broke into the house to try to steal furnishings before the estate sale. She's obviously unbalanced."

"I don't think so," Merijoy said. She opened her crocodile Kelly bag and extracted the Polaroid photograph of the table Hargreaves had sold to Liz Fuller. "Recognize that?" she asked.

Hargreaves flipped it backward and forward on his desk. "It's apparently the table I sold you."

"It's apparently the table you sold *me*," Liz Fuller said, leaning forward.

"And it's an exact copy of the one I bought," Merijoy added, picking the photo up from the desktop. "So you see, we have a dilemma."

"Hard to believe there might be two Empire card tables made on the property at Beaulieu," I couldn't resist pointing out. "You blew it, Lewis."

He slid back in his chair and closed his eyes, sighing the sigh of a thousand martyred men who'd grown weary of dealing with hysterical women.

"I have no idea what you're talking about," he said, gazing calmly at Merijoy. "I've never seen this Fuller person in my life. And I certainly did not sell her anything like an Empire card table."

"You did though," I said. "I saw it myself. In her shop in Bluffton. The day after you sold it to her. I recognized it as the same one I'd seen at Beaulieu during the memorial service."

Liz reached into the pocket of her jumper and pulled out a carefully folded piece of paper, which she placed neatly in front of Hargreaves. She sat back then and folded her arms across her chest. "That's the bill of sale. Your handwriting, on L. Hargreaves stationery."

Merijoy leaned over and examined the bill with interest, totally feigned, since she'd already seen it earlier in the day. She went again to the pocketbook, as we'd rehearsed, and pulled out her own bill of sale, which she slapped on top of Liz's.

"Busted," I said lightly.

"This is absurd," Hargreaves said. "Merijoy, are you honestly accusing me of selling forgeries?"

"I'm accusing you of dishonestly selling forgeries," Merijoy said.

"Me too," Liz added.

"Ditto," I said.

"And do you want to know what really steams me, Lewis?" Merijoy asked, crossing her legs. "I am just really, really annoyed that you charged me *three times* as much for that table as you charged Liz."

"I told you, I've never seen her before," Lewis cried, his face reddening. "You know my reputation, Merijoy. I would never do anything as unscrupulous as what you've described. And I'll tell you something else. This is slander."

He pointed a finger at me. "And I know just who's stirring it up. You! A third-rate burglar."

"Careful," I said. "The original charge against me was criminal trespass. But even that was dropped. So if you want to find out about slander, just try calling me a burglar again. I'll slap a lawsuit on you so fast your head will spin."

"It's all ridiculous," Lewis said, reaching into his desk drawer. He pulled out a checkbook and started writing. "But Merijoy, if you're dissatisfied with the table, I'll be more than happy to refund your money and take the table back."

"Oh no you don't," Merijoy said. "You think I'm that big a fool? There's a museum conservator from Jacksonville headed up here today. He's going to take a look at my table and tell me what he thinks."

"If it's a fake, he'll figure it out," I said. "His name's Bennett Campos. An authority on nineteenth-century Southern furniture, and a vicious gossip."

"Benny Campos?" Hargreaves looked slightly ill. "The man hates me. He'd do anything to cast aspersions on my reputation."

"Too bad," I said.

Hargreaves chewed his bottom lip. "Your table is real, Merijoy. You can have it looked at up and down, but it's the genuine article. I wouldn't have dared try to pass off a copy if it was going into a museum."

"And mine?" Liz asked.

"A skillfully made modern representation," Hargreaves whispered.

"A phony," Liz said. She pounded the desktop with her fist. "I knew it."

Hargreaves was scratching away at his checkbook again. He finished with a flourish, ripped the check out, and handed it across to Liz.

"This was all an unfortunate misunderstanding," he said. "I honestly believed you would realize that certainly nobody would sell an antique of that quality for as little as five thousand dollars. It would be absurd. I just assumed you knew your table was a reproduction."

"Bullshit," Liz said, looking down at the check. "Ten thousand dollars. Twice what I paid for it. Is this what you'd consider hush money?"

Hargreaves winced. "I'd like the table back. So that there can be no further misunderstandings. The money will pay for the inconvenience of contacting your clients and having the piece shipped back to me."

"No way," Liz said. "I'm not letting you off the hook that easy."

"What do you people want from me?" Hargreaves whined. "This is all so ludicrous. I can't believe what you're accusing me of doing."

"Just so you know," I said. "I've seen your little phony furniture factory. The one down by the Port Authority?"

His eyes widened.

"Yeah," I said. "Cute little setup you've got over there. How long have you been at it, Lewis?"

"You're crazy," he sputtered. "A ragpicker. A junk monger. You're nothing."

"I'm not a millionaire antique dealer like you," I admitted. "But I know what I saw, and I saw that workshop. And I saw that fake table you sold Liz here, as well as the original while it was sitting in Anna Ruby Mullinax's house. And I know all about your arrangement with Gerry Blankenship to skim the best pieces from the estate, as well as to strip Beaulieu of its original woodwork and moldings."

"Nonsense," Hargreaves said weakly.

"Did you have to pay Blankenship a franchise fee—for the copies you made of the Beaulieu pieces?" I asked.

He looked up sharply.

"Oh," I said. "Blankenship didn't know, did he? Or he would have demanded a piece of the pie, for certain, the greedy pig."

Hargreaves stood up. "Are we done here, Merijoy? Do you intend to keep the table?"

"I'll keep it," Merijoy said. "And I'll let you know what Bennett Campos says. But I think you still have some private business with Weezie."

"And with me," Liz said, tearing up the check he'd given her. "I'll have to do some fancy explaining to Peg Follachio when I call her and ask her to ship that table back to me. I don't think this piddly little old check of yours will come even close to what it'll cost me in time and inconvenience."

"Tell her you've discovered the table was infested with powder-post beetles," I suggested. "State law says it has to be burned, to keep the infestation from spreading."

"Good idea," Liz said. She looked at Hargreaves and stuck out her hand. "Twenty thousand ought to about cover it."

"Outrageous," he muttered, but he started scribbling in the checkbook again.

He slapped the check on his desk, ignoring Liz's hand. "Are we done here? I have a screaming headache."

"I'm done," Merijoy said, standing up and smoothing her skirt.

"I'm going to the bank to cash this check," Liz said, following Merijoy to the door. "And if it's no good, I'm going right from the bank to the police department."

"It's good," Hargreaves said, pressing his fingertips to his temples.

CHAPTER 67

*H*argreaves sat back in his desk chair and gave me an appraising look. His colorless lips twisted into a smirk. "What's your interest in this whole affair?"

"The Moses Weed cupboard," I said. "I want it."

He laughed. "As my grandmother used to say, 'wantin' ain't getting.'"

"I saw the price on the piece the night I went into Beaulieu," I went on. "And I'm prepared to pay that price."

"What makes you think I have it?" Hargreaves asked.

"You have it," I said. "So let's stop playing games. I'm prepared to pay you the original price for the Moses Weed cupboard, which was fifteen thousand dollars."

He crossed and then uncrossed his legs. "If I did have it, we both know that's the wholesale price. It will bring three or four times that at retail."

I raised my chin and ignored his smirk. "I never pay retail."

"Why would I sell it to you?" he asked. "If I had the piece."

"Because I know about your counterfeiting operation. I saw it in action, and so did two of my friends who were in the warehouse. I have copies of your bills of sale to Merijoy and Liz Fuller. I can prove what you were up to."

"Then why not tell the police?" His voice was taunting.

"The police are interested mostly in violent crime," I said. "But my clients, antique dealers up and down the East Coast, would be very interested in hearing about your little enterprise. Don't you think?"

"What you're proposing is blackmail," Hargreaves said.

"Someone with a criminal mind like yours might see it that way," I said. "I'm merely offering you a fair price for an antique."

"And you'd keep your mouth shut?" he asked.

"Only if I'm sure the enterprise has been shut down," I said.

"Oh, it's shut down," he said bitterly. "Merijoy Rucker will see to that. She's a one-woman gossip mill. If she says anything to anyone in her circle of friends, I'm done."

"She's not anxious to let people know she was cheated," I pointed out. "And I'm not anxious to let the Moses Weed cupboard slip through my fingers again. I'd say it's a win-win situation. Wouldn't you?"

"The cupboard isn't in Savannah," he said, drumming his fingers on his desktop.

"You sent it somewhere to have it copied?" I guessed.

He frowned. "It needed some restoration work I can't get done around here. It's at a cabinetmaker's shop in Alexandria, Virginia."

"I have a truck," I said. "Tell me the address. I'll go pick it up."

"I've already paid the man fifteen hundred to repair some damaged boards on the back of the cupboard," Hargreaves said. "So the price has gone up."

I swallowed hard. "No. I won't pay more. And if I find out your cabinetmaker has been making copies of the cupboard, all bets are off. I'll go public with what I know about your phony furniture. The Chatham District Attorney's Office can open an investigation into your business dealings. And I'll bet the IRS would be interested in looking at your past tax returns. You did declare all the income from the counterfeiting operation, didn't you?"

He thought for a moment, then picked up the phone and started dialing.

"Andrew? It's Lewis. Have you started working on that cupboard I sent you? No? That's fine. Just leave it be. I've sold it as is. The buyer says she'll pick it up herself."

"Next week," I suggested.

"Next week," Hargreaves repeated.

He hung up the phone, wrote an address on a piece of paper, and handed it across to me.

"Thank you," I said, giving him a gracious nod. "A pleasure doing business with you, I'm sure."

"This will be the last time," Hargreaves said.

"Of course."

CHAPTER 68

*H*as he said anything about me?" I asked BeBe. She was helping me paint the carriage house in a show of solidarity.

The team's current goal was to have my shop open by November 1. And it was already October now.

"Who?" She was painting the trim around the front window in what had been my living room.

She knew exactly whom I meant. "Daniel."

"He barely speaks to me, let alone mentions your name," BeBe said. "I tried to apologize. Honey, I groveled. And you know God did not give BeBe Loudermilk a groveling gene."

"Is he seeing anybody?"

She pretended to be interested in a crack in the plaster, studying it, turning her head this way and that to get a better view.

"Nobody important," she said finally.

"Who is the slut?" My face burned. In the weeks since Daniel had gone out of my life, I'd made up countless fantasies about him. He was hurt, desperately hurt. And so alone. In my fantasies, he cooked nonstop, dicing and slicing, sautéing away his misery. Or he worked on the Tybee beach house, brooding and alone, obsessing over Sheetrock and cabinets and tile backsplashes. There were no other women in my fantasies of Daniel's post-me life.

"She's nobody," BeBe said. "If she weren't the best waitress I'd ever seen in any restaurant on the planet, I'd fire her in a minute."

"She *works* for you?"

"She's got a really funny-looking chin," BeBe said. "And serious depilatory issues. But with tits like hers, I guess guys can overlook a little goatee."

"You're not making me feel better," I said. "What's her name?"

"Her name is not important," BeBe said.

"If you don't tell me, I'll kill you."

"Since you put it like that, it's Michelene."

"Tell me she's not French."

"Not really French. Sort of Alsatian, I think."

"Same thing. Is she blond?"

BeBe stepped back and gave the wall we were painting an appraising eye. "I think we're going to knock this booger out with only one coat, don't you?"

"At least tell me she's not a natural blond," I pleaded.

"Usually that shade of blue eyes goes with that shade of blond hair," BeBe said. "But maybe she's a mutant. I really couldn't say."

Swell. The one love of my life was dating a blue-eyed natural blond French waitress who could balance a cocktail tray on her tits.

"I want her terminated," I said, dipping my roller into a pan of Benjamin Moore Decorator White. (Eggshell finish.)

"Don't ask me to do that," BeBe said plaintively. "Michelene is the best waitress I've ever seen. The customers adore her. Especially the men. My wine business is up thirty percent since she came to work for me. I can't just fire her."

"I don't want her fired. I want her assassinated," I said, staring moodily at the stark white walls. "Are they sleeping together?"

"I wouldn't know," she said, trying for demure. On BeBe, it was not a good fit.

"Well, what do you think?"

"If Daniel's getting laid, it's not helping his personality any," she said. "God, what a crank."

"Is that a yes or a no?"

She considered. "If they are sleeping together, it's not exclusive."

"Does your mama know about your uncle?"

I nodded and smiled. "She even had James and Jonathan over for dinner. We warned him ahead of time, and he had half a pack of Pepcid as an appetizer. You know Jonathan. He's so proper, so Southern. He raved about Mama's meatloaf. Now she makes him one once a week. He just sticks them in the freezer. I told him when he has enough he can get some of her couscous and build him an addition onto James's den."

BeBe inspected her nails and flicked a spot of paint from her white overalls. "You going to Merijoy's big wingding tonight?"

I grimaced. "I promised her I would come. It was the only way to get her to help me corner Lewis Hargreaves. And you know Merijoy. She never forgets a promise. God. Why did I ever get mixed up with that woman?"

"Because she helped you get the goods on Hargreaves. And helped you get your mitts on that cupboard of yours."

I dropped my roller in the kitchen sink and began rinsing it out.

"OK. It was worth it. I never in my life thought I would sell a single piece of furniture for that kind of money."

"Seventy-five thousand is serious money," BeBe said. "Does Randy Rucker know how much Merijoy paid for that thing?"

"He knows," I said. "Merijoy likes to pretend it's a big game, keeping secrets from him, but Randy is totally gaga over her. And I think he's really pretty proud that she single-handedly raised the money to buy Beaulieu *and* tracked down so many of the original furnishings. Besides, the Ruckers are so rich, seventy-five thousand is pin money to them."

"Are you taking a date?"

"Are you?"

"Emery Cooper." She actually blushed when she said it.

I whooped. "Emery! I thought you had a moratorium on dating newly divorced men."

"The divorce papers were final a year ago Tuesday. I made him show them to me. And his wife is getting remarried. She's taking the kids and moving to Atlanta."

"Is this getting serious?"

She fluffed her hair so that it fell behind her ears, and for the first time I noticed the earrings. Diamonds. At least a carat apiece.

"BeBe!" I gave her a hug. "Does this mean what I think it means?"

"It does if you think a gift of diamond earrings means a gentleman can expect an especially cordial welcome at the end of an evening," she said, fluttering her eyelashes.

"Are you going to marry him?"

"Depends."

"On what?"

"On how soon he sells that mortuary," she said, shuddering. "I can't be married to a man who plays with the dead."

"Can I be the maid of honor?"

"Who else?" she said. "I was counting on you baking the wedding cake too. Now what about tonight? Are you taking a date?"

"James volunteered to go with me," I said. "Jonathan has to work late because he has grand-jury presentations tomorrow. To tell you the truth though, I'd just as soon stay home."

"No way," BeBe said. "You two can double-date with Emery and me. We'll pick you up at seven-thirty. Wait 'til you see the darlin' little Bentley Emery took delivery on last week."

"I guess," I said, drying the roller off with a paper towel. "What's the dress for this thing, anyway?"

"The invitation says black tie, so I'm wearing a cocktail dress. Strapless. And my hair up, so everybody in town will burn with envy when they see my diamonds."

"Great," I said. "The only cocktail dress I own is the one that fell to shreds that night at the Ruckers'."

"Borrow one of mine," BeBe said. "I've got a whole closetful of things. Some of 'em still with the price tags hanging off 'em."

"I don't know," I said. "I'd feel funny wearing your dress."

"But you don't feel funny running around town wearing some dead lady's dress you found at the Goodwill?"

"That's different," I said. "Those clothes are vintage."

"Mine are vintage too," she said. "There are even a couple dresses left over from my first marriage. Now *that's* vintage. I'll gather some things up and drop them by for you this afternoon. All right?"

"All right," I said finally. "Can I borrow your diamond earrings too?"

"Never."

CHAPTER 69

I was sorting through a box of old sterling flatware when BeBe burst through the door of the carriage house. She had a plastic garment bag in one hand and a Saks Fifth Avenue shopping bag in the other.

"Here's the dress I promised you, shug," she sang out, dropping both on the back of a chair.

She unzipped the garment bag and held up a supershort black sequinned slip dress. It still had the store's price tags dangling from an underarm seam.

I glanced at the tag and shoved the dress away. "Six hundred dollars! I can't borrow something this expensive, Babe. What if I sweat on it or something?"

BeBe laughed. "Honey, this dress is designed to make *other* people sweat when you wear it. Sweat, laugh, and cry 'Take me, Jesus.'"

I hung the dress on the outside of the closet door and eyed it critically. "I don't believe you had this just hanging in your closet. It isn't even your size. It wasn't my size either, until just lately."

BeBe toyed with her diamond earrings. "I bought it ages ago. For inspiration. To lose weight. But I can't diet. There is no way I'm giving up butter and cream and chocolate just to get into a size four. So that's it. I'm doomed. A size six for life."

"A sad pathetic fate," I said sarcastically. "And you really think I'll look all right in this rig?"

"You'll be fabulous," she said airily, handing me the shopping bag. "I threw in a few other things too. See you at seven-thirty."

I spent the rest of the afternoon working on the shop. Garrett, the window man, came over around four to install a pair of arched Gothic-type windows I'd picked up for seventy-five dollars at a demolition sale on Reynolds Street a couple years earlier. The windows had been gathering dust in Mama and Daddy's garage since then, just waiting for me to find a use for them. I winced as Garrett's sledgehammer fell its first blow on the old brick sidewall of the carriage house, but as the hole grew, I could see this was the perfect spot for a display window for the shop.

By the time he finished, it was late. Nearly seven. I took the stairs two at a time and breezed in and out of the shower. I ran some mousse through my wet hair and took a little extra time with my makeup. Then I dumped the contents of BeBe's shopping bag out onto my bed.

The "few extra things" she'd tossed in consisted of a package of ultra-sheer black stockings, a pair of high-heeled black evening sandals, a tiny gold evening bag, and a jewelry box containing a pair of dangly antique jet earrings.

I held my breath as I slid the sequinned dress over my head and struggled with the zipper. BeBe had gotten ripped off big time with the dress. I'd have been willing to bet there wasn't too much more than a yard of fabric in it.

I fastened the sandal straps and took a final turn in front of the mirror, nearly tripping from the awkwardness of the high heels.

I looked, I thought, like a hooker. A high-priced one, thanks to BeBe's expensive taste, but a hooker nonetheless.

Somebody was knocking on the door downstairs.

"I'm coming," I called. I picked up my house keys and lipstick and dropped them into the little evening bag, then tottered precariously down the steps to the front door.

"Good heavens," Uncle James said, blushing.

"Just let me grab a jacket or something," I said, rummaging through the contents of the hall closet. The choices were nil. Finally, I grabbed an old embroidered and fringed black silk shawl from the top shelf and draped it artfully around my shoulders.

"Better?" I asked.

"Depends on who you're asking," James said. "Personally, I think you look lovely either way."

I gave him a quick grateful kiss on the cheek. "I'm glad BeBe talked me into going tonight after all. It'll be fun having you as my date."

"Maybe you'll find somebody more appropriate at the party."

"Never," I said, linking my arm through his.

Emery Cooper's silver Bentley gleamed like new money under the streetlight.

"Isn't this fun?" BeBe cooed, leaning over from the front seat after James had helped me into the back. "Just like a double date."

"Whee," I said.

"You certainly look beautiful tonight, Weezie," Emery said.

I'd met Emery once or twice before. He was in his early fifties, with thinning dark hair and a narrow face that gave him the look of a born mortician, except for the surprise of dark eyes that were fringed with luxuriously thick long black lashes.

"That's an amazing dress you've got on there," Emery said mischievously.

"Be good now," BeBe said, giving him a playful punch on the shoulder. "You're taken."

"I was trying to be charming," Emery protested.

"There's a thin line between charming and lascivious," BeBe said primly.

The four of us chattered away about nothing until Emery paused at the turnoff for Beaulieu.

"Oh my goodness." BeBe barely breathed the words.

The old wrought-iron gates to the mansion had been rehung and newly painted. A white-haired black man in black tails, top hat, and white kid gloves waved us through the gate with a grand gesture.

"Wow," I agreed. The long shell drive had been freshly raked. The construction equipment was banished, and each of the live oaks on both sides of the drive was covered in tiny white lights that twinkled in the gathering dusk.

"I haven't been out here since I was a teenager, and my daddy brought me with him to make the burial arrangements for Miss Anna Ruby's sister," Emery said, slowing the Bentley to admire the view. "It really is magnificent, isn't it?"

"Would you look!" BeBe said, leaning forward and pointing as the mansion came into view.

The outside of the house was crisscrossed with scaffolding, but the scaffolding had been adorned with more lights, and long white silk ribbons were tied in floppy white bows at every corner.

The house already looked perkier, its sagging corners propped up with new framing, the old tabby walls cleaned up and repointed. Gleaming new green-black shutters hung from all the windows, which had also been reglazed. All the overgrown trees around the house had been trimmed back, and there were new beds of blooming flowers peeking out from around the foundation.

"That Merijoy," BeBe said. "Isn't she something?"

A line of cars was already drawn up in the drive, and more liveried doormen were helping people from their cars.

"Isn't it elegant?" BeBe asked, nudging me as we trooped up to the veranda of the house.

"I can't believe what she's already accomplished," I agreed, looking around the foyer.

The heart-pine floors had been cleaned, sanded, and waxed, and they gleamed now in the light of hundreds of candles placed in heavy silver candelabras around the mostly empty rooms. Missing moldings had materialized, copies of the originals.

There were arrangements of camellias and roses and magnolia leaves placed strategically around, but Merijoy had wisely decided to let Beaulieu's stately old rooms speak for themselves.

"Look." BeBe elbowed me again and pointed to a wall opposite the fireplace in the front parlor.

There, cordoned off with velvet roping, stood the Moses Weed cupboard. The elm boards glowed warmly and the cupboard's shelves were now filled with blue-and-white Canton china, much the same as the Canton ware that the Mullinax family had once displayed with such pride. With the exception of a long cloth-covered table being used as a bar, the cupboard was the only piece of furniture in the room.

"It's wonderful, Weezie." I turned. Merijoy was standing beside me. She took my hand and squeezed it. "Can you believe it? Can you believe how wonderful the house looks? It's like a fairy tale, don't you think?"

"It's magnificent," I said, giving her a hug. At the same time, it occurred to me that Merijoy Rucker's life was like a fairy tale. But her enthusiasm really was infectious.

After we chatted with James and BeBe and Emery for a while, Merijoy dragged me into the hall to see a painting she'd bought. "It's not from Beaulieu, of course," she admitted. "But it's by a low-country artist, and from the eighteen eighties, so I thought it would be perfect for the house."

We were standing in front of the painting, which was a river scene, sipping champagne, when I spotted Daniel Stipanek. He was dressed in a tuxedo, deep in conversation with a woman I didn't recognize. I almost spit out my wine.

"What's he doing here?" I whispered.

Merijoy gazed across the room.

"Who? Daniel? He's catering the food tonight. And he's only charging us his cost. Honestly, Weezie, he is so scrumptious in that tux of his. I could just eat him up. Couldn't you just eat him up?"

I couldn't take my eyes off him. Especially since the woman he'd been talking to had turned around now. She was blond, with amazing cleavage. It had to be Michelene.

"Weezie?" Merijoy tugged at my arm. "Is something wrong? You two make the cutest couple I've ever seen."

She saw the stricken look on my face.

"Don't tell me you've broken up."

I nodded mutely.

"Oh no," she moaned. "What happened?"

"We had a fight." It sounded stupid, even to me.

"Well, you've just got to get back together," Merijoy said. "He's too cute. You can't just let him wriggle off the hook, honey."

"He's already wriggled," I said. "And from the looks of things, somebody else has him hooked now." I looked around the room to find James, but the place had gotten so crowded that all I could see was a sea of black tuxes and cocktail dresses.

Merijoy and I exchanged air kisses and I wandered away to find my "date." Suddenly, the fun had gone out of the evening.

"Weezie." BeBe had materialized at my side. "Did you see who's here?"

"Daniel," I said. "He's catering the party."

"Well, I *knew* that," BeBe said. "He's using the equipment at the restaurant."

"I saw him in the living room, nuzzling up to that Michelene person. He's wearing a tux. And he looks gorgeous, of course."

BeBe swept me up and down with her fake eyelashes.

"Weezie, honey," she drawled, "I hate to break it to you, but you look twice as gorgeous as he does. Every man in the room, except Emery, of course, has his eyes on you tonight."

I looked down at my cleavage and tried to yank up the bodice of the dress. "But I don't want every man in the room. I want Daniel."

"Then stop all this whining and sniveling and do something about it," BeBe snapped. She gave me a little shove. "Go talk to him. Flirt with him. When he sees you in that dress, I guarantee he'll forget all about that idiotic fight of yours."

"Not Daniel," I said. "He forgets nothing. He even remembers the bathing suit I wore when I was seventeen."

She sighed dramatically. "All right. Have it your way. Go into hiding. Be miserable. You're an adult. Do what you want."

"Thanks a lot," I said.

I walked away before she could offer any more unsolicited advice. After all, I reasoned, why should I take relationship advice from a woman with three failed marriages?

Merijoy and her host committee had set up a buffet in the dining room. I suddenly remembered I'd had nothing to eat since a banana and a mug of coffee fourteen hours earlier.

The food, I had to admit, looked incredible. A tall white-clad chef carving a steamship round of roast beef stood at one end of the table. At another end, a Japanese chef was hand-rolling sushi to order.

I picked up a small glass plate and started grazing. Barbecued shrimp on a skewer, tiny goat cheese and sun-dried tomato tartlets, and miniature fried grits cakes topped with carmelized onions crowded my plate. I added a sliver of smoked salmon atop some black bread, topped with capers.

I was just popping a grape into my mouth when James walked up. "Listen, I'm sorry, but I've got to leave."

"Fine," I said. "I'm ready anytime you are."

He shook his head. "No. I've got to leave right now. Janet just beeped me. Denise Cahoon is in serious trouble. Janet is picking me up out front, and we're going straight over to the police department."

"What's wrong?" I asked.

"Denise found out Inky's girlfriend is driving a new Jeep Cherokee, and she had a meltdown. She went down to the newspaper, snuck upstairs to the composing room, and shot the place up pretty bad."

"My God," I said. "Was anybody hurt?"

He grinned. "Fortunately, she hit Inky in the ass. He's a pretty bulky guy. The girlfriend took a bullet in the hand, but another bullet went astray and hit the composing-room foreman in the leg. He lost a lot of blood, and he's still in surgery at Memorial."

"You go on ahead," I said. "Don't worry about me. BeBe and Emery will take care of me." He touched my shoulder and then was gone.

I watched as he moved briskly through the crowd toward the front door, then I turned around and started the hunt for BeBe and Emery.

But the rooms were swarming with people. The house was awash in tuxes, sequins, jewelry, and big hair.

I finally caught sight of Merijoy on the veranda, deep in conversation with a portly man with a bad toupee. He looked vaguely familiar.

She waved me toward them. "Eloise!" she called, flashing a huge smile. "I want you to meet Baxter Howell."

So that's how I knew him. From the Baxter Howell Cadillac ads on television. On the commercials, he wore a crown on top of his toupee and swept through the dealership proclaiming himself the "Caddy King of the Coastal Kingdom."

"The Caddy King!" I said, laughing. "I just love your commercials."

He took my hand and kissed it. "And I just love your dress."

I laughed uneasily and shifted my shawl up around my chin.

"Baxter," Merijoy said, "Eloise is one of my old classmates from St. Vincent's Academy. She's the one who found us that magnificent cupboard in the front room."

"How nice," Baxter said, taking a sip of his highball. "You're a young lady of exquisite taste, I can tell."

"Excuse me for interrupting," I said. "Merijoy, have you seen BeBe?"

Merijoy looked stricken. "Oh, Weezie. I guess she couldn't find you to tell you she was leaving. Emery had a family emergency. They left about fifteen minutes ago."

"A family emergency? One of his kids?"

"No," Merijoy said. "It was his little sister. Melanie. She was working downtown at the newspaper, and some deranged woman broke into the place and shot her in the hand. Can you believe it?"

"Emery's sister is Inky Cahoon's girlfriend?" The world really was too small.

"Who?" Merijoy was the confused one now.

"Never mind," I said, patting her hand. "The thing is, Uncle James had to leave in a hurry too. So it looks like I'm stranded."

"Nonsense," Merijoy said. "You can ride back to town with us. Of course, we're not leaving for hours yet. We're having a midnight breakfast buffet, you know."

It was only ten o'clock. My toes, cramped into BeBe's spike-heeled sandals, screamed in protest.

"That sounds nice," I said lamely.

Baxter Howell had turned away to talk to someone else.

"Listen, Weezie," Merijoy said, lowering her voice, "Baxter Howell was absolutely starry-eyed while you were talking to him. He's going to become a sustaining sponsor for Beaulieu, at ten thousand dollars a year for three years."

"I'm glad," I said.

I headed for the powder room, which was off the front hallway. It was really a tiny, closetlike bathroom that had been hurriedly papered and painted in time for the party. I slammed the door shut and locked it. It smelled like candle wax and wet paint.

I fixed my hair and put on some more lipstick and started to unstrap my shoes. If I was going to make it another two hours, I had to get out of those torture traps.

I closed the commode lid and sat down. I was drowsy from the heat and the wine. Before I knew it, somebody was knocking discreetly at the door.

I lurched to my feet and struggled back into the damned heels.

Outside the door, an elderly woman was hopping up and down, waiting to get in.

"Sorry," I said. I sped away down the hall to get away from her.

And ran smack into a black-clad figure toting a huge silver tray of dishes and glasses. My heel caught in the runner. I lurched forward and took the tray carrier down with me.

The tray went left. And the delicate champagne glasses and plates of leftover food went—everywhere, but mostly all over me.

"Damn it," I muttered, feeling the chill of champagne soaking through the dress.

"Goddamn it," the waiter growled. I knew that growl. I quit brushing canapes off my dress and looked up. It was Daniel. Now the chill wasn't just from the champagne. I shivered.

"I'm sorry," I said, scrambling to stand up so I could give him a hand.

He waved my hand away and picked up the tray and stood there staring down at the mess.

"I'll get a broom. I'll clean it up," I said. "I'm really sorry, Daniel."

He flicked a bit of endive from his tuxedo lapel and frowned. "Sorry. Seems like I've heard that somewhere before."

CHAPTER *70*

I stopped blotting my dress with the edge of the shawl and looked at him with as much dignity as I could muster. Which wasn't much, considering I had bits of Brie dangling from my earrings.

"You don't have to be so snotty," I said quietly. "It was an accident, you know. I certainly didn't mean to . . ."

"Hurt me," Daniel said. He reached out and straightened the strap of my dress, which had slipped off my shoulder.

"You're soaked," he said, with the ghost of a smile that made me shiver even more. "I think your dress is shrinking."

I looked down and made a valiant effort at hiking up the top. A piece of shrimp toast was plastered to my left breast. I brushed it away. "The dress is ruined," I said. "And it isn't even mine. Six hundred dollars. Down the drain."

He looked shocked. "Really?"

"It's BeBe's. She loaned it to me. It was brand new." I shrugged. "Oh well. Is there a dustpan and broom in the kitchen?"

"Probably," he said. "I need to get this cleaned up before somebody else slips and gets hurt. Why don't you stay here and wave people away while I get the stuff?"

"All right," I said.

A minute later he was back with a mop and a broom and a garbage pail.

"I can't sweep in this dress," I said apologetically as he got busy cleaning up the glass.

"I'm surprised you can even walk in it," he said, glancing up at me.

"I knew I should have stayed home tonight," I said, rubbing my arms for warmth.

"I heard you bought the townhouse," Daniel said, dumping the glass and broken china into the trash can. "Have you moved in yet?"

"Sort of. Most of my stuff is over there. But I'm still sleeping at the carriage house."

He raised one thick eyebrow in a question.

It was a question I didn't feel like answering just then. Or ever.

"OK," I said briskly. "Look. Send me the bill to have the tuxedo cleaned. It was all my fault. Guess I'll go catch a ride home. See ya."

I gave him a cheery little finger wave.

"I saw your uncle leave over an hour ago," Daniel called after me.

I turned around slowly. "He had an emergency. But Merijoy can get somebody else to give me a ride back to town." I started walking again. I could feel a run zipping its way up the back of my left leg. My toes squished in the wet sandals.

"I'm going back to town," Daniel said. "If you want to ride with me."

"I thought you were serving a midnight buffet. It's not even eleven yet."

"Another caterer is doing the breakfast," Daniel said. "And I've got the Guale van. I have to drop it off at the restaurant and pick up my truck there. So you're on my way."

"Do you have room?" I was thinking about the Alsatian milkmaid. Michelene.

Now he looked annoyed. "Did I just offer you a ride? Of course I have room. Now, yes or no?"

"All right. Yes. Thanks."

"Good. Meet me out front in ten minutes. I just need to make sure everything's been loaded into the van."

I spent the next ten minutes back in the powder room, trying to rinse the champagne out of my hair and repair my makeup.

It was mostly a lost cause. I'd only brought along lipstick, and there hadn't been room in the tiny evening bag for a comb or brush.

By eleven o'clock, I stood, huddled under my damp shawl, near the front steps to Beaulieu. I heard a mewing and looked down. A tiny black kitten brushed back and forth against my sandal. He'd probably mistaken me for a vat of Little Friskies.

I let the cat lick a bit of crab dip from my shoe. Don't get yourself worked up, I cautioned myself. You're a mess. He has a girlfriend. He's just giving you a ride out of pity.

Who was I kidding here? The hell of it was, I'd take anything, even a dose of pity, from Daniel Stipanek.

He pulled around to the front door in the big white van with the words "Guale—A Southern Bistro" painted on the side. He hopped out, came around, and opened the passenger-side door for me. He might hate my guts, but he was still too polite to let a lady open her own door.

"Thanks," I muttered, hoisting myself up and onto the seat. He got in behind the steering wheel, glanced over, and grinned wickedly. I looked down. My skirt was hiked up almost to my crotch.

"My pleasure," he said, looking away quickly.

"What does your girlfriend think about your leaving the party early to give me a ride home?" I asked.

He gave me a blank look. "Girlfriend?"

I placed the shawl over my lap, draping it so it reached down to my knees.

"I thought you were dating a woman who works at the restaurant," I said.

"Not any more." He threw the van into gear and sped down the shell road in a cloud of dust.

I pursed my lips together tightly and clasped my hands in my lap. So much for my effort at polite conversation.

Daniel pulled out onto the pavement at Skidaway Road and barely slowed down for the stop sign. We were almost to Thunderbolt before he spoke again.

"You're really something, aren't you?"

I stared straight ahead.

"What's that supposed to mean?"

He pounded the dashboard with his fist. "You know damn well what I mean. What was that crack about my girlfriend? Have you had BeBe checking up on me again?"

Well, duh. BeBe was my best friend. Of course I had her checking up on him.

"Don't flatter yourself," I said. "I happened to notice you talking to that blond waitress tonight. You looked pretty cozy. I just assumed . . ."

"You just assumed she's a bimbo, because she's blond and a waitress, and therefore I must be screwing her," Daniel said, shaking his head. "Well, you're not even half right. We dated a few times. Michelene is no bimbo. She's really quite bright. She has a degree in art history. We just didn't have much in common. My being a lowly cook and all."

I bit my lip. It had been a mistake to think things could ever be right again between us. Daniel still had a chip the size of a two-by-four on his shoulder. Nothing would ever change that.

"I didn't think that," I said stiffly, and then stopped. I could feel tears welling up.

Before I could let out a sob, though, Daniel swerved the van hard left, across two lanes of oncoming traffic, and into the parking lot at the Skidaway Liquor Store. He slammed on the brakes, and I slid clear across the leather seat and nearly into his arms.

"Damn it, Weezie," he said, his voice husky. He pulled me to him. "Let's stop playing games. I'm lousy at this. I don't give a damn about Michelene. Or anybody else. I dated her because I knew BeBe would run and tell you. I wanted to make you jealous."

"Why?" I pulled away from him.

"I guess I wanted to hurt you like you hurt me. But it's no good." He was kissing my neck. "You taste like champagne."

I reached up and ran my fingers through his hair. Something stuck to my thumb. It was fishy smelling. "I think you've got caviar in your hair."

He laughed and kissed me hard, this time on the lips. "God, I missed you," he said, framing my face with his hands.

"I missed you too," I said. "I was stalking you for a while there. Driving past the house at Tybee."

"I saw you once," he said. "I almost called you that night, but I was too stubborn."

His hands roamed over my body, and I didn't make a move to stop him, even though we were parked right out in front of the liquor store, with people pulling up in their cars and walking right past us.

I heard another laugh, muzzled because his face was between my breasts.

"What is it now?" I asked.

He held up a tiny pea-shaped object between his thumb and forefinger. "Caper. We keep this up and we'll have our own midnight buffet."

"We keep this up and we'll get arrested for public indecency," I pointed out. "It's not that I want you to stop, sweetheart. It's just that I think there are better places to do this."

"You're right," he said reluctantly. "My place or yours?"

"My place," I said, without hesitation. "The townhouse."

He looked surprised.

"I didn't want to stay there alone," I said haltingly. "I thought it was because of Caroline. But I think maybe I was wrong. Maybe it wasn't her at all. Maybe it was me. I just wasn't ready yet."

He put his arm around my shoulders and drew me closer. Then he turned the key in the van's ignition. "Is that something I could help with?"

"Would you?" I asked, a little shy. "Would you spend the night with me at my new house?"

"Depends," Daniel said, pulling back onto Skidaway Road in the direction of town.

"On what?"

"On what you're serving for dessert. I've already had my appetizer, you know."

I reached over and started popping the tiny mother-of-pearl studs on his tuxedo shirt.

"Oh, it'll be sweet," I promised. "Very, very sweet."

A READING GROUP GUIDE
to

Savannah Blues

AN INTERVIEW WITH MARY KAY ANDREWS

Q. You went from journalism to novel writing. What demands does the novel form make that journalism does not, and vice versa?

A. Point of view and voice are such an important part of fiction writing, but in journalism, the point of view is generally that of an objective bystander. One reason I wanted to try fiction was that I longed to pour some passion, or emotions, into my writing. Journalists are trained to look passively at all sides of an issue, present the pertinent information, and move on. Part of the function of a working journalist is that of gatekeeper, of deciding what information is relevant and what is not. The novelist is free to tell one person's story, warts and all, and to imbue that story with all the trimmings that usually fall away from nonfiction.

Q. Why use Savannah for the setting and not your hometown of Atlanta?

A. I'd written eight novels set in Atlanta, where I've lived for the past twenty years, and still have lots of story material, but Savannah, the city where I lived as a newlywed, where my first child was born, kept calling me back. Atlanta is so typical of the New South, always looking forward to the next challenge, the next deal. But in Savannah, the pace is slower, and so much depends on the past. It's a place where secrets linger, and memory counts.

Q. You also mention that you asked to be locked up by the deputies at the Chatham Correctional Institute "for authenticity's sake." What in particular did you learn from the experience, and what did you pass on to Weezie's character?

A. Thanks to the cooperation of the local district attorney and the sheriff, I was able to go through the booking process at the jail in Savannah, from arrival at the "sally port" to the end experience of being bailed out. I was surprised at how dehumanizing the experience was—being patted down, searched, having your possessions seized and locked away, being photographed and fingerprinted. Even being forced to wear "jail-issue" rubber thongs. Weezie was particularly horrified at the humiliation of the entire episode, and of having the whole world know she was a jailbird.

Q. Are you still an antiques picker? What was your best find?

A: Antiquing starts as a hobby, and if you stay with it long enough, it becomes a lifelong addiction. Rarely does a weekend pass that I'm not out "junking." I still sometimes pick up such a great bargain that I end up selling it to a dealer. One of my best finds ever was a French majolica asparagus dish, which I bought at an estate sale in my neighborhood for 75 cents. I sold it to a dealer at the old Elco flea market here in Atlanta for $75, and at the next month's show, he had the dish marked $500!

DISCUSSION QUESTIONS

1. Discuss Weezie's character. What are her values? Her fears? Her ambitions? Does she change in any fundamental way by the end of the novel?

2. The first chapter sets up one emotional triangle—the ex-wife, the husband, the girlfriend. Discuss Weezie's marriage to Tal: Was it a good marriage? What went wrong? At the beginning of Chapter 7, Weezie says, "Right after Tal announced he was in love with somebody else and wanted a divorce, I was so depressed, all my friends were afraid I was suicidal. I ran around and did all the things women do when their lives are shattered into little pieces." In your own experience, what are those things? Yet even after all Tal has done, Weezie still entertains thoughts of reconciliation. Do you find her postdivorce emotions for him typical or unusual?

3. Bebe Loudermilk also makes an appearance in the first chapter. In what respects is she the archetypal best friend? Of all the people who form Weezie's support system, do you think Bebe is the strongest member? Why or why not?

4. Besides the chemistry between Weezie and Daniel, what do they have in common? What weighs in against this relationship lasting? What does it have going for it? What's your long-range prognosis?

5. Weezie's mother Marian has been drinking for years. What event forces Weezie to face the reality of Marian's alcoholism? Do you find what happens to Marian after the intervention to be convincing or not?

6. What does the plantation Beaulieu represent? Is it worth saving? Should great old houses such as this one be preserved? Nearby Charleston, South Carolina, has an aggressive preservation program with very strict regulations forbidding the demolition or alteration of older buildings. Do you think such a program should be instituted nationwide? How much of our heritage should we save?

7. Is Savannah unique as a city? What contributes to its special character? Can you think of any other city that would have served as well as a backdrop for this story?

8. Weezie's antiquing embodies this past decade's enthusiasm for the yard sale, garage sale, flea market, *Antiques Roadshow,* and eBay. What do you make of this phenomenon? In the 1950s, for example, few people wanted old things. Everyone wanted new furniture, new homes, new appliances. Today's chic vintage clothing was once called "hand-me-downs." Speculate on the reasons for this change of perception.

9. Provenance, or a record of origin for an antique, is important in proving its authenticity. Fakes abound in *Savannah Blues,* from furniture to people. In what way is nearly everyone in the novel a fake—and who becomes authentic, or true to themselves, by the end of the book? Do you think self-deception is always destructive?

Here's a sneak preview of

Little Bitty Lies

by Mary Kay Andrews

Available in hardcover

from HarperCollins

Chapter 1

Mary Bliss McGowan and Katharine Weidman had reached a point in the evening from whence there was no return. They had half a bottle of Tanqueray. They had limes. Plenty of ice. Plenty of time. It was only the Tuesday after Memorial Day, so the summer still stretched ahead of them, as green and tempting as a funeral home lawn. The hell of it was, they were out of tonic water.

"Listen, Kate," Mary Bliss said. "Why don't we just switch to beer?" She gestured toward her cooler. It had wheels and a long handle, and she hauled it down to the Fair Oaks Country Club pool most nights like the little red wagon she'd dragged all over town as a little girl. "I've got four Molson Lights right there. Anyway, all that quinine in the tonic water is making my ankles swell."

She thrust one suntanned leg in the air, pointing her pink-painted toes and frowning. They looked like piggy toes, all fleshy and moist.

"Or maybe we should call it a night." Mary Bliss glanced around. The crowd had been lively for a Tuesday night, but people had gradually drifted off—home, or to dinner, or inside, to their air conditioning and mindless summer sitcom reruns.

Bugs swarmed around the lights in the deck area. She felt their wings brushing the skin of her bare arms, but they never lit on Mary Bliss, and they never bit either. Somebody had managed to hook up the pool's PA system to the oldies radio station. The Tams and the Four Tops, the same music she'd listened to her whole life—even though they were not her oldies but of a generation before hers—played on.

She and Katharine were the only adults around. Three or four teenaged boys splashed around in the pool, tossing an inflated beach ball back and forth. The lifeguard, the oldest Finley boy—Shane? Blaine?—sat on the elevated stand by the pool and glowered in their direction. Clearly, he wanted to lock up and go to the mall.

"No," Katharine said, struggling out of her lounge chair. "No beer. Hell, it's early yet. And you know I'm not a beer drinker." She tugged at Mary Bliss's hand. "Come on, then. The Winn-Dixie's still open. We'll get some more tonic water. We'll ride with the top down."

Mary Bliss sniggered and instantly hated the sound of it. "Well-bred young ladies never drive with their tops down."

Katharine rolled her eyes.

The Weidmans' red Jeep stood alone in the club lot, shining like a plump, ripe apple in the pool of yellow streetlamp light. Mary Bliss stood by the driver's door with her hand out. "Let me drive, Kate."

"What? You think I'm drunk?"

"We killed half a bottle of gin, and I've only had one drink," Mary Bliss said gently.

Katharine shrugged and got in the passenger seat.

Mary Bliss gunned the engine and backed out of the club parking lot. The cool night air felt wonderful on her sweat-soaked neck and shoulders.

"I can't believe Charlie gave up the Jeep," Mary Bliss said. "I thought it was his baby. Is it paid for?"

"What do I care?" Katharine said, throwing her head back, running her fingers through the long blonde tangle of her hair. "My lawyer says we've got Charlie by the nuts. Now it's time to squeeze. Besides, we bought it with the understanding that it would be Chip's to take to Clemson in the fall. I'm just using it as my fun car this summer. We're having fun, right?"

"I thought freshmen weren't allowed to have cars on campus," Mary Bliss said.

"Charlie doesn't know that," Katharine said.

Mary Bliss frowned.

"Shut up and drive," Katharine instructed.

The Winn-Dixie was nearly deserted. A lone cashier stood at the register at the front of the store, listlessly counting change into her open cash drawer. Katharine dumped four bottles of Schweppes Tonic Water down on the conveyor belt, along with a loaf of Sunbeam bread, a carton of cigarettes, and a plastic tub of Dixie Darlin' chicken salad.

"Y'all got a Value Club card?" the cashier asked, fingers poised on the keys of her register.

"I've got better than that," Katharine said peevishly, taking a twenty-dollar bill from the pocket of her shorts. "I've got cash money. Now, can we get the lead out here?"

The fluorescent lights in the store gave Katharine's deeply tanned face a sick greenish glow. Her roots needed touching up. And, Mary Bliss observed, it really was about time Katharine gave up wearing a bikini. Not that she was fat. Katharine Weidman was a rail. She ran four miles every morning, no matter what. But she was in her forties, after all, and the skin around her neck and chest and shoulders was starting to turn to corduroy. Her breasts weren't big, but they were beginning to sag. Mary Bliss tugged at the neckline of her own neat black tank suit. She couldn't stand it the way some women over thirty-five paraded around half naked in public—as if the world wanted to see their goods. She kept her goods tucked neatly away, thank you very much.

Mary Bliss made a face as she saw Katharine sweeping her groceries into a plastic sack.

"Since when do you buy chicken salad at the Winn-Dixie?" she asked, flicking the tub with her index finger.

"It's not that bad," Katharine said. "Chip loves it, but then, teenaged boys will eat anything. Anyway, it's too damn hot to cook."

"Your mother made the best chicken salad I've ever tasted," Mary Bliss said. "I still dream about it sometimes. It was just like they used to have at the Magnolia Room downtown."

Katharine managed a half-smile. "Better, most said. Mama always said the sign of a lady's breeding was in her chicken salad. White meat, finely ground or hand shredded, and some good Hellmann's Mayonnaise, and I don't know what all. She used to talk about some woman, from up north, who married into one of the Coca-Cola families. 'She uses dark meat in her chicken salad,' Mama told me one time. 'Trailer trash.'"

"She'd roll over in her grave if she saw you feeding her grandson that store-bought mess," Mary Bliss was saying. They were right beside the Jeep now, and Mary Bliss had the keys in her hand, when Katharine shoved her roughly to the pavement.

"What on earth?" Mary Bliss demanded.

"Get down," Katharine whispered. "She'll see us."

"Who?" Mary Bliss asked. She pushed Katharine's hand off her shoulder. "Let me up. You've got me squatting on chewing gum."

"It's Nancye Bowden," Katharine said, peeping up over the side of the Jeep, then ducking back down again. "She's sitting in that silver Lexus, over there by the yellow Toyota. My God!"

"What? What is it?" Mary Bliss popped her head up to get a look. The Lexus was where Katharine had pointed. But there was only one occupant. A man. A dark-haired man. His head was thrown back, his eyes squeezed shut, his mouth a wide *O*, as if he were laughing at something.

"You're crazy, Katharine Weidman. I don't see Nancye Bowden at all." She started to stand. "I'm getting a crick in my calves. Let's go home."

Katharine duckwalked around to the passenger side of the Jeep and snaked herself into the passenger seat. She slumped down in the seat so that her head was barely visible above the dashboard. "I'm telling you she's in there. You can just see the top of her head.

Right there, Mary Bliss. With that guy. Look at his face, Mary Bliss. Don't you get it?"

Mary Bliss didn't have her glasses. She squinted, tried to get the man's face in better focus. Maybe he wasn't laughing.

"Oh.

"My.

"Lord."

Mary Bliss covered her eyes with both hands. She felt her face glowing hot-red in the dark. She fanned herself vigorously.

"You're such a virgin." Katharine cackled. "What? You didn't know?"

"That Nancye Bowden was hanging out in the Winn-Dixie parking lot giving oral sex to men in expensive cars? No, I don't think she mentioned it the last time I saw her at garden club. Does Randy know?"

Mary Bliss turned the key in the Jeep's ignition and scooted it out of the parking lot, giving the silver Lexus a wide berth. She would die if Nancye Bowden saw her.

"It's called a blow job. Yes, I'm pretty sure Randy knows what Nancye's been up to. But you can't bring yourself to say it, can you?" Katharine said, watching Mary Bliss's face intently.

"You have a very trashy mouth, Katharine Weidman. How would I know what perversion Nancye has been up to lately?"

"I guess y'all were down at Seaside when it happened. I just assumed you knew. Nancye and Randy are through. She moved into an apartment in Buckhead. He's staying in the house with the kids, at least until school starts back in the fall, and his mother is watching the kids while Randy's at work. Lexus Boy is some professor over at Emory. Or that's what Nancye told the girls at that baby shower they had for Ansley Murphey."

"I had to miss Ansley's shower because we took Erin down to Macon for a soccer tournament," Mary Bliss said. "I can't believe I didn't hear anything, with them living right across the street. The

Bowdens? Are you sure? My heavens, that's the third couple on the block. Just since the weather got warm."

"Four, counting us," Katharine said. "You know what they're calling our end of the street, don't you?"

"What?"

"Split City."

ALSO BY
MARY KAY ANDREWS

SAVANNAH BREEZE
A Novel

ISBN 0-06-056467-9 (paperback)

A brief but disastrous relationship with the gorgeous Reddy, a con man, causes Savannah belle BeBe Loudermilk to lose everything. All that remains is a ramshackle 1950s motor court on Tybee Island.

Breeze Inn is a place where the very classy BeBe wouldn't normally be caught dead, but what choice does she have? Soon Bebe has the motel spiffed up and attracting paying guests.

Then there's a sighting of Reddy in Fort Lauderdale, and BeBe decides to go after him.

"Mary Kay Andrews has perfect pitch when it comes to endearing, smart-mouth heroines."
—Anne Rivers Siddons

"Andrews lays on lots of Savannah atmosphere and Southern charm."
—*Boston Globe*

SAVANNAH BLUES
A Novel

ISBN 0-06-051913-4 (paperback)

A delightful, witty novel with a delicious revenge-against-the-bimbo-who-stole-your-ex plot. After a rough divorce, Weezie's husband is awarded their house in Savannah's historic district. Relegated to the carriage house, she must sit by and watch as her ex moves his "perfect" new girlfriend in.

"A great heroine, steamy Savannah setting, a hunky chef, antiques galore. It doesn't get any better than this."
—Susan Elizabeth Phillips

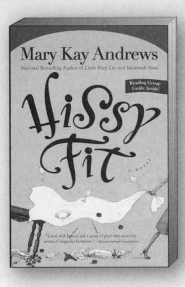

HISSY FIT
A Novel

ISBN 0-06-056465-2 (paperback)

The night before her wedding, in the middle of the rehearsal dinner, interior decorator Keeley Murdock finds her fiancé and her maid of honor in a compromising position. Keeley throws the hissy fit to end all hissy fits.

"A good old-fashioned romp with a modern Southern belle taking no prisoners . . . entertains on many levels."

—*Nashville Tennessean*

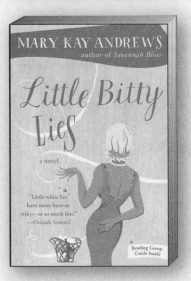

LITTLE BITTY LIES
A Novel

ISBN 0-06-056669-8 (paperback)

Mary Bliss doesn't realize her marriage is in trouble until her husband and their funds disappear. She decides her course of action is obvious: stage her husband's death and claim the insurance money.

This comic Southern novel highlights all the important things in life: marriage and divorce, mothers and daughters, friendship and betrayal, small town secrets—and a great recipe for chicken salad.

"A breezy story . . . brimming with good spirits and feisty humor." —*Booklist*